Cre

Volume 2

# The World Turn'd Upside Down

### Seth Irving Handaside
(Neal Friedman)

Historium Press

THE WORLD TURN'D UPSIDE DOWN

COPYRIGHT © NEAL FRIEDMAN 2024
PUBLISHED BY HISTORIUM PRESS 2024

THE SECOND BOOK IN THE SERIES

ALL PERSONS PORTRAYED IN THIS WORK OF FICTION ARE FROM HISTORICAL ACCOUNTS AND/OR FROM HISTORICAL DOCUMENTS, OR FROM THE AUTHOR'S IMAGINATION. AUTHOR MAINTAINED THE HISTORICAL VERBIAGE THROUGHOUT AS SHOWN IN HISTORICAL DOCUMENTS.

ALL RIGHTS RESERVED. NO PART OF THIS PUBLICATION MAY BE REPRODUCED, STORED IN A RETRIEVAL SYSTEM, OR TRANSMITTED IN ANY FORM OR BY ANY MEANS, ELECTRONIC, MECHANICAL, PHOTOCOPYING, RECORDING OR OTHERWISE, WITHOUT THE PRIOR PERMISSION OF THE AUTHOR.

HARDCOVER ISBN 978-1-962465-78-6
PAPERBACK ISBN 978-1-962465-79-3
EBOOK ISBN 978-1-962465-80-9

HISTORIUM PRESS

# CONTENTS

1. His Excellency, General Washington — 7
2. JW Joins the Rebellion — 12
3. Alex Gets Ready — 14
4. Patrick Henry @ C.C. — 17
5. King George III — 20
6. Gates Elaborates — 22
7. Johnny Goes Home — 26
8. A Winded Tale — 29
9. Howe in Command — 37
10. Manhattan Island — 39
11. General Howe — 47
12. TJ & D of I — 49
13. Burr Arrives at Headquarters — 55
14. Colonel Henry — 59
15. Right-hand man — 62
16. Reality — 65
17. AH — 74
18. Prelude to Battle — 77
19. Flight or Fight — 85
20. My Honoured Friend, Reverend Knox — 89
21. "Billy" Howe — 92
22. Sir Henry Clinton's Plan — 97
23. The Great Escape — 99
24. GW on Manhattan — 102
25. The Brits Are Coming — 109

| | |
|---|---|
| 26. A Decision | 115 |
| 27. Governor PH | 120 |
| 28 GW Retreats | 126 |
| 29. Henry Clinton | 129 |
| 30. Beating A Retreat | 131 |
| 31. Schuyler and Gates | 134 |
| 32. AH in Retreat with GW | 138 |
| 33. "The Congressing Generals" | 140 |
| 34. Lee's Capture | 149 |
| 35. Burgoyne Goes Home & Hamilton Rising | 153 |
| 36. Ready or Not | 157 |
| 37. Wilky's Adventure | 160 |
| 38. Jane, David and Fort Edward | 166 |
| 39. Burgoyne's Army | 174 |
| 40. Politics | 178 |
| 41. St. Clair to General Washington | 181 |
| 42. GW learns of loss of Fort Ticonderoga | 186 |
| 43. B in Thought | 193 |
| 44. Castleton | 196 |
| 45. The Wolf Le Loup | 199 |
| 46. Jane at Fort Edward | 202 |
| 47. Journals, Dairies, Letters | 207 |
| 48. British Advance | 209 |
| 49. Lt. Colonel Burr | 218 |
| 50. At his Fort Edward House | 224 |
| 51. St. Leger | 227 |
| 52. JW Rambles | 233 |
| 53. Reflections AB | 236 |
| 54. Left Alone | 245 |
| 55. 1st Battle of Saratoga | 249 |
| 56. Charles Lee's Plan | 257 |

| | |
|---|---|
| 57. In-Between | 259 |
| 58. General Burgoyne sends a message to Foreign Secretary | 261 |
| 59. War of Words | 265 |
| 60. Burgoyne & 2$^{nd}$ Battle of Saratoga | 268 |
| 61. JW relates 2nd Battle of Saratoga | 275 |
| 62. Loss of Burgoyne | 283 |
| 63. At Monticello | 285 |
| 64. PH Another Term | 287 |
| 65. The Bastard Confers with the Butler | 290 |
| 66. Wilky Dtirs the Pot | 296 |
| 67. Lee's Treason | 303 |
| 68. Franklin Makes a General | 305 |
| 69. France Makes a Treaty | 310 |
| 70. Wilky Saves Washington | 329 |
| 71. Love Enters | 332 |
| 72. The Gone Man | 338 |
| 73. Burr Enters Law | 342 |
| 74. Wilky Does Arnold | 345 |
| 75. Sir Henry's Plight | 349 |
| 76. Love, Hate and Treason | 354 |
| 77. West Point and the Chesapeake Bay | 363 |
| 78. Yorktown | 369 |
| 79. Wilky Goes West | 383 |
| About the Author | 389 |

# Chapter 1

# His Excellency George Washington

"Proceed, great chief, with virtue on thy side,
  Thy ev'ry action let the Goddess guide.
  A crown, a mansion, and a throne that shine."
  With gold unfading, WASHINGTON! Be thine.-Phillis Wheatley

At the wealthy loyalist John Vassall's abandoned three-story Georgian mansion in Boston, the Commander of the revolutionary army, General George Washington, lived in high style with two cooks, a steward, a maid, a washerwoman, eight others with unspecified duties, several slaves, and a personal tailor. His generals and others were constantly coming and going from dawn to dusk. His soul passed over the contradiction between his lifestyle and the army, informing the 2nd Continental Congress that "the monthly expenses of this Army amount to nearly 275,000 dollars, and the clothing sent to the Quartermaster General is not sufficient to put half our Army into regimentals."

*How is he to equip a fighting army?* he thought as he glanced around, his forehead furrowed, and another distressing matter dropped on his mind: "Payment to the troops was several months overdue, and the new militia will need tents and cloth for making shelters."

With an overloaded plate, he further informed Congress, "It is believed that British General William Howe was sending people out from Boston who had been deliberately infected with smallpox so that they might pass on the disease to Americans in the surrounding area."

*Are there no bounds to decency?* Washington thought. Realizing respected behavior was a casualty of war, he shrugged and wondered why he once wanted to wear an English uniform.

Clad in a waistcoat, breeches, and size 13 shoes with buckles, he sat in a French gilt-wood side chair by a plated window at Vassall's mansion. Staring at the view of the Charles River, his mind briefly wandered to his Mount Vernon estate. With 11,000 British troops and some 1,000 loyalists held in check because General Israel Putnam fortified the higher ground above Bunker Hill, called Breed's Hill, British superiority was turned upside down.

Cannons fired on the British forces in Boston, forcing them to attack as they advanced up a steep hill toward the American fortifications. (British casualties: 1,054) Unfortunately, the Americans ran out of powder and retreated.

Continental Army Brigadier Nathanael Greene commented, "I wish we could sell them another hill at the same price."

Washington believed the British intended to regroup and invade Manhattan and Long Island and shuddered at the thought that British control of Manhattan would jeopardize the vital line of communication between New England and the rest of the rebelling colonies.

Looking into Washington's eyes, the thin, hawk-faced, dark-haired Charles Lee knew his general's reputation rested on the Hudson River-Lake Champlain corridor.

After consulting with Lee, the commander-in-chief ordered him to Manhattan Island to survey and plan for the city's defense. They devised a multilayered plan, having troops stationed and prepared to fight in different parts of the city.

After arriving in February and standing twenty yards from the Hudson, Lee concluded that without command of the sea, the island of Manhattan must fall to the British.

"What to do with this city I own puzzles me," he wrote to General Washington. "It is encircled with deep, navigable water; whoever commands the sea must command the town."

The only question in Lee's mind was whether the Americans should make the British expend great effort to capture the city.

Washington's gray-blue eyes glared as he realized he must lead his soldiers to victory or face humiliation. He marched his unpaid soldiers from his Cambridge headquarters to New York on April 4, 1776, leaving behind beef, lamb, roasting pig, wild ducks, geese, turtles, fresh fish, plums—a favorite of his—peaches, barrels of cider, brandy, rum by the gallon, and a forest of limes to thwart scurvy.

On April 14, General Washington arrived and knew he must devise a plan to fortify the Hudson River and thwart the British from controlling that strategic area. A contorted expression appeared on the general's face as he realized that if he failed, the northern colonies would stand separated from the south, his reputation ruined, and his ragtag army severely disadvantaged.

Charles Lee interrupted his thoughts as the sun decided to shine after a day of rain. Resolved to talk to his commander, he said, "I think it is vital that you know about the British generals."

"Speak, sir."

"Howe has a face that some people describe as 'coarse' and often lacks self-confidence. I consider him a soft and ineffective leader whose aristocratic background makes him indulgent to a fault."

Washington filed Lee's words in his mind, detecting a note of anxiety in Lee's voice.

"Clinton is hypersensitive, capricious, irritable, and unable to accept criticism. Cornwallis is an overweight, pompous, preening servant of King George III. Burgoyne reeks of ambition, pride, and rashness, often responsible for his failure. And Carleton's talents lie more in administration and diplomacy than war."

Washington shook his head and was about to speak when Lee said, "Controlling the Hudson River is vital to our war effort."

"On both sides," responded Washington.

"I am sure it's been in the minds of the British," said Lee, "before their siege on Boston."

"Rest assured," said Washington, "I understand its strategic location and status as an important port."

The town of New York stood upon the point of a narrow neck of land between the East and North Rivers, and Lee surmised it not to be more than a mile wide for six or seven miles back.

Realizing that both rivers met a sufficient depth of water for ships of any burthen, he ordered the construction of Fort Lee on the Jersey side and Fort Washington on the New York side, twin forts on opposite banks of the Hudson in the spring.

The strategic town with a population of 26,000 later became the nation's first capital for a short period.

"One could," he told Washington, "easily command Manhattan Island with artillery fire from Brooklyn, but unlike Bunker Hill, deep navigable water separates Brooklyn from New York." Hesitating, he absently rubbed his left cheek with his writing hand.

"Both sides," he continued, "east and west of New York, are wide open and reach far north."

Shaking his head, Washington knew control of the sea was critical, but the rebel forces were without ships. His mind turned silent as he "ordered the rebel army to build a defensive system."

His spine stiffened as he waded through Lee's words: "Forts on both East River banks from the Battery to Hell Gate, hoping they would contain the British, and another line of entrenchments (except where there were marshes) to fortify the North River from New York to Little Bloomingdale near Greenwich and a line of redoubts and works that stretched from Jones's house across the island from Lespenard's and Mortier's home." Washington shifted in his chair as he learned, "Near Bayard's Mount is the only work of consequence that stands, a well-finished fort of sod called Bunker's Hill. The many remaining works nestled to one's amusement rather than warfare."

General Israel Putnam arrived in New York on the evening of April 4 to assume command after General Lee left New York on March 7 and now commanded in the south, with Lord Stirling taking temporary control.

Letting out a breath, Putnam immediately began further fortifications and supplemented the defensive structures initiated by Lee.

His optimism made him expect the fortifications to menace British vessels in the New York harbor.

By ship from Boston on March 17, 1776, the British sailed north to the safety of Halifax, Nova Scotia. Spending most of his time thinking over his options, Washington's army, in mid-April, started to leave New England for New York. Upon arrival, he assumed command and inspected the works, urging further continuance and extension.

A grin flashed as he observed fortifications that stretched to Red Hook, which stood on the southern end of Brooklyn's peninsula.

General Washington then ordered the East River to be made more secure, attempting to close the North River to the British.

His Excellency watched as the patriots tore apart the city's streets to save it from the British, believing he had erected a military fortress.

He assigned General Greene to command Brooklyn Heights, which his generals believed must be held at all hazards. No one disagreed that the key to the defense of New York was Long Island, the part directly across the East River.

Of crucial importance was Brooklyn, which stood on Jamaica Road, inland from the ferry landing, situated on the northwest end of Long Island.

Three hundred yards from the river stood an eminence that sloped gently to the waterside, the once-imposing De Lancey mansion, now called Fraunces Tavern, a popular hangout for the rebels at Broad and Pearl.

Its main entrance was from the east, and at the rear—on a level with the drawing room, a dozen feet or so above the sloping hillside—was a broad veranda commanding a view westward to the Jersey highlands and southward down the bay, clear to the hills of Staten Island.

The grounds resembled an English park, planted with clumps of Lombardy poplars and an impressive row of locust trees. Immediately about the house was a tall hedge of box.

## Chapter 2

# James Wilkinson Joins the Rebellion

At the confluence of the Potomack and Monocacy rivers, the summer solstice air pressed upon a group of men and women. "Hot," murmured the waiting patients, their shadows growing in length, their hands swatting at mosquitoes under the gleeful yolk of late afternoon.

James Wilkinson stood inside the log cabin, having learned to bleed and purge impurities from the body in medical school in Philadelphia. Now, he was concocting a potion of rhubarb, hemp, mota, and chicory for a patient with a severe headache, carefully measuring the ingredients.

With a keen eye for refinement, his grandmother boasted on his return to Maryland, "He has inherited a gracefulness of address and ease of manners."

At nineteen, he settled into medicine in March/April of 1775. After the Battle of Lexington and Concord, his days of watching geese skimming upon the river's waves and a summer thunderstorm whipping the virgin forest, were replaced by a passion for arms, overtaking his thoughts like a herd of elk trampling the ground. He wrapped his arms around the rebellion. It haunted his every thought. He rode sixty miles round trip to attend drills of a rifle company. In July of 1775, not three months after setting up his medical practice, the news of Bunker Hill and Washington's command of the army shot into his ears.

Cocking his head, his face aglow, he beamed at the thought of going to war. Like many of his generation, he pounced on a career of arms. "At my expense," he told his mother, "I must skedaddle to the rebellion's voice."

In the late summer of 1775, he arrived at Cambridge as a volunteer and joined a rifle company commanded by Colonel William Thompson of Pennsylvania. Learning they lacked artillery supplies and possessed only enough cartridges for twenty-four rounds a man, he looked up, his expression more incredulous than sanguine. He commented to a fellow volunteer, "On entering the camp near Boston, the familiarity that prevailed among the soldiers and officers of all ranks, from the colonel to the private, struck me as odd. I observed but little distinction. I could not refrain from remarking to the young gentlemen I made acquaintance with; the military discipline of the troops was similar to the civil subordination of the community where I lived."

Somewhat dazed and struck by the unexpected, he surveyed the camp, struggling to find any order, the color emptying from his face. At night, by candlelight, he grabbed his quill and wrote home. "The Continental Army, of which General Washington took command at Cambridge on July 3rd, 1775, rated at 14,500 militaries. Without a shade of uniformity in its organization, pay, dress, arms, or exercise," he grimaced, "Destitute of subordination and discipline, and fluctuating from day to day at the caprice of the men, inclined them to absent themselves or to rejoin their colours."

After an hour, he finished his letter, "The British army under General Gage in Boston consists of twenty regiments of the line, estimated at less than 10,000 men."

With a happy, charming face, one that would make his grandmother smile, he went to sleep.

Battles. Battles. Swelling and melting like wax through his dreams.

# Chapter 3

# Alex Gets Ready

On June 25, 1775, Robert Troup burst through the door of the library at King's College, looking for Alexander. He eyeballed his roommate at a corner table, scrutinizing William Blackstone's *Commentaries on England's Laws*.

Alex, distant and bemused, looked up as Troup approached. "Something you need to tell me?"

"Quick, General Washington's carriage, pulled by a team of white horses, is approaching."

Alex followed his friend as they mingled among spectators, watching Washington and General Phillip Schuyler proceed down Broadway under a warm and brilliant sun.

Admiring the purple sash across Washington's uniform and the ceremonial feather emerging from his hat, Alex elbowed Troup, "Our destiny awaits."

Two months later, Alex and fifteen King's College students roped ten large cannons, dragging each to the liberty pole on the Commons to prevent their seizure by the British.

"Safe now," said Troup.

With a half-laugh, Alex rubbed his hand over his chin, disappointed that there was no stubble of hair.

The British warship *Asia* fired grapeshot and cannonballs upon the students. The bombing resulted in an enormous hole in the roof of Fraunces Tavern and sent thousands of New Yorkers fleeing from their beds into the streets.

While hauling off one of the cannons, Alex had given his musket to Hercules Mulligan, who left it at the Battery—the location most exposed to the *Asia's* heavy shelling.

"Where are you going, Alex?"

"To get my musket, my war awaits me."

"He went off," Hercules said to Troup, "as the bombardment continued, with as much unconcern as if the vessel did not exist."

During the following fall term at King's College, Troup sat beside him, resting a hesitant hand on his friend's shoulder. "You will need to find a new publisher for your essays."

"Why?"

"A mob just carried off the press of the *New York Gazetteer*."

Rejecting the information as absurd, Alex pictured the feisty publisher, who wore a silver wig, facing the mob.

Alex turned his head and stared at Troup with a frown as visible as a full moon. They rushed off to judge the situation for themselves.

Troup observed the lines on Alex's face—carved with determination outside the entrance of Rivington's premises.

With a steady glance, Alex stared at the vandalized room with a cold, calculating gaze, saying, "Freedom of speech died at the hands of those who try to control one's right to state their opinion."

Troup knew that "right" now stood even more precious to Alex; their eyes gleamed with disbelief, knowing they would never forget the sight.

Alex raised his chin, looking down, his face as purple as a plum. "Might does not make right."

"The violent nature of mob rule cares not," replied Troup, whose jaw tightened.

With a scowl that distorted his face, Alex said, "Disorder among the masses offends my balance of liberty and order."

Years later, they still spoke in disbelief when mentioning Rivington, who acted as a spy for General Washington during the Revolution. It felt odd to Alex not being printed in Rivington's paper, but he realized matters were out of his hands and now wrote in John Holt's *New York Journal* without a word to Troup.

More practical, he decided to forge and cultivate his thoughts. In another paper, *The Monitor*, Alex urged his fellow patriots against "a groveling disposition."

Fearing this would lead them "from the rank of freeman to that of slaves," he hammered home his view. While still a student, he attended drills at St. Paul's Churchyard every morning, wrote an essay every week for three and a half months in the *Journal*, and began his legal studies, immersing himself in William Blackstone and Sir Edward Coke.

After his last *Monitor* essay on February 8, 1776, he wrote to the Reverend Hugh Knox at St. Croix. "It is uncertain whether it may ever be my power to send you another line. I am going into the army, and perhaps ere long may be destined to seal with my blood the sentiments defended by my pen. Be it so, if heaven decrees it. I was born to die, and my reason and conscience tell me it is impossible to die in a better or more important cause."

On a bright and sunny day, February 23, 1776, Col. Alexander McDougall recommended Mr. Alexander Hamilton for Captain of a company of artillery based on the premise he could muster thirty men, the window of his ambition wide open.

According to Hercules, he recruited twenty-five that first afternoon and soon sixty-eight. They wore blue coats with brass buttons, buff collars, and white shoulder belts strapped diagonally across their chests. Under his command, he delved into his St. Croix fund to equip the unit.

With a nostalgic feeling inside, Troup beamed with joy for his friend, knowing glory awaited him, for he turned off the civilian road onto the private lane of war. The twenty-one-year-old Alex accepted the assignment on March 14, but not before rejecting an offer to serve as Lord Stirling's military aide as a Brigade Major.

General Nathanael Greene, an ex-Quaker and former hardware man from Rhode Island, observed Alex putting his troops through parade exercises and stopped to converse with him. He looked so young, thought Greene, so frail, standing in his uniform, with his hair mussed from the evening wind.

Invited to dinner, Alex impressed Greene with his military knowledge, liking how his mind split off and ran in all directions. Who did not believe in magic?

"His learning," Greene relayed to Henry Knox, "is intuitive."

Alex's military company constructed a mud fort with twelve cannons on Bayard's Hills' high ground. He then led one hundred men in a two-hour nighttime attack with artillery and small arms against the Sandy Hook Lighthouse outside New York Harbor.

"The best news of the day," he wrote Knox, "was that the war I hoped for arrived on my terms."

# Chapter 4

# Patrick Henry @ C. C.

**P**atrick Henry's daughter, Patsy, raced toward him with wet eyes some days before he was to leave his home at Scotchtown for another session of the Continental Congress. "Mother is dead."

His eyes swelled as he thought of the twenty-one years of marriage to his beloved Sarah, who had given him three sons and three daughters.

*How was he to bear the change?* he thought. A hole existed in his heart. The man of many words fell silent for days, his lips in a frown.

In early May 1775, accompanied by an armed escort to prevent his arrest, he departed for Philadelphia, passing under storm clouds that hovered over the Blue Ridge Mountains. He turned his head, divided between tears and memories, thinking of Sarah. "I will make you proud."

As he watched the delegates to the Second Continental Congress make their way through Philadelphia's crowded streets to Smith's New Tavern, his frown slowly faded.

Before entering, an awareness shot through Patrick's body—a date with history awaited him. Words often said to him by Sarah.

His heart raced as he looked at the two-story building shaped like a cross. Although he preferred the isolation of the countryside, he admired the decorative gables and pediments on all four sides.

"Let us ferment rebellion under the true banner of liberty of conscience," he said to fellow members.

"How should Congress proceed?" asked John Adams.

"It would be a great injustice if a little island should have the same weight in the councils of America as a great one," said Henry.

Samuel Adams, his round face glistening with a halo of sweat, said, "Some of the delegates feign patriotism."

"Quacks in politics who would intimidate the populace," added Richard Henry Lee. "What we need," said John Adams, "is a man who speaks with the passion and language of a town meeting."

The men's heads turned to Patrick, who desired a spirited rejection of English policy. Waiting for the Congress to come to order, Samuel

Adams made an impatient sound, eager for the session to begin.

Finally, the gavel sounded, and the debate began on the convention floor. "How dare this Assembly, like some foreign imperial power," sneered a New York delegate, "sit in judgment on the decrees of the British legislature."

Heavy-eyed, Henry viewed the link between freedom and suppression tighten. In his chair, blowing on his coffee, he watched the delegates with heightened curiosity.

"I wonder," said a member with a large, dark, blemished face and receding hair, "whether some degree of respect is not always due from inferiors to superiors, and especially from children to parents?"

The chamber's anxiety rippled through the blue-eyed Patrick, who thought of all the times he sat under a tree, living with wild things, thinking about the future and what awaited him.

"No Englishmen, no Scots, no Britons—only a set of wretches dare to complain," said another delegate.

Patrick gazed at his fellow members, their brows furrowed, looking like tired children.

He rose on July 10, 1775, wondering if the delegates truly desired freedom. "Many men's eyes," he paused, "float in the clouds and fail to see the benefits of freedom. The subtleties of despotism wear many vestments, some of which can be glamorous and attractive."

Perched on his chair, jealous as a rejected lover, Jefferson thought Henry had covered some of this territory in the House of Burgesses.

"Something exists sweeter than life and something larger than peace, and if I may be bold enough to interpolate, something safer than security. The liberty of every citizen of a free country and, as a child of nature, must be honored."

Watching the representatives from the corners of his vision, Jefferson witnessed Henry curve his words, achieving their desired effect: the earth was no longer flat.

"It is no longer a question of Parliament's right to tax but of its right to govern. There is no longer any room for hope under this system. If we wish for freedom, we must fight!—I repeat it, sir, we must fight! An appeal to arms and the God of Hosts is all that is left to us."

Some delegates from New York twisted in their seats, staring at Henry, considering his words treasonous. *Hang him for treason,* they thought.

"Is life so dear and peace so sweet," continued Patrick, "that we accept the price of chains?"

A few of the delegates from Pennsylvania glowed like ghosts on Halloween night.

"Guard with jealous attention the public liberty."

He surveyed the delegates from left to right and then back again. "Suspect everyone who approaches that jewel."

Jefferson observed a sign of pleasure on Henry's face, remembering Patrick failing in so many ways but begrudgingly knowing Henry was now up to the task.

"The King acts as a tyrant, a fool, a puppet, and a tool to the ministry." He paused. Several seconds passed. Some sense of fury surrounded him, coupled with a hot dose of patriotism. He could not have expected a more spirited approval of his oration. Several voices yelled from the back of the assembly, "Give us liberty or death!"

Patriotism leaped into the veins and exploded in the minds of most delegates.

For a moment, he thought he heard Sarah's voice. Standing frozen for a moment, he wondered what lay over the next hill. *The innocent will not suffer anymore,* he thought.

With conviction, he said in an entirely different voice, "Separation and armed resistance, now! It is not possible to couple empire with liberty."

"Without individual freedom, we have nothing!"

## Chapter 5

# King George III

"May George, beloved by all the nations round,
    Live with heav'ns choicest constant blessings crown'd!
    Great God, direct and guard him from on high,
    And from his head let ev'ry evil fly!
    And may each clime with equal gladness see
    A monarch's smile can set his subjects free!" - Phillis Wheatley

In early September of 1775, King George III knelt, his hands clasped at the royal chapel in St. James' Palace, built by Henry VIII on the site of a former leper hospital.

Glad he had moved the family from the uncomfortable and too-cramped Tudor palace, he prayed for guidance. An admonishing chill raced up his spine, making him straighten his shoulders.

"The rebellious war becomes more general and turns toward establishing an independent empire."

His distress sliced deep. "What shall I do, Father?" Shifting his weight from his left knee to the right, he wheeled awkwardly but corrected his balance. He glanced up at the windows, admiring the light pouring in, rainbow-tinted by the glass.

He smiled a superior kind of smile, considering for a moment, then nodded.

"I need not dwell upon the fatal effects of the success of such a plan. The object is too important, the spirit of the British nation too high, the resources with which you have blessed us too numerous."

He paused, thinking about how to turn adversity into advantage.

"To give up so many colonies that we planted with great industry, nursed with great tenderness, encouraged with many commercial advantages, and protected and defended at much expense of blood and treasure, I shall not."

Like the wing of a bird of prey, a thought flapped across his mind. "If only Lord Bute stayed by my side." He laughed softly.

He knew that the plague of politics would continue to touch him, leaving him vulnerable.

"It now becomes part of wisdom, and (in its effects) of clemency, to put a speedy end to these disorders by the most decisive exertions."

Sighing, he widened his eyes, hoping for divine inspiration. Seeing the colonies running their hands over his rule, he shrugged and grimaced, though it was a mask.

He then heard, "Increase your naval establishment and significantly augment your land forces, but in such a manner as may be the least burdensome to your kingdoms."

# Chapter 6

# Gates Elaborates

**B**irthed in 1728 to the much older housekeeper of the 2nd Duke of Leeds of England, who should know more about the desire for glory than the son of a housemaid?

Horatio Gates, a thick, barrel-chested man of 50, whose job was to help organize the myriad of state regiments that composed Washington's army, barked out orders. He thought himself very efficient in managing the camp at Cambridge.

At a soirée given by Washington for his officers at his residence on Brattle Street in the summer of 1775, Gates sat across from Nathanael Greene, whom he studied. Standing up, his wire-rimmed glasses sitting on the tip of his nose, he glanced around the room before sitting again. He informed anyone who would listen, "Burgoyne considers himself a man of wit, fashion, and honor, a fine dramatic writer, and an officer whose courage endures beyond question. The only thing that rattles through the thick skull of John Burgoyne is his quest to achieve fame."

Gates' muscles, especially around his mouth and eyes, twitched slightly, the image of Burgoyne stuck in his mind. He laughed. The tone of his voice changed, and he spoke at a quicker pace. "Many aspects of his life Burgoyne enjoyed, but none more than public recognition. When, as a member of the House of Commons, he demanded an investigation of the East India Company, alleging widespread corruption by its officials, he basked in notoriety."

Greene rolled his eyes, successfully stifling a chuckle. "From a personable standpoint, Burgoyne invited criticism. My godfather, Horace Walpole, told me in a friendly way, 'Burgoyne is the illegitimate son of Lord Bingley,'" Gates continued. "He relied on competent authority from the loose tongue of a jealous woman."

"You know much about him," Greene said.

"Yes, I feel I must; destiny stands before us."

"Really," said Greene, who had enough of Burgoyne but not Gates, whose mind itched to pick up a sword.

"Born in 1722," Gates continued, "his father was the second son of a third Baronet. He was educated at Westminster School in London, where he befriended Thomas Gage and Lord James Strange, the eldest son of the eleventh Earl of Derby. The latter would influence his life and fortunes."

Without a word, General Israel Putnam, who commanded the Army Center at Cambridge, took a seat across from Gates. He blinked and scratched his unshaven face, knowing a good tale awaited.

"In August 1737," Gates resumed, "the Baronet entered the British Army by purchasing a commission in the Horse Guards. He became known for his fashionable attire and earned the nickname 'Gentleman Johnny.' He sold his commission in 1741 but returned to the army four years later by buying a cornet's commission in the 1st Royal Dragoons. A year later, promoted to Lieutenant, he finished the conflict as a captain."

Gates paused, pleasure radiating from his face. He smiled, but his eyes avoided his comrades. He breathed in the scent of fall that wafted through the open windows.

Softly breathing, he said, "The aroma is sweeter than usual." His listeners each took a whiff and nodded in agreement.

The past blew through Gates' mind and opened his memory. Feeling his way, he asserted deliberately, "Johnny and I served as fellow junior officers in the same British regiment in 1745, and I had to intervene and save his ass. I knew I should have objected more strenuously when he was promoted to Lieutenant, but I remained silent despite my better judgment."

Both men gave him an amused look, each thinking he talks at length but says little of value.

"After the War of the Austrian Succession in 1748, he wooed the daughter of Lord Derby, who thought him a weasel. That is an apt description, for he did have short legs and an elongated body and neck. The couple eloped in April 1751, but the Baronet, steeped deep in debt, sold his commission and moved with his wife to France. Returning to England in 1755 with a year-old daughter, the couple reconciled with Lord Derby, who gave his daughter a 400-pound annuity and expectations of an estate of 25,000 pounds."

He chuckled and laughed again, taking another sip of claret. Greene and Putnam's faces morphed into a look of blank bewilderment. Their eyes showed a mixture of amusement and shock.

"Upon a horse, he dashed through Portugal, Spain, and France during the Seven Years' War in Europe. Some good reviews came his way, and he entered politics as a hardliner 'Tory' and Bon Vivant. He encountered no trouble in forming alliances in his stance against the colonies. Lord Chesterfield took him to task for an audacious remark concerning the American colonies, but any criticism left no impression." Gates cleared his throat before saying, "The bastard played in the war. It evaporated quicker than dew on the grass under the morning sun."

Putnam squinted, suppressing an impulse to speak up.

Greene shot Gates a cold glance that the latter chose to ignore. He watched him continue to unhook his tale.

"By his knack of ingratiating himself to all ranks, the King promoted Gentleman Johnny to major general on May 25, 1772. Deep with conceit, he bided his time, wrote a play, and hoped for military intervention in the troublesome British colonies in America. His arrogance grew tall as a majestic apple tree."

Greene interjected, "It will only produce spoiled fruit."

With a brittle smile, Gates proceeded. "Parliament passed the Tea Act on May 10, 1773, 'to lend a hand to the East India Company by giving exclusive rights to sell tea' (actually to avoid bankruptcy). It imposed no new taxes on the American colonies, and Burgoyne thought it strange that prominent men in British America feigned more anger than a cuckolded husband."

"He, like many others in the mother country," said Putnam, "failed to realize that a tax is a tax is a tax."

Both men showed surprise at Putnam's words.

Towards the conclusion of Washington's soirée, Gates assembled young officers. "As you might recall, on December 16, 1773, British officials denied permission for three ships to sail back to England and began preparations to seize the vessels for nonpayment of the tea tax." Greene and Putnam's eyes beamed, amused by how a cat plays with a mouse.

"A group of some 50 men, under the direction of Sam Adams, dressed more like clowns than Mohawk Indians, boarded the vessels. They split open 342 chests and threw them into the harbor while a crowd, full of spirits, cheered from the dock, shouting its approval."

"Really," both men said without looking at him.

Biting the inside of his mouth, Gates peered at the two generals through his wire spectacles. Repeating himself, he asked, "Did you know the jovial Burgoyne wrote a play?"

They nodded to amuse themselves and said, "What was it called?"

*The Maid of the Oaks.* Refusing to give up his story, Gates said, "While he hoped for military glory in the troublesome American colonies, his play debuted on November 5, 1774, to both good and bad reviews. The leading female character's name was Elizabeth Hamilton."

Greene mused at the name Hamilton, thinking of Alex.

Putnam, trying to imagine writing a play, dismissed the idea and longed for the next battle. He then snarled, "No glory in fighting when you fight for the wrong."

"When you see your friend," said Greene, "tell him to stick to writing plays if he seeks glory."

# Chapter 7

# Johnny Goes Home

The playwright lingered in Boston, his stay stretching into annoying seconds. His head uncocked, his face not bright, as lifeless as a wilted garden. Wanting a new place in the fight against the rebels, he wrote in his notebook, "Oh, sun, how I hate your beams. My talents as a general lie fallow."

Busy making notes at a tavern, he pulled another pint of beer. He thought his commander, Howe, was content with having him act as his private secretary while the powerful skyward king of day shone—but not on him.

At Cromwell's Head in School Street, he glanced towards a barmaid, studying her up and down, her high cheekbones reminding him of his mistress, Peggy, at Westminster. He thought of her firm, round breasts pressing into his bare chest.

Wondering if the barmaid had a rebel lover, his thoughts turned to the rebel army in Boston.

Mumbling into his ale, he said, "Their army is the most wretchedly clothed, and as dirty a set of mortals as ever disgraced the name of a soldier."

An altercation between two privates over the barmaid interrupted his ramblings.

Contrary to his usual activities, he lowered his drink and glared at them. "I do not like seeing soldiers fight over a woman."

The two men stopped, laughed at their relapse, and resumed more serious drinking.

The playwright looked at his hands and held them out, thinking they existed to caress a woman's body. *Use words, not fists*, he mused.

After another drink, he continued his observation of the Continental Army. "They would rather let their clothes rot upon their backs than be at the trouble of cleaning themselves." Later that evening, he wrote to his wife, Charlotte: "In charge of the rebel army is George Washington, who employs two cooks and a staff of ten, not including several slaves."

Getting his wish, Burgoyne left Boston for England to report on the state of affairs on December 5, 1775, on the *Boyne*, the King and Lord North agreeing to this before his coming to America.

The wind blew the ship to England in three weeks. Often at dusk, he stood on the bow with the wind at his back as the orange orb set within the distant blue-green plain, dreaming of glory.

He imagined himself standing without a care on a cliff above a thousand leagues' precipice through the vast expanse of time. His bravado echoed to the limit of space in ten directions. The pain of glory and its thirst cut like a knife in the wound of his pride. Bewildered by ego and unaware that his intolerable vanity would roast the fate of others.

The *Boyne* landed at Portsmouth the day after Christmas, 1775.

Though his wife, Charlotte, lay stroked by death's fingertips, he chose to tread the path of ambition, his merry sounds ringing around.

Spending many hours and days with the King and his minister, George Germain, he moved for command. With his forehead muscles tight, Burgoyne said, "I caution against underestimating the rebels' skill in forest fighting and urge you to provide more soldiers." The King, surveying a herd of fat oxen in the distance, listened to Burgoyne absently. The rattling opinions of all were a noise that resulted in naught, but Burgoyne was promoted to lieutenant-general and would be Carleton's second in command.

His heart strived for a knighthood, but the blackness of a moonless night was soon to appear.

With vanity stamped on his face, he sailed on the *Blonde*, a frigate conveying Brunswick troopships on March 30, '76. Stealing the truth from himself and leaving himself soulless, he never saw his wife again.

Sheltered from the North Atlantic's buffeting headwinds in the rear of the convoy, he contemplated plenty, for the voyage took eight weeks. Forever gazing at the skies, knowing Charlotte's blush-like innocence was gone, along with her original brightness.

From that moment on, he never saw the good that surrounded him. He wrote in his journal, "Since man was born, the grasp for the rose has left a prick. Not one of us is born solid."

When he arrived in Quebec on May 28, '76, he failed to appreciate the water's harmony amidst the fragrant whiffs of spring, his ambition hard at work.

While chasing the regressing rebels, he observed in the distance two men, Benedict Arnold and a young man, as they escaped on the water from St. John. He wrote home that Carleton missed every opportunity to capture the Americans while they retreated from Canada.

"But for the timid and cautious generals," he wrote, "the war could have been won this campaign."

The playwright returned to England after the campaign of '76 shut down, his health preferring England's winter and its doors. Manhattan Island, in possession of the British, the Americans hanging about in Canada, and everything in between these points in jeopardy for the rebels. Though the rebels' pot of freedom simmered, the British did not understand that no shortage of oxygen necessary for liberty and prosperity existed. Try as they might, they failed to dampen the fire within the rebelling nation. Nor could they fathom why the rebels fought against their mandates. They needed to recognize that their actions strengthened a people who desired to be free; they chased their tail, not understanding that British regulations failed to hinder the rebels' daily free exchange.

It was always more than just about tea.

# Chapter 8

# A Winded Tale

**B**efore attending President John Adam's inauguration as a guest of honor and commander of the U.S. Army on March 4, 1797, James Wilkinson opened an invitation. It read, "General Wilkinson, the Senior Officer of the U.S. Army, is invited to spend the weekend with New York Senator Aaron Burr."

He glanced back to the last time he spent a weekend at Richmond Hill with Burr, who enjoyed hosting informal parties, suppers, and musical soirees — mirth and jests were his delight. His pleasantry, wit, and joy were contagious, and his nature was generous and accessible.

The General admired that Burr received his friends with the greatest empressement and was always in excellent humor.

He barked out an order to his subordinate," Have a box of Cuban cigars sent to Senator Burr."

As the hot and humid afternoon advanced, you could see many guests bidding their farewell through the open windows. There remained with Burr, his daughter, Theodosia, the young Washington Irving, his older brother Peter, and General Marinus Willet, who was made of "good thread."

They gathered under the veranda with the soft sound of the Hudson cooing in the background. General Wilkinson sat ensconced upon a high-backed stuffed chair. Sitting straight as a pine tree, in full uniform, gold epaulets were on his broad shoulders, his headpiece was decorated with filigree, and his spurs and buttons were glistening brass. He treated the gathering with tales gleaming from sonorous lips.

The guest of honor took particular delight in reveling the young Miss Burr with stories of his "service" in the revolutionary war.

He wiped the sweat from his forehead with a hand-stitched handkerchief given to him by his wife, Anne, his eyes surveying the audience.

"I arrived late summer 1775 at the camp as a volunteer and joined a rifle regiment commanded by Colonel William Thompson, a short, gray

-haired, and very undignified gentleman of Pennsylvania. We lacked artillery supplies and had only enough cartridges for twenty-four rounds a man. And let me tell you, most bright flower," his eyes fixed on Burr's daughter. "I observed little distinction between the soldiers and the officers."

Father and daughter eyed each other, Theo blinking in astonishment.

"I took part in Washington's attacks in the hills and heights overlooking Boston with no rank but Mister."

You performed your duties faithfully and energetically," added General Willet.

The General felt too innocent to argue, and with his words ready to fire, he said, "In March of 1776, I was made a captain of the 2nd Continental Infantry and assigned as an aide to General Nathanael Greene."

Catching Theo's eye, Wilkinson winked, then grinned at the infatuated young girl.

"I went with General Greene to New York, where I took command of an infantry company."

The General paused, thinking to himself as if looking back in time.

"As the army's discipline was lax, and in the militia nonexistent," Wilkinson informed Theodosia and the young Irving, "an incident occurred. A Yankee farmer with the rank of Lieutenant, twice my age, refused a command to march. I ordered him arrested, but the regiment's men refused to obey. I informed the rascals I would proceed from left to right, running every man through with my sword until they obeyed orders or my strength failed longer to support me. My resolve succeeded, and the Lieutenant submitted to arrest. The men were drilled in accordance with the Royal Irish, and I bore the reputation as a competent and rigorous drillmaster. General Washington heard of the incident and recommended me in his dispatches to Congress."

"Your opportunity arose when General Washington," said Burr, who looked at Theo and Washington Irving, "upon hearing that the expedition to Quebec had come to naught, sent four regiments under Brigadier-general Sullivan to aid Arnold in his siege upon Quebec."

Wilkinson smirked before continuing. Yes, and I, an untested youth, became attached to one of five regiments subject under marching orders for Canada and then to Montreal to reinforce General Philip Schuyler."

Thus, he began his rise like a phoenix from the ashes of obscurity, Burr realized.

"About this time," said Wilkinson, "you," he eyed Burr, "left the military disaster of Canada and looked for active service before I, the doctor-soldier, arrived."

"Yes," replied an amused Burr, "I did not possess the temperament to be around the morose Benedict Arnold after the failure of the Quebec campaign."

Wilkinson shook his head and tapped his finger on his glass of Madeira in a positive manner as he spoke. "In the spring of manhood," he leaned towards Washington Irving, "I led a New Hampshire company from New York up the Hudson to Albany where my corps rendezvoused and were reviewed by Major-general Schuyler. My orders were to march to St. John's, where I found the post without garrison or commandant, "infested" with stragglers from the army. Without written or verbal orders beyond this destination, I assumed command."

Washington Irving observed an expression of satisfaction spread over the General's jowly face as he continued, "I marched for La Prairie with upwards of one hundred strong. My official regiment consisted of 86 non-commissioned officers and privates and others I had taken who acknowledged to be soldiers."

The sound of a random mosquito or three caught Wilkinson's attention momentarily. Gracefully, he turned to Burr's daughter, "Miss Burr, on entering some woods along the way, swarms of mosquitoes attacked me, more numerous than ever beheld on the banks of the Mississippi. I proceeded to three leagues above St. John's, where we found quarters in a Canadian barn.

Early the next morn, my eyes became affixed on the rapids of St. Lawrence at La Prairie; the island of St. Helena, the city of Montreal, and its mountains forming a picturesque background. This French-speaking village consisted of half a dozen humble wooden houses and a church." The eyes of Washington Irving were enraptured by the General's signs, gestures, and general animation, envisioning Shakespeare's Iago.

"I learned of a river which we marched along, crossed a creek, traversed woods and at a summit perceived an Indian village inhabited by the Cachnawaga tribe of the Iroquois, who acknowledged Colonel Lewis, the issue of a negro and a squaw, for their chief. And he was commissioned by General Washington. Through an interpreter, I pointed to La Chine, the head of the rapids of the St. Lawrence. With information gained from the colonel, I marched towards Montreal three miles distant, where I was received by Colonels Brown and Williams."

"Fortunate indeed," said Burr with feigned enthusiasm.

Wilkinson stared at him in suspicion giving the remark a respectful exit.

The conversation stalled and faded away into silence. Burr shook his head to clear it out.

"Excuse me. What were you saying?"

"Arnold, at the time, was on a visit to Cachuawaga," said Wilkinson. "The reduced garrison welcomed us with outstretched arms. Their situation appeared perilous."

He turned from "Theo" and looked at the youthful Washington Irving and winked before turning back to the vigorous and fresh daughter of Burr, intoning with the tenderness of a spring bud adorning a barren branch. We were a force of 450 men, crouched shoulder to shoulder in a small garrison, low on food and ammunition, without the prospect of reinforcements, and the enemy on the march. I felt it was my duty to inform my superiors of the situation. I wrote what could be my "last letter" and addressed it to General Greene."

At midnight at La Chine, on the Twenty-Fourth of May 1776, about 12 miles from Montreal, "The Wilkinsonian Quill", his writing instrument struck an oil well of ink. It was to be a stroke that would be scribed numerous times and was similar to the one he would write to President Jefferson in 1806.

He need not strain to find words; they flowed like the great Mississippi. We are now in a sweet situation. A part of the garrison at Detroit, in conjunction with the Indians and Canadians, to the amount of 1000 men, have made themselves masters of Colonel Bedel's regiment, who were stationed about nine miles from this place – General Arnold, with a handful of men, have been throwing up a breastwork here, in order to stop the enemy's progress, and indeed mediated a plan of attacking them–we cannot now muster more than 350 men – we shall be attacked within six hours. Their drums were heard this evening at our camp – But the morning dawn – that morn, big with the fate of the few, a handful of brave fellows. I shall do my part – but remember, if I fall, I am sacrificed. May God Bless you equal to your merits – Vale!"

Theo's brow fluttered like a stalk of corn in the wind. Her tongue gently wet her upper lip — the child-woman fastened in wonderment. Irving's vigorous and fresh eyes surveyed her, his face smitten by love.

The letter made it to Greene, then to Washington, and finally to Congress, with comments from shocking to genuinely alarming.

A note of historical accuracy: the nearest British troops were three days away, and 500 Americans soon marched into Arnold's camp. Washington heard from General Schuyler on the Tenth of June '76, "I am happy that Captain Wilkinson's Conjectures were not realized."

The Captain, none the worse from his nullified demise, was handy to agonize that Arnold possessed great celebrity and became attached to him at the end of May in Montreal. Within a few days, Arnold appointed him as his aide-de-camp.

"Reinforcements arrived under General Wooster," continued Wilkinson, "but Arnold became outraged. He felt that Wooster had not consulted him or something to that effect and asked to be relieved. He came to command at Montreal. This would not be the first time the hot-brained Arnold would take insult."

Wilkinson stopped speaking as he stared at his audience, almost daring them to say something, but they remained silent.

"By the spring of '76, smallpox, dysentery, scurvy, and rheumatism had ravaged 1000 of the Americans in Canada." Needing to step back and clear his memory, he poured himself some Madeira.

"Burr," that was how Wilkinson liked to address Colonel Burr, "Dispirited with their commander, Philip Schuyler, who traveled forth between his Albany and Saratoga homes but not on the ground of Canada; our forces were in retreat."

Wilkinson saw annoyance in Burr's face and smiled at him, a charming smile that made him look much younger.

"You knew about retreat."

The Colonel remembered being with Washington's army at Long Island in the summer of '76, always stepping backward.

"On assignment for Arnold," Wilkinson informed the gathering, "I embarked on board a twelve-oared batteau with dispatches for General Sullivan. My progress retarded by a strong wind ahead that caused a considerable swell in the river. Upon hearing the reports of cannon fire, I reconnoitered and soon came to realize that the enemy was near; when I approached with my men to within 200 yards of the village of Varenne, I observed the enemy turn the corner of the street and realized that they were now within fourteen miles of Montreal, without General Arnold's knowledge."

He gave a dignified little nod before he paused, then took another sip of Madeira, stood up, squat like a shrub oak, "I inclined to the right," his body jerked, "leaped a fence," his legs lifted slightly, "and under shelter of a copse of wood, retreated as fast as the men could run, keeping the wood between the enemy and me. I left the men in charge of a sergeant, mounted a horse bareback, which I discovered at the door of a wind-mill, and rode full speed to Longuille where at the point of my sword, I extorted a paddle and launched a canoe with the assistance of a Canadian from the beach, into which I jumped, and with much labor gained the opposite shore and about six o'clock reached Arnold's quarters who were exceedingly surprised by my report, having just received word of General Sullivan's retreat from Sorel and did not contemplate crossing St. Laurence before the next morning, which would have been too late."

Wilkinson paused and drank another glass of Madeira, swooshing it in his palette before continuing.

"Arnold ordered me to Chamblee, twelve miles, to report to General Sullivan the situation and request a detachment to cover his retreat by La Prairie. Upon reaching Sullivan, it was acknowledged, on all hands, that a detachment was necessary to cooperate with Arnold. After some deliberation, I was sent with instructions to Brigadier-general Baron de Woedtke, who commanded the rear, to make a detachment of 500 men to cover General Arnold's retreat. After marching for several hours, and I might add wet to the skin, covered with mud, I threw myself down on the floor of a filthy cabin and slept until the dawn of day."

Wilkinson threw up his hands in mock horror. "Not the kind of man to rest for a moment longer than I have to, I inquired in the morn for de Woedtke. Informed by Lieutenant-colonel William Allen of the 2d Pennsylvania Regiment, 'no doubt the beast was drunk and in the front of the army.' He then put his arm on my shoulder and looked me in the eye, 'This army, Wilkinson, is conquered by its fears, and I doubt whether you can draw any assistance from it; but Colonel Wayne is in the rear, and if anyone can do it, he is the man." Chuckling, he stepped back in time, needing to clear his mind from the Madeira.

"Within half an hour, I met the gallant officer, with whom I had made an intimacy at New York. Wayne was as much at his ease as if he was marching a parade of exercise. He confirmed Allen's report respecting de Woedtke. A plan was put into force, but after walking for two miles, we met an express, which informed us that Arnold had escaped from Montreal and on his retreat to La Prairie. I followed Wayne along with his men. We quickly proceeded to the rear of the army now at Chamblee, where I observed some consternation as General Sullivan's camp thought the enemy was approaching. Exertions to prepare for battle were observed, but at the same time, numbers were seen to seek safety by flight. Through his pulled-out glass, Colonel Wayne enjoyed the panic his appearance had produced."

Burr snickered at the story and started to make some joke, but Wilkinson looked at him curiously. "You are very irreverent, Burr." His tone was light, and he was teasing him.

"Two days later," continued the General, "on June 18, '76, Sullivan and Arnold's men reached St. John's in the morn, where we moved up the Sorel in the afternoon of the same day. The instance after the last boat but Arnold's had put off; he mounted his horse, and I mine. We proceeded two miles down the direct road to Chamblee and met the advance of the British division under Lieutenant Burgoyne. We galloped back to St. John's, stripped our horses before Arnold shot his own, and ordered me to follow his example, which I did with reluctance. As the night's first stars glistened the front of the enemy approaching, we took leave of the faithful chief of the Cachnawaga tribe, Colonel Lewis, the only Canadian who accompanied the army in its retreat from Canada. We watched as he retired precipitately into the adjacent forest."

Burr rolled his eyes as the well-fed figure of General Wilkinson continued his story.

"During this episode, General Thomas died of smallpox, and General Sullivan succeeded him. The latter had procured all the vessels and boats at St. John's and destroyed the rest, allowing the sick, retreating Americans not to be pursued across Lake Champlain by the British, who were prone to advance slowly. We reached Crown Point. The entire army of the Congress crossed under the scorching sun of July in leaky boats without beds of straw, with no food but raw salt pork, often rancid, and hard biscuit or unbaked flour, no drink but the fetid water of the stagnant muddy lake."

"As a point of reference," Willet informed Theo and Irving, "the needy were established at the South end of Lake George, fifty miles in distance. Without enough men to defend Crown Point, the Army of Congress fell back to Ticonderoga."

A pause engulfed the Patriots. No one spoke, but all thought of the men who passed beyond the boundaries of time to the eternal unknown.

General Willet raised a glass, "To those who came to reside in tents, sheds, or miserable bush huts and in every abode a dead or dying man."

Glasses clinked. The gleaming eyes of the men who fought the English despot were as proud as a bride's father.

Washington Irving envisioned, "Thirsty for a taste of liberty, the bare feet of the rebel army blistered upon the road, their palates waiting for the entree of freedom."

"My brave general," I said to Arnold, "extending an open arm while walking with him, allow me to steady the boat for you. Arnold, with a New England stare, said to me, 'After you, Major.'"

Irving then imagined the two Sorcerer's Apprentices jostling.

General Wilkinson, with bowels of passion, turned to the wistful Irving, "Young man, he had an indignant look in his eyes, and he resisted, my proffers of service, pushed off the boat with his own hands and thus indulged the vanity of being the last man who embarked from the shores of the enemy."

In a letter written to a correspondent, Arnold had sworn that if the army retreated from Canada, he would be the last man to depart. To Captain Wilkinson's chagrin, he was a man of his word.

The present General of the American Army turned to Theo, sipping more Madeira into a brain already in high spirits, and explained how the escape from the enemy was of great value to the whole cause of independence.

"You see, the fate of our independence rested on the successful escape from Canada. By what slight thread was the issue of the revolution suspended at this moment? If our Canadian army suffered defeat, it is not improbable that the dubious question of independence, not yet decided at that juncture, would have been negatived, or possibly a negotiation opened with the British commissioners and reconciliation with the parent state might have followed."

Irving realized Wilkinson lived for the opportunity and hungered for glory, his velvet tongue pleasing his superior's senses, their pulse, their ego, their pride. They could not get enough of his words.

The hard-of-cheek soldier paused in reverence to the escape from Canada. His revolutionary comrades sighed concurrently.

"The flight from Canada," continued Wilkinson, "did appear miraculous or countenanced by Sir Guy Carleton. Instead of harassing our rear, interrupting the march, and forcing the Americans to a general action or putting them to the rout, Carleton hesitated. His tardiness gave our army time to retire without losing either men or stores. The bulk of the army, fewer than 3000, entered the dilapidated Fort Ticonderoga in early July '76."

His eyes narrowed for a heartbeat, then broadened.

"Be it not forgotten that the revolutionary Americans choose not to be an anvil to the hammer of despotism. There was a sense that the Revolution was an idea bigger than any patriot could know and greater than all individual aspirations. It was an unknown guiding force that controlled the universe whose time had come. Proof positive that when citizens pursue their purposeful actions, free from the edicts of tyranny, they will allocate scarce resources for productivity. Future prosperity is the result of unleashed uniqueness."

Leaning forward, the General grasped another glass of wine.

"Though the stew of freedom in upper New York boiled poorly," he announced, "it would produce martyrs and heroes for time immemorial."

# Chapter 9

# Howe in Command

The British siege of Boston ended when the rebels seized Dorchester Heights in the spring of 1776 with the mounted artillery secured by Colonel Knox. After replacing Gage as head of the army in America, the new commanding general, William Howe, moved quickly and regrouped at Halifax in Nova Scotia. He was now left to superintend his actions and quicken his career. How could Gage have been so deceived, he thought? Looking back as well as he could, he realized that Gage had taken up the idea of holding Boston and made everything bend to it.

Howe wrote Sir Henry, telling his subordinates to test the loyalists in the south and coordinate an attack. "I will have under my command thirty-thousand soldiers in the best possible spot for using them."

Hope bubbled up in Howe's soul for the first time since assuming command.

"Yes, New York has the strategic advantages that Boston lacks, replied Sir Henry. "The command of the Hudson and an easy overland route to Canada."

Sir Henry enjoyed communicating with Howe, helping him with his strategy.

"Control this route," he said, "and the rebellion can be cut in two and reduced to piecemeal."

Understanding Sir Henry's advice, Howe nodded. "Once I take Manhattan, the American force will be pinned down in southern New York and New Jersey."

"Exactly, general," wrote back Sir Henry, "and the Canadian army will advance against Washington's rear."

"He will have to retreat from the line of the Hudson," wrote Howe, "and see New England isolated from the middle colonies or risk his raw troops in a decisive battle."

"Which is desired as it is the most effectual means to terminate this expensive war," replied Sir Henry.

To Howe, a soldier, standing in the center of a confusing situation, his thoughts lifting to glory. He decided to have another glass of brandy.

"Everything hinges on Sir Guy Carlton," wrote Sir Henry, "advancing far enough to threaten the enemies rear; if not, the rebels can dispute their backcountry, inch by inch."

A flicker of nervousness crossed Howe's face, but the liquor calmed him.

"If he does," continued Sir Henry, "I shall not despair of taking Carleton by the hand in Albany and there singing Te Deum for a cursed war finished."

So much for the war, he decided, and relaxed his hand on the glass before saying, under his breath, "A man can only win a battle if the circumstances are right."

# Chapter 10

# Manhattan Island

Montgomery's route back down to Fort Ticonderoga served as Burr's guide. The land was nothing but dense forest, swamps, and mosquitoes, the sun bronzing his idealism, his thoughts fluttering between the past six months and what future fate lies on his path.

He enjoyed the exhaustion of soldiering and its consequences; "death on the battlefield, a more noble outcome than to die by ennui."

In a week, Schenectady's outskirts, a terrain abounding with rocks, stretched before his eyes.

A remoteness crouching on the border of civilization was unsettled, nothing but barren pines. He viewed a house or two on the road, the land closer to the town, somewhat improved.

Relatively narrow roads and loose logs hugged the bridges, making them dangerous to pass. The status of the more significant part of the people mirrored the actual state of the tenancy.

He ascertained the town, 350 or so houses, sat alongside the Mohawk River, a branch of the Hudson. At a tavern, he overheard a conversation that the land was treasured and sold for 40 to 50 dollars per acre.

The day's topic was the Patriot's past success at Bunker Hill.

Toast after toast saluted Colonel Prescot, who seized in the night the high ground of Breed's Hill for the patriot cause under British eyes, thus allowing the rebels to command the harbor of Boston.

Though a young, seasoned veteran of twenty who served in the attack on Quebec "with distinction," it seemed to him that militarily, this was a blunder by the Americans. The British, who commanded the sea, easily could have controlled Prescott's rear and both flanks.

As he observed during his nearly fourscore of years, rashness's limits are not bound by ignorance.

The difference between genius and stupidity is that genius has its limits, he mused. Luckily for the Patriots, General Howe ordered repeated head-on attacks and suffered significant British loss.

This British General intrigued Burr.

When leaving Boston, Howe felt compelled to leave behind ammunition and supplies which he should have destroyed.

Two hundred or so cannon, lots of powder, thousands of muskets, and military stores of various kinds found their way into the grateful rebel army's hands. What made a British General blunder like this? The thought rumbled through Burr's mind.

Furthermore, the tongue of rumor spoke that he had left behind a mistress.

Burr guessed he was not as skilled at making war as he was at making love. "The beauty of a woman," he said to himself, "does not make a man wiser." An old saying galloped through Burr's mind. "Never make stupid mistakes, only very, very clever ones."

Something in his lifetime, he came to comprehend.

Albany being his destination and only 16 miles distant, he rode his mount and arrived in the capital of the county of the same name in a couple of hours.

The old low Dutch architecture of the 400 Houses grimaced at him; two Dutch and one English church were no friendlier.

On a hill above the town stood a decayed fort. He sent a look of attentive sorrow.

Two enormous and handsome houses adorned each end of the city. One belonged to General Schuyler, the other to Mr. Rensselaer. Two men were unknown to him then, but little did he know they would impact his life a decade later.

He immediately realized that Roman blood flowed in his veins as he rushed to find a suitable house with a bath; the water, though cool, penetrated his mildew-stained pores.

Generally, he was a man who liked to be clean. When he was, he responded to the throbbing of his stomach. A hot and delicious soup concocted of local fish (a plentiful supply existed from the Hudson River rock & perch & from the springs large trout.) And a roasted chicken followed by grilled sausages browned in sweet onions.

He wiped the plate clean with warm bread from the crackling hearth.

Some berry claret and goat cheese followed; he did not think he ever ate as much nor enjoyed it more.

Fresh blankets folded across a wool mattress and pillows stuffed with feathers greeted him as he entered his garroted room. A single oil lamp flickered, sending shadows dancing upon his washed face.

His dreams floated in his head that chilly June night. There was not a better time in his life as far as he was concerned.

The Fresh Water or Collect Pond just east of Broadway and north of the Commons, which lay above the extremity of old New York in 1776, bathed his subconscious. He floated in the water, his young body cooled, the frogs croaking and the crickets cricking, and hearing the hissing of the large springs that fed the clear, sparkling deep pond, which exemplified a garden of Eden in his green mind.

In 1796, John Fitch sailed an 18-foot long, six-foot beam Steamboat with square stern and round bows powered by a twelve-gallon potboiler in the Collect.

The boat circled several times at a speed of six miles an hour.

In time, tanneries and breweries used the Fresh Water Pond's water and soiled its chastity.

When in exile from Mr. Jefferson's twisted reach in 1808, a canal was dug, and the oasis drained. In 1811, the year before he returned to New York, progress had filled in the Collect. A channel remained until 1820, when development covered and paved over it.

They now call it Canal Street.

Awaking in the early morning, he retired from Albany's fertile town after learning that a place on General Washington's secretarial staff awaited him, but this would not do. He would rather resign than be a clerk. He wanted an active-duty post. The mere idea of coming face-to-face with quill and parchment cowered and shook him to the bones.

Onboard a sloop heading south, the tide favorable but much rain and wind ahead, Burr dreamed of glory, but the wind began to blow hard, remarkably hard, and having made only a few miles, the craft returned to Albany.

Boarding again the following day as the crimsoned sky turned to ash, a fair but very light wind and tide became his friend. Off he was the Island of York reflecting in his memory.

When the boat came to anchor near Clermont, he and others fished. All they did was yank the rod back, and in an hour, they secured several dozen excellent white perch for their meal.

They procured milk, fruit & vegetables upon the land, leaving a pleasant feeling in their stomachs and satisfaction in their minds.

The night wind refused to breathe. Major Burr focused on keeping his eyes aimed at his future with a stark calm in the air. He feared that morrow would cough a contrary wind impeding his southward voyage. The next morning, he waited to board the sloop until an S. E. wind rustled the sails. At ten o'clock A.M., with the southerly wind still fresh and fair at their backs, the boat trimmed along against the tide.

He spent midday reading and lolling in his birth, but the environs of

Manhattan fought the words on the pages.

Feeling confident he would make it down if the wind continued, but at two P.M., the wind began to shift and assumed a temper.

Barely making it to Newburgh, yet near enough to the entrance to the Highlands, he stood for a moment, considering his options.

He decided to make a run for it and proceed by horse thru the mountains, Hackensack his destination.

The roads, much worse thru the Gap of the Mountains than he was led to believe, he decided to re-cross the North River and caught another sloop.

A brisk breeze whisked him to Dobb's Ferry, 25 miles from New York, a most idyllic repair to quote an aid to Washington, Tench Tilghman, whom he would soon meet.

He noted that the Jersey shore, bounded by a perpendicular ledge of rocks about 50 feet in height, came close to the water's edge. The New York shore was a gradual ascent upon which many Gentlemen's Seats and Farm Houses sat.

He lamented, "No time or way to stop and visit my family."

The sloop arrived on the upper tongue of Manhattan at King's Bridge.

He stared hard and fiercely at it for an instant, filing it in his memory.

The town of New York stood upon the point of a narrow neck of land between the East & North Rivers, and he knew it not to be more than a mile wide for six or seven miles back.

He understood that both rivers met a sufficient depth of water for ships of any kind.

Splitting his time, he looked at Fort Lee on the Jersey side and Fort Washington on the New York side.

The ramblings of Don Quixote filled the pathways of his mind, but no Sancho Panza stood at his side. He decided to circle the island to assess information on its new fortifications under construction.

He walked south on the old Boston Road and veered east before Harlem Lane, taking a shortcut towards the Village of Harlem. He could smell the East River in the distance.

Sheep and cattle grazed to his left and right on the smooth grass as rabbits' white cottontails bobbed far and wide. While meandering under the hard-green fruit of an orchard, blue jays screeched at his unwanted presence as the running water's sound throbbed steadily.

He wished for a canvas and brush, but his implements were a sword and gun.

From Harlem, he walked south and traversed several streams that emptied into Kip's Bay. He rested momentarily at the Sunfish Pond, thoughts returning from his youth. When he looked at his reflection in the water, he noted his expression was undoubting. He sighed, "No sense in looking for complications."

Inland from here, Kip's farm flourished on the old road to Kings Bridge, where various mouth-watering fruits glowed like stars from this garden of Eden in the night. Delight sprang into him as he tasted some of the crops. "This fertile land is now the trademark of progress."

He continued observing the yellow sunlight bending in the wind as fallen pale green leaves rippled under his small feet. The shrubs, trees, flowers, and everything in between shimmered in the gentle gust.

Climbing a steep hill, he partook in a cold drink at Wolfert's tavern, the farthest outlying dwelling on the island's Eastside.

He repaired from the tavern, the yellow-orange light of the sun splashing beneath his feet. Nearing the Tea Water Pump, an oasis near the High Road, he crossed the Old Kill by the Kissing Bridge and stared at the old white fort opposite the Tea Water Pump.

From the light that protruded from a gap in the bridge's rough wooden planks, he remembered sitting under it with Emily, a blazing yellow streak on her hair. Her side hushed her polka dot dress as her silky elongated fingers crossed his brow, the warmness of her succulent lips inviting him.

He ran his tiny, soft fingers through her peach-colored hair. She spoke with her pale green eyes as the light reflected on the bracelet of her firm left wrist. They kissed her first.

This spot marked the end of town on the East side until the close of the Revolution.

A young girl in her early teens sprawled under a peach tree in the present-day foreground. Her russet hair stood as a beehive, bare velvet arms as soft peach fuzz, eyes the green of unripe apples, and lips full and inviting. Lazily, she pulled daisies from the shaded ground as a young black cur chased a rabbit in the distance.

His thoughts crisscrossed -Was he remembering Emily, or was this some lost dream born of his mind?

A puffed-up innocent cloud, pure and white, gradually grew into a vast dark storm; the sky angered, and the swollen clouds belched.

An avalanche of loud drums resounded from the lusterless blackness of the horizon. Heavy rain fell hard to the ground, producing a constant tap, tap, tap. Brown and swollen streams began to run from the thickly wooded slopes.

The sudden torrent ended just as suddenly, and he proceeded close to the East River, passing Crown Point on his way to the Battery, which spanned the lower end of Broadway.

Passing the James De Lancey estate between Bowery Lane and the East River's foot, he recalled the racetrack and stables for breeding racehorses, which vanished by progress's march.

As a small lad, he often dreamed of riding the most elegant stallion far afore of the field before an awed crowd.

From a distance away, the slate roof of the King's Arms Tavern (now called the Burns' Coffee House), still wet from the rain, glistened like the amber coals of a hot winter fire from under the harsh sunlight that reappeared.

He stopped there, saying nothing as he watched the customers move about the room.

Opposite it, he gazed at Fort George, where the Sons of Liberty, under Marius Willet, met to plan the overthrow of the English government.

He swallowed. "Go to Hades," he uttered as he thought of the King.

On the East and West of the Old Fort rested Market-field and above it the Bowling Green.

Butterflies danced silently as clouds, their wings effortless as the afternoon morphed into tranquility.

Parenthetically, by 1790, the fort was removed and replaced by the two-story Government House, and the Battery was extended.

"A portico," projected before the Government House, "covered by a pediment; upon which is superbly carved in basso-relievo, the arms of the State, supported by justice and liberty, as large as life. The white arms and figures are placed in a blue field, and the pediment stands supported by four white pillars of the Ionic order, which are the height of both stories."

Little did he know then that the State's future arms would chain his life's circumstances.

The road to Greenwich he knew well. It skirted the water and crossed above a causeway at Lispenard's Meadows and the Manetta Brook. A favorite fishing location, which tumbled to the Hudson while swarms of trout leaped in the foam under the hot sun. No matter how mad or low, his uncle Timothy's frown sank, "Matty," and he knew it would turn upside down when they returned home with their catch.

He proceeded north with Brooklyn Heights staring at his back, high above the shimmering water. But his feet took him the long way; up Broad Street, the clip-clop of horse's hooves hummed steadily from the wide cobblestone street.

His thoughts were bound up in the glory of Caesar.

He realized that one could easily command Manhattan Island with artillery fire from Brooklyn, but unlike Bunker Hill, deep navigable water separated Brooklyn from New York.

Both sides, East and West of New York, were wide open and reached far north.

Shaking his head, he knew control of the sea was critical, but the rebel forces were without ships to speak of.

He liked returning to his youth's familiarity and active campaigning, for the British would want to take control of New York and its surroundings. Here was the place Aaron sensed would draw him to honor.

Major Burr learned at the King's Arms Tavern that the rebel army began a defensive system. By building forts on both East River banks from the Battery to Hell Gate, they hoped to contain the British.

He observed another line of entrenchments (except where there were marshes) fortified the North River from New York to Little Bloomingdale near Greenwich. Near Bayard's mount was the only work of consequence that stood, a well-finished fort of sod called Bunker's Hill.

The many remaining works stood to one's amusement rather than armed conflict.

Fortifications stretched to Red Hook, which stood on the southern end of Brooklyn's peninsula.

General Washington desired that the East River be more secure and attempted to close the North River to the British, which Lee later told Burr was impossible.

Washington assigned General Greene to command Brooklyn Heights, which his generals believed must be held at all hazards.

No one could disagree that the key to the defense of New York was Long Island, the part directly across the East River.

Of crucial importance was the Brooklyn part, which stood on Jamaica Road, inland from the ferry landing, situated on the Northwest end of Long Island.

After leaving King's Arms Tavern, Major Burr crossed Grand Street, observing works east and west in construction to hinder the enemy if they landed above the North River shore. The most crucial aspect was the defense of Long Island and, thus, Brooklyn.

Few mansions stood in the middle of the island, but where they did, the future needs of war required a General to bed in an abandoned loyalist home.

The wealthy then lived near the rivers' steep and abrupt banks on each narrow island side. Nature abounded. Sycamore, elm, oak, chestnut, wild cherry, peach, pear, and plum trees grew above Chatham Street, the town's boundary, flourishing within this landscape of winsomeness, artichokes, tulips, and sunflowers.

# Chapter 11

# General Howe

> Howe, with his legions came,
> In hopes of wealth and fame.
> What has he done?
> All day, at Faro play'd
> All night, with the whores he laid,
> And with his bottle made,
> Excellent fun.

General Howe set sail for New York with a convoy of 110 down the blue Atlantic, "their tall masts piercing the sky before the swoosh of the wind."

Reaching the rendezvous off Sandy Hook in Monmouth County, New Jersey, he dropped Anchor and waited for the stragglers to catch up.

Anticipating an attack, General Washington ordered his soldiers to "lay on their arms in their tents and quarters.

"They must be ready to turn out at a moment's warning," he told an aide, "as there is a great likelihood of it."

On July 2, Howe moved his armada inside the bay and landed on Staten Island without opposition. A glimmer of amusement crossed his face as he watched the soldiers, who had been cooped up on shipboard since March 17, leaping, wrestling, running races, and rolling on the turf.

Delegations of loyal Tories flocked to General Howe's headquarters. Sixty men from New Jersey carrying muskets reported that five more men would follow the Crown's services.

"They tell me," a delegate said while drinking coffee, "the Tories want peace;"Howe listened with one ear as he was anxious for the arrival of his brother, Admiral Howe.

Soon after the coming of Admiral Howe, General Henry Clinton returned from Charleston with 2000 men after an unsuccessful attempt against the town. Shifting his feet, Howe winced at the news.

"What will be your fighting force?"

Howe took a satisfying breath. "10,000 seamen and a land force of over 32,000. They are well-armed, well-found, well-fed, well-clothed, and well-trained, but my brother and I want to offer reconciliation with General Washington."

"I want to make real concessions to the colonies if they will lay down their arms," said Howe, "I am fighting for peace."

The delegate seemed impressed.

"I must do much damage before the enemy considers my terms. But if I completely suppress the rebellion, it will cost England more to garrison troops here and keep them suppressed than the colonies are worth."

Plenty more ideas circled Howe's mind with arguments for and against his plan.

## Chapter 12

# TJ & D of I

Sixteen days after leaving Monticello for Philadelphia, Thomas Jefferson took residence on May 23, 1776, at the bricklayer Jacob Graff, Junior's three-story house at the Southwest corner of Seventh and Market streets.

Suffering from a splitting headache after his mother's death, he struggled to read, write, and think; John Locke and Montesquieu were resting on a table by his bedside. And with his wife pregnant again, he worried about her health. A few days later, he found himself on his hands and knees at his boarding house, looking for Martha's letter, which the wind had blown off his writing table. He yearned to touch her silky skin, smell her tumbled hair, admire her soft curves, and feel her moist lips. He missed the pianoforte, the harpsichord, and the dancing at Monticello.

He found the letter, and most of his focus done, he added a note before sealing it, "The Continental Congress in Philadelphia is readying for the coming conflict." He swallowed any more words and rose, seeing independence, still rough, the house, half-done, with walls and stairs yet to come.

Rounding the corner, he went through the Pennsylvania State House's back door and heard men in the cloakroom. He spotted Elias Boudinot and Samuel Chase chatting. "I do not know what to say." Chase threw up his hands.

The majority of the Assembly, waiting to meet, he assumed; he rendered what passed for a chuckle before walking towards the great room.

"Not much longer now," John Adams boasted to a group of men. "Washington's army in New York, ready to kick ass."

Jefferson ambled over and heard Patrick Henry say fast and loudly, "Liberty is pure Virtue, and if the British cannot learn this simple truth, the hell with them."

Adams nodded and, in a moment, expounded, "Our revolt was

effected before the war commenced. It was in the hearts and minds of the people."

Jefferson's beliefs brushed over his, a pleasing feeling that stirred the juices of his ambition. He opened his mouth to speak but thought otherwise.

"This radical change in the principles, opinions, sentiments, and affections of the people," continued Adams, "is the real American Revolution. A revolution without a prior reformation would collapse or become a totalitarian tyranny." Samuel Adams responded in a crackling and raw voice, "My sentiments exactly!"

At the end of the first week of June, Mr. Jefferson found himself listening. The debate over independence was in full swing at the Continental Congress, with Pennsylvania, Maryland, Delaware, and New York holding back on seceding from England.

He did not miss his books and the quiet as the weeks passed. The day of committees, votes, talk, and more talk invigorated Jefferson, but the constant bickering annoyed him.

He reminded himself achieving freedom was business and picked himself up until he learned about his wife's unfavorable situation; she suffered another miscarriage. Putting his sorrow aside, he attended a conference with John Adams, Richard Henry Lee, and George Wythe, the quartet thinking it prudent to wait for the four states to agree on saying goodbye to the mother country.

Pausing at the door of liberty, Congress put off the vote until July 1.

Committees were organized to draft a declaration, set guidelines for negotiating a foreign alliance, and prepare for the new government.

"You should pen the grand statement," Jefferson said to Adams.

"I will not," said Adams, who choked out a snicker.

"You should do it."

"Oh! No," replied Adams, who continued to look at Jefferson's bland face as the Virginian tried to get out of doing the writing.

"Why will you not? You ought to do it." Said Jefferson.

"I will not."

"Why?"

"Reasons enough."

Jefferson shot his hand up before Adams could continue. "What can be your reasons?"

"Reason first, you are a Virginian, and a Virginian ought to appear at the head of this business.

Reason second, I am obnoxious, suspected, and unpopular. You are very much otherwise. Reason three, you can write ten times better than I can."

"Well, if you are decided. I will do as well as I can."

With "thanks," Jefferson took a quill from Adams and slid the project into his mind.

Looking forward to savoring the experience of making dry sentences dynamic, mixing adverbs and adjectives and nouns, he put his forefinger to his lips.

"Very well," said Adams, "when you have drawn it up, we will have a meeting."

With a soothing bottle of Bordeaux on his small wooden desk in his private parlor, he relaxed., thinking of the philosophers of the Scottish Enlightenment. He read James Wilson's tract *Considerations on the Nature and Extent of the Authority of the British Parliament*, which negated Parliament's control over the colonies. He paused momentarily, flicked back the hair draped over his face, and decided to write to his wife.

"My dearest Patty,

I have not heard from you for two posts. I hate not hearing and fear the worst. I am torn between my duty to you and my public commitment to remain in Philadelphia. I must admit I feel drawn to political life, yet I long to be home with you and my family.

I have been assigned to draft a declaration of independence, but my headache throbs day in and out, poetry and prose challenging to summon.

Realizing my goal primarily consists of one thing, and one thing only, a justification of the separation of the Colonies from Great Britain.

Therefore, in a defense of the rights of revolution in respect of the condition of the original thirteen States, I decided to model my words on a recently received draft of George Mason's Virginia Bill of Rights.

As I am under a deadline, Congress ordered that it be sent to the several assemblies, conventions, and committees, or councils of safety, and to the several commanding officers of the continental troops. I asked Ben Franklin to read it, and he replied in the affirmative."

Taking a deep breath, Jefferson extended his arms. He shifted his fingers to his eyes, the memory of Martha dancing clearly in his mind.

Continuing his letter to Martha, he wrote, "Much of the preamble of my declaration, if not in substance, in form, is taken as the occasion justifies; for I must divide my time between writing and executing congressional duties.

My mouth waters, for the peaches must be ripe, and I long to hold you in my arms.

Your devoted and loving husband, Thomas."

The following day, he sent his slave, Jupiter, a note to the lodgings of Benjamin Franklin: "The enclosed paper has been read and with some small alterations approved of by the committee."

"Will Doctor Franklin be so good as to pursue it and suggest such alterations as his more enlarged view of the subject will dictate?" Eyebrows lifting, Franklin read the document, and his mind returned to the beginning of the second paragraph, *We hold these truths to be sacred & undeniable and crossed out, "sacred & undeniable," and put in "to be self evident.*

At that moment, Franklin remembered King George III, who refused to read the colonist's pleading to be free from Britain.

Remembering, he chose to wage a cruel war against human nature, violating the sacred rights of life and liberty in the persons of distant people who never offended him. He captured & carried them into slavery in another hemisphere, incurring a miserable death in their transportation thither, his face turned crimson, breathless with anger.

His dislike for England heightened as he read, "This piratical warfare, the opprobrium of infidel powers, is the warfare of the Christian King of Great Britain."

Franklin's mouth opened and closed as he dragged his writing hand over his balding head, seeing the King's face jumping and skipping with disdain when informed of the colonies' declaration of independence.

Delighted with the high tone and the flights of oratory, Franklin knew the passage condemning the slave trade would not fly.

He smiled as he read Jefferson's harsh language.

"Determined to keep open a market where Men should be bought & sold, he has prostituted his negative for suppressing every legislative attempt to prohibit or restrain this execrable commerce. And that this assemblage of horrors might want no fact of distinguished die, he is now exciting those very people to rise in arms among us. To purchase that liberty of which he has deprived them by murdering the people on whom he has obtruded them: thus paying off former crimes committed against the Liberties of one people, with crimes which he urges them to commit against the lives of another."

Introduced on June 28, 1776, a Friday debate began on Monday, July 1, on Jefferson's draft of a Declaration of Independence.

The delegates, well aware their assemblage constituted a treasonous event, set it aside, clinging to liberty.

Franklin and Jefferson sat beside one another, watching silk-stocking-legged Congressional members swat horseflies from a nearby stable with handkerchiefs. The flies buzzed in all directions through the Pennsylvania State House.

Jefferson pulled a pair of silk gloves from his coat pocket, a present from Martha, and put them on.

"And to think," said Franklin, "what history will say about this."

Before Jefferson could answer, Franklin's gloved hands clasped a giant fly.

"Shall we send it to the King with our compliments?" Asked Franklin.

Jefferson smiled and turned to the pleasant voice of fellow Virginian, the six-foot-four-inch Benjamin Harrison, who John Hancock described as "noble, disinterested, and generous to a very great degree."

"I shall have a great advantage over you, Mr. Gerry, when we are all hung for what we are now doing. From the size and weight of my body, I shall die in a few minutes and be with the Angels. But from the lightness of your body, you will dance in the air an hour or two before you are dead."

Franklin smirked. "He looks like he loves good food."

"And good wine, I can attest to that."

Franklin gave Jefferson a slow, sly smile. "Well, when we adjourn, let us return to his lodgings."

"He would be honored, Dr. Franklin," said Jefferson.

Catching Jefferson's eye, Franklin winked.

"Adams informs me," said Jefferson, "that his pleasantries steadied tough committee sessions."

Half-amused, Franklin leaned back in his seat. "I see why he acquired the nickname, the Falstaff of Congress."

As they both toyed with spending an evening with the "big guy," the debate turned to Jefferson's censures against the English people and slavery.

Dr. Franklin observed Jefferson biting his tongue and turning his sad eyes from the corner of his face.

"When I was a journeyman printer," said Franklin to the Virginian, "one of my companions, an apprentice hatter, having served out his time, was about to open shop for himself. His first concern was to have a handsome signboard with a proper inscription. He composed it in these words, 'John Thompson, Hatter, makes and sells hats for ready money,' with a figure of a hat subjoined. However he would submit it to his friends for their amendments. First, he showed it to thought the word

'Hatter' tautologous because followed by the words 'makes hats,' which showed he was a hatter. It was struck out. The next observed that the word 'makes' might as well be omitted because his customers would not care who made the hats. If good and to their mind, they would buy them, by whomsoever made. He struck it out. A third said he thought the words for ready money were useless, as it was not the custom of the place to sell on credit. Everyone who purchased expected to pay. They were parted with, and the inscription now stood, 'John Thompson sells hats.' 'Sells hats!' says the next friend. 'Why, nobody will expect you to give them away. What, then, is the use of that word?' It was stricken out, and 'hats' followed it, the rather as there was one painted on the board. So the inscription was reduced ultimately to 'John Thompson,' with the figure of a hat subjoined." Jefferson burst out a hearty laugh.

The next day, July 2, after more debate under Chairman of the Whole, Benjamin Harrison, the resolution for independence was adopted and, on July 4, ratified.

Jefferson wrote to Patty, "My task was to express the American mind and to give to that expression the proper tone and spirit called for by the occasion, but I believe Congress marred my composition."

The Pennsylvania Evening Post published on July 6, the Declaration on its front page, and on July 8, it was declared publicly in front of the State House in the city of brotherly love to a cheering crowd that chanted, "God bless the free states of North America."

## Chapter 13

## Burr Arrives at Headquarters

From the King's Arms Tavern, Aaron wrote Sally, "Some men called Tories were carried and hauled about through the streets, with candles forced to be held by them, or pushed in their faces, and their hands burned; but on Wednesday, in the open day, the scene was by far worse; several, and among them gentleman, were carried on rails; some stripped naked and dreadfully abused."

Shaking his head, he continued, "I heard that some of the generals, especially Putnam and their forces, tried to quell the riot and make the mob disperse."

Displeased, he rushed off to Washington's headquarters, the recently built Mortier mansion on Richmond Hill in Greenwich (on Barrow Street at the junction of Varick and Van Dam Streets near Lispenard's Meadows), the lowering sun's rays reflecting from the windows into his eyes.

Never having seen the completed structure, he murmured, "This general picked a magnificent house for his headquarters." He admired the commanding view from its elevation and knew he wanted to live there someday.

And he did. Years later, he decorated the front walls of the wooden building of monumental architecture and a lofty portico supported by Ionic columns with pilasters of the same order. A Palladian ornament distinguished its whole appearance, though sober became his.

His daughter, Theodosia, and adopted daughter, Natalie, practiced ballet in the ballroom.

He put a handsome gateway at the entrance, made many plantings, and carved a small lake into the landscape. It became known as Burr's Pond, later a favorite place for skating. Just for the record, John and Abagail Adams lived at Richmond Hill before the U. S. capital moved to Philadelphia.

The Adams consisted of the stock of his grandfather, Jonathan Edwards, cold, arrogant, and dogmatic, a world apart from what he wanted to become.

But back to the subject, Burr and Washington.

Seeing broad-shouldered Washington again, up close and personal, he looked the same. Clean-shaven, in brilliant military dress, slouched behind a desk lost in thought. His brow furrowed; his mouth twisted in a way that told Burr he possessed few friends.

Burr observed papers and maps stacked in every possible way and Washington's tiny spectacles perched on his large, thick nose, which blushed that warm moist day. His long hair pulled back in a queue in a military manner and held tightly with a ribbon amused Burr.

His hands were enormous, as were his bones and joints leaving Burr standing in awe as sunlight shot through a large window, bursting and flickering over Washington's dark lines that perched above his gray eyes, which were lodged far apart. High round cheekbones adorned a freckled face that blended with a few scars from smallpox.

He did not look the part of Apollo nor like a God, thought Burr, who waited five full seconds, his ear cocked for any sound of recognition.

"Sir," he announced, "Major Burr, reporting for duty."

The general looked up at him and rose. They stood. The Virginian's head tilted downwards, one cold gray-blue eye giving Burr a once over while the other stared at snippets of daylight hanging above the green-blue North River.

Standing erect as a statue, Washington never momentarily relaxed from his military posture or attitude.

He motioned Major Burr to two chairs before a window facing the river.

Enormous black boots with studded gold stars adorned his feet, size thirteen, deemed Burr, resting on the wood floor. He guessed his height, six feet two inches.

From the window, Burr's diminutive stature reflected on him. He sensed the general regarded him as a mere child.

He let out a sigh that ended with a slight giggle. He blushed at his relapse and then resumed a more serious countenance.

Troubled gray eyes contrasted with Washington's strong face. From his hoarse throat came, "Have a seat, Major."

Burr observed his hands that substantially exceeded the typical size, later learning that he had to have his gloves made to order.

His mouth was full and complex, with lips so tightly compressed, a pain shot through Burr as he observed him; Burr's natural cheerfulness under temporary gloom.

"May I speak freely, sir?"

He smiled ever so slightly, a rare event the Major would soon learn, and many defective teeth stared at him.

"Proceed, Major."

"I seek an active duty."

Burr thought Washington looked annoyed. "What is your point, Major?

"As a youth, I traversed Manhattan Island, and I know it."

"So."

"Before coming to headquarters, I surveyed the island up, down, and around. There is much activity, and I would like."

He cut him off with a cold stare and then spoke gruffly while glaring at the sparkling windowpane rather than what lay beyond it.

"My staff serves me at my pleasure and in accord with my wishes." No matter how firmly Burr ordered his mind to stay calm and focused, one thought ran through him.

*Why am I here?* He did not consider that being a clerk to the general might be more critical than engaging in battle.

His commander did not care that he had skiffed along the Elizabeth River. Or sometimes took Thompson's Creek into the Auther Kill and boated over to Staten Island in his youth.

Or when there, tramped, traversed, and crossed every field and orchard.

Burr averted eye contact though Washington's pupils glowed like the flames of candles. As wisps of fog swirled inward, the Major, to himself, refused to let him dissolve his military ambitions.

He believed that the general possessed the coldest eyes, small and transparent, and nothing behind them from that moment forward.

After leaving Washington's headquarters, Major Burr walked to the Hudson with bitter, cold exhaustion. He let it empty into the North River.

As he mingled with Washington's staff officers in June of '76, unaware of the future, his mind frothed with suggestions." Twenty miles west of Sag Harbor on Long Island, 100,000 cattle and sheep blanket Shinnecock's sandy hills.

"In the eastern part of the island, the fruit of abundant orchards sparkle in the noonday sun, and grapes crisscross the fields."

He knew the island of Manhattan and its surrounding locality as Galileo did the stars.

Unfortunately for Major Burr, his knowledge of the landscape and his opinions, he believed, were wasted on Washington's sterile, methodical mind.

He clung to the knowledge that he knew his stay would be short with the commander-in-chief. John Hancock promised to find him a position where he could participate in active campaigning instead of writing letters to Congress, but still, his urge to impress stood out. "The land of Long Island produces more of the food than the entire province of New York," he told an aide to Washington, who relished a blank expression.

# Chapter 14

# Colonel Henry

While at the second Continental Convention in Philadelphia in the May of 1775, Henry, his bright smile still dulled from the loss of his wife, buried himself in a bevy of military activities.

"Never remake the same mistake twice," he told a colleague, "and certainly not against the British."

With fierce eyes, he began to learn the strategy of war, and an imaginative and spiriting thought entered his mind.

"I would welcome command of the First Regiment of Virginia," he told his friends.

A contingent in Virginia opposed him, "You are totally unacquainted with the art of war, and that such a person is very unfit to be at the head of troops who were likely to be engaged against a well-disciplined army, commanded by experienced and able generals."

"I have preached for months we must fight and want to engage in the field of war, preferably on horseback, leading troops."

By a narrow margin, he became Colonel and commander of the First Regiment "Of all forces raised, or to be raised, in the colony." His name brought recruits, especially among the rank, file, and junior officers. It appeared to him the most satisfactory agreement in the arrangement.

Most of his men wore hunting shirts and farm clothes and became known as "the Shirtmen."

Everything was in short supply – firearms, gunpowder, bullets, shoes, leggings, clothes, and blankets. Patrick observed old rugs serving as blankets, and his men brought their "squirrel guns."

The men thought he had a way about him, "Downright honest," one man said.

"I am happy you approve," said Patrick, grinning, "but I trust I am not deficient in leading you."

"No," said the men standing together about him.

A company from Culpepper County wore green hunting shirts stitched with "Liberty or Death" across their chests, a flag exhibiting a coiled rattlesnake, and the words "Don't tread on Me." With bucktails in their hats, tomahawks, and scalping knives tucked in their belts, they were mistaken for hostile Indians. Frightening the locals, one of the fiercest-looking savages was Lieutenant John Marshall, future head of the Supreme Court.

Saying nothing when he heard on November 7 that the British Governor, Lord Dunmore, proclaimed, "All slaves free can bear arms," he observed anxiety in the Virginian gentry, who believed Dunmore's forces would grow "like a snowball." Patrick wished to appease it.

"It might be distressing for the moment," he said as he stepped back, "but you need not think about it; the slaves lack the means to seek freedom." Even the man whose words untied his country from the autocracy of the Brits continued to see white as good and black as bad. The man of freedom remained silent when two runaway slaves hailed a boat on the York River only to find out it was not British and were captured and shot.

Unfortunately for Henry, the president of the Committee of Safety, Edmund Pendelton, wanted to relieve him of command. He made his rank subordinate to every Colonel with a Continental command through sleight of hand, forcing Colonel Henry to walk away from his command of the First Regiment of Virginia.

Offering him their sincerest thanks, Henry's men expressed their poignant sorrow to this glaring indignity, and an uneasiness sprang among the soldiers, who stated they wanted Henry as their leader or they would leave, mutiny hanging as the morning mist.

Patrick bit the bullet of being driven from command and carried the day, "Lay aside this imprudent resolution and continue in the service. The Patriot cause is all-important, and nothing should hinder its success."

He told his friends, "He regarded his soldiers like many gentlemen who met to defend the country. He exacted little more from them than the proper courtesy among equals."

As rain spilled down, Pendelton's replacement for Henry, Colonel Woodford, allowed the "Shirtmen" to liberate the wine cellars and the taverns after invading Norfolk; the drunken looting sizzling for several days the case for liberty.

Trying to suppress the news, Pendelton praised Woodford for his excellent judgment and discretion, but the proper sense of the people opposed such conduct and closed their eyes to the hypocrisy.

Not a gentry member, Henry could not buy or receive a military title. Politics deprived him of command, failing to understand that men's loyalty and respect can overcome the enemy in a battle. Colonel William Christian believed that Henry would have conquered the mystique of command with his usual speed and concentration.

Throughout his life, Patrick refused to use the title of Colonel.

"Virginia has two frontiers," he told his brother-in-law, "one bordered by a wilderness of savages, the other by a sea of enemy ships."

'Politics does not understand the reality of our situation," said Christian.

Patrick tried to exert joy but remained skin-tight. He looked up and into the bold brown eyes of his friend. "Discarded like a spent bullet."

He trotted old Shandy upon the muddy road home, his head bent low against the strong wind, his chin touching his chest. His dreams of military glory shattered, and his pride scared.

Virginia's militiamen disliked being away from home for too long as the war progressed without a natural-born leader like Henry. They were uncomfortable serving under Continental officers and resisted draft orders from the Continental Army, becoming reluctant to aid the patriot cause in any way and were tired of giving supplies – through impressments and taxes – freedom taking a step back.

## Chapter 15

## Right-Hand Man

3/4 a mile from a wooded bluff of Brooklyn, hidden from view from the tip of Manhattan, Washington built a sizable square bastion, Fort Sterling, with eight cannons to rule the East River-his eyes, bright as he skimmed over the structure.

"It surveys all: the harbor, the rivers, and the topography of New Jersey," he told his staff."

The East River, a saltwater estuary a mile wide and challenging to navigate due to its swift, contrary currents and six-foot tides, boosted Washington's confidence, fire, and spark, burning his vision.

"The narrow channel of the East River that passes into Long Island Sound is called Hell's Gate," said one of his aides. "It is dangerous to ships because of its strong tidal currents and rocks."

"Our advantage," said Washington. His aides noticed the intensity of his gaze as he studied the fortress.

Burr chimed in, "But the North River or Hudson is greater than two miles wide and is impossible to keep the British from navigating."

Washington glared at Major Burr.

"We must," said the general who sighed long and deep, his noble shoulders ascending, his eyes going hard and hopeful, "make things difficult for the British."

"We risk, Sir, of being boxed in and spreading our forces too thin," said General Israel Putnam.

He knew that but refused to be mortified, surmised Burr. "The defense of New York," said the Commander, "requires the army to keep Long Island and Brooklyn Heights from the enemy."

He surveyed his staff, never realizing his erroneous policy would sacrifice many worthy souls in the summer of '76. "I want several thousand troops on Long Island under the command of General Greene."

His officers knew that meant approximately a third of those near New York. Their breath became terse; their heads went light as the order cemented into reality.

Defensive fortifications sprang up in every direction a head turned.

Three principal forts inhabited Long Island: Fort Putnam (after Rufus Putnam), Fort Greene with six cannons overlooking Jamaica Road, and Fort Box (after Major Daniel Box, an officer under General Greene), and strongholds stood at the southeastern end of the Brooklyn lines near the head of Gowanus Creek, and east of the small village of Brooklyn.

Eying the completed forts as a child might a birthday present, Washington explained to his officers, "The objective is to supplement Fort Sterling's defense, perched on Brooklyn Heights."

Hypnotized by power, more construction took place under the orders of the commander-in-chief at Red Hook, called Fort Defiance, some three miles to the right of Fort Putnam, and on the banks of the Hudson, Fort George, and at the East River, at Whitehall dock.

Below it, at Jeffery's Hook, was built a strong redoubt, and about the same distance to the North, another defensive structure came into being. Twenty-four cannons and smaller artillery and mortar were mounted on these fortifications.

In conjunction with Fort Lee opposite the Jersey side of the Hudson and Fort Washington on the New York side, Washington said, "This should thwart British ships from sailing up the Hudson."

Trying to get some perspective, he fought to find a way to make sense of it, understanding he was the commander-in-chief. He frowned, disregarding his reputation for optimism.

The Patriots were busy beavers at every nook and cranny of Manhattan Island. They drank his command like a thirsty camel in the desert.

On June 22, 1776, Burr moved to General Putnam's headquarters at the foot of the Battery, where the Kennedy house stood at No.1 Broadway. Fort George's entrenchment flanked the mansion while its garden meandered to the Hudson River's beaches.

Major Burr wrote Sally, "Washington granted my request for active duty and transferred me to General Putnam. The good and farmer-warrior possesses few pretensions. We have a relationship based on mutuality and utter honesty. The canny and fearless fighter of Breed's Hill likes to drink and revels in me with his stories. The Connecticut Yankee lacks polish but stands in contrast to the arrogant, aristocratic Washington whose military family consisted of several aides."

As deep and true as his desire for glory, he informed Sally, "I must pass on success if it means I must pander or feign respect to advance in rank – A Major I will be. I am "Old Puts" right-hand man and like it that way."

After setting the letter aside, Sally gave her husband a gentle look. "Tapping, I think Aaron found his mate."

For his good "old General" in early July, he went on recruiting trips and inspected the troops. His thoughts, command, and entire mind rose like a phoenix.

He twitched, a quick gesture of discontentment when he spotted a solitary ship coming down the North River on the morning of June 29. After a few seconds, curiosity ripened like a summer peach through him, but then a frown covered his face.

"General," Major Burr said to Putnam, "the British Royal Naval ships are classified according to how many guns are aboard and given a rating. Greater than 74 guns are line-of-battle ships, rated one, two, or three, and none have arrived."

Putnam shrugged a sigh of relief. "Fine by me."

"Forty-four to twenty guns on a single gun deck are frigates, which are three-masted, square-rigged ships and rated accordingly from four to six."

Putnam sat back, drumming his fingers, impressed with Burr's knowledge." Other British vessels are bomb ships, brigs, schooners sloops, and tenders which are commanded by either a commander or a lieutenant and not rated."

## Chapter 16

# Reality

On a bright, sunny summer day, robins chirped short, high sounds as British transport after transport dropped anchor in the Narrows, a body of water that linked the upper and lower bays of New York and separated Staten from Long Island.

"General Putnam," said Burr, "I received information from Washington's headquarters, "Our people are firing with the nine pounders at the Narrows but have not heard where they have done any execution."

His general looked relaxed, and Burr observed a glow about him. Then again, he usually did when a battle loomed.

"Forty-five ships have anchored," the Major announced to General Putnam. "their masts resemble a forest of trimmed pine trees."

"By evening, the forest grew," Burr wrote to Sally, "to more than a hundred ships standing tall in the Lower Bay of Sandy Hook, ten miles beyond the Narrows.

The views of the wooded shore of Staten Island were now dotted with the white tents of the recently arrived British forces under General Howe's command. Over 400 vessels were in the harbor within seven weeks and 30,000 troops were camping on Staten Island."

On July 2, Burr and Putnam observed some of the British fleet sailing through the Narrows and landing troops on the eastern shore of Staten Island. From no headache to a throbbing one, Putnam refused to succumb to the explosive pressure in his head. Thinking of the upcoming battle, it subsided.

Early the next morning, an enemy party headed by General Howe landed on Staten Island, and a spy informed the Patriots, "All the Troops ashore, about 2,300, march'd along the North side of the Island by Deckers Ferry, and part advanced to Elizabeth Ferry, Richmond, etc."

Burr rushed to tell Putnam on the morning of July 4, "10,000 enemy forces landed on Staten Island and set up an encampment there." He thought Putnam giddy over the prospect of a battle, no headache this time.

On the evening of the ninth of July, the American brigades in New York gathered at the Commons. The Declaration of Independence was read. Loud huzzahs serenaded the bold document. Major Burr listened to the stirring words of liberty, never guessing that his future would be determined by its author, Thomas Jefferson, whose bright hazel eyes beamed from his freckled face.

Their time together in politics allowed Burr to see that his thin lips hid an even shallower smile.

And beating in his chest was a heart colder than icy streams in winter.

Burr would come to know he had an opinion on everything and believed what he said to be the truth.

To do this or that, Jefferson would cast a hint to a devoted follower through the corner of his eye, only taking a look at his face.

When talking about Hamilton, his veins knotted at his temples, and his face resembled a red beet. He could roll his followers into a ball or flatten them; it mattered not, and he directed without his hand being seen.

Burr understood that sincerity in Jefferson was no more possible than dry water or wooden iron.

In 1800, Burr would make him president through his diligence and integrity, but Jefferson's twisted hand wrapped his honor into alleged deceit. Smug and sympathetic symbolized the Virginian's superior skills.

He was the man who always looked at you from a soft to vibrant face Burr observed, but little did you know that he was trying to find out where to stick the knife.

What the Sage of Monticello did to Washington and Adams through his newspaper henchman, Burr shrugged off as the opposition's fate.

In time, he learned the great Sage considered anyone other than Madison and Monroe the enemy. In Burr's old age, looking back over the hedges of time, all might have been forgiven had not the man possessed the humor of a corpse.

After reading Jefferson's Declaration on the 9th, speeches came and patriotic shouts advanced, but the participants' lungs gave way, and the great mass of patriots rushed to the South of Broadway on the Bowling Green. Once there, Burr turned around, jolted when he watched them storm the 4000-pound gilded lead statue of George the Third, which showed the King in the garb of a Roman emperor mounted on a horse. Thousands of hands pulling ropes tumbled it down.

"The delirious crowd," Burr wrote to Sally, "cut off the nose, hacked the wreath of laurels from the brow, shot a bullet into the head, and took the odious prostrate symbol up to Fort Washington intending to mount it on the truck of the flagstaff."

There is a famous fable that the King's statue went to the home of Oliver Wolcott, Governor of Connecticut, in Litchfield, his wife, and daughter making 42,000 bullets that were fired at the British as "melted George," history must manage a disbelieving laugh at the yarn.

"Three Regiments of Connecticut militia Light Horse Lee," Burr continued to Sally, "Men of reputation & of property, arrived in New York under the command of Lieutt Colo. Seymour on July 11 as the setting sun bronzed their smiles. On impulse, near-sighted Washington wanted the men only on the condition they could leave or send back their Horse" much to their chagrin. The General told his staff, "There is not enough forage on hand or to be had than is absolutely necessary for the use of our Working and Artillery Horses."

"They were discharged," Burr wrote, "by the unrelenting commander a few days later because they refused to perform the common fatigue duties of a soldier."

Washington's staff, on July 12, informed General Putnam, "At about half after three o'clock this evening, Two of the Enemies Ships of War, one of Forty and the other of Twenty Guns, with three Tenders weighed Anchor in the bay opposite Staten Island."

Burr watched as *The Phoenix* and *Rose* rapidly sailed into the Hudson River with a favorable wind to their backs and an inviting tide.

"Look at that," he said as the ships were soon abreast of Red-Hook.

Bad, he decided. Very, very bad.

The noise from the Battery shattered the morning silence, and all the Batteries, for three Miles on end, opened fire upon them till they sailed past entirely.

Every thought that did not revolve around the British, particularly an armed foe, was a struggle for Burr. He stepped back as the enemy kept a warm fire the whole of the time on the rebels - tho' with no effect - several Patriot shots hulled them.

In his report to Putnam, he recorded that in the fray, "We lost six Men by our Guns, carelessly. When abreast of Mount Washington, 12 miles above the town, Genl. Mifflin gave them a Warm Reception - but did them no great damage."

Receiving communication from Washington's headquarters, Burr handed it to Putnam.

"Our generals thought the British view was to cut off our communication with our Northern Army around Albany. My view entails that they knew our batteries are impotent and will make plans accordingly."

No point in telling us that, Burr decided. We know that.

"Without sea power," said Major Burr, who angled his head and grimaced. "New York should not be defended; the risks are too great."

Putnam's instinctive cry for battle roared. A fire consumed him. "Orders are orders."

With his mind still opening up to the situation, Major Burr stared at his General. They watched as the British ships shot cannonballs into the small town's defenseless houses, where they exploded and rolled down the streets.

Hearing the shrieks and cries of those poor creatures running every way with their children, Burr studied Putnam.

"This is truly distressing," said his general.

With his eyebrows lifting, Burr watched the smoke from the patriot cannons fill the air thicker than a morning fog and the smell of sulfur reek from one end of the Island to the other.

The Major let a gasp that ended on a hesitant snicker as he departed on an errand for his general, who listened to more than two hundred shots fired by the patriots but without avail.

By dusk, Burr returned and reported, "The enemy ships moored at Tarrytown, thirty miles above our army, ready to cut off supplies and promote Loyalist sympathy."

Putnam considered as he waited for inspiration. "Sometimes, I wish I was back in Salem Village farming with my father." But then reality set in, "Damn it, I want the battle to begin."

Major Burr learned of a most original proposal submitted to Washington and his generals as the British showed the rebelling patriots their muscle.

Entitled, "A Plan for Attacking Staten Island in different places so as to Form a General Attack upon the Enemy's Quarters."

At a council of war on July 12, Washington asked his generals, Putnam, Spencer, Green, Heath, Stirling, Scott, Wadsworth, and Heard, "Whether, in our present Situation, such a measure is advisable." It was agreed unanimously that it was not.

Burr told Putnam, "This is an egregious error to me. The strength of the rebellion must be hit-and-run warfare."

Putnam snorted, smelling blood and sweat, not distasteful to his mind.

Major Burr failed to say to his general, "The basic problem is that Washington never commanded a regiment, much less an entire army. "It is not surprising that such a bold move could be agreed upon."

A lesser plan to alarm the enemy was put forth by Washington, where General Mercer would confer with Major Knowlton, who had reconnoitered the Island and knew it well. This Plan was well known to "Old Put" and as Major Burr was intimate with his general, its details became privy to him. He was to be involved in its execution, but inclement weather led the rebels to "relinquish the Enterprize."

Watching more British ships continue to moor: five on July 25. On July 26, eight boats were seen in the Offing standing towards the Hook; Burr heard that Washington learned that Men of War & Tenders on the 29th were still up River.

Burr scanned the Hudson and heard a whoosh as more enemy fleet appeared. Reading Colonel Hand's Reports, "Nine ships, four Briggs & two Sloops at the Hook came in last evening and that Two Briggs came up to the Narrows, and one went down, "It is rather obvious, really," Major Burr said to General Putnam, "that the British have us in a vice."

"On August 1," Burr said to Putnam, "45 ships arrived with Generals Henry Clinton and Charles Cornwallis. And if they needed it, the British forces received another 21 ships on the fourth, 100 ships total in ten days."

After a moment's thought, he withdrew, and General Putnam murmured, "God help us."

Word circulated throughout the Army that three dozen Tories were known to have been exploring the south side of Long Island at the entrance to Jamaica Bay by Plumb Island. Burr could feel the trap being set. Between Red Hook on the North and Yellow Hook on the South was Gowanus Bay's cove on the eastern shore of Long Island. Most British fleet was anchored at Yellow Hook, directly across the Narrows from the Watering Place on Staten Island.

He reported to Putnam, "30 transports, under convoy of three frigates, put out to sea on August 7. They could go around Long Island and thus cut off an American retreat from the East River."

As the days advanced, Major Burr noticed the men's brows furrow, their mouths twisted in a way that told them the future was not their friend.

He noticed the fear among the officers of being entrapped, "On this tongue of land, where we ought never to have been."

On the morning of August 12, the sight of the British fleet in the offing produced a lump in the rebel soldiers' throats.

By evening, their number consisted of 107 Sail.

"This large fleet," Burr wrote to Sally, "entered the harbor with the

Sails crowded, Colors flying, Guns saluting, and the Soldiers both in the Ships and on the Shore continually shouting."

Burr took a deep breath, "I might add no way a comforting sight to the aghast rebel army."

An aide to Washington disclosed the words of Washington to Burr. "He had long religiously believed that a vessel with a brisk wind and strong tide cannot unless by a chance shot be stopped by a battery."

What would be the effect of the entire British fleet on the defense of New York? Burr contemplated. The thought of victory and the distance to liberty a universe away.

"It was an untenable situation," Burr wrote to Sally, "and the British General could have ended matters right then and there. With 30,000 seasoned and well-equipped men, a large load of artillery, and cavalry, he could advance from an undefended rear while the Navy bombarded safely from the water."

"For the several posts on New York, Long & governors Islands and Paulus Hook," Burr told Putnam, "we have fit for duty 10,514 - Sick present 3039 - sick absent 629 - On Command 2946 on furlow 97 - total 17,225."

General Putnam informed headquarters, "Our posts too are much divided having Waters between many of them and some from Others fifteen Miles."

Burr knew that Washington did not need good eyesight to see in almost every barn, stable, shed, and even under the fences and bushes hide the sick. Their countenances were an index of the dejection of spirit and their distress.

"With this the reality," Burr continued to Sally, "and almost no artillery nor mounted men, (due to his ignorance of rejecting the Connecticut militia Light Horse) General Washington thought he could defend an expanse of water and land covering 30 miles, vulnerable to attack from the front, rear, and flank."

He held his quill in his hand, then wrote, "The odds are better for catching a flying pig."

"For reasons unknown," Burr said to Putnam, "General Howe moves in mysterious ways; I think he wants to dazzle (bombard, shock, and awe) us as if that would put an end to the conflict."

Putnam frowned.

Burr contemplated the situation, returning to his point, "He is free to concentrate his attack at any point. With a superior force, he can easily divide our scattered forces."

On August 12, another 100 ships anchored, and General Putnam learned through Colonel Hand that "about Eight O'clock yesterday evening Hessians were landing on Staten Island to a considerable Number."

Putnam leaned back as his fighting spirit sprinted to life.

"The ships have bobbed in perfect tranquility," Burr wrote to Sally, "for five weeks while their awnings stretched, and their sailors tanned in the sunshine until August 18.

All in all, 120 cannon, though always proving ineffectual, waiting for the forces of King George."

He rose and adjusted his grip on reality as he weighed the situation. *Not good*, he thought.

The next day, Burr watched as General Washington surveyed his establishments and stood proudly. The general thinking of glory and the distance to victory.

Burr learned from one of Putnam's aides, "Most of the Troops that come over here are strangers to the Ground, Undisciplined and badly furnished with Arms - they will not be so apt to support each other in Time of Action."

The Patriots ascertained from a report made by escaped patriot Captain Alexander Hunter, "That about 8000 Hessians have arrived, and five Thousand more Hessians are expected in a few Weeks - that the whole Force is supposed to be about 26 or 27000. That it is expected an Attack will be made in Eight or Ten days and not before. That it is believed in the Fleet that General Washington is weak and has not more than 15000 Men in New York and Long Island."

"Lacking in artillery," Burr noted for Sally, "without mounted horsemen, unfamiliar with the lay of the land and, of course, with no naval support, General Washington continued to ignore reality.

He stared the situation in the face and wanted to make a stand believing the enemy granted us much time to collect our strength and erect the necessary Works of Defence. The excessive danger of the situation never dawned on him." The situation looked awkward to all but Washington, who longed to prove his worth and overcome his insecurity. "No doubt in my mind of defending this place," was Washington's very words."

When resting his mind, Burr felt annoyed. He thought Washington tempted fate, and 32,000 well-armed enemy troops were assembled on Staten Island, a population higher than America's largest city, Philadelphia.

"To make matters worse, the oppressive heat has caused," he noted to Sally, "a camp fever in the patriot cantonments."

Major Burr informed Putnam "That to protect the heights of Brooklyn, Washington would have to divide our impotent force. In an emergency, one portion could not assist another. The entrenchments around Brooklyn are key and should be concentrated around lines of the strongest defense, not spread out over a six-mile stretch. At least 8000 men were needed to defend the interior works at Brooklyn and another 8000 on the exterior lines before Flatbush."

Putnam formed a tight fist on his right hand and wanted to strike out but refrained.

"Of course," continued Burr, "this is assuming the best-case scenario, the enemy would oblige Washington by attacking his front and ignoring to attack his flank and rear."

"Damn it all, yes, Major, I suppose you are right, but my job is to follow a command."

Burr stopped and turned, recognizing that ideas must proceed with actions or stand askew to them. Progress limps along, getting somewhere, even if it is not the place it is aimed for.

On the morning of the 18th, Major Burr took it all in as the *Phoenix* and *Rose*, men of War with Two Tenders, availed themselves of a favorable and Brisk Wind. They sailed down the river and joined the fleet (near Staten Island); several Batteries fired at them in their passage, but again without any beneficial effect.

General Mercer, stationed at King's Bridge, forwarded two matters of intelligence regarding the enemy:

1. "British can go round the East end of Long Island into the Sound to cut off communications between Long Island and the Main."

2. "Land above the Town which means they expect to secure General Washington & the Army without firing a Shot."

On August 20, General Greene became dangerously ill, and Washington put John Sullivan, a recent arrival from Canada, in his place as commander of the troops on Long Island.

"You think all it takes is four stars and an order? He knows nothing of the land," said Major Burr while making notes for General Putnam.

Burr snapped the pencil he gripped into two, hurling both parts to the floor.

"Washington now believes," Putnam told Burr, "the enemy will attack Long Island and to secure our works there, if possible, and simultaneously another part of their Army is to land above the City - Nor is it possible to prevent them landing on the Island."

Wanting something to pound on, to beat senseless, Major Burr clenched his fists.

"He told his Generals," said Putnam, "attempt to harass them as much as possible.

*Risking everything just to harass*, thought Major Burr.

His eyes narrowed as he wondered if this was some psychological scar from his days in the French and Indian War.

The Major wanted to get out and breathe some air before the force of Washington's ignorance made him scream.

He turned to the facts and was disappointed, the situation roaring like a lion. He concluded that General Washington boosted himself up in arrogance, straddled his ignorance from behind, and dug his fingers into defeat.

# Chapter 17

# AH

The air, thick with the fragrance of summer, flowers blooming in every direction, at the Battery with an unobstructed view of the British vessels' thick masts, Hercules turned to Alex with a look of worry.

"Good thing Congress declared independence," said Alex, "at least if they hang us for treason, future generations will know why."

With a quizzical look, the tailor and future spy for General Washington shook his head, "Damn, the harbor resembles a wood of pine trees."

"When we kick their asses," replied Alex, "we will have plenty of wood for winter."

On the night of July 9, Alex dreamed; in the dream, he was in his youth on St. Croix contemplating greatness. The following morning, he and Hercules stood at the Common.

"We are back to where you first spoke," Hercules told Alex.

"Not that long ago," mumbled Alex, who smiled, remembering the crowd's applause as he listened to Jefferson's manifesto read aloud, 'The United Colonies are Free and Independent States.'

"I would have worded it differently."

On July 12, Captain Hamilton barked orders as four of the biggest cannons in the rebel arsenal fired on the ships sailing up the river: the *Phoenix*, a forty-four-gun battleship, and the *Rose*, a twenty-eight-gun frigate.

One of Alex's cannons burst, killing six of his men and injuring several others.

"What happened?" Alex yelled at Hercules.

"The men neglected to swab out the sparks and powder after their previous firing."

Too stunned to react, Hercules failed to tell Alex that some men were hungover from whoring and drinking the night before. Blinking away a tear, Alex gritted his teeth, "War is a filthy business."

Ambrose Serle, General Howe's secretary, mocked the patriot army as "the strangest that was ever collected: old men of 60, boys of 14, and blacks of all ages and ragged, for the most part, compose the motley crew."

By August 17, only five thousand out of a population of twenty-five thousand remained in Manhattan. A long string of emptiness swelled the morning air.

Returning to their temporary home in Manhattan, Robert Troup, leaning on the doorjamb, observed Alex's distress.

Hamilton avoided his gaze, wanting to take a walk around the gardens.

"What's wrong," asked Troup.

Wringing his hands, Alex said, "How can we defend Brooklyn Heights against a British attack?"

Troup frowned at him, blinking against the moonlight streaking through a window.

Alex picked at the edge of his quill in the foyer. "I am quite tired thinking about this. I sat for two hours this afternoon and failed to conceive a plan to stop the British."

"What does Hercules think?"

"He and the Reverend John Mason, over dinner, suggested writing an anonymous letter to the General urging a tactical retreat, and he would deliver it to an aide of Washington."

Troup heard Alex taking a deep breath.

The anonymous letter fell on deaf ears.

Troup kept a look at Alex, fascinated by his concern. "I need sleep," he said. "Do what you do best. Write."

Later that evening, sleep captured Alex's eyes; he pictured singers and musicians sauntering into an imposing Greek palace with ionic columns on Brooklyn's heights, ready to perform a dramatic work.

Ares waved the audience to sit.

Poseidon smirked benignly before announcing, "The Great Escape of Washington."

Cymbals shook the gilded walls, and daylight streaked upon the Continental Army.

Athena announced, "Not since Moses parted the sea was there a body of mortals more in need of a miracle."

Disgrace or danger requires our attention.
Draw the sword, not a question

Leave the fear of defeat on the shelf
The honor of freedom is life itself
Abandoning it is to accept servitude
The bounds of moderation feud
Sometimes the body of liberty requires retreat
To fight another day, to a further drumbeat
From the fiery and destructive passions of a master
Liberty climbs above itself to avoid disaster.
Through acts of bravery and heroism, the arms of liberty drum.

Usually, the wind blew southwest at this time of year, which would have carried the enemy ships up the East River, placing them in front of Brooklyn. But the God of War, Ares, implored Zeus to blow the wind northeast, thwarting the ships under the command of Sir Peter Parker to reach their destination.

One small ship managed to get up the river and bombarded the western Brooklyn line of the Patriot's defective battery at Red Hook. Alex's face turned sunset red, wanting to take a great leap of faith and move from the inevitable.

A small group of Washington's aides came to his door that evening. They glanced back as they walked away, watching their general looking for the quiet face of inspiration, believing he had no intention of settling for less. How could they have been so deceived?

Indeed, divination in warfare guided Washington's light as the noise of combat crisscrossed Manhattan Island's waters, ceasing for the time being.

Washington's eyes opened, gazing straight into the Hudson, the general learning to be rather glad that such a moment came.

## Chapter 18

# Prelude to Battle

As Major Burr meandered at dusk from the Kennedy house's gardens at the Battery's foot to the Hudson River's beaches on August 21, the entire horizon became black as coal. He stood for a moment with a clenched jaw, concentrating his eyes on the sky, considering making a run for it but continuing casually, hoping for a cleansing. As he reached the mansion's front door, the rain dropped faster—a heavy thunderstorm burst. It lasted for several hours, with uncommon lighting, one hard clap after another until after 10 o'clock.

"Three officers, viz., one Captain, and two Lieuts." Burr wrote to Sally, "was killed in one of the Camps; they were all Yorkers; and one soldier of the New English People was likewise killed in a house in the square; several others were hurt, and the mast of one of the row gallies smash'd to pieces."

It amused the Major that the religious among the American army took it as an omen. He imagined his grandfather, Jonathan Edwards, off yonder with a smug look as he tilted the sky.

"It was," he continued to Sally, "as if the electricity of the stationary storm was drawn to the oversupply of arms scattered about the vicinity of Manhattan Island. I wonder what old Ben Franklin would have thought?"

The day after the storm, on August 22, after lingering for seven weeks during the best campaigning weather, General Howe ceased the balls, fireworks, and games.

He ordered his subordinate, General Henry Clinton, to cross the Narrows amidst heavy thunderstorms with an advance guard. The rebels, thinking the weather too severe for British movement, allowed them to land unopposed. Soon afterward, more of the British army crossed the Narrows, and 10,000 enemy soldiers with 40 cannons landed on lower Long Island at Gravesend Bay.

"They marched unhindered," Burr told Putnam, "across the low, cleared grounds and stopped near the woods at Flatbush within three miles of our lines."

Putnam's teeth ground. Burr waited a few seconds for his general to compose himself. He gave his general a long searching look before saying, "Howe's army possesses the plains from the river to the villages on the flatlands of Long Island."

The coming conflict raged within Putnam. Like Beowulf, he wanted to fight the Dragon even though he was old.

"Howe's experienced force," said Burr, "with forty pieces of artillery and a cavalry regiment, is now poised to attack Brooklyn."

General Putnam's lips curved.

When he learned that Lord Cornwallis on the 23rd took a post in the village of Flatbush, reflectively, he said, "Bring them on,"

The British army extended from the ferry at the Narrows through Utrecht and Gravesend to the village of Flatbush.

"I heard that headquarters," said Burr, "believes their force now well near 15,000 and growing."

The stark reality of how to oppose a vast army of experienced veterans with about a third of many men, many raw, scattered apart over too many miles, hit Putnam and Burr.

"The British General Howe no longer lingers," uttered Major Burr.

Swearing at first, Putnam said, "He will learn we are very welcoming."

They laughed at their chitchat and returned to a more serious consideration of their situation. The foreplay of war, a skirmishing constancy, stretched their clock's hours.

On August 24, the austere Virginian General replaced the recently arrived General Sullivan, who had replaced the ill General Greene with General Israel Putnam as commander at Brooklyn.

On the same day, Sir Henry Clinton began a scouting expedition with Lord Rawdon and Sir William Erskine, an aide to Howe. Finding that the rebels were poorly posted, he drew up a plan of attack. He proposed an active corps march to the Jamaica Pass at night, advance through it at dawn, and come in behind the enemy. At the same time, the British would storm the ridge of hills and move eastward while part of the army pinned down the enemy in the center, and the navy in the East River threatened their communications, harassing every quarter before the main attack burst on them from behind.

At first, rejecting the plan, Howe changed his mind and endorsed it the next day, the 25th.

On Sunday morning, the 25th, Major Burr, "Old Put," and six battalions ferried to Brooklyn. Once there, Putnam sent Burr out to inspect the works on the Island, and he reported, "Militarily, it is suicide to combat the British."

"Washington seems utterly unaware that his army is in an impossible situation," said Burr, "he covers his mind with gross ignorance, the face of a man overcome with the reality about to face him."

"General Putnam," said Washington, "The irregularities" of the troops now under your command must be righted."

Putnam eyed him momentarily, holding his tongue, knowing his soldiers were outnumbered at least seven to one.

"The militia is timid and ready to fly from their own shadows," said Washington, who refused to issue a withdrawal to the Island of Manhattan. He worried harder that day than he had ever in his life.

These were not cheerful facts, thought Burr, and the sight of the British army surrounding them did not further confidence. The regiments were powerless due to the General's disregard for the facts. Burr then sat with Putnam, who was always agreeable and obliging and spoke kindly of everybody, but Burr knew he was distraught.

By Sunday night, the 25th, 5,000 Hessians crossed the Narrows from Staten Island, bringing Howe's army to 20,000.

Burr reported to Putnam that Howe camped that night at Graves End. His general was thinking of the coming invasion, *like a million shooting stars*.

Informing Putnam, Burr said, "It was apparent to all and even the blind that almost, the whole of the enemy's fleet has fallen to the Narrows, and from this circumstance - the striking of their Tents at their several Encampments on Staten Island."

"Old Put" sat back and thought of the plow he left in a field in Pomfret, Connecticut.

"We are led to think," said Burr, "they mean to land the main body of their Army on Long Island and to make their Grand push there."

Intrepid Washington discussed with his aides, and rightly so, about a British feint to draw more troops to Long Island and weaken the patriot forces in New York.

He set about being simple-minded and ignorant at the eleventh hour, not cutting the mustard of command.

Clinging to the foolish belief that victory, if unfortunately, it should decide in favor of the enemy, should not be purchased at a very easy rate.

He risked the loss of his entire army.

The Commander informed Putnam, "The entrenchments from the village of Brooklyn to Gowanus Cove on the South to Wallabout Bay on the North, consisting of a mile of creeks and morasses on either flank, must hinder the approaching enemy and be vigorously defended by your force."

Putnam watched Washington's face lengthen and his mouth uttering the voice of naiveté.

Told of this by Putnam, reality blew through Burr's mind and piled up against the hope of his future.

"The distance between Graves End and our entrenchments is eight miles," said Burr, "between these two, about five miles from Graves End and three miles from Brooklyn, is a heavily wooded ridge, the Heights of Guana.

"Brigadier General Samuel Parsons described," said Putnam, "the Heights as a natural barrier that ran northeast in length about 5 miles or so, which terminated in a small, rising land near Jamaica; through the hills are three passes. One near the Narrows, one on the road called Flatbush Road, and one called Bedford Road. These passes are through the mountains or hills, easily defensible, being very narrow, and the lands high and mountainous on each side and are the only roads which can be passed from the South side of the hill to our lines, except a road leading around the easterly end of the hills to Jamaica."

"If we must, we must," said Burr, who glanced around, noting the looks on the soldier's faces.

"We must place," said Putnam, who looked out of character – nervous and irritable, "On each of these roads a guard of 800 men, and east of them in the wood. Place Col M. with his battalion to watch the motion of the enemy on that part, with orders to keep a party constantly reconnoitering to and across the Jamaica Road."

Putnam stopped suddenly, and Burr caught him looking out as if to see how he should proceed. "Place the sentinels as to keep a constant communication among the three guards on the three roads."

On the pass beyond the road that ran north from Flatbush to Bedford stood a line of American forts and parapets that defended Brooklyn; General Sullivan sent there the early morning of the 26th.

"Since their landing upon Long Island," the American commander-in-chief informed his aides, "the enemy has not had in their power to do on account of the Wind, which has either been a head or too small when the tide has served to position their ships to the back of Brooklyn Heights."

Is it ignorance or arrogance, reflected Burr as he looked at his Excellency, that made Washington think the wind would always blow warmly upon his countenance?

After several seconds of complete silence, Putnam said, "I suppose he has his reasons."

Burr pursed his lips and nervously scratched his scalp as he tried not to contemplate that the earth and sky drained the Virginian of all sense.

Washington, who stood under the dancing sun, his gray eyes tangled in shortsightedness as the birds screamed in the damp green trees, had more sail than ballast.

To Burr, he seemed deaf to the acoustics of time, space, and common sense.

Once the British landed at Graves End with 10,000 British soldiers and 40 cannons, the Brooklyn entrenchments should have been reinforced and mounted horsemen stationed at the passes. The roads were constantly under surveillance. With 5,500 men never seeing battle, only six artillery pieces, and no horsemen to bring communications to and fro, Washington decided to risk an engagement, one that could lead to his utter demise.

"At least 15,000 men with adequate artillery are needed," Burr said to Putnam.

Burr meditating, it would not have taken Hannibal's mentally disabled son long to realize that this strategy was untenable, but not Washington.

When informed that Washington expected "Old Put," with only 3,000 inexperienced men behind the Brooklyn works, and General Sullivan, with three thousand men patrolling outside the fortified lines, to thwart the seasoned British army, Burr shook his head.

"The rugged terrain, General Putnam," said Burr, "prevents efficient communication, and in some places, the dense woods limit the view to a hundred feet."

Washington's actions rationalized Burr was as translucent as a house of glass. "He knew not what to do, for as we know, he had never commanded an army in battle, and his officers were green."

This soon became quite apparent through the transparency of reality. "Square-shouldered Washington," said Burr, "with an over-glorified mien, expected Lord Stirling to defend Martense Lane Pass east of Gowanus Cove. And General Sullivan to protect the Flatbush Pass, which crossed the ridge before the village of Flatbush, and Colonel Miles' reinforcements to patrol the Bedford Pass."

The enemy advanced by the road from Flatbush to the Red Lyon. It stood about three miles south of the Brooklyn ferry at Gowanus Road's junction, which went from Brooklyn to the Narrows.

Washington informed Putnam to order Lord Stirling to march.

Haslet's & Smallwood's met the enemy with two regiments,

advancing from the Martense Lane Pass east of Gowanus Cove. While on the road to the Narrows, daylight bloomed, and the rebel forces proceeded to within a half-mile of the Red Lyon, where they joined Col. Atlee with his regiment.

The opposing armies engaged until nearly eleven o'clock.

Instead of waiting in his lines, Washington ordered his force to meet the superior corps, not leaving his generals in the happiest moods.

Prescot at Bunker Hill stayed within his lines as the foolish enemy marched into his line of fire. Putnam received orders to send General Sullivan's forces to guard against the enemy advancing between the Flatbush and the Bedford pass.

The rebels learned these skirmishes were just feints by the British, and life turned very complicated in a brief time.

Clinton's soldiers marched shortly before midnight on the 25th, reaching the pass at Jamaica at dawn on the 26th. Finding the left of the Americans not so well secured as it should have been, they took the opportunity to reach the ground, which gave them a great advantage.

The British passed through this narrow opening, ironically, the most accessible pass to defend. Left essentially unguarded with five inexperienced officers on horses who were supposed to thwart a possible invading enemy, the British now outflanked the Americans the morning of the 27th.

Waiting for Howe, who arrived two hours later with the main column, the generals advanced westward towards Brooklyn." I urge caution and to form a line," said Howe, "in case we meet opposition." "I assure you," said Clinton, "that not having prevented us at the gorge, they will not take any position. The affair is surely over." "The enemy," replied Howe, "will open upon us when we reach the village of Bedford." "We are there," said Clinton." Are you certain," asked Howe." Ask the guide."

Howe turned to the guide.

"Yes, general." "Victory," said Clinton, "lies ahead." He pointed to the rebel position in Brooklyn. Without any resistance and behind the rebel's left wing, which collapsed at the first attack, Washington's right wing gave way. The American army fell behind the lines defending Brooklyn. "I have no information," said Howe, "about the strength of the enemy's position." Remembering what occurred at Bunker Hill, he sided with caution." I want a siege, not an assault." "The rebels are ready to be taken," said Clinton. "I see it in their eyes. They are panic-stricken, and their defenses useless. Their back is to the water, and our army is in front of them." The British General refused, and after repeated orders from Howe, Clinton called off the assault, groaning ferociously. Wanting victory desperately, the hunger for battle consumed him, but it moved beneath his grasp. "I sense trouble lies ahead," he said.

The British generals held "too many opinions that spoiled their strategy," and this manufactured a lack of coordination. Timing is always a critical issue; they rarely saw eye to eye, shadows moving with them, and in them, they glowed certainty.

Howe, a pedestrian general, lacked confidence he could take on Washington in a decisive battle without help from the Northern army, still haunted by his costly victory at the battle of Bunker Hill. He took pride in taking charge of the right wing of the attack personally but frowned that his first two assaults were repulsed by the Patriots, his third gaining his objective.

*****

Howe recalled that when Clinton was ordered to Boston with British reinforcements to strengthen their position, he believed everything hinged on whether Carleton advanced far enough to threaten the rebels' rear. After the battle, Clinton wrote, "A dear bought victory; another such would have ruined us." Disgusted with the situation in Boston, he sailed to the Carolinas in January of 1776 to assess military possibilities. His naval fleet and 1500 men landed near Sullivan's Island and bombed the rebel forces but to no success. Rejoining the main fleet, he participated in General William Howe's attack on New York in August of 1776, victory tasting delicious.

Burgoyne realizing the wilderness between St. Lawrence and the Hudson, made carrying on the war "a damned affair," informed his superiors, who smiled and shifted to another subject, ignoring him.

In the Summer of 1776, Burgoyne, eager to join Clinton and Howe in NY, wanted to help Carleton prepare for an invasion from Canada. Sailing up the Saint Lawrence River to save Quebec City, under siege by the Rebel Army, he led forces under General Guy Carleton, assisting him in forcing the Continental Army from the province of Quebec. Carleton's gratitude remained on the floor. Burgoyne stared at him until, saluting him and stalking away without a word. After Carleton won the naval Battle of Valcour Island, Burgoyne wanted him to lead the British forces onto Lake Champlain and capture Fort Ticonderoga, but Carleton thought otherwise. Burgoyne sighed and let his shoulders droop as the air warmed. A toad, he thought, is more valuable than him.

Always thinking of what happened at Bunker Hill, Howe aimed to dislodge the enemy at the least possible cost in men, regardless of the cost in time. He dug deeper into his decision as time passed.

Having failed to exploit Clinton's plan for victory, Clinton did not criticize him, though he knew he would have acted differently.

He declared to Cornwallis, "I cannot bear to serve under him."

Cornwallis let Howe know Clinton's feelings.

Henry Clinton sailed for England on January 13, 1777, and contested for control of the northern campaign, but Burgoyne received the reigns by King George. This led Clinton to request to resign, but the king dispatched him back to New York to serve again as Howe's second in command. To appease his ego, the king granted him a knighthood.

## Chapter 19

# Flight or Fight

Always thinking of what happened at Bunker Hill, Howe aimed to dislodge the enemy at the least possible cost in men, regardless of the cost in time. He dug deeper into his decision as time passed. Henry Clinton told Guy Carleton, "his heart pumps blood through his body, "but not to his brain." "People use their legs to walk," responded Carleton, "but Howe uses them to remain stationary." By the early evening of August 27, 1776, with" Old Put" at the besieged Fort on Brooklyn Heights, Putnam noticed that Burr's hair was untidy for him but not as untidy as the dire situation of the rebellion. After learning that Washington stood pondering his grave situation, Major Burr's fingers rushed over his scalp, looking tidy to his general.

Washington advanced through his options and left no answer satisfactory choice because numerous British ships were anchored within Sandy Hook, south of Staten and Long Islands, he was left hoping to cooperate with the forces on the ground and sat down to conjure a miracle.

"Why does Howe wait to order a full assault, asked Washington to General Putnam, who informed Burr of this question. The eyes of the general and major stared at the ground as it would speak to them.

"It is one of the world's great mysteries," said General Putnam as he informed Major Burr of more of the details of his meeting with Washington.

Burr took Putnam's notes and looked through them. His spelling was as bad as his handwriting, and many letters were reversed, foil as final.

"I think Howe wants us to surrender, said Putnam, who let loose a torrent of profanity, "Damn the son-of-bitch to a fiery hell; they are bloody, snaked-eyed bastards.

Burr flushed a deep crimson and turned his head to look into "Old Puts" eyes before saying, "To repatriate as loyal subjects of the crown without resentment,"

"A slight family misunderstanding," said Putnam, who lifted one of his hands and brushed his thinning hair. Burr, amused by "Old Puts" humor, not a common occurrence.

"A crushing defeat would leave acrimony and plant future seeds of rebellion," said Burr. Scratching his chin, Putnam said, "Howe's generalship is one of the world's great mysteries."

"A riddle riding an oblique four-legged conundrum," replied Burr.

Putnam laughed. "Yours is more reasonable than most of them," he said, shooting his Major a large and lofty smile from the ground to the gray sky.

Most patriots spent the night of the 27th shivering in a puddle of sweat spawned by fear.

During the early morning of the 28th, constant skirmishing occurred between the opposing forces. The Americans' stomachs ached from hunger, and their spirits were lower than the shallowest tide. Burr observed many stopped speaking and put their hands over their faces. He thought of a couplet:

*what could have been*

*while drinking East Indian tea*

Washington took a deep breath with his army's back to the East River and the wispy wind blowing hard into their faces. He ordered 1300 troops over from New York under the command of General Mifflin. One of the regiments, commanded by Colonel John Glover of Marblehead, Massachusetts, mainly consisted of sailors, fishermen, and boats. Men who "could trim a sail and pull an oar."

A heavy rain and hail storm came on by the afternoon, attended by thunder and lightning, arresting any British advance.

Major Burr glanced involuntarily towards the high wind and strong tide that slapped the rocks below the Heights of Brooklyn as the awful boom of thunder spoke harshly far into the evening.

The Gods, thought Burr, trying to impress each other. They must astonish and have their amusement. General Washington slept for a few hours, thinking of the British in a dream standing over him. His heart pounded as he tried to rid his insecurity, only to be awakened by an aide.

At 4 A.M., in the washed-out ink of August 29, a full consciousness returned to him. He liked the smell of early morning and took stock of the situation, wanting to make a stand against the British. He evinced divine hope that tents might be secured to cover his bathed men. There were few things that he knew. He knew that thwarting the Brits was a beacon that would shine on him.

The mid-morning found storm clouds waning upon Hicks Street, just south of Joralemon Street, in Brooklyn. The general summoned a council of war, which met at the large framed house of the absent Philip Livingston. Its gardens are the most beautiful ever seen in America.

Major-Generals Putnam and Spencer and Brigadier-Generals Mifflin, McDougall, Parsons, Scott, Wadsworth, and Fellows were in attendance by afternoon. They surrounded him, trying not to look grim.

Trying not to admire the colonial mansion's beautifully carved woodwork and ornamental ceilings and the Italian marble chimneypieces sculptured in Italy, the attendees considered themselves lucky. They knew the field would be lost if the British had advanced previously. A dense fog now covered the land and sea, thwarting the movement of Howe's ships. Meanwhile, Howe blinked and took a vacation from command; his eyes glittered with anticipated gratification as he thought of going off to a lover's lap.

The rain danced on the ground the afternoon of the 29th, more precipitation than anyone could remember, leaving the men standing up to their waist in water.

The middle-aged Putnam told his commander, "If the wind sufficiently picks up, the tide will no longer thwart the British warships, allowing them to sail up the bay from Sandy Hook to destroy our defective batteries at Red Hook, where Fort Defiance stands."

"After this," said Spencer, "nothing can prevent them from bombarding the two batteries, Grand and Whitehall, on the tip of Manhattan and anchor in the East River. If this occurs, the army would be surrounded and fatally trapped."

More British ships anchored at Flushing Bay on the Sound, allowing land troops on the East side of the Harlem River to take control of King's bridge, the key to the Island of Manhattan.

Evident to all for weeks, Joseph Reed, Washington's adjutant-general, having an intimacy with the General, undertook to give his opinion. Though he felt, "This might not be acceptable advice."

Washington frowned at Reed, not liking initiative even in those he fancied.

The Council of War "Unanimously agreed to leave Long Island & its Dependencies & remove the Army, without baggage or tents and almost without victuals or drink, to Manhattan."

Washington, doomed to silence, was unable to share in the decision. The chagrined warrior closed his eyes, longing for the fields and luster of Mount Vernon. In his heart, he supposed they were right.

Major Burr's General, 'Old Put,' a man of few but succinct words, later told him, "Convinced by unanswerable reasons, Washington resolved to take flight." But how, thought Putnam?

Burr smirked as he listened, feeling Washington swallowing the word "retreat."

# Chapter 20

# My honoured friend, Reverend Knox

"I thought you would like a narrative," wrote Alex to Reverend Knox, "of my late involvement in a battle."

"Asked by the hard-drinking Lord Sterling to help man some cannon, I went to Long Island on Monday morning, August 26.

Quickly, we learned by the return of some of the scouting parties that the English were in motion and coming up the Island with several fieldpieces.

Three thousand men received orders, chiefly from the Pennsylvania and Maryland troops, to attack them on their march. About sunrise, they meet up with a very extensive body of them.

The assault from this flanking force began amid a clear and cloudless sky at nine A.M., the 27th. This unopposed force under Howe outnumbered the whole American army. It was now in the rear of the American detachments under Sullivan and Sterling, who rushed forward to defend the direct western routes.

Yours truly and my men, with few cannons to defend ourselves, set up in an orchard.

On the enemy's approach, we gave them a very severe fire.

We kept this up for a considerable time until we were near surrounded.

We then retreated to the woods.

The overweight and rheumatic Lord Sterling, who commanded, immediately drew us up in a line and offered them intense battle in an authentic English taste.

The British army then advanced within about three hundred yards of us and began a heavy fire from their cannon and mortars, for both the balls and shells flew very fast, now and then taking off ahead.

Ordered not to fire until the enemy came within fifty yards; the patriots stood their fire coolly and firmly, but the British declined to come any nearer, although treble in number.

In this situation, my men and I stood from sunrise to midnight, the enemy firing upon us most of the time.

By a route never dreamed of, the main body of the British army surrounded the rebels and drove within our lines. Ordered to withdraw, we fought through the enemy on every field and road. We retreated a quarter of a mile before being fired upon by an advanced party of the enemy. In our rear, we received fire from their artillery. Our men fought with more than Roman courage, and I am convinced they would have stood until they were shot down. We forced the advanced party, which first attacked us, to give way. Through an opening, we got a passage down to the side of a marsh, seldom before waded over, which we passed, and then swam a narrow river, all the time exposed to the enemy's fire.

The whole of our battalion's right-wing, thinking it impossible to pass through the marsh, attempted to force their way through the wood. They were almost to a man killed or taken.

The Maryland battalion has lost two hundred and fifty-nine men, amongst whom are twelve officers: Captains Veazey and Bowie, the first certainly killed; Lieuts. Butler, Sterrett, Dent, Coursey, Muse, Prawl; Ensigns Coats and Fernandes; who are killed, or who prisoners, is yet uncertain. Many of the officers lost their swords and guns.

Generals Sullivan and Sterling were surrounded and surrendered to General De Heister, Commander in Chief of the Hessians.

Through an interpreter, the smiling Heister is said to have imparted to Howe, according to a captured British Lieutenant, "The gluttonous inebriate you told me about, Sterling, is my prisoner."

Alex's mind jumped to his father passing out drunk on a Sunday afternoon in St. Croix. "With a frown on his face, according to this source, Howe said, 'I will have to listen to the vain and pompous son of a bitch; maybe we should return him to the enemy.'

"Colonels Atlee, Miles, and Piper are also taken. About one thousand men are missing. We took a few prisoners. By this Lieutenant, we understood they had about twenty-three thousand men on the Island that morning.

Most of our Generals viewed the battle with glasses upon a high hill in our lines. When we began our retreat, they could see the enemy we had to pass through, though we could not. Many of them thought we would surrender in a body without firing. When we began the attack, General Washington wrung his hands and cried out, Good God! What brave fellows I must this day lose!

To quote the men, 'We received a severe flogging.'

"More than a third, 1,500 men, were killed, wounded, or missing out of an engaged body of 3,500.

Six hours of daylight remained, and we waited for our doom. The American cause was due to set with the sun, but by 2 P.M., the fighting suddenly ceased.

Washington's army was isolated from the main body in New York, with a superior enemy force in front and the British navy in his flank and rear.

Howe just had to attack, his victory assured. To quote one of the soldiers, the Brooklyn lines were 'unfinished in several places. So low that the rising ground immediately without it would have put it in the power of a man at 40 yards Distance to fire under my Horse's belly whenever he pleased.'

"I must get some shut-eye."

Your friend,

Alexander Hamilton

N.B.

"Feel free to submit this to the Royal Danish American Gazette under an unnamed correspondent if you feel it is worthy."

# Chapter 21

## "Billy" Howe

Awake, arouse, Sir Billy
    There's forage in the plain
    Ah, leave your little Filly,
    And open the campaign.
    Heed not a woman's prattle,
    Which tickles in the ear
    But give the word for battle,
    And grasp the warlike spear,
    Behold each soldier panting
    For glory and renown
    To them no spur is wanting
    March, and the day's your own

A brief account of the British General, the real saviour of George Washington, and the truthful progenitor of the United States are appropriate. He allowed victory to leap out of England's dominion, racing around the colonies.

While in England in exile in 1811, his second stay there, Aaron Burr sojourned again, as he did three years earlier, at the home of the kind Jeremy Bentham.

After dinner, or was it supper, one of the guests, a noted wit and classmate of General William Howe, exclaimed, after the second round of drinks, "Though so silent nobody knew whether he was or not."

A grin adorned Burr's brow as he chuckled a little awkwardly.

"The taciturn "Billy," continued the wit, "was a Whig whose family embodied America's warmth. Howe's slain brother's monument once stood in Boston as a tribute to a British man held in high esteem." He died in the French and Indian War when 40,000 British soldiers served in British America against France."

Burr spun around to face Howe again, listening to the past. Both recognizable and outlandish, animated and agonizing battles swept through and over his memory.

"Of course," the wit informed, "Billy' did not want to crush the rebellion but gently defeat it. He wanted the Americans not to harbor a grudge and to return amicably to the nest of Mother England."

Burr said, "Any general than Howe would have beaten Washington, and any other general than Washington would have beaten Howe."

He paused and smiled to himself, looking backward.

A reserved chuckle followed, the English not letting their humour fill the room.

"Billy's" classmate informed the gathering, "When the now Lord "Billy" (not Sir "Billy" anymore) arrived in Philadelphia, a stunning, flashing blonde noted for her playful nature, Mrs. Elizabeth Loring, the former Miss Lloyd of Boston, became his mistress."

Burr recalled her name.

"Mrs. Loring was at his side, whether at the faro table, the playhouse, or the dancing assembly. She remained so during the rest of the General's residence in America. Her husband, Joshua, was appointed by Sir "Billy" to the lucrative position of Commissar of American prisoners at the close of 1776. He pocketed his guinea a day and rations of all kinds for himself and his family.

There were not less than 10,000 prisoners (sailors included) in New York's British lines.

Loring appropriated to his use, nearly two-thirds of the rations allowed the prisoners.

He starved about 300 of the poor wretches to death before an exchange occurred, which was not until February 1777.

The hundreds alive at the time were so emaciated and enfeebled for want of provisions that numbers died on the road on their way home. Many lived but a few days after reaching their habitations." Burr straightened and listened to the tale from Howe's class informant.

"Billy's" severest critics, the staunch Loyalist Judge Thomas Jones, described Billy's lady as "the famous and celebrated Mrs. Loring, who as Cleopatra of old lost Mark Anthony the world, so did this illustrious courtesan lose Sir William Howe the honor, laurels, and the glory of putting an end to one of the most obstinate rebellions that ever existed."

Burr ascertained that the large six feet, dark-complexioned, affable Lord "Billy" liked his glass, lass, and cards.

"With Mrs. Loring, he gambled away hundreds of guineas."

His old classmate toasted his childhood companion, raising his gilded glass as the coal-burning hearth's blood-red wall warmed the room.

> "wine glinting in crystal glasses
> another day coupled with mirth
> Golden balls and silver laces
> securing the king's sovereign earth."

After the host's guests retired, Bentham shot up his hand before Burr spoke. Having gone straight to Bentham's head, the wine asked with caution and respect, "Tell me about your impressions of Howe and Washington."

Measuring his words thoughtfully, for Burr was conversing with one of the great minds of the time, took a deep breath, sat straight, and sipped some wine.

"Both Generals," he explained after gathering courage, "wanted success but chose to achieve it by a wish to avoid making mistakes."

Bentham sat back with open ears.

Burr's mind swooped out of the sky, over the fields and mountains as he plodded over the past, between the two generals, flanked by examples, late into the night.

"Both failed to push advantages that a bolder mind would have taken."

He paused a moment, his words brewing in the recesses of his imagination.

"Howe did not adhere to the successful military command code, pursue the enemy with full vigor whenever found."

Burr's tone was unlike anything in his memory, curiously objective and matter of fact, as a sage's voice.

"General Howe, once bitten by his three charges up Breed's Hill, always chose to err on the side of caution, and luckily for America, he cautioned too often in 1776 and 1777, missing opportunities to end the revolt." With his voice and intonation changing, Burr explained. "Washington only needed to avoid being caught in a position that would lead to a decisive defeat and major reduction of his army. It was amazing how often this military genius, the modern Julius Caesar, cast this dictum to the wind and left himself open to humiliation."

Bentham stepped into the story.

He remembered telling acquaintances that the thirteen colonies were vast during the revolution. Sir "Billy" does not have enough men to police the areas he could win and go on to battle in another place.

"Lucky for you, Burr," Bentham announced in a heckling voice. He lifted a glass for a toast.

"The British government was unwilling to commit the resources in hard currency or men to complement the military strategy necessary to thwart the march to self-government."

After clapping glasses, Burr admitted to his friend.

"Washington, our country's savior, finally came to understand that he should never risk an ultimate defeat after the Battle of Brandywine,"

Bentham cocked his head sideways as though not wanting to miss any details.

"Time was on the side of the rebels."

The candles threw their shadows, distorted, on the coved ceiling as Burr thought he uttered his last remark before retiring for the evening.

"This determination was a spectacular acquirement for Washington, and I did not think it within him.

Howe did more to lose the war than Washington did to win it."

"Colonel Burr," said Bentham, "I need more of your thoughts."

"This Loring was a monster! - There was not his like in human shape. He exhibited a smiling countenance and seemed to wear a phiz of humanity but has been instrumentally capable of the most consummate acts of wickedness, which were first projected by an abandoned British council clothed with the authority of a Howe, murdering premeditatedly in cold blood near or quite two thousand helpless prisoners and that in the most covert, mean and shameful manner at New-York. He is the most-mean spirited, cowardly, deceitful, and destructive animal in God's creation, and legions of infernal devils, with all their tremendous horrors, are impatiently ready to receive Howe and him, with all their detestable accomplices, into the most exquisite agonies of the hottest region of hellfire."

Burr paused and then recalled the snows of winter melting and running off down the little brooks of New Jersey with pleasant gurgling sounds. Wildflowers poked up through the leaf mold and spread their pretty petals to the sun's grateful warmth as the sap rose in the trees, the buds swelled, and birds came and mated and built their nests." Bentham's attention was captured.

"As long as the rebels held the forts on the Delaware, food transports could not be brought to Philadelphia for the British from their boats. They only had a week's food supply and ran the forts' gauntlet by night. Washington never realized the vital power that the possession of these offenses placed in his hands. Instead of manning and strengthening them, he paid no attention to them for two vital weeks after the Battle of

Germantown. Still, he wanted a battle with his undisciplined men against the well-trained forces if the British were securely entrenched behind redoubts. Fort Mifflin was garrisoned by only thirty militia, and others were neglected, half-finished, ill-garrisoned, unsullied, and unsupported. They held out for six weeks, and General Greene felt that Howe was on the verge of evacuating Philadelphia if the forts held out for another week."

Bentham poured Burr another glass of wine. Burr took a slow, steady sip.

"After Burgoyne's defeat, the rebels should have rushed to the Delaware River forts' defense with the captured guns and ammunition. Another surrender stood in the cards, but Gates refused to help Washington and was glad George received the blame.

When Clinton operated his offensive operations in northern NY, Howe ordered him to send them to Philadelphia. 'Good God?' he exclaimed, 'what a fair prospect blasted.'He abandoned all he had won, leaving Burgoyne outnumbered and surrounded by three to one."

A smile as wide as the Atlantic Ocean draped Burr's face." All through the winter of 1777-78," he said, "Billy sat in his quarters surrounded by his large army, while Washington encamped a few miles away, wasting from disease, desertion, and lack of the barest necessities of life at Valley Forge. The enemy was too vulnerable, but General Howe failed to exert the necessary skill. He did not march; he did not grasp the warlike spear; he did not open the campaign. Billy did not leave his Filly. He did not arouse. In a military sense, he did not even awake. He put the war behind him and threw himself into having a good time." Burr remembered when Washington retreated through New Jersey; the British numbers sufficiently drove him with the most remarkable ease. But orders were wanting.

"The British Commander-in-Chief, Howe, diverted himself in New York, feasting, gaming, and banqueting."

# Chapter 22

# Sir Henry Clinton's Plan

"Washington forces are in a desperate situation," said Clinton, who straightened his eyes on Howe.

"Explain," responded Howe, whose head ached from a hangover.

"They are in what amounts to a bottle, with its neck the Harlem River, and you can cork it because we command the surrounding water."

Thinking of the bottle of Bordeaux he uncorked last night, Howe tried to listen.

"You must move against Kingsbridge by way of Randall's Island and the Bronx to cut off the escape route and drive in the cork."

Howe believed Clinton looked starry-eyed.

"The rebel army's only choice would be starving, surrendering, or trying to escape to New Jersey and drowning in the Hudson."

Studying him, Howe thought he was too opinionated."

"Whenever an army composed, like this, of rebels, in a situation so alarming, it can never recover. It loses all confidence in its chief: it trembles whenever its rear is threatened."

"The enemy is evacuating the city, and my single aim is to speed their departure. The navy wants docking facilities as soon as possible to refit the men-of-war."

Clinton blinked. Here it comes, he thought, *his grand plan*.

"I propose a double assault on Manhattan: at Kip's Bay and northeast of the city's limits."

"Sir, I would land further north near the East River and the Harlem confluence."

"No, the troops would be too near the treacherous waters of Hell Gate.

Clinton tilted his head as he blew out a heavy breath. He wanted to laugh.

"The attack must concentrate on Kip's Bay, and you will command the advance guard."

Howe thinking, when criticized, Henry Clinton took it as a personal insult and tried the patience of his colleagues.

"The rebels are entrenched on the shore. Without covering fire from the navy, the plan is both dangerous and misdirected."

Howe's temper, harnessed through years of patience and determination, said, "Kingsbridge is the key to victory."

Clinton thought *Howe's plan was a small thing besides his alternative.*

"Landing at Kip's Bay," said Clinton, "offers real dangers but only limited success."

"Striking at Harlem has its dangers, from tide rips," replied Howe.

"But offers infinitely more," said Clinton, "the destruction of the enemy."

"The enthusiastic spirit of the opposition must soon subside," concluded Howe, "and that the inexhaustible resources of Britain will ultimately triumph."

## Chapter 23

# The Great Escape

Knowing Howe's indecision, Henry Clinton arrested the cessation of the strife, for Clinton took it as a personal insult that Howe did not allow him to assault the rebels at Brooklyn; his look trying the patience of his commander.

"The American forces were left defenseless," wrote Clinton to a friend in England, "if Howe allowed me to storm through the lines the afternoon of the 27th, for the East River lay at Washington's back and escape impossible."

Washington, the rank amateur in war, stood as the grandmaster of retreat, a brilliant tactical feat of war! Burr, to his dying day, shook his head and questioned any praise upon him as a military man.

Apologists for Washington cite Greene's illness and the incompetence of "Old Put" as the reasons for the loss of Brooklyn Heights. But the Commander spent August 24 in Brooklyn and gave written instructions for the plan of operations.

After telling "Old Put" what to do, "Meet the enemy head-on," he glanced back at his soldiers. "I want to inflict heavy casualties on the British when they advance through the wooded hills and then retreat to the entrenchments of Brooklyn."

*But those entrenchments are in poor repair,* thought General Putnam, who held his tongue while looking at the Heights.

Washington lifted his head and stared down at him. His eyes were narrow but focused on his, not wanting any questions but absolute obedience.

All this could only be done with an accomplished leader on the spot, competent staff, experienced soldiers, and good communication between the various posts.

When Washington turned down the cavalry sent in July by Governor Trumbull of Connecticut, he erred. Believing the expense of feeding their horses, though the countryside was abundant with foliage, he shunned a broad defense that needed good communication and mounted horsemen.

A few dozen soldiers in the saddle on his army's flanks would have allowed Sullivan and Sterling on the morning of August 27 to be forewarned and, in all likelihood, avert their capture.

Inexperienced in handling large bodies of men, Washington's most fatal error was in accepting the battle in the first place. His pride lingered on the blanket of the battlefield. It was the first thing that penetrated his decisions.

Thus, the famed General risked his army in a stand over Long Island; without sea power. It did not matter whether the British attacked from Long Island or north of Tarrytown.

Once Howe's immense force landed on Long Island, Washington should have retreated to New York and beyond instead of preparing to harass the foe in a disadvantageous engagement. His insecurity allowed him to make stupid decisions. *You cannot repair stupid*, Burr thought.

Allowing a trap to be set he opened the door to defeat.

The cutting remark of the historian Van Tyne that Washington possessed "little genius and not much aptitude for war" seems appropriate.

The retreat began amidst a heavy dew on Thursday, August 29, at dusk. As the rebels walked in the mud towards the river, the smell of fear hung in the air. General Putnam assisted General Alexander McDougall, who once delivered milk in New York and served as a tailor's apprentice after going to sea. Together in the rain, they coordinated the departure from the Brooklyn Ferry, the shortest distance between Manhattan and Brooklyn.

Putnam ordered the Indian allies to wail their war chants and beat their drums throughout the night. This caused the neighborhood dogs to howl as the Americans hurried into boats that ferried them to Manhattan. "That matters were in such confusion at the ferry," McDougall informed Hamilton, "is undeniable and that it was impossible to get within a quarter of a mile of the ferry, the rebel crowd was so great, and they were in such trepidation that those in the rear were mounting on the shoulders and clambering over the heads of those before them are the facts."

"I heard," said Alexander, "that they were speechless and silent, sometimes grasping hands to keep companionship."

"A fabrication," growled McDougall, "from a tissue of dirt held together by the dust of undeserved bravado."

At first, Washington's lip quivered as Zeus teased his army. He was producing an unfavorable northerly wind that negated the sails and required the men to be slowly rowed in staggered groups. Then, Zeus shifted the wind westward, allowing Glover's Marblemen to use their sailing boats, which sped up the two-mile broad withdrawal. They rowed the entire Rebel forces: men, artillery, wagons, and horses, across the East River to Manhattan.

Putnam observed McDougall's concerned face, doubting the army would successfully make it.

Burr found himself busier than a waiter at Fraunces Tavern as he helped Putnam manage the feat. First transported were the cannons, ammunition, supplies, and horses, Then the wounded, and finally, the remaining cold, wet Brooklyn army. He watched the quarter moon peeping in and out as the rebel army, always in their lines, surreptitiously rowed to safety. At 6 a.m., the last boats sailed off. For hours Burr and Putnam's eyes were mostly open; till the men's crossing of the East River was completed. The lingering, tumultuous hours impassioned him and gained him the further respect of "Old Put."

At daylight, the ever-friendly Zeus, along with the bare-shouldered Hera, Queen of the heaven and sky, at his side, puffed on a seegar, exhaling a mass of mist that hung like branches of a forest of willows over Brooklyn Heights.

It obscured the water while sheltering the last of the escaping patriots.

At dawn on the tip of Manhattan, Burr watched the sun figuratively and metaphorically burst forth.

After the fog broke, the disbelieving British viewed the saved Continentals, beyond musket shot, hurrying from the ferry landings to Rutgers' farm.

The rebels made suitable noises, and the British General said with a queer kind of regret, "I should very much like to do this again."

# Chapter 24

# GW on Manhattan

At the tip of Manhattan Island, cold shadows shimmered in the breeze on the forenoon of August 30 as the sojourned faces of the liberated patriots felt the rush of the calm wind after slipping away from the British. The life and death of the situation in Brooklyn relaxed at the forefront of the minds of the soldiers.

Washington stood with a frame of mind thinking a little too well of himself. Trying to look unconcerned, he shifted from leg to leg, wanting to redeem himself in his officer's eyes as a hard rain blew across his face.

Major Burr lifted his quill with a nod, noting in a letter to Sally, "The merry tones on drums and fifes have ceased, and they were hardly heard for a couple of days. It seemed that a general damp spread and the scattered people's sight up and down the streets was indeed moving. Many looked sickly, emaciated, cast down, &c.; the wet clothes, tents - as many as they had brought away - and other things were lying about before the houses and in the streets to dry; generally, everything seemed to be confused."

Burr lifted his head, struggling for the right words. "General Howe on August 31 marched his Army to Newtown, nearer Hells Gate, and the Sound. General Washington now believes that the American Army is collected, without Water intervening, while the enemy can receive little assistance from their Ships. In contrast, ours are connected and can act together: They must affect a landing under so many disadvantages."

*Washington's mind always left Burr bewildered; the space in it is limited*, he thought. The Major pulled down more of his thoughts for Sally. "The General left Long Island and Brooklyn Heights because his divided force was unable to resist the Enemy in any one point of Attack, fear of having his communication cut off the main (of which there seemed to be no small probability), the extreme fatigue his Troops were laid under in guarding such extensive Lines, without proper Shelter from the weather."

With an inward shrug, he continued, "Yet all the same conditions exist in trying to hold Manhattan." Hoping Washington would still improve his mind through much study, he knew the Virginian never read more than a few chapters from any book he surveyed.

He choked on his thoughts, laughed, and shook his head.

"Logic never seeded in the infertile mind of this Virginia planter. Howe can now strike at any moment, and if he did, our Army would have to leave New York in much confusion immediately."

The rebel command remained in a state of vexation. Still, they did not know that General "Billy" Howe, with his brother Admiral "Dickie" by his side, dined in the afternoons, sipping brandy and reminiscing about the good old days.

Billy whispered with great delight to his brother. One brother's cheerful look and manner, establishing the others as Ares, the God of War, delayed them from attacking through Dionysus, the god of intoxication.

Still needing to learn his lesson, Washington now attempted to hold Manhattan Island from the British, a useless objective being that the British controlled Brooklyn Heights.

The very next day, he shunned the advice of General William Heath, "There is a great Probability that the Enemy will throw over a Body of Troops from Flushing or Somewhere near that Place as it Can be done with the greatest of Ease."

His Excellency ignored the opinion of General John Morin Scott, "I believe that despite the precautions that have been taken to shallow the entrance into the East River, the Enemies ships may force their way into it. Should that not be the case, they have the Command of the City from Long Island. Their Ships perfectly command the North River. I have reason to believe that their Troops are filing off to the Eastward; and I make no doubt that under Cover of their Ships of War, now in the Sound; they will possess themselves of the Heights opposite King's Bridge woods. By this Manoeuvre, we shall be encircled with the same Kind of danger that We had Reason to apprehend on the other side of the Water, the Apprehension of which induced Us to retreat."

General Washington put his temper aside, hoping he looked casual, but a frown tarnished his brow. By no means did he wish to disregard his generals' advice, but he wanted no assistance. After an impatient glance, he shoved the past retreat out of his mind.

"A strong Garrison," continued Scott, "in the King's bridge works & Woods; and retreat of the Army into Westchester county is our nest option. The City will, in that Case, be evacuated."

Not giddy over the prospect of retreat, Washington glared at Scott.

"I think that the Method I propose," said Scott, "will prevent the Enemies encircling us; and enable us to keep up a good communication with the Eastern States."

Washington's large, callous, thick, protruding ears were deaf to any suggestions.

A most severe risk Washington now undertook. He decided not to escape to the highlands but to defend a nonstrategic position with the American Army, a very soft 20,000 stretched from the Battery to King's Bridge.

On September 3, an aide informed Washington, "The British ran a ship past the City up to the East River."

Washington sat with downcast eyes and a glob of affliction on his lips, thinking it was now a question of whether to defend the City or evacuate it and occupy the substantial grounds above.

An aide chimed in, "Every exertion has been made to render the works both numerous and strong, and immense labor and expense has been bestowed on them."

"The city must be obstinately defended," said General Washington, who now listened with half an ear.

He wrote Congress the opinion among his senior officers was that the town of New York should be burnt to the ground. But Congress did not wish the City left in ashes.

Even John Jay, not a military man, understood that a defensive war should be the American objective among the highlands' passes and defiles. He ventilated to those who would listen, "I cannot forbear wishing that a desire of saving a few acres may lead us into difficulties."

Washington looked at his aides, grinned, and divided his troops into three divisions under Putnam, Spencer, and Heath. Who was he kidding?

"Many of the soldiers," wrote Burr to Sally, "belonging to the Battalions, that suffered the most, in the Action on Long Island are much dispirited, & often muttering Expressions that they have lost their Officers, lost their Blankets, & have no money, & the like. One-half of the General George Clinton's Brigade are at Mount Washington: sick, without the want of covering, and suffering much."

Coming to their senses, the enemy advanced eastward on Long Island, opposite Hell's Gate.

Burr watched most of the rebel army march north towards an intensely illuminated skyline with hues from A to Z.

It stared at them from Harlem, the objective of the advance.

The strongly lit expanse of blood-orange leaves shimmered before the rebel army as it slowly recollected itself. Old Put's division consisted of Parson's, Scott's, James Clinton's (Glover's), Fellow's, and Silliman's brigades. Their objective was to protect the East River up to Fifteenth Street. The defense fell to Spencer's six brigades that extended to Horn's Hook and Harlem. Heath's two units guarded Kings Bridge and the Westchester shore. Thus, the entire length of Manhattan Island, from the Battery (farthest south) to Kings Bridge, stood in defiant but tenuous arms, a distance of fifteen miles.

Washington informed General Heath, "The most Salutary consequences may result from our strong encampment at the post on the Jersey side of the North River, opposite Mount Washington on this Island."

Heath lifted his brow, feeling his bruised palm, and determined he needed some thinking to do.

"This," said Washington, "should be begun & carried on with all possible diligence and dispatch."

The general's order was issued on September 2.

The *Rose*, a forty-gun British frigate, covered British troops' landing on Governor's Island.

It sailed up the East River with several flatboats to the mouth of Newtown Creek near Turtle Bay at night.

By nightfall on the third, British troops landed on Blackwell's Island under the *Rose's* auspices.

Fabricating historians tell us that Washington possessed "evidence of military genius such as has seldom been surpassed in modern warfare history." But the rebel army from August 27 to September 15 was at the whim of the opposition. Washington was a slow man who needed more instinct to do the right thing at the correct time, offensively or defensively.

Trying to imagine some "brilliant stroke" to save the day, he possessed no idea what this might entail.

Right from the start, Washington falsely believed that by commanding Brooklyn Heights, the British navy could be kept out of the East River, and he could defend New York. Yet, despite Brooklyn Heights, his flank was vulnerable from both sides, and he should have realized the situation's futility. The British could have cut the rebel army in two through their navy and the lack of patriots.

What is unimpressive is that he thought his plan was reasonably based on his experiences in Boston.

Yes, both towns had a harbor, but there ended any similarity.

His genius was as a politician. A man can fall in love with power if he lets himself, but he always remained a patriot for liberty.

Washington's generals kept imploring him to consider the facts. General Greene wrote, "The object under consideration is whether a General and speedy retreat from this Island is Necessary or not, to me it appears the only eligible plan to oppose the Enemy successfully and secure our selves from disgrace."

Washington snapped the pencil he held in two but read on.

"We have no Object on this side of Kings Bridge. Our Troops are now so scattered that one part may be cut off before the others can come to their support. . . Tis our business to study to avoid any considerable misfortune. And to take post where the Enemy will be Obliged to fight us and not we them."

Greene paused, knowing Washington would be upset when learning what was known on Monday, the ninth.

"The enemy are encamped in three divisions, One at Newtown, which is Head Quarters, One at Flushing, and One at Jamaica. The Hessians are at Newtown. That 1500 wagons are employed in Bringing across the Boats &c. That an Attack will Soon be made Somewhere east of Hell Gate."

More news soon reached Washington. Thirty means of transport and three Pilots proceeded unnoticed through Hells Gate. At sunrise, the British landed two light infantry battalions at Montresor's and Buchanan's Islands opposite Harlem.

Narrowing his eyes, Washington ordered the removal of the sick, the stores, and ammunition and marched men towards Harlem Heights, but not before taking the bells out of all the Churches.

On September 10, a report surfaced. "The Enemy has been all this Day landing Troops on Montrosure's Island where there appears to be a very large number of them & Sentries all around the Island."

Montresor Island stood at the mouth of the Harlem River. New York could not be defended, yet Washington stood proudly, still waiting for divine inspiration.

Was he waiting for Zeus to whisper in his ear?

On September 11, 1776, Benjamin Franklin, John Adams, and Edward Rutledge met with General Howe and his brother, Admiral Howe, but the meeting did not bring peace.

Also, on the 11th, Robert Hanson Harrison, an aide to Washington, observed to General Heath that the General was "fully sensible that you are deficient in Men which is not only the case of your post but to every Other, and which he well knew would inevitably be the consequence, when It was determined that our defense should be divided and extended to so many Objects."

Let it not be said that Washington was ignorant of his precarious situation. He was sure he was correctly facing the upcoming battle and that his strategy beat normally.

Finally, he agreed to listen to General John Morin Scott and other General Officers to consider the Army's situation.

"So critical & dangerous. . . I think it a mark of Wisdom to reconsider Opinions upon Subjects of high Importance whenever so many respectable Gentn request it as have signed above me. Therefore, I heartily concur with them in the above-mentioned Application to reconsider my stance."

By nightfall, two battalions of British troops stood fully equipped at Buchanan and Montresor Islands, which lie in the Harlem River's mouth, which runs out of the Sound into the North River.

Abnegating himself to his council of war, General Washington abandoned the City on September 12.

Most of the troops were to march speedily to King's bridge to secure a line of retreat. "Old Put," with a garrison of four thousand men, was temporarily left in charge of the City, his headquarters still the Kennedy House at No. one Broadway.

They were to hold the enemy at bay from a landing at either of the Batteries. The troops on the East River were to keep the ground until "Old Put" could leave for Harlem Heights.

But the weakest defense point was the middle of the island at Kip's Bay.

General Heath bespoke the absurd view against evacuating New York, "it being too strategic to the American cause."

Against a fire sunset, "Four British ships, one of which was a two-decker, ran by the city up to the East River" on the 13th."

General Washington ordered Spencer's six brigades to take up the line from that point to Horn's Hook and Harlem.

With two brigades, Heath was to watch King's Bridge and the Westchester shore. Having not recovered from his illness, Greene and his old troops, under Nixon and Heard, temporarily did duty with Spencer's command.

On September 14, the British sent three or four ships up the North River to Greenwich. Much of his army was late that afternoon at King's Bridge and Harlem Heights. Having turned sensible to needing to evacuate from New York, Washington moved up to Harlem Heights with the army's remainder. He told his aides, "If it is deferred a little longer, I flatter myself. All will be got away, and our Force be more concentrated &, of course, more likely to resist them with success."

Howe began crossing the East River late Saturday afternoon, the 14th, with eighty British flatboats filled with two divisions, 4,000 British and Hessian soldiers. They anchored in the East River below Kip's Bay while the rebel army removed cannons and stores from New York. That evening, five frigates, six means of transport, and one hundred barges defied rebel guns.

The trap was ready to spring, and Sir Henry Clinton expected Howe to close the door and allow him to lean against it.

# Chapter 25

# The Brits Are Coming

On September 15, Major Burr, outside the Kennedy House at the foot of Broadway, and Captain Hamilton beside the fort at Bunker Hill watched the moon subside. As the sun rose, birds began to chirp, mother nature's alarm clock signaling the arrival of a new day. Hamilton blinked, thinking since the dawn of time, the best time to charge the enemy is with the sun at your back.

Burr folded his arms before filling his lungs with the morning's fresh air, reflecting on life and death, admiring the magnificent beauty of a spider's web, waiting to catch its first meal of the day.

Under the abundance of light on the Hudson River, three British warships, the *Renown*, *Repulse*, *Pearl*, and the schooner *Tyral* sailed northward. The scent of the morning air was as sweet as a newborn mother's milk.

At 11 A.M., five British warships, the *Phoenix*, *Roebuck*, *Rose*, *Carysfort*, and *Orpheus*, began firing for an hour from a few hundred yards of Kip's Bay.

American soldiers were buried under their breastworks. Those still above ground fled like rats from a sinking ship.

"The houses on York Island shook, and the sound was terrible," an occupant inside said. The burning brush, dust, and artillery fire left a sharp and robust smell throughout the air and obstructed the view.

Washington's eyes flew open from his new headquarters at the Morris Mansion (eventually owned by Burr's second wife, Eliza Jumel). He moved there the night before from Richmond Hill.

Realizing his military error, he told Putnam to retreat the ten miles to Harlem Heights and his Excellency then rode off towards the smoke in the sky.

"Old Put," upon hearing the same bombardment, also rode towards the smoke over Kip's Bay, knowing his troops would be in extreme danger if the British landed successfully.

Meeting Washington around noon, near Murray Hill at the

intersection of the Bloomingdale and Kingsbridge Roads, they proceeded towards the East River.

They fell upon troops retreating en masse from the advancing British.

The tall and short men towered in rage, attempting to rally the cowardly soldiers, but it would have been easier to suspend Newton's laws of motion. As the rebel army retreated northward to Harlem Heights, General Putnam ventured south in search of his men.

A mighty irregular heptagonal redoubt stood at Bayard's Hill, west of the Bowery, where Grand and Mulberry streets intersected.

Mounting eight nine-pounders, four three-pounders, and six royal and coehorn mortars, it viewed the city on one side and the approach by the Bowery on the other.

Silliman, meanwhile, took a post with Knox in and to the right of Bayard's Hill Fort.

Captain Alexander Hamilton, who commanded a post near New York and fought with the rear of the army, heard the bombardment and soon smelled the sulfur in the air.

An angry colour flushed on his cheeks.

He learned that General Knox and some of his men escaped to Powle's Hook by boat.

The general's appetite for food prevented him from making the winding march of at least twelve miles to Harlem Heights. He commented to a fellow officer, a favourite and an idolater of Washington.

"More men of merit in the most extensive and unlimited sense of the word are needed and that the bulk of officers of the army are a parcel of ignorant, stupid men." After the Revolutionary War, Knox advocated for a military academy to "teach the art of war."

A white flag was displayed on Bayard's Hill Redoubt by loyalist citizens, and in the afternoon, a detachment from the fleet took possession.

After their departure, Captain Hamilton surrendered his heavy guns, and his company's weaponry was among the last of the army that left the city. Swept along in this retreat to the heights of Harlem with his cannon and his company of New York artillery, he frowned with Brigade-Major Fish.

Upon the cessation of the British bombardment around noon, Clinton and Cornwallis, in eighty-four boats, led four thousand British and Hessian troops and descended upon the shores of Manhattan Island at Turtle and Kip's Bays, about 3 miles above the tongue of the tip of Manhattan. A soldier said they looked like "a large clover field in full bloom."

General Henry Clinton, one of the first upon the shore, led his troops inwards toward Murray Hill but halted as ordered. Watching the remnants of the enemy in sight, he waited for the main body to join him, muttering that chance of victory slipped by again.

Major Burr, in the city with the remainder of Putnam's command, realized early on that the troops would be caught in a trap if the British extended their lines across Manhattan. He assumed the authority to move them north, away from the Battery.

The high summer sun beat down upon the patriots, sweat glistening on the colorless faces of the men as the sweltering troops, and Burr hurried north on Broadway.

Meeting near Murray Hill, "Old Put" informed Burr, "The enemy owns the main road leading to Kingsbridge,"

"We must use the route of Bloomingdale," said Burr, "to avoid them."

"A brigade," said "Old Put," "under Colonel Silliman is unaccounted for."

"The enemy will soon stretch from the East to the North Rivers," said Burr, "preventing escape to our men below."

"As you knew the terrain, Major, look for the lost brigade as I march with the men northwest towards Harlem Heights."

While walking through the thickly forested Manhattan in a drenching rain, Captain Hamilton lost his baggage and one cannon, which broke down, his arsenal down to two mobile fieldpieces pulled by horse and hand.

Burr did not ride for long before he spotted a makeshift fort, "Bunker Hill" (in honor of the famous engagement at Charlestown).

Perched on Bayard's Hill Redoubt at Grand & Mulberry Streets between Broadway and Bowery Lane, he galloped to the troops a mile above the Commons.

Finding that Colonel Silliman commanded them, he said, "Colonel, you must make an immediate withdrawal."

Silliman tightened his lips and nervously scratched his head.

"You have no moment to lose and will surely be captured unless you retreat."

"I agree but refuse, as my orders are to hold the redoubt unless I am ordered otherwise."

Burr observed his forlorn statement, thinking of a way for him to leave.

"I will do my best to fight off the enemy."

Reading his eyes, Burr jumped on his horse and rode a short distance to where he could not be seen.

He then galloped back to the entrenchment, calling Colonel Silliman, "Withdraw immediately under orders."

Silliman at once obeyed, his eyes telling Burr he understood.

With the lost brigade in hand, they marched northwest to join "Old Put" close to the New Bloomingdale crossroad.

Noticing a column of British infantry descending upon their right, Major Burr galloped to inform "Old Put, who dared to lead where any dared to follow.

Their rear attacked, and Colonel Jabez Thompson of the regiment died on the spot, the only loss before they filed off to the left.

General Putnam issued orders, encouraged the troops, and flew wherever he was needed with his horse covered in foam. Burr guided the forces along the rough, stony, uneven Bloomingdale Road.

Stone walls and trees partially obstructed them from the eyes of the enemy. Through the swamps and by way of the woods west of Broadway to Greenwich, they hurried.

Taking the less traversed North River Road that bordered the river bank to Bloomingdale Road, to the upper part of the Post Road, they hid in old familiar haunts when in sight of the enemy.

By mid-afternoon, another 9,000 of the enemy arrived at Kip's Bay and joined in the fray but did not pursue their advantage. At the same time, most of Washington's army exited in a "miserable disorderly retreat" towards Harlem Heights.

Eventually, the British encamped from the East to the North River at Striker's Bay: between the Seven & Eight-mile Stones, under the command of General Henry Clinton.

With Burr leading the vagabond patriot forces, they zig-zagged through the enemy but sighted; the enemy fired at the rebels, and a few men fell.

With 300 of his men, Colonel Silliman took a hill to combat the British.

On seeing this, the enemy fled. The patriots relaxed and smiled as they secretly continued their flight.

"The soldiers," according to Colonel Humphreys, "had been fifteen hours under arms, harassed by marching and countermarching in consequence of incessant alarms, exhausted as they were by heat and thirst (for the day proved insupportably hot and few or none had canteens, insomuch that some died at the brooks where they drank."

Arriving at Harlem Heights, four miles below Kingsbridge well after dusk, it was supposed by Washington and the command that Silliman's brigade were prisoners.

After reaching Harlem Heights in the dark, a silent Alex sank to the ground in an abyss of anguish

"That night," said Colonel David Humphreys, who served under General Putnam, "our soldiers, excessively fatigued by the sultry march of the day, their clothes wet by a severe shower of rain that succeeded towards the evening, their blood chilled by the cold wind that produced a sudden change in the temperature of the air, and their hearts sunk within them by the loss of baggage, artillery, and works, in which they had been taught to put great confidence, lay upon their arms, covered only by the clouds of an uncomfortable sky."

The American army rested there, some between Harlem Heights and King's Bridge and the rest at King's Bridge. Another narrow escape was accomplished, all the labor in creating works of fortification was for naught.

That night the wind blew hard amid heavy rain as the aroma of dankness whiffed the cold autumn air, the spirits of the patriot army dripping into the wet ground.

The next day, a brief skirmish occurred at Harlem Heights, known as the Battle of Harlem. Generals Greene and Putnam led the main attack against 5000 enemy soldiers.

Colonel Thomas Knowlton's Connecticut regiment severely mauled several hundred British light infantry.

The tattered, ill-clad patriot soldiers held their own, and the British retreated.

Washington then fortified Harlem Heights, and his army secured a very advantageous position, which Howe chose to respect, the encounter reviving the spirit of the patriot army.

The rebel army waited, expecting the British to follow up on their success, but again, the Greek gods exerted a tranquilizing effect on the cautious mind of General Howe.

During this hiatus, Washington observed Alex's special organizational abilities as he watched him supervise the building of an earthwork.

Entering into a conversation, he invited him to his tent, a shadow from his past lingering in one corner. Washington received an impression of his military talent, and the General and Alexander developed a rapport.

Nicholas Fish told Hamilton, "The general's shoulders are broad enough for these great duties, and his faith and resolution remain unshaken."

"I hope so," said Alex, "the fate of America hangs in the balance."

But, when it came to noting Burr's deeds on the march to Harlem Heights, in the general orders, his name remained amiss.

No point in complaining, he decided; Washington wanted only officers around him who ushered praise. Until his death, Burr's tongue was never soft regarding the Virginian.

## Chapter 26

# A Decision

In the fall of 76,' Thomas Jefferson faced a decision in Williamsburg. Go to Paris as a delegate with Benjamin Franklin and Silas Deane to represent America's interests in creating an alliance with France or stay in Virginia and be with his wife, her health prohibited her from accompanying him on his mission. He spent days glancing back and forth between Martha and a letter to the Continental Congress, with an occasional ride through Monticello's hills. "What will you do now, husband?" "I cannot leave you and go to France." "Our country must ally with France, or we will lose the war. Britain is too strong." Thomas looked at his wife and knew that, given her health, he might never see her again if he left for France. "I love you; I love my family. I love my new nation. If I stay, I can have all I love by my side." Martha, too weak to get up and run into his arms, let loose a simple smile while bracing herself on the arm of a chair. He put his hand on her forehead, massaging it gently. Writing to John Hancock, "No cares for my person, nor yet for my private affairs would have induced one moment's hesitation to accept the charge." Sweat broke out on his forehead. After a few moments, a thought came to his head. Hearing a sigh of pain from Martha, he finished the letter with, "But circumstances very peculiar in my family's situation, such as neither permits me to leave nor to carry it, compel me to ask to leave to decline a service so honorable and at the same time so important to the American cause." As 1776 ended, Jefferson learned from a correspondent on the Delaware River, "The enemy are like locusts." He went out, seeking the comfort of his garden and eating some sweet cherries. That should have gratified him, but it did not. He heard from Richard Henry Lee, "The British under John Burgoyne, with 10,000 men, chiefly Germans, plan to attack Virginia and Maryland and put the Southern and Middle colonies under military government." Washington informed his friends in Virginia that the military situation was critical. "No man . . . . Ever had a greater choice of difficulties and fewer means of extrication himself than I have." Hearing of this, within the pit of Jefferson's mind, fear lurked, unchained, and growling as he stood facing his library's gas light.

Later that day, Patty, feeling better, stood by Thomas's side under the winter twilight. They were alone, Jupiter, his personal slave, off on an errand.

"Tell me," Patty asked her husband, "do you remember any instance where tyranny was destroyed and freedom established on its ruins among a people possessing so small a share of virtue and public spirit?"

He shook his head. "I recollect none." As a delegate to the General Assembly of Virginia, the tall, prominent Thomas Jefferson, author of the Declaration of Independence, met the small, understated James Madison, known to his classmates at the College of New Jersey as "Jemmy." Years later, Washington Irving described Jemmy as "but a withered little apple-John."

"James," said Jefferson, "It does not speak well of the power of God if he needs a human government to shore him up."

Jemmy pushed at the gates of his mind, which opened quickly, with a practical creaking, and replied, "The necessity of freedom of conscience is paramount."

"Traditional Christianity is superstitious and unreasonable," replied Jefferson.

The little man hesitated and put his words off for a moment or two. "As you well know," he said, "It is a crime in our beloved Virginia not to baptize infants in the Anglican church."

The sniggering voice of the church burned in Jefferson's mind. "Dissenters are denied office, civil or military; children can be taken from their parents if the parents fail to profess the prescribed creeds."

"I," said Jemmy, "have heard Baptiste ministers preaching from within prison walls."

"Well, to make a long story longer, I," said Jefferson, "defended Reverend John Ramsay for getting drunk drinking the sacrament wine."

"Beware, my friend," replied Madison, "cries for religious liberty will bring on severe contests."

Jefferson's jaw tightened. "Honest men must stand firm."

"Jemmy" heard the command, his eyes fixed on Jefferson's animated face.

"Funds," continued Jefferson, "should not be used to support an established church."

"Nor to tie civil rights to religious observance," added "Jemmy."

"Yes," said Jefferson, "It leads to a spiritual tyranny."

With their minds locked and their needs fused, they swore to bring about religious freedom in Virginia. Reputations were falling; gentlemen were shouting, clutching at petitions spreading across Virginia for relief from the Anglican Church by the end of '76.

"The severe wrath from honest men but zealous churchmen," Jefferson told Patty, "baffles me."

Finding a hidden strength, she pulled him closer. "A law that protects the Jew, the Gentile, the Christian and Mahometan, the Hindoo, and infidel of every denomination must be my goal."

Cradling his face in her hands, she kissed him.

The tall man approached his short partner at the General Assembly in late 1776. "We must amend the law on slavery. The freedom of all born after a certain day, and deportation at a proper age." Alarmingly, the proposal chimed with "Jemmy's" thoughts on Virginia society that, for a moment, entirely threw him off his mental balance.

"Why not retain and incorporate the blacks into the state," asked "Jemmy," "and thus save the expense of supplying, by the importation of white settlers, the vacancies they will leave?"

"Deep-rooted prejudices entertained by the whites," said Thomas, "ten thousand recollections, by the blacks, of the injuries they have sustained; new provocations; the real distinctions which nature has made; and many other circumstances, will divide us into parties, and produce convulsions which will probably never end but in the extermination of the one or the other race."

"Jemmy's" eyes shifted apart before attempting to speak, but no words flowed from his small, soft lips. He shook his head.

"It is inconceivable to me," said Jefferson, "that free whites and free blacks can live side by side peacefully.

Shivering some, "Jemmy" thought regretfully of the happy hours of Dr. Weatherspoon's class on Moral Ethics at the College of New Jersey.

"Nature, habit, opinion," said Jefferson, "have drawn indelible lines of distinction between them."

"Jemmy" looked down, hiding his view from Jefferson, wondering if he wanted to help get this done. "We know that among the Romans, about the Augustan age especially, the condition of their slaves was much more deplorable than that of the blacks on the continent of America."

Later that week at the Assembly, with "Jemmy's help, Thomas decided to rid Virginia of primogeniture and entail, slavery put on the back burner.

"They are," said Jefferson, "archaic laws which compelled wealthy landowners to pass their property to a single heir, creating, in his words, "a distinct set of families, who being privileged by law in the perpetuation of their wealth were thus formed into a Patrician order, distinguished by the splendor and luxury of their establishments."

He profited from this system, never emptying some of his pocketbooks, and sharing his inheritance with his younger brother. Together Jefferson and Madison continued to survey the entire legal code of Virginia. They wished to limit the death penalty to murder and treason, create a public education system, and shorten the time for foreigners to become citizens. Mulberry Lane, a housing and business street, sat atop his 872-foot mountain. His extended family received instruction in music and dance, minuets, and country dances. But Jefferson, who hammered home the need for public education to the legislature, never set up a school at Monticello for the black coopers, smiths, nail makers, brewers, cooks (professionally trained in French cuisine), glaziers, painters, millers, and weavers. As a guest at the home of a gentry neighbor with his slave, Jupiter, he heard about an incident told by the host.

"In the evening, my wife and little Jenny had a great quarrel in which my wife got the worst, but at last, by the help of the family, Jenny was overcome and soundly whipped."

Heat flashed into his eyes, but Thomas held his tongue. He *thought blacks secrete less by the kidneys and more by the skin's glands, which gives them a potent and disagreeable odor. They seem to require less sleep. After hard labor through the day, a black will be induced by the slightest amusements to sit up till midnight or later, though knowing he must be out with the first dawn of the morning. A* rush of emotion came into his eyes as his thought continued.

*"Their existence appears to participate more in sensation than reflection. To this must be ascribed their disposition to sleep when abstracted from their diversions and unemployed in labor. An animal whose body is at rest and who does not reflect must be disposed to sleep, of course. Comparing them by their faculties of memory, reason, and imagination, it appears that, in memory, they are equal to the whites; in reason much inferior. I think one could scarcely be found capable of tracing and comprehending the investigations of Euclid; and that in imagination they are dull, tasteless, and anomalous."*

In a future conversation with Burr, who rushed down to Monticello from Philadelphia while roaming the land to get the Virginian elected president in 1800, the conversation turned to slavery. "Most of them indeed have been confined to tillage," said Jefferson, "to their own homes and their own society."

Studying Jefferson, Burr wondered where the conversation was going.

"Many have been so situated that they might have availed themselves of the conversation of their masters." *Really*, thought Burr. "Many have been brought up to handicraft, and from that circumstance have always been associated with the whites."

"Their life like clockwork," said Burr.

Jefferson held back a glare. "Some have been liberally educated," declared Jefferson.

"Who are the some?" asked Burr.

Jefferson sipped more of his wine, ignoring the question, and went on. "Are not the fine mixtures of black and white, the expressions of every passion by greater or fewer suffusions in the one, preferable to that eternal monotony, which reigns in the countenances of the other."

For the next hour, Burr listened and observed Jefferson drink several glasses of Bordeaux.

"Does not the immovable veil of black cover all their emotions?" A cry of horror burst within Burr. "Their flowing hair is a more elegant symmetry of form." As the evening drew on, Jefferson's words became more troublesome.

"Their preference of them declares their judgment in favour of the whites."

*Ignorance must be borne*, thought Burr, for the day of enlightenment, is waiting for the right leader.

"As uniformly," said Jefferson, "as is the preference of the Oranootan (orangutan} for the black women over those of his own species."

Burr shrugged as Jefferson finished speaking.

## Chapter 27

## Governor PH

"The man of desperate circumstances," wrote Lord Dunmore to the British ministry, "who had been very active in encouraging disobedience and exciting a spirit of revolt among the people for many years past," assumed the office as the first Governor of the Commonwealth of Virginia on July 5, 1776.

Forsaking his buckskin, the once "uncouth woodsman," dressed in a scarlet cloak, black-small clothes, silk stockings, silver-buckled shoes, and a newly dressed wig, he pledged to serve the glorious cause as a private citizen.

Addressed by friends and enemies as "Your Excellency" or "Your Honour," his Quaker friends wished him to declare all men equally free and establish a plan for the gradual emancipation of the slaves.

The legislative's restraints on the executive were so tight that the governor was not allowed to debate policy or make it. Establishing a plan for the gradual emancipation of the slaves was beyond his horizon, but he never looked in that direction.

Learning that General Washington needed help defending Long Island, Governor Henry ignored the state Constitution and the House of Delegates, assuming the powers he needed to defend liberty.

Sending 700 men of the First and Second Virginia regiments northward, they reached New York too late but he ordered more men and materials to Washington.

Washington wrote to the governor, "Your correspondence will confer honor and satisfaction, and whenever in my power, I shall write to you with pleasure."

Tapping his finger on the letter, Henry beamed as he read, "Our defeat on Long Island and the evacuation of New York was of prudence and necessity. The troops are, in some measure, dispirited by these successive retreats. The evils of short enlistments are detrimental to our success, and I urge the establishment of a permanent body of force."

Henry's shoulders moved in a quick, determined gesture. "I will," he said to himself.

"Secure your towns and houses on navigable waters," Washington wrote, "I expect Virginia to furnish the Continental Army with fifteen battalions."

"I must have six armed sloops," Henry told the House of Delegates, "to protect the entrances to inward waterways and prevent British ships from sailing upstream to pillage our river-front villages and plantations."

"Need we inform you, Your Excellency," said a delegate with a thatch of gray hair, "that you are exceeding your constitutional powers?"

"Well, sir, I want to be appointed chairman of a new Navy Board."

The Delegates smirked and thought of not standing aside.

"Or I will resign as governor."

Some Delegates glanced at their desks and the stacks of paper with resolutions to put into effect.

Henry opened six new shipyards and assembled a navy of seventy ships, crewed by 600 seamen using his new authority, and recruited 300 soldiers to combat British attacks on coastal towns and plantations. And he sent ships carrying tobacco to the West Indies to barter for needed gunpowder and salt.

Writing the governors of Cuba and New Orleans, "I need not inform you that these states are not free and independent, capable of forming alliances and of making treaties."

Virginia received many goods from Havana to New Orleans and then overland to Williamsburg.

Governor Henry assumed control over every area of Virginia's war effort to the disdain of some members of the House of Delegates,

He informed the War Office in Philadelphia that Washington's army was retreating across New Jersey. "I have issued the necessary orders this morning that the Troops of Horse (six) shall be marched to join General Washington."

He wrote Richard Henry Lee, "I have procured ten tons of lead, which are ready to be delivered for the use of the Continental Congress."

And he informed the president of Congress, John Hancock, "We have a gun factory at Fredericksburg."

Directing the war effort, Henry worked twenty-four hours a day, and collapsed with a malarial fever that incapacitated him.

Sick, he slid down from the office and left for home.

Resting on Scotchtown's high ground, away from the swampy lowlands' mosquitoes, he enjoyed the warming sun, and the short shadows, and read books on war. He yearned for Williamsburg and kept informed of Washington's movements.

Visited by the tall, strapping twenty-four-year-old George Rogers Clark, who wanted arms and gunpowder for Virginia's western settlements, Henry listened.

Henry admired his buckskins and remembered his skins and the somewhat uncouth but charming youth he once lived.

"We need more than just verbal support," said Clark, "in resisting the British and restless Indians."

"Yes, but the assassins of the Indians must be brought to justice. Having to leave woodsmen there to fight the Shawnees prevents their joining General Washington to strike a decisive stroke for independence."

"I agree with you about the importance of bringing these wicked men to justice."

"A precedent should not be established involving Virginia in a war whenever anyone in the backcountry shall please."

Clark took the words Henry handed him, scanned his face, and understood them.

"I will," said Henry, "send you a letter to the Executive Council recommending they help you."

"If we give you the powder," said a representative, "we might be censured by the House."

Little by little, Clark learned of the politics Henry mentioned.

"And we might," said a different council member, "be held responsible for restitution." *Nonsense*, Clark thought, his eyes calm and level.

"If the frontiersmen would stop encroaching on the Indian land and respect the treaties and agreements, you might not need as much powder."

"The British have sent agents to incite the Indians to go on the warpath against the scattered frontier settlements."

"The brutal murder of the Mingo chief, Cornstalk, under a flag of truce," said another delegate, "along with his wife and all their children, including a babe in arms, still leaves a prejudice against the western settlements."

Clark's hands tightened into fists, and he took a long breath.

"We will give you the powder on two conditions."

Clark's eyebrows shot up.

"First, we will make you a loan, and you will be responsible for the money

Second, you have to transport the powder yourself."

"It is beyond my power to convey the powder at my expense such a long distance through enemy territory.

Let him be annoyed, they thought.

"Well. I am sorry. The Kentuckians will find protection elsewhere."

"Really, young man."

"I have no doubt we can get it."

Six weeks later, on September 17, Henry returned to Williamsburg, informing the legislature that his "low state of health still prevented him from attending his duties."

Back home at Scotchtown, he kept abreast of the legislature's inefficiency at this critical period, and they were astonished that he chose to occupy the position of governor.

During Henry's absence, Thomas Jefferson emerged as a House leader, repealing laws requiring dissenters to pay taxes to the Anglican Church. He abolished fines for not attending church at least once a month but neglected military affairs, leaving the coastline "naked and defenseless."

Returning to Williamsburg in mid-November, Henry helped the Executive Council overcome Virginia's limited resources and military needs.

Washington wanted him to "Muster fifteen battalions and produce officers and soldiers. Militiamen can fight Indians but not hold the field should the British invade."

In his order to Henry, Washington sent a pamphlet by Thomas Paine of the Continental Army.

"These are the times that try men's souls. The summer soldier and the sunshine patriot will, in this crisis, shrink from the service of their country; but he that stands by it now deserves the love and thanks of man and woman. Tyranny, like hell, is not easily conquered; yet we have this consolation with us that the harder the conflict, the more glorious the triumph. What we obtain too cheap, we esteem too lightly: it is dearness only that gives everything its value. Heaven knows how to put a proper price upon its goods, and it would be strange indeed if so celestial an article as FREEDOM should not be highly rated."

By December of 1776, the varied interests of the legislature left Virginia disturbed and distressed. They considered for a moment, then shook their heads.

Thomas Jefferson, who was tending to his sick wife at Monticello and not parked in the House of Delegates, proposed creating a "Dictator."

The exterior of the legislation was rough and needed landscaping. Still, friends of liberty at Williamsburg, Richard Henry Lee, and George

Macon, did not mention this scheme to establish a dictator.

Governor Henry's power emanated like a sculpture out of stone, granted an expanded command by the Virginia House of Delegates.

Making requisitions, paying for supplies, ordering troop movements, and raising additional battalions, he was as "busy as a ticking clock."

He received a warning, "Departure from the constitution of government, being in this instance founded only on the most evident and urgent necessity, ought not hereafter to be drawn into precedent."

"Whatever fears are swirling around the House of Delegates must be controlled," he replied, "No one has all the answers."

Jefferson, highly critical of the legislature's authorization, asserted five years later that Henry and the delegates attempted to create "a dictator, invested with every power legislative, executive, and judiciary, civil, and military, of life and death, over our persons and over our properties."

Over the rim of his glass of wine, Mr. Jefferson referred to Henry as "all tongue without either head or heart" and involved with "crooked schemes."

In 1816, he stated in the fourth volume of the History of Virginia, written by his neighbor, Frenchman Louis Girardin, "Mr. Henry was the person in view for the dictatorship is well ascertained."

Some wounds scar over, but in the case of Jefferson, they fester. Behind the scenes of the past, he pulled strings, playing with history.

Writing to Richard Henry Lee, "The terrors of smallpox, added to the lies of deserters and want of necessaries, are fatal objections to the continental service." Henry learned then that pragmatism justified the threat to liberty the British army presented. He held adversity in his hands, trying to appease the fears of the legislature.

Receiving Washington's orders to promote an aggressive inoculation campaign, he ordered the Virginia troops to receive a shot when they enlisted. While in Philadelphia for the Continental Congress, he received a vaccination from Dr. Benjamin Rush without pausing.

Filling the army ranks created tension between Washington and Henry over how to accomplish this.

Henry looked at reality and sighed.

Wanting to raise volunteers for six to eight-month terms. Washington informed him, "I want a professional army I can train, discipline, and count on to stay long term."

It was well past the time to debate Washington. He checked any impulse to disagree.

"I defer," wrote Henry, "to the General's opinions on military matters."

## Chapter 28

## GW Retreats

While eight or nine British ships of war were in the North River on the night of September 20, a fire erupted in New York in a low-class, wooden barroom and brothel on the pier near Whitehall.

There were but few inhabitants in the city, and the flames, for a while unchecked, spread rapidly.

All the houses between Whitehall and Broad Streets up to Beaver Street burnt to ashes. When the wind veered to the southeast, it drove the blaze toward Broadway.

Destroying all on each side of Beaver Street to the Bowling Green, it crossed Broadway and swept all the buildings on both sides, as far as Exchange Street.

On the west side, it burned almost every building between Morris Street and Partition Street, devouring Trinity church and destroying all the buildings towards the North River.

Burr watched from the Heights of Harlem and thought the lower world resembled an inferno.

"The whole air red. . . . It raged all the night, and till about noon consuming the fourth part of the city. . . the bells being carried off, no timely alarm was given; the engines were out of order; the fire company broke. . .if the wind had shifted to the west, as it had the appearance a couple of times, the whole city might have been destroyed."

What should have been by design was ordained by fate. The gods bestowed their blessings on the American commander-in-chief.

Approximately five hundred buildings turned to ash out of four thousand houses in the square mile town of New York.

For nearly three weeks, the British rested, not choosing to make a significant movement, the Gods at work again.

Day after day, the autumn horizon boasted a panoply of rust, orange, and bright red as the Hudson sparkled and undulated under the lazy arching yolk's brilliant light.

Upon Burr's urging to boost morale and replenish supplies, "Old Put" ventured out into the Harlem plains.

He carried off an ample grain supply before dawn on a misty morning with several wagons.

The Virginian, Captain Daniel Morgan, who just returned from Canada as a prisoner, arrived and was promoted by his fellow Virginian, General Washington, to Colonel. Burr realized the Virginians; "They stick together."

Morgan, the officer, who failed to seize the initiative at Quebec by neglecting to advance through an unguarded gate, allowing the enemy to re-gather, rose in rank as Burr attended to his duties under "Old Put."

Washington admitted, "At no time since General Howe's arrival at Staten Island has my force been equal (in Men fit for duty) to his.

To this cause, the patriots were obliged to occupy posts to secure communication with the Country. The intended mode of Attack was to be attributed to the retreat from Long Island and the Evacuation of New York.

With the assistance of the enemy's ships, the British intended to draw a line around Washington and cut off all communication between the City and Country if he stayed in New York.

The tranquility of this perfect coexistence ended on October 9, and three British

warships heading north passed quickly. Forts Washington, ignoring the American efforts to block the river with "sunken hulks and a submerged chain of spike-studded logs.

The American cannons wantonly fired, but the enemy ships steered close to the Jersey side and anchored at the Tappan Zee, off Tarrytown.

Again, the American effort to hinder the enemy's movement came to naught.

One had to question the feasibility of holding the forts if they could not thwart the British Navy's mobility. The British intended to outflank Washington by landing a large force north of him at Throg's Neck landing.

After dusk on October 13, Major Burr rushed inside to where "Old Put" sat.

"At Throg's Point, Sir, eight miles east of Kings Bridge where the East River converges into the Long Island Sound, the British landed."

"How many ships?"

"Nine, full of men, went up the Sound in the evening."

"What about the land along the road and across the adjacent fields that were full of stone fences that Washington thought would hinder the enemy's forward movement on the main road."

"Useless, Sir."

"Your orders are to attend to all the works and necessary places of defense from Headquarters to Mount Washington and obstructions in the Hudson."

"The British General is trying to hem our rebel force in again with a line in our rear."

"Our lines were extended to East & West Chester."

On October 12, Howe moved his army north to outflank Washington at Throgs Neck. He landed successfully, but his forces were bottled up on the Neck, sometimes an island depending on the tides.

Washington withdrew north to White Plains, and the British slowly followed. It took Howe ten days to arrive in White Plains. On October 28, the British troops captured Chatterton Hill, to the right of American lines. Washington soon withdrew to New Castle, and Howe did not follow.

# Chapter 29

# Sir Henry Clinton

At White Plains, Clinton left with the rear guard to cover the rebels' retreat to Dobb's Ferry, venturing to change the stipulated route of march, but received a brief message from Howe, "Do as I told you."

He yelled with a shiny forehead and quick, wandering eyes, "I cannot bear to continue to serve under him."

From where he stood, leaning against a maple tree, Cornwallis heard Clinton's vitriol.

"I would rather command three companies by myself than hold my post as I have done the last command in his army!"

Cornwallis smiled and relayed Clinton's words to Howe the next day, who paused for a moment, "I shall never forget them."

Steadying himself, "Clinton said, "I want to pursue Washington's New Jersey retreating army and eradicate it before reaching the Delaware River."

"How," said Cornwallis.

"By a three-pronged attack. Howe would advance across New Jersey, attack Philadelphia, and the fleet and a contingent of troops would clear the Delaware. This plan would close on the rebel capital and Washington's army."

Hearing of the plan and thinking it was inept, Howe removed it from his mind, more out of spite than on its merits.

General Clinton suggested, "Put me ashore on the Jersey coast to engage and block the retreating rebel army until Cornwallis arrives."

Looking at Howe's blank expression, he knew his commander had rejected the plan.

Clinton then proposed that the fleet carry him up the Delaware, land at Philadelphia, disperse the Continental Congress, and harass Washington's rear.

"We can win the war, now, General," said Clinton, who wanted to blaze in glory.

As he rummaged his mind for a proper reply, his tact slipping, Howe said, "Stop knocking on my door; it goes unheard."

Clinton refused to be silent, "The war can be won on the Delaware."

Howe, thinking he needed to be rid of Clinton, said, "Rhode Island." Still, Clinton blurted out before he could continue, "Common sense suggests concentrating our force for a final effort, not dispersing it by sending me to Rhode Island."

"I want a base of operations at Newport that can threaten the mainland."

"It is late November, hardly a propitious season."

Clinton observed Howe's spotless fingers intertwine for a moment.

"General, you strike, not at the heart, but the ground under the enemy."

Wanting to be rid of him and dream of a lover, Howe yawned.

"You seem less concerned with defeating the enemy and more concerned with bringing about their absence. You pushed them off Bunker Hill; you pushed them into northern Manhattan; you maneuvered them into Westchester, then across the Hudson, without bringing Washington to action."

"My orders are to win victory and negotiate peace. Like my brother, the Admiral, says, "The assignment is an awkward dualism, for we are to act simultaneously like lions and like doves."

It was astonishing to Clinton that this man giving orders was his superior.

Trying to refrain himself, Clinton said, "Land battles do not produce conciliation but increase the rebels' desire to resist. Blockading their commerce can sap their resistance."

Clinton's face grew suddenly grim.

"Too many posts in New Jersey," he said to an aide before sailing for Newport. "The enemy can hit us and run, and a single one might have serious consequences."

Howe ignored the advice and pushed the posts westward to the Delaware.

Abandoning himself to the situation's demands, he lit a cigarette and crossed his legs with a genuine joie de vivre as he dined with his inamorata.

## Chapter 30

## Beating a Retreat

So it began. "Washington issued orders on October 17," Burr wrote to Sally, "to alter our position" and, except for a thousand men who defended Fort Washington, the American army "egressed" from their position north to White Plains." Telling himself to forget about it, Burr looked forward. The seed of liberty needs time to sprout.

"Old Put" having received orders at White Plains to reinforce General McDougall, but before he reached McDougall, 7000 British arrived on October 28, 1776, and flanked the American force." He needed to set it aside but not before telling Sally, "Old Put's" men, well-positioned behind stone fences and trees, covered the retreat of McDougall's troops while engaging the enemy."

Fuming over the retreat, Alex took a position with two field pieces upon a rocky ledge at Chatterton Hill above the White Plains River. He took delight as the British tried to cross the river; his artillery flashed repeatedly, sending them down to the river's edge.

After regrouping, the enemy forced Hamilton and his men to abandon the hill but not without the patriots inflicting substantial losses on the enemy. It lifted Washington and his downtrodden army's spirit. His aides noticed his eyes flicker.

Fall, now in full hue, as Burr, Putnam, and Hamilton scrutinized the sour taste of retreat. The army marched north towards New Castle into a strong wind that threw heavy rain in their faces, the enemy not following and well sheltered.

On November 3, the British pulled back, leaving Washington to guess their next move. He stood, hands in his pockets as he studied his situation, invading New Jersey his conjecture. Preparatory to this event, the stout Virginian ordered "Old Put," "With your 4,000 men, cross the Hudson and march as far as Hackensack and wait for further orders."

The numbers always varied by the end of the week, with 6,000 to 8,000 troops; General Howe turned his army south to finish evicting the Continental Army troops from Manhattan.

The patriots who guarded the grounds outside Fort Washington were driven within the walls of the Fort by the well-trained British and Hessians.

The gallant, undermanned American soldiers were compelled to surrender by late afternoon, and nearly 2800 prisoners were doomed. A task Howe accomplished at ten in the morning, Saturday, November 16, Generals Washington, Putnam, Greene, and Mercer watching from the Hudson's East side at Fort Lee.

Many rebel soldiers suffered and died in the military prisons, unheated barns, and sheds of Manhattan and enemy ships. The most notorious prison ship was the "*Jersey,*" brought in to incarcerate the captured Americans.

Large quantities of blankets, tents, arms, tools, brass, and iron cannon, which could have been used during the ensuing winter, were lost to the English.

Forefront in Washington's mind was that he cared more for a fighting reputation than hit-and-run tactical warfare. He pounded his foot on the ground for a moment, closed his eyes, and envisioned his failing prestige. He thought of Congress as his insecurity rose like the moon.

Trying not to feel dejected, Major Burr wrote Sally, "New York must go. It is a necessary consequence. Good comes from bad; Congress is now levying a new army."

*War is war,* he thought. *Whoever can grab it?*

"The barbarities by the Hessians are false, incredible flights into fancy," he noted. "Our cause is the most important revolution that ever took place. We may indeed be called favored people." He ended his letter with, "The British hold us in utter contempt, thinking they can force our lines without firing a gun. They have dismissed Bunker Hill."

A repeat performance occurred at the recently constructed Fort Lee three nights later as 4,000 foes scaled (a bold move) the Palisades, a steep near perpendicular footpath,

Howe had performed a similar move 20 years earlier in Quebec during the Seven Years War. (Burr advocated the same tactic to General Montgomery during the American siege of Quebec at the end of December 1775, but it failed to occur). Receiving notice of this daring plan, Washington ordered his men to abandon the Fort. Its tents, still standing and kettles boiling on the fire as the smell of forsaken breakfast greeted the entering adversary. Also left behind were almost all the artillery, a thousand barrels of flour, tents, arms, picks, shovels, and food.

Another route became official, and Washington closeted his insecurity, trying to find a way to thwart the British. His body was as strong as a wild boar, but his military acumen mouse-like.

Long Island, the loss of the town of Manhattan (first from the Battery to Chatham Street and then the complete island), and the retreat from Fort Lee echoed through the colonies.

His grim face grew grimmer as his reputation sank like lead in water; he blamed others and refused to take responsibility. "What do I have here," he asked himself. "How much longer can I keep balancing inexperienced men on this tightrope."

General Lee lobbied Congress, telling his friends, "I am the nation's savior."

Joseph Reed, Washington's closest aide, touted praise of Lee.

Washington and his staff became suspicious, imagining cabals and plots, leading to what Burr described as "party business," which he avoided in his year-long tenure with Putnam.

"It takes time," Washington told his friends at Congress, "for an army to establish roots.

The British hounds chased the rebel army into New Jersey, and when the enemy's advance guard entered Newark, the patriot's rear guard exited.

Retreating with the army of Washington, Burr passed through Elizabethtown on the way to the far side of the Raritan River at New Brunswick, Cornwallis nipping at their heels, hoping they would linger.

As the rear guard of the rebel forces crossed the river, Cornwallis' superior, fast-approaching army suddenly halted; the assault was ordered to stop until the arrival of "Sir Billy" with reinforcements. He was dumbfounded and, for a moment, wanted to set the order aside but paced around, restless.

Luck worked its magic for the Patriots, or was it the lap of a lover of Howe? "Billy" did not arrive for seven days, and the fleeing rebel army crossed the Delaware River as the Redcoats viewed the last of the rebels boated to safety.

The rebels did their work well, leaving no boats existing for miles in either direction on the river for the enemy to use.

"It is said," Burr wrote to his sister, "that General Howe could calculate with the greatest accuracy the exact time necessary for the enemy to make his escape."

Burr let out a gasp that concluded with a chortle.

"I must say," he said to himself, there is much truth to that statement."

## Chapter 31

# Schuyler and Gates

As a young man, Philip Schuyler led a local company in the forest fights during the French and Indian War. His motto was "Better to show than tell what you can do," he was always conscious of keeping the family name above reproach.

Living at the northern end of the Hudson River's great waterway, the fur trade headquarters, the gateway to Canada, and Lakes Champlain and George, he breathed Albany's terrain.

Whether on the bare, bone paths near Albany or in a birch canoe on the Hudson, he journeyed in a manner that made the passers-by smile, for he was liked and respected.

The forest was his second home, and he always thought of it.

His years in northern New York as a soldier, then land developer required him to be innovative. Putting his money where his mouth was, he was the first to cultivate hemp and flax, increasing the value of his lands at Saratoga.

Elected to the Continental Congress in 1775, he served until he was appointed a Major General of the Continental Army in June. Taking command of the Northern Department, he planned the invasion of Canada—fame, he thought, over the next hill.

Along with their fortune, the Schuyler family of New York bequeathed to their oldest son, Philip, a predisposition to rheumatic gout. This illness attacked him when he needed all his strength and removed him from the military expedition to Canada in late 1775. Standing against a maple tree, he placed Richard Montgomery in command of the invasion and shrugged off his disability.

Schuyler looked strong with color in his cheeks when not debilitated by gout. He stood out with thick, black eyebrows and a healthy, rugged appearance. His domain, the tiny village of Albany, and his mansion sat halfway up a bank opposite a ferry on the Hudson, a half-mile south of Albany.

Knowing the tools of war that would be needed by the rebels while campaigning in the forests and waterways, the functioning of the Northern Department for the rebellion rested on his broad shoulders.

Though not a professional soldier, his ingenuity allowed him to solve new and exacting problems. With steady fingers, he tied on the apron of a jack of all trades.

He was his quartermaster, commissary, and recruiting officer. Tents, arms, powder, food, clothing, and medicines were the first orders of necessary supplies ordered by Congress to equip an army, but Schuyler added to that list: tools for the gunsmith, blacksmith, carpenter, and boat builder; rope, oakum, nails for the boats that needed construction; and shovels and pickaxes for entrenching against the forthcoming force.

"I see my strength as an organizer of men and a provider of food and arms," he told his friends at Congress. "In the English army, I served as a commissary."

His detractors said, "You lack experience as a commander in battle."

He sat down, facing them, "I deserve the honor of the commander of the Northern Department of New York."

"An army needs to be raised, clothed, armed, fed," he said.

He turned, his face full of pride, eyes glittering with determination so fierce he knew the outcome.

The choice fell on him.

He went about the task through his knowledge, business connections, and relations with the Indians of northern New York. He did have a reputation for having a hard head; a mule was less stubborn.

As Aaron Burr knew, "It took more than honor to command and win a battle."

Horatio Gates was short, stocky, ruddy-faced, bespectacled, and mild-mannered.

"An old granny," according to Colonel Troup, who said, "The General suffered from a gastronomical ailment, for he consumed too much of the food out of jealousy."

Having removed to America in the early 1770s, he purchased an estate in Berkeley County, Virginia, west of the Blue Ridge. A self-taught scholar well-versed in history, the Latin classics, and the correct political principles of being a Whig.

Without a pang of doubt, the Revolution appealed to him.

A military base graced his manners and deportment. He considered himself hospitable, generous, just, and inflexible in his attachment to his friends. On May 16, 1776, he received the rank of Major-General.

"My strategy," he told those within earshot, "is to fight the enemy I served under in the past."

He paused for a moment. "We must Defend the main Chance; to Attack only by Detail; and when a precious advantage offers."

It was no wonder that he and the hot-brained and impatient Arnold would grow apart.

The New England delegates in Congress were active and influential in Philadelphia, and their chief, John Adams, chairman of the board of war, was in a position to carry out their designs.

A delegate said, "Congress is not helping the situation in the northern department when you appointed Gates to command the forces in Canada."

"Really?" said Adams, "I shall try not to laugh."

"Gates will use this as a wedge which would lead to the higher and coveted command of the northern department."

"Worry about power. Worry about wonder," said Adams.

Gates replaced General Sullivan, who had successfully conducted the retreat from Canada.

On June 25, 1776, Schuyler heard of Gates' appointment to Canada's army command.

He invited him to his home.

The latter arrived at Albany, pleased with his complete and independent powers to command Canada's army.

"The army," said Schuyler, "is no longer in Canada but in New York under my command."

Schuyler watched chagrin drape the face of Gates and felt his heart sink like fishing sinkers into the Hudson and knew he wanted to mount the stairs of power, his ego, wide as a child's smile.

Gates announced, "I consider myself the senior officer in the Northern Department and refuse to sit idle on a technicality."

The proud Dutchman's face turned stiff; though uninspired, he fought to keep his chin up.

The matter landed on Washington's desk for clarification, who forwarded the problem to Congress.

In his mind, Schuyler did not crave power for power's sake. Thoughts of duty enveloped him.

He heard the footsteps of Gates rushing towards his gate of influence, wondering what concrete solution he should adopt.

Benedict Arnold, with Major Wilkinson, arrived in Albany in late June. Though one of the smaller colonies ranked seventh in population, New York was most important strategically to the enemy.

It separated New Jersey, Maryland, Virginia, and the Carolinas from New England.

Wilkinson assessed the situation without needing eyes to observe the quest for power between the aristocrat and Gates.

Unready to burn bridges, he inched towards General Gates and established a relationship with General Schuyler's aides, David Varick and Brockholst Livingston.

They informed him that the ministers to King George coveted control of northern New York and the Hudson.

Immediately, he realized the importance of the man in command in northern New York. Scents of power surrounded him.

Colonel Arnold was at the bottom of the totem pole for power in northern New York, and Wilkinson lay down in the sphere of Gates, realizing he could offer more.

It was astonishing that the nearly twenty-year-old gained his affection and, with the skill and artfulness of Machiavelli, maintained a relationship with Schuyler and Arnold.

The rattling noise of Congress heightened the situation. They were like ravens and carcasses: tearing and being torn.

Schuyler and Gates would soon understand they were characters in a French farce.

Until Congress clarified the problem, Gates demanded that through the fertile mind of Wilkinson, his instructions gave him independent control of the troops.

By semantic maneuvers, Gates assumed command and ignored Alexander Hamilton's future father-in-law. Congress informed the former that they intended to have him command the troops while in Canada. With the forces on the Southside of Canada, they had no design to invest him with a command superior to General Schuyler.

Thus, a farce in the best tradition of Moliere's The Flying Doctor took the stage in a modern adaption entitled "The Congressing Generals."

The fate of northern New York for the next sixteen months became increasingly feverish and confused. Both Gates and Schuyler were excellent in elucidating and wished to be the lead actor in the Northern Department's command. Each had ravens at Congress to pick the other's carcass.

Factions like flesh flies are naturally drawn to particles of excrement and settle within the body politics' unconsciousness, where its metastases.

Cunning and deceit became the modus operandi as the army became entrapped in partisan politics, anchored in jealousy instead of consideration.

# Chapter 32

# AH in Retreat with GW

Though retreating from the British, Washington desired to fight them at the Raritan River, near New Brunswick but changed his mind when he looked at his bedraggled troops. Observing Alexander Hamilton protecting them with his cannon posted high on the river bank, he said to an aide, "I am charmed by the brilliant courage and admirable skill of Major Hamilton. He directed a battery against the enemy's advanced columns that pressed upon us in our retreat by the ford."

In a letter to Congress, the General praised the "smart cannonade that allowed my men to escape," though he did not mention Alex by name.

Hanging his head, shamefaced, the General toyed with an idea.

Deciding to cross the Delaware River into Pennsylvania, he informed Congress on December 20, 1776, "Ten days more will put an end to the existence of our army who lack winter clothing, blankets, and morale."

From the look in his eyes, his aides knew he needed to do something daring to rally his troops. Some thought, was he mad, or what.

After his heroics, Alex lay bedridden at a nearby farm due to recurring health issues. With lowered eyes, he sat up momentarily, vulnerable and guilty. Upon hearing of Washington's plan for Christmas Eve, he rose from his "long and severe fit" of illness and left his bed to fight.

With less than thirty men left in his company, part of Lord Stirling's brigade, they marched towards Washington.

At midnight assembled in cargo boats draped with ice, Washington's men polled their way across the Delaware River. Marching eight miles through a heavy snowfall with his cannon, Hamilton and his two cannons discovered an exhausted Hessian detachment who did not get much sleep for over a week because they expected an attack by the rebels.

Cannonballs flew in all directions as Washington's soldiers advanced, the snow deadening their footsteps.

Over one thousand captured Hessians. The news spread, and patriots rejoiced everywhere. The country fell in love with Washington and left the past behind.

Alex thought it over for three winks before he wrote the Reverend Knox, "The fire from my artillery company helped to force the surrender of many enemy soldiers."

A senior officer noted, "Boldened by his only success, Washington attacked the British at Princeton on January 3, 1777, capturing two hundred enemy prisoners."

As his aides watched him smiling, the General bellowed, "It is a fine fox chase, my boys."

"Well, do I recollect the day," said a friend, "when Hamilton's company marched into Princeton. It was a mode of discipline; at their head was a boy, and I wondered at his youth, but what was my surprise when struck with his slight figure, he was pointed out to me as that Hamilton of whom we had already heard so much."

He set up shop in the college yard opposite Nassau Hall. His cannon pounded the brick building as he remembered the College rejecting his request to enter and advance "with as much rapidity as his exertions would enable him to do." Legend purports that a cannonball sliced through a portrait of King George II in the chapel.

"I noticed," a veteran officer related, "a youth, a mere stripling, small, slender, almost delicate in frame, marching beside a piece of artillery, with a cocked hat, pulled down over his eyes, apparently lost in thought, with his hand resting on a cannon, and now and then patting it, as if it was a favorite horse or a pet plaything."

The British soldiers deserted their position and surrendered. When hearing this, General Howe seated near an amour, her oval knee touching his. "What is going on in the world?" he asked.

She listened, scratching her head as Howe told her, "Washington's army set up quarters at Morristown, New Jersey." Beaming, General Washington let out a long breath, his aides knowing he did not have to feel apologetic anymore.

A tender, unthreatening expression adorned his face as he stepped forward.

# Chapter 33

# "The Congressing Generals"

The second night of the small gathering at Burr's Richmond Hill house never made it to bed. Young Washington Irving, his brother Peter, General Willet, and Theodosia were wide of the eye as Wilkinson destroyed their desire for sleep.

General Willet, the oldest, tended to rest his eyes.

"My life," announced Wilkinson, "did not present a uniformly smooth current. It was irregular, startling, at times rambling and digressive but never, I trust, dull or inanimate."

The truth was he did not move within the narrow lines of conventionalism and often transgressed the limits of morality. His life was fraught with fancies and shadows and, if written, would seem farfetched.

As the rich, pervading, and aromatic smoke filled the air like fog, the once young but never naive soldier's body was in motion. With a cigar in one hand, the other with glass, his eyes darting from side to side, and his memory afire.

Sitting with bright eyes and a trace of mockery on his lips, Washington Irving glanced over at Theodosia as she sipped from a cup of tea.

Relishing the role he played in politics, war, and preparations for the Northern campaign, Wilkinson expounded.

"With Arnold detracted by allegations of 'looting' while in Canada, I assumed responsibilities at Fort Ticonderoga and dealt directly with General Gates."

From roaming eyes, a grin spread like wildfire over his face.

"The fort at Crown Point was being prepared to receive nearly 2500 men, survivors, most sick from the Canadian fiasco. Crown Point was nine miles from Fort Ticonderoga. Much responsibility was conferred on me. From my medical training, I knew what was needed."

Young Irving wondering did not know if he was relaying the truth or lying.

Theodosia's lips parted and closed before she dragged her hand through her lush coils of hair. With her maturing curves and skin luxuriously in the gaslight, Irving wanted to cuddle next to her.

"Tired of serving on Arnold's staff, immersed in routine duties, I was."

He stopped and turned some as Burr stared at him.

"True enough," said Colonel Burr, who never missed serving as Arnold's aide-de-camp.

"On my own account, I conducted reconnoitering excursions but could not accept behavior on his part that I considered dubious, for I believed that he had plundered the merchandise of Montreal merchants under the pretext of providing for the officers of the army. Captain Scott, a reduced officer of Jersey, transported the goods to Albany and sold them to General Arnold, who pocketed the proceeds. When he gave up command of the right wing of the army for that of a flotilla on Lake Champlain, I embraced the occasion to retire from his family."

*Point taken,* thought Burr, who shifted in his chair with a pang of doubt.

"Gates, so impressed with my reconnaissance and activities, appointed me on July 20, '76, to a major of the brigade to the troops destined to take possession of Mount Independence, just to the south of Lake Champlain and to the east of the northern end of Lake George."

He trailed off and pressed a hand to his temple.

"Here, I pitched my tent amidst its native forest."

General Willet shook his head, remembering the damp ground under the trees.

"I remained with the brigade until the beginning of September when Brigadier-general de Roche Fermoy took command, and I was transferred to that of General St. Clair, but my dear friends," his eyes resting on young Irving and Theodosia, "be aware of Fate."

His left eye either blinked or possibly twitched, his consternation blushed, and sweat appeared on his brow.

"Whilst actively engaged in the duties of my station – preparing for the reception of the enemy, and every heart panted for the clash, I was suddenly struck down by a typhus fever which prevailed with great violence and swept off more than a thousand of our troops. I was removed to the South end of Lake George."

Wilkinson choked out a laugh.

"Let it be known that while there, one pale eye and the other opened in confusion and dolefulness. What on earth is going on? I wondered. I forgot the journey, the British, the Indians, the war."

Theo narrowed her eyes, Irving wanting to guffaw ferociously.

"I thought my father was talking even though I rested in a strange room. I did not understand; for I was in a state of mind where the past obstructed the present."

Burr looked over at Willet and grinned, listening with half an ear.

"A young woman entered with a tray of cold towels and placed them on the bedside table.

"How are you feeling today?" She said.

"Struggling to open my mouth, I gasped silently and passed out like a woman on a scorching summer day with a tight corset.

Her delicate hands, I learned, placed the cool towels on my forehead as she prayed for my recovery."

Burr listened intently, imagining that his father stood at the door staring at him in the General's mind.

"Dreaming I was still at home, I seemed to talk to my father's firm, callused hands, folded on top of a quilted rainbow blanket. Occasionally in broken words, a few harsh commands were uttered from his blistered lips. Suddenly I shook my head and breathed out as my consciousness closed. The flames of a high fever scorching my soul."

The general turned to the half-awake Willet and smiled, "My general had assigned the senior medical officer, Doctor Jonathan Potts, to keep me alive at any cost. Despite this attention to medical art, I was on the last extremity; every hope of recovery had expired. Consigned to the grave, a coffin was prepared. Life trembled over the verge of eternity–the immortal spirit having fled its mortal tabernacle. After six days of semi-conscience and feverish, drifting in and out of sleep, I started coming around. That morning my temperature dropped. It was only then I felt a desire for life."

Irving studied his face, seeing a sense of bravado. He wanted to besiege him with questions but refrained.

"Fortuitously, my youth and spirit prevailed. Resting on a bed of straw in a wagon, I was removed to Albany where under the fostering care of P. Van Rensselaer, Esq. and his amiable lady, and the tender attentions of General Schuyler, I joined the living."

Willet shot his hand up. "A toast to our general."

Wilkinson refilled his glass.

Irving thought someday, he must use Wilkinson's character to start a good, thick, old-fashioned novel. He did as the fleeting thought remained with him.

"My bed rested next to a window overlooking Pearl Street, Albany. The smell of death was gone as the fragrance of the tall green elm trees that lined the street wafted through the open window. The loud voices of children in the house reinvigorated my spirit. I enjoyed seeing them playing outside betwixt the green trees. An older woman carefully watched them as she sat at a nearby table shining silverware.

In very feeble health I was unfit for regular duty until December 5, and I did not recover my wonted strength until the spring."

Sitting there quietly, Willet recalled that his brigade under St. Clair marched towards General Washington and that Wilkinson became attached to Gate's staff during his sickness. In early December, seven of the regiments were ordered by Congress to re-enforce General Washington's army that lay somewhere between New York and Philadelphia.

Willet's memory stalled until he remembered the date (December 12), Wilkinson volunteering to message Gates detailing his plans to Washington. While heading ahead to locate Washington, he heard the General had crossed the Delaware. "Being resourceful," said Wilkinson, his pupils enlarged as he took another long puff on one of Burr's long cigars, "I could not find a boat to follow. As Artemas Ward had resigned, I sought out the second in command, Charles Lee. After questioning anyone who looked loyal to our cause, I found Lee, late that night, sleeping at a tavern in Baskingridge on December 13, 1776. I ascertained that Lee had planned an attack on the British post at Princeton. Washington, having reached the nadir of his military career, Lee hoped a successful attack would place him in command of the army by Congress."

He turned to Theo and young Washington Irving, "Lee, earlier in his life, lived as a Native American and married a Seneca. His Indian nickname, "Boiling Water," fitted his aggressive behavior."

Irving split his eyes between Wilkinson and Theo, wanting to slip an arm around her shoulders.

"General Washington considered him the first officer in Military knowledge and experience in the whole army."

Burr, who sat a little distance apart by the writing desk, did not participate in the general conversation-which; however, he followed with quiet attention and nodded in agreement.

"I requested an answer to the letter from Gates, but he put me off till the morn. Unfortunately for Lee, I noticed a British force marching towards the inn while completing his reply to Gates. I went upstairs and secured myself in an advantageous place, awaiting the enemy with a dirk and gun, determined to fight should they appear but I am out of sequence." Burr wondered if the rambling Wilkinson knew the beginning, middle and end of any tale he told.

"Upon receiving Lee's letter, Gates proceeded to Delaware and, on

December 20, 1776, arrived at Washington's headquarters near Coryell's ferry." His fingers tightening as he looked up at Washington, Gates turned down the command at Bristol his fellow Virginian offered him.

Accompanied by Major Wilkinson, he rode off towards Philadelphia to his wife's waiting arms and the ears of "The Congressing Generals" nearby at Baltimore.

"He informed his "ravens" that instead of vainly attempting to stop Sir William Howe at the Delaware, General Washington should retire to the south of the Susquehanna and form an army."

During this episode, Gates and his "recovered" companion alighted at a city tavern, the General charging Major Wilkinson with a letter to Washington.

Looking at Theo with his intense brown eyes, Wilkinson said, "Washington's troops had been retreating through the Jerseys' without cavalry, carrying what little they had, without tents, tools, camp equipage, magazines, half-clothed, badly armed, debilitated by disease, disheartened by misfortune and worn thin by fatigue. I proceeded in quest of the troops, whose route was easily traced, as there was little snow on the ground, tinged here and there with blood from the feet of the men who wore broken shoes."

Willet remembered they were preparing to be ferried across the icy Delaware River, which was swept by high winds, Washington risking all in a surprise attack on the enemy at Trenton, New Jersey, on the morning of December 26, 1776.

"When the General received the letter, he exclaimed with solemnity, 'What a time is this to hand me letters!'

"I answered that I had been charged with it by General Gates."

"By General Gates! Where is he?"

"I left him this morning in Philadelphia."

"What was he doing there?"

"I understood him that he was on his way to Congress!"

He earnestly repeated, 'On his way to Congress!' and broke the seal. I could see in his eyes that he knew his authority was in jeopardy. For the esteemed man, Gates's letter just intensified his desire to succeed in this risky maneuver. For General Washington's power was melting like snow before the sun."

Wilkinson took one big breath and began to pace. Illuminated by this memorable episode, he said to Theo and the young Irving, "Washington challenged the force of the current, the sharpness of the frost, the darkness of the night, the ice made during the operation, the high wind. All these elements rendered the passage of the river extremely difficult."

*The World Turn'd Upside Down* | 145

Wilkinson pressed his hand to the side of his face.

The flashback of that spectacle played back all too clearly in his head.

"I have never doubted that he resolved to stake his life on the issue."

The verbose soldier, full of wind, titled his head somewhat back and, with a smile ever so slight, poured another glass of port, took a quick swallow, his red lips aflame.

Burr, amused by Wilkinson's energy, blew concentric smoke rings that dissolved into a halo over the latter's head.

Flooded with spirits, he continued in a slow elaborate manner, "During the attack, I served as a courier between St. Clair's Brigade and Washington. Upon learning his strategy was successful, Washington took my hand and observed, "Major Wilkinson, this is a glorious day for our country."

And Burr thought of General Washington as well but not with kind thought.

"One thousand Hessians captured," said Wilkinson, "and cannon, shot, and gunpowder, and another hundred enemy killed."

Irving thought, *saved from disaster, what a story to write.*

"A Tory," said Wilkinson, "admitted several days after the battle that the rebels had given up the cause as lost. Their late successes have turned the scale, and now they are all liberty mad again."

Peter Irving said, "To supplement his victory, Washington launched another surprise attack a week later on a British garrison at Princeton."

"A bloodier battle, the enemy lost," said Wilkinson, "nearly four hundred, and we routed three battalions of their infantry who occupied the town."

"In the space of a week," said Irving, "Washington won back control of New Jersey."

"Up in front as usual," said Wilkinson, "I nearly died when a ricocheting ball from the stone walls of Nassau Hall caromed towards me at the battle of Princeton on January 3, 1777."

"I believe," said Irving, "The ricocheting cannonball was fired by Alexander Hamilton," whom Burr recalled took pleasure in firing his cannon against the school that refused him admission.

"I stood watching the enemy file out of the building," said Wilkinson, "and surrender while about two hundred other soldiers of the British escaped by running like a blur at top speed towards Brunswick. I cannot recall ever seeing men move that fast in my life.

We suffered only forty casualties."

Assuming the air of a father of a newborn, General Wilkinson informed Theo and the young Irving, "The American community began to feel and act like a nation determined to be free."

The General suddenly turned, "We were the little band who faced the storm when the summer soldier and the sunshine patriot hid their heads."

Burr raised his glass, "Yes when many tin soldiers thought they were generals."

Glasses clinked. "Generals lacking in brass," noted the young Irving.

After the two victories, General George Washington's army proceeded north, setting up winter headquarters at Morristown, New Jersey. On January 6, the hills surrounding the camp offered him a perfect vantage point to keep an eye on the British army, headquartered across the Hudson River in New York City. Its position also allowed Washington to look after the roads leading from the British garrisons in New Jersey to New England and Philadelphia's roads—where the shepherds of the American Revolution quarreled and attempted to govern.

At this time, General Washington offered Major Wilkinson a lieutenant colonelcy under Colonel Nathaniel Guest in one of the sixteen battalions authorized by Congress on Friday, December 27, '76.

It came to Burr's attention, some years later, through Colonel Clement Biddle, that Lieutenant Colonel Wilkinson turned down Washington's first command.

"Who were you to serve under," asked Theo" Colonel Guest, a gentleman," said Wilkinson, "bred on the southern frontier. There would be a difference of education which might be prejudiced to the harmony of the corps."

From a curled lip that turned to a slight smirk, General Washington informed the young man.

"The command is to remedy the defects of lax discipline and polite manners; although Colonel Guest was rough, he was a brave and good man."

Thinking there are two types of people, those who can charm and promote their careers and those who belong in the scrap heap. The fearless one pressed the issue on the future president "Washington let me choose whom to serve under. Colonel Thomas Hartley became my immediate superior. We acted together in Canada." Wilkinson nodded as young Irving looked at him.

"I repaired to Maryland with authority to appoint officers to three companies and proceeded to select platoon officers for the companies, Captain Benjamin Stoddert, a friend of my youth and age; Captain Richard Wilson of Queen Ann County, an esteemed and respectable acquaintance; and Lieutenant Henry Carberry." His fingers tightened as he ventured unto the past,

"I," said Wilkinson to the gathering at Richmond Hill, "returned to Philadelphia, the regimental rendezvous, at the beginning of March and renewed my intimacy with General Gates, who was in command.

I met my "Nancy," Ann Biddle, the most accomplished and respectable of the fair sex again."

Wilkinson sighed, remembering how glad he was to be in the company of "Nancy," whom he cuddled next to.

"She brought out a courting Distemper," he reported to Theo as he winked at her.

It seemed Irving's eyes saw things differently. A streak of jealousy surfaced on his brow.

While he wooed "Nancy," her younger sister, Lydia, was courted by Doctor James Hutchinson, a fellow medical student with Wilkinson in Philadelphia before the rebellion started.

During Gates' audition for Congress, Wilkinson suggested he take credit for Arnold's maneuvers in delaying Carleton on Lake Champlain Gates jumping at the opportunity.

"As the snows gave way to spring buds in 1777, Congress found an excuse to reprimand Schuyler, and off went my Gates to take command at Ticonderoga with St. Clair under him."

The official change of authority of the Northern Department occurred on March 25.

The fact that it was done with a bare quorum and the New York delegation was not present mattered little to one of the "Congressing Generals."

Not aspiring to be an extra, Schuyler went to Philadelphia in April 1777, desiring to redeem his honor, "all that stands in their journals injurious to me must be expunged, or I quit the service."

Receiving a standing ovation on May 22, Congress directed Major-General Schuyler to proceed to the northern department and take command there immediately. He performed exceptionally well, and his mood suddenly brightened. The door ajar and Schuyler rushed in.

Gates opened his eyes wide, knowing what the expression on Schuyler's face meant. The war between these two inflated bags of skin continued; there was no shortage of vanity.

This venality in Congress is proof positive of the evil that politics does to democracy. Petty bickering is one thing, but this sideshow spoke volumes when the revolution hung by a thread.

*Politics is rattling noise,* thought Burr, *opinions of no value that lead to the bleeding of humankind.*

.

## Chapter 34

## Lee's Capture

"I am looking for General Lee's whereabouts," said James Wilkinson to a man with large, callous, thick, protruding ears.

The man nodded and smiled, putting two and two together, thinking that must be why the military guard surrounded the tavern.

The Tory pointed northeast, 'In that direction.' Before returning home, he hurried off to inform the British of his suspicion.

"I rode the fifteen or twenty miles the night of December 12 and found Lee lodged in White's tavern at Baskingridge, New Jersey. I awoke the General, who got out of bed, thrusting an old flannel gown over his nightclothes. The words flashed back into his mind.

"I have a message for you from General Gates."

"It can wait till morning, grunted Lee"

"Sir, your sentries are posted far from the tavern."

Lee glared at him.

"Are not you disturbed?"

"What I am troubled about is that you woke me up."

"Lee returned to his room, needing to recover from his earlier eating, drinking, and womanizing the following day soon to come." Wilkinson stopped for a moment, gathering himself mentally on how to tell the stories.

"The following morning, having breakfast with his French aid, Lee informed me in a dressing gown and slippers, 'Washington should be conducting a hit-and-run campaign against the enemy rather than trying to confront a professional army in open battle.'"

Wilkinson pursed his lips as he took him in, and the face he offered was warm and soft.

"I have made things unsafe behind the British lines," said Lee, "and they must deploy extra troops to guard against my raids."

Wondering if he should hitch his wagon to Lee, Wilkinson nodded in approval.

"I disturb their support line and often capture small escorted and baggage wagons. Two days ago, I appropriated 1,000 sheep and hogs from their commissariat and captured several patrols and individual dragoons. From these captured soldiers, I gleaned important military information."

Lee's eyes changed like a warrior's when his plans became crowded with success and ambition. He stretched out his long legs.

"I am planning an attack on the British post at Princeton." "I withheld the information that Washington already attacked Princeton." Wilkinson whipped around his back to the Hudson.

"Knowing that Washington had reached the deserved nadir of his military career, I surmised that Lee hoped a successful attack would place him in command of Congress's army.

I knew well that he must appear to agree. I shifted and beamed at Lee"

Bowing in consent as Lee began drafting a letter to Gates, "Entre nous a certain great man is damnably deficient. Unless something happens, which I do not expect, our cause is lost. Our counsels have been weak to the last degree."

"As Lee finished the letter, I heard hoofbeats on the road and, looking out of the window, saw a troop of red-coated British soldiers riding rapidly up to the house."

Wilkinson fetched more wine from the table giving himself a moment to think.

"With the wine still singing in his head, Lee instructed me to deliver the letter to Gates, but then the Brits surrounded the tavern, shooting two guards and informing the innkeeper, Get General Lee, or we will burn down the house." Wilkinson jerked his head back as he said, "I saluted the general and rushed upstairs as he departed the inn.

"What a curious coincidence," said Harcourt as Lee approached him.

"You look familiar," said Lee.

"I served under you in Portugal."

Lee began to laugh and mumbled a string of profanity,

"Are you still the brave but somewhat irascible soldier?" asked Harcourt.

"I beg you to spare my life," Lee said, "with a look of horror."

"Well, old fellow," said Harcourt. "That is not my decision."

Lee's eyes darkened, and he shivered.

"It is a great shock to your nerves finding yourself captured."

The British dragoons crowded around him and seized him, crying out that he was a deserter from the British army and wanted by General Howe.

Lee knew what that meant; there was more than humiliation in his capture and possibly a disgraceful death!

"Will you allow me to get dressed?"

"There is no time for the hero of Charleston to dress."

Lee rubbed his temple, trying to find words to convince him.

"Tie him to a horse like a cattle thief."

"Where are you taking me?"

"To the British camp and General William Howe in New York."

Riding along hatless and clad in an old flannel wrapper amid the jeers of his captors, he was packed off to New York on Wilkinson's horse.

The entire episode of encircling the house, the shooting, the capture of Charles Lee, and riding off with him took four minutes and occurred at ten in the morning. About 200 paces from the house, Lee's corps arrived late to save their General.

Lee's adjutant general, a French colonel, was also captured. With only one horse, the French Colonel rode with a servant of Colonel Harcourt. The aide indignantly protested that this was beneath his dignity in a letter to General Howe. The French!

Upon his arrival in Manhattan, Lee was treated with the same "courtesy" as he had been by his captors at White's Tavern.

"I regard you as a traitor and will wait for England's orders,: said Howe.

Captivity, aged Charles Lee. At first, he worried that he might be tried and shot by General William Howe as a deserter and then fumed that Congress and Washington were not doing enough to free him.

Confined in the Council Chamber of City Hall, "one of the genteel public rooms in the city, square, compact, tight, and warm," he concluded the colonies could never achieve victory. A continuation of the conflict only weakened America and Britain.

A sentry stood at the door, and firewood and candles were provided for him, and he ordered dinner every day from a public house, sufficient for six people, with what liquor he wanted and of what kind he pleased. He had the privilege of asking any five friends to dine with him daily and at England's expense.

Writing to Washington, "I am likewise extremely desirous that my Dogs be brought as I never stood in greater need of their Company than at present."

"Your dogs," replied Washington, "are in Virginia. This circumstance

I regret, as you will be deprived of the satisfaction and amusements you hoped to derive from their friendly and companionable dispositions."

## Chapter 35

## Burgoyne Goes Home & Hamilton Rising

As Burgoyne stood at his wife's grave, a sadness overcame him. He accepted her death, but being left out of the command at the siege of Boston in 1775 still left him gloomy. He resented being ignored by Carleton in Canada, and it made his blood boil.

"My two stints in America were a box office flop," he said, "but I promise you, Charlotte, this will change."

Sitting at Boodle's on 28 St. James's Street, Johnny, with a unique dramatic style, announced, "The damn bastards are as clueless as an explorer wearing two eye patches."

It was going to take time, he thought to get what he wanted – command.

Rising, he sauntered to the bar, complaining throughout the evening about his superiors, "They lack a regard for my talents." Day after day, the well-built, bright, pleasure-loving soldier appeared throughout London amidst the topic of the day, the politics of the American Question, "Without much to his credit, nor the satisfaction of the court," said one of his critics, "He received what he deserved."

Criticism flowed from his puffy lips, even to Charles Fox and the Opposition, for he knew all the Ministers. "I have plans for invading New York from Canada. . ."

Fox cut him off. 'I will arrange for my friends in Parliament to meet with you."

The Court bought his affected dissatisfaction with the war in America.

Burgoyne's rank and pay grew without a single question raised in the House of Commons; fifteen men were added to each company of his regiment (all to his profit).

Four cornetcies (a commissioned cavalry officer rank in the British army) were given to him to sell and "an extraordinary promotion for his late wife's nephew, Mr. Stanley."

But the hierarchy of aristocracy intervened,

Stanley's promotion ceased due to the Secretary of War's partiality to Captain Stanhope, Lady Harrington's son, over whose head Stanley would have risen.

At Brook's on Christmas Eve, Charles Fox saw it in his eyes, heard it in his voice, thinking that Burgoyne and the King were like Rome lying in sleep.

Gentleman Johnny bet Fox 50 guineas that he would be back in a year, victorious.

He struggled with his temper as Parliament debated little on America.

Having the ear of the king, whom he often met, Burgoyne, more often than not, noticed the king admiring a sterling silver tea set.

He told the king and Germain, "The enemy will be in great force at Ticonderoga. Different works exist of admitting twelve thousand men, and they can occupy Lake George with considerable naval strength." "Give us your strategy," said the king.

He put on paper for Germain *"Thoughts for the Conducting the War from the Side of Canada."* Burgoyne, like the ministry, wanted to tear the rebellion in half. The settled plan was a three-fold attack against northern New York. He would lead the main army to the upper Hudson by way of Lakes Champlain and George, while Colonel Barry St. Leger, with British regulars and Indians, 1700 in total, would fight their way down the Mohawk Valley, and Sir Henry Clinton would march north from Manhattan.

*****

In 1777 General Washington summoned Generals Alexander McDougall, Nathanael Greene, and Lord Stirling.

"Gentlemen, there is a vacancy in my staff."

His generals grinned, thinking they knew who should staff it, their eyes open.

"Do you have any suggestions for whom might fill the position?"

They watched him pace around the room in his stiff military gait.

The three-hundred-pound, former Boston bookseller Henry Knox entered, eying platters of food as he sat between Greene and McDougall.

Knowing Washington lacked verbal flow, Knox asked, "Why the silence?"

"With me, it has always been a maxim rather," Washington said, "to let my designs appear from my works than by my expressions."

"I repeat, gentlemen," his eyes scanned his three generals, "I need someone to cope with an unending flood of paperwork from Congress and the state legislatures."

"There is only one person alive who meets the requirements," said Knox as he bit into a leg of mutton.

"Is he a fluent wirer?"

"Yes," said his generals in unison. "Major Hamilton."

Washington sent a note to Alex, inviting him to join his staff as an aide-de-camp.

On March 1, the appointment became official, and Major Hamilton, already encamped at headquarters, obtained the rank of lieutenant colonel.

Sitting on the side of his bed that night, drumming his fingers, he wrote Reverend Knox in St. Croix, "For several months, the war has produced no military event of any great importance, allowing me to recuperate from an illness." Amused, he continued, "In the four years since I arrived in America, I have become an aide to the country's most prominent man."

The twenty-two-year-old Alex smiled but yearned for a field command and shirked off second thoughts about being a clerk at a new desk. Washington's proxy strutted and beamed a grin for the first time in days, knowing that all the managerial skills from his days as Cruger's clerk qualified him for the position.

Writing to McDougall on March 10, "His excellency had been sick, and I hesitated to disturb him but now recovered, I find he is bothered with matters which cannot be avoided that I am obliged to refrain from troubling him on occasion, especially as I conceive the only answer he would give may be given by myself."

Looking up, Alex took a long breath, believing his mother would be proud, and lifted a brow; the organizing problems of running a war suiting him. To shuffle the recruiting logistics, promotions, munitions, clothing, food, supplies, and prisoners was child's play for Alex.

He thought for Washington, as well as executed orders. Most of Washington's field orders were in his handwriting.

"The pen for our army," said Robert Troup, "was held by Hamilton, and for the dignity of manner, the pith of matter, and elegance of style, General Washington's letters are unrivaled in military annals."

James McHenry, an aide to the general, would say, "Hamilton aided our chief in giving to the machine that perfection to which it had arrived previously to the close of the revolutionary war." His authority remained unabashed as the General allowed Alex to ride with him in combat, go off on diplomatic missions, interrogate deserters, and negotiate prisoner exchanges.

Washington's subordinates knew that he was the "principal and most confidential aide" of the general.

Sitting back, his eyes bright and sober, he wistfully calculated he would lead the army by summer. With hope and skill mixed into a firm dough, he let his dreams rise.

Dances, parades, and reviews sometimes excused him from the exhausting schedule, and at night, he engaged in conversation with the four to six aides that slept in one room.

"Fine words, "Hammie." I wonder where you stole them."

"Well, at least, I never have been known to use a word that might send a reader to the dictionary."

"Did I tell you "Ham" that I like your new hairstyle; it makes your nose look normal?"

"You have delighted us long enough," said Alex.

"You're funny in how you make people laugh at you."

A look invaded Hammie that made him tender.

"You are pretty in the picture Charles Willson Peale painted of you."

Alex shrugged. "Remember, on his visit here at headquarters. The portrait of you, a miniature on ivory."

"We did not recognize you!"

Alex feigned puzzlement for a moment.

"I thought I looked dignified in my blue-and-buff uniform with gold epaulets and a green ribbon, my hair cropped close, my nose long and sharp, and my gaze so serious."

The aides glanced up, saw he was serious, and laughed.

## Chapter 36

# Ready or Not

As morning dawned on Montreal, the roll of drums and clamor of bulges roused the sleeping inhabitants.

Burgoyne's mistress, her hair tied back with his red scarf, the only clothing on her, attempted to make the messy bed.

Seated erect with his back to her, the general wrote in a flowing manner at a cluttered table, taking great delight in dotting the i's and crossing the t's.

In a coy voice, she asked, "What are you writing? Mon general." He pivoted in his chair and, with a bemused look, glanced at her unclad body. He began to read in French, "It is my design while advancing to Fort Ticonderoga, and during the siege of that post, for a siege I apprehend it must be, to give all possible jealousy on the side of Connecticut. If I can, by stratagem, lead the enemy to suspicion, my views are pointed that way after the reduction of Ticonderoga. . ." His mistress, like a bird of prey, approached him. Her tender hands encircled his chest as she whispered, "Mon Cheri, my lovable gamester likes to play the war's diversion, always striving to be one step ahead in the contest."

He lifted her left hand and nibbled on her forefinger's tip harder than he should have.

In reaction, the fingernails of her free hand left a red line on his chest. She tried to make light of it, but he turned to her, "Machiavelli taught that one could make your opponent suspect by a maneuver. In my case, after the reduction of Ticonderoga, I want the rebels to think my views are pointed that way. It may make the Connecticut forces very cautious of leaving their frontiers and much facilitate my progress to Albany." Extremely contented, she gave him a slow, sultry smile.

A grin as wide as the ocean adorned his face. He looked at his watch and sighed, thinking he should take her arm and carry her back to the bed. He felt a stirring in his loin.

She emitted a sudden, unrefined snort, and his loins retreated.

Again. in French, he said, "I have sworn to the King and his Majesty's ministers that whatever demonstrations I may endeavor to impose upon the enemy, I shall make no movement that can procrastinate my progress to Albany."

"Mon general," she bit her lips as she stared into his eyes, "I like a hell-bent man. You do not need a compass to know what direction you must go. Hail Caesar." He rose in reverence to Julius, but pressing thoughts sallied forth, "Damn the scattered troops, the currents, the winds, the roads, the want of materials for caulking the vessels, the inactivity, and desertion of the Canadian corvees."

"You should not take it personally, Cheri; contingencies exist to block mankind's progress." His most significant need, horses and carriages for the bare transport of provisions and tents, lingered in his mind like a tax collector or dog in heat.

"Do not forget, mon general, that the water has been your friend. But you will be without the luxury of water carriage at Fort George or any other place where you dock your army." "The path becomes my enemy," he said.

"Cheri, your destiny is not a matter of chance but your choice. Do not wait for it."

"Do you foresee the future?"

"Your destiny is as sure as a baker kneads flour." He absorbed her prophetic words and then picked up the Quebec Gazette. To his surprise and mortification, he read his campaign's exclusive design almost as accurately as if copied from the Secretary of State's letter. His caution was such that no man knew the secret until last night's staff meeting. His thoughts then brushed aside the fact that his army fell short of the strength computed in England. The added want of the camp equipment, clothing, and other necessary articles took the wind out of his sails.

"I am nevertheless determined," he informed his mistress, "to put the troops destined for my command immediately in motion, and, assisted by the spirit and health in which they abound, I am confident in the prospect of overcoming difficulties and disappointments."

He recalled a recent letter to Germain, "How deficient in justice and honor I would be without mentioning the sense I entertain of General Carleton's conduct. Though he was anxiously desirous of leading the military operations out of the province, his deference to his Majesty's decision and his zeal to effect his measures in my hands is equally manifest, exemplary, and satisfactory."

He did not mention that with some smugness and a matter of facts, he happily handed Germain's dismissal letter to Sir Guy Carleton, who was not pleased.

On June 1, 1777, more warships and transports arrived in Quebec.

On July 29, 1777, eight weeks later, a grin streaked across his face. He commanded 39 sail, eleven British infantry companies, 450 Jagers of Hesse-Hanau, 4000 British regulars (light infantry and grenadiers), and a large mercenary force of 3000 German brutes in heavy boots, rattling swords at their sides. With plumes upon their heads under the command of Baron Friedrich von Riedesel, nearly 500 artillerymen with 130 brass guns, 500 loyalists, and 400 fierce Indians tattooed from head to toe soon proceeded southward to Fort Ticonderoga. Featherbeds, culinary exotics from the European continent, and too numerous everything-in-between thought necessary by the aristocratic Burgoyne and his entourage accompanied the expedition. Last but by no means least were hundreds of female camp followers, officers' wives, etc. He wrote Carleton, "A breach into my communication must either ruin my army entirely or oblige me to return in force to restore, which might be the loss of the campaign. Ticonderoga and Fort George must be in very good strength to prevent a breach, and I must have posted at Fort Edward and other carrying places. These drains, added to common accidents and service losses, will necessarily render me inferior in point of numbers to the enemy, whom I must expect always to find strongly posted. I ask pardon for dwelling so much upon this subject and have only to add my request to your Excellency to forward the other companies as expeditiously as may be." Carleton refused to honor his request, knowing this put Burgoyne in a disadvantageous position; he enjoyed setting up consternation and not dropping down to aid him. "Sorry," he said to himself as he rested his fingers on his lips, amused.

The army under Burgoyne needed to set up a house in Albany, but no arrangements existed for moving the field artillery by land. Neither carriages nor horses could be procured on the other side of Lake Champlain nearer than Albany.

He exited his bedroom from a romp with his mistress, his hair still uncombed and his shirt only half-buttoned.

And as for his loin, the deed of 1387 doth explain:

I, John of Gaut

Do give and do grant

Unto Roger Burgoyne

And the heirs of his loyne

All Sutton and Potton

Until the world's rotten

# Chapter 37

# Wilky's Adventure

"Marching north to join Gates," Major Wilkinson announced to Burr and his guests at his weekend at Richmond Hill, "I was no longer a youth but an experienced soldier. Yes, I lacked command in battle, but I served the contest by my extensive scouting and intelligence gathering."

He hesitated for a moment remembering the campaign of 1775-1776. "I partook in active

service then between the Atlantic and St. Lawrence as a staff officer. I put into motion the commands of my superiors who possessed the more tactical and strategic skill."

Of utmost importance to him, Burr surmised that he navigated General Washington's aura, who approved his mount from a volunteer to a lineal rank of lieutenant colonelcy and its emoluments.

The lieutenant Colonel, like himself, made his "novitiate" in arms' at his own expense.

By joining Gates, he took a demotion in rank. Burr recalled that General Armstrong, 'the hero of Kittanning,' upon hearing of this phenomenon concerning military men, declared, "Will wonders never cease, while lieutenant-colonels of the line resign to become majors on the staff."

"My whole soul," said General Wilkinson, "became devoted to the cause of my country. I was, of course, emulous of distinction, but it was more the distinction of service than that of rank."

Burr thought military distinction upon an honourable means also ran through his blood during the War of the Revolution, but it stuck in his heart like a lead weight.

"At the later end of April 1777, I arrived in Albany," said Wilkinson, "and was dispatched by General Gates with authority to examine and regulate the chain of communication with Fort Ticonderoga and to take command of said fort as brigade major."

He waited a moment to bring up the suspense. Irving shot Theo a glance.

"I was under authority to inform my general of the state of the garrison and every material occurrence. I put to paper three letters between the 16th and 26th of May on this matter. My conclusion was that the fort was defenseless and abandonment of it obvious."

Wilkinson believed St. Clair and Schuyler were unfairly put to task for succumbing to this oblivious conclusion. Only the fools in Congress wanted to engage the British.

Intrigues and plots, the lifeblood of politics, continued circulating in Congress and led "The Congressing Generals" to restore Schuyler to command of the Northern Department over Gates on May 22. The intrigues and plots of the Adams faction that put Gates in command on March 25 were rescinded.

After yielding command, Horatio Gates scampered from Albany to Congress for another act of "The Congressing Generals."

"General Schuyler,' Wilkinson said, 'send Arthur St. Clair to take command of Fort Ticonderoga on June 5." On the twelfth, he greeted him.

Wilkinson remembered St. Clair standing quietly, observing the badly armed, poorly clad, small garrison without magazines.

"Congress fails," said Wilkinson, "to send the 10,000 troops requested by Schuyler and Gates. St. Claire's shoulders drooping from the weight of command.

"Due to a rumor," said Wilkinson, "that the British were sending a large portion of the army to Howe in New York, the naive minds at Congress improvidently neglected the fort as it did not impose any immediate concern to the safety of the Northern Department."

On June 10, "Wilkinson" learned of his appointment to deputy adjutant-general by Gates at Fort Ticonderoga. "Yes, yes," he said to himself. "Finally."

"Dispirited by jealousies in the Northern Department," he wrote to his beloved general, "the perfidy of mankind truly disgusts me with Life. I do not wish to breathe the air with Ingrates, assassins, and double-faced Villains."

Prejudiced by the New England troops for keeping his headquarters in Albany, never commanding the troops in person in the previous campaign, being of Dutch descent, and identified with the New York side of the quarrel over the Hampshire Grant, Schuyler did not fit in.

They did not trust him, observed Wilkinson then, and it did not help that he failed to practice the art of popularity on many occasions.

"When Gates arrived the previous spring," continued Wilky, "a Captain Vidney had observed the miserable state of despondency and terror, but that Gates raised the men as if by magic. They began to hope and then to act."

"Something Philip Schuyler," said Burr, "never accomplished from his estates' comforts."

The storyteller charged forward with more detail about the upcoming British invasion, Washington Irving studying General Wilkinson's mannerisms.

"In Mid-June, General Schuyler visited Fort Ticonderoga, a star-shaped fort," said Wilky. "He informed me that he would like a share of my regard for Gates.

Always eager for esteem, Wilkinson established a professional relationship with him. With mutual trust affected, Schuyler sought Wilky's opinions regarding the fort. He told him, "As you can see, general, the soldiers at Fort Ticonderoga are a naked, undisciplined, badly armed, unaccounted body of men." Taking a long, long breath, he continued.

"I then advised Schuyler that he should hold a council of war which he did. It decided:

1. Defend as long as possible, then move to Fort Independence.
2. Have Bateaux in readiness if Independence became untenable."

He stopped. Theodosia noticed a quizzical expression appear on the General's face. With a feeling of wonder, he explained, "But pertinent to these two resolves were:

1. How to move the troops from Ticonderoga to Independence in the face of an enemy that had driven them out of the former?
2. How would the Bateaux be preserved for retreat if the forts proved untenable?

On June 20, Schuyler returned to Albany without addressing these concerns. I presumed to hope for the best".

Hope springs eternal, thought Washington Irving.

"I could see," said Wilky, "that we were on the edge of disaster from the slightest push."

As a shooting star zipped across the horizon above the Hudson, Wilkinson fully jumped aboard his tale, firing detail after detail to his listeners.

"I suggested to my general a brigade occupy the old French lines on the height to the north of the fort of Ticonderoga. These lines were put in good repair and had several entrenchments behind them, chiefly calculated to guard the northwest flank, and were further sustained by a blockhouse. Farther to our left was a post at the sawmills, which stood at the foot of the carrying place to Lake George, a block-house upon an eminence above the mills, and a blockhouse and hospital at the entrance of the lake."

Thoughts of pride enveloped Wilkinson. Perhaps there is justice, after all.

"Upon the right of the lines, and between them and the old fort, were two new block houses and a considerable battery close to the water's edge. On the opposite bank of Ticonderoga, on the east shore of Lake Champlain, stood Fort Independence, of considerable eminence and star-shaped."

Sensing the confusion in Theo's eyes, he said, "This is where the lake narrows to the dimension of the river."

She gave him a quick smile.

"My chief industry and greatest force was employed upon Mount Independence, which is a star for, high and circular, upon the summit, which was Table Land. It was made of pickets and well supplied with artillery and a large square of barracks within it.

The foot of the hill, on the side which projects into the lake, was entrenched and had a strong abattis close to the water. This entrenchment was lined with heavy artillery, pointed down the lake flanking the water battery, above described, and sustained by another battery about halfway up the hill."

Sensing the confusion in Theo's eyes, he said, "On the west side of the hill ran the main river, and in its passage was joined by the water which comes down from Lake George."

Cuddled next to her father, she gave him another quick smile.

"Since the previous autumn, I had been laboring to construct a great bridge of communication between the two forts. A bridge that the enemy could not reconnoiter. It was supported by twenty-two sunken piers of large timber at nearly equal distances; the space between was made of separate floats, each about fifty feet long and twelve feet wide, strongly fastened together by chains and rivets and also fastened to the sunken piers. Before this bridge was a boom, made of very large pieces of timber, fastened together by riveted bolts and double chains, made of iron an inch and a half square. On the east side of the hill, the water forms a small bay, into which falls a rivulet."

Burr was impressed by his stalks of detail, seeing qualities in Wilkinson that he never imagined.

"After having encircled in its coarse part of the hill to the southeast.

The side to the south could not be seen and was inaccessible to the enemy.

Yes, we labored hard to strengthen Ticonderoga and expected to give a vigorous resistance there. On Lake George, some vessels were built."

Wilkinson paused, patting himself on the back.

"On June 30, we learned the British advanced corps, consisting of the light infantry and grenadiers, the 24th regiment, some Canadians and Savages, and ten pieces of light artillery, under the command of Brigadier General Fraser moved from Putnam Creek, where they had been encamped some days, up the west shore of the lake to Four Mile Point, being within that distance of the fort of Ticonderoga. The German reserve, consisting of the Brunswick chauffeurs, light infantry, and grenadiers under Lieutenant Colonel Breyman, was moved at the same time to Richardson's farm, on the east shore, opposite Putnam Creek."

Wilkinson grimaced as wide as a barn door.

"Our commanders left Sugar Hill, opposite Ticonderoga on the southern side of the discharge from Lake George into Lake Champlain, unfortified.

John Trumbull, notable for his historical paintings, and I discussed the significance of this. The military importance of this elevation towered beyond question. Arnold, Gates, Wayne, and Trumbull all stood on the hill, as did I. Schuyler thought it wrong to throw away labor in preventing an evil that could never happen. This is where the time, effort, and money should have been expended, and John Trumbull tried to show the importance of this, but it would not penetrate the minds of his superiors."

With a quizzical look, Wilkinson said, "On the 25th, I wrote to Gates, 'I prefer death to capacity, but the event as it will, I shall not disgrace my acquaintance. Oh, that you were here! The fertility of your soul might save this important pass."

Standing beneath the veranda at Richmond Hill, Wilkinson looked out, and expelled a long breath.

"By July 1, 1777, the whole of the British army made a movement forward. Soon Brigadier Fraser's corps occupied the strong post called Three-Mile-Point, on the west shore; the German reserve the east shore opposite the army encamped in two lines, the right-wing at the Four-Mile-Point, the left wing nearly opposite, on the east shore.

The *Royal George*, and *Inflexible* frigates, with the gunboats, were anchored at this time just without the reach of our batteries and covered the lake from the west to the eastern shores."

Wilkinson shook his head, remembering what a depressing sight.

"The British gunboats moved forward, and the boom and one of the intermediate floats were cut with great dexterity and dispatch; Commodore Lutwidge, with the officers and seamen in his department, partaking the general animation, a passage was formed in half an hour for the frigates."

He stopped and did not talk anymore. The door of 1777 closed, Irving observing sadness floating upon his eyes. "I hope," said Wilkinson, "I have shown you the events that led to the fall of Fort Ticonderoga.

## Chapter 38

# Jane, David and Fort Edward

The drama concluded, and the curtain fell on the history of the Northern Campaign in New York in 1777, but Wilkinson took second fiddle to a young woman.

In upstate New York, circa 1900, there would come to be a group of researchers and historians obsessed with the death of the beautiful Miss Jane McCrea.

Wilkinson thought, "She was plain-looking."

Beauty resides in the eye of the beholder.

This cult in New York searched for records that did not exist. They could not report the facts because there were none. They did address each other's contradictions and filled in the gaps with their creative imagination, easing their minds. Something that Burr experienced all too well in his life.

As much as they praised each other's work and supplied answers based on their fancy, they misstated the only pertinent fact besides her name. They declared: The Date of the Death of the Fair Maiden of Fort Edward" the Sabbath of July 27.

When in exile in England in 1812, Burr talked further, into his past, past the deep gardens of politics, with their partisan shadows. He declared to Jeremy Bentham. "How can we trust history? It is left chiefly in the hands of imaginative writers."

A lesson exists about the role of historians in the lives of Jane McCrea and Aaron Burr.

A crow will perch on a tree. Settle with an eye on its surroundings and straighten a folded wing, but the historian will not do the same.

Historians:

1. treat sources without fidelity (say things that the records do not)
2. ignore records that contradict the origins of their argument
3. report more than what the documents say
4. are blind to the contradictions and do not fill in the gaps with facts

During Burr's four years in exile, his ideas reverted to his treatment before and after his alleged treason. The voices sounded closer and then withdrew. Should he have foreseen such a circumstance?

The agitation he experienced, realized Bentham, on learning that the loud and overpowering dictum of partisanship raised considerable emotion. It shot across the turbulent atmosphere of his life that goes with the territory of leadership.

How high must the disappointment be, thought Bentham, who inquired no further?

Enough said.

The misty gray-blue eyes under the straight eyebrows of Loyalist Lieutenant David Jones focused on General Burgoyne as the gilded green sun faded over the valley through which lay the proposed route of Burgoyne. David's intimate knowledge of the country led him, his brother, Jonathan, and sixty men to volunteer their services to the British at Crown Point.

Honoured with commissions in the British service, Jonathan as captain and David as a lieutenant served in the same company. David followed his heart and turned away from the revolution, leaving behind his love, Jane "Jenny" McCrae, and risking their future life together.

Jenny, who resided with her brother, an officer of the revolution, oozed guilt about David's love, a problem she chose to ignore. They found themselves struggling with those who decided to support the revolution—the plight of many Americans who walked the line of uncertainty. No joy or innocence there, however. The colors and brushstrokes blurred.

David watched General Burgoyne welcome more than four-hundred Indians from remote parts of Canada decked with feathers and war paint at St. John's on June 21 in Boquet's Valley.

He thought the war paint on the Indians was not inviting, but it was hard for him to avert his eyes.

He promised to write to Jenny about his life as a soldier. How would he describe this, he thought—a puzzle to be solved. Awake and excited, his fellow soldiers, the generals, and camp followers' faces pressed against the brisk dusk air as their eyes bulged at the near-naked Indians. David Jones' mind turned elsewhere, floating on his love's wings, Jane McCrea, seeing her soft white skin that showed a rosy flush when he winked at her.

Wondering did she understand that he wanted a life with her. Brilliant, luxurious, and happy, he caught himself frowning. He shook his head. What was he doing, leaving her alone with a war heading her way?

The General bestowed a ceremony of great pomp towards "his Majesty's savages," who were chiefly of the tribes of Algonquins, Ottawas, and Iroquois; Lieut. Jones's mind returned to the feast at hand. Fascinated by the Indians, who sang their traditional songs in exulting language, his eyes followed their movements.

What do they mean? He thought. These crazy, violent, beautiful motions?

Listening with astonishment to an interpreter, he learned they dwelled upon the extent of their history and their fathers' ancient glory with each step and gesture.

David experienced his breath turning short; his head went light as his eyes soared to rude pictures of the deer, the squirrel, and the oak, imprinted on their bodies.

Later that night, he looked up and smiled a bit, wondering if time stretched out for Jane or if an hour was only a second. He then wrote to his love, who resided near Fort Edward with her traitorous brother, John. How would he deal with him in the future, he pondered?

He told her, "I watched the war dance, Jenny, the entire band moving in a circle, whooping, brandishing their tomahawks, imitating the act of scalping, of laying in ambush, the sudden attack, the struggle, the carnage, and the victory, thus representing how they would vanquish the enemies of their great father beyond the sea."

He stopped for a second before continuing. "I worry for you and your safety in these horrid times."

David neglected to say that he shivered and realized the Indians chilled him to the bone.

"I heard General Burgoyne, through an interpreter, deliver a highly prosaic address to our new allies. "I represent," he said, 'the great father beyond the great lake. The collected voices and hands of the Indian tribes over the vast continent are on the side of justice, law, and the King. Warriors, you are free! He raised his voice to a high screech. Go forth in the might of your courage and your cause, strike at the common enemies of Great Britain and America–These disturbers of public order, peace, and happiness—Calling themselves the rebels, he laughed. They are the destroyers of commerce, parricides of the State.

Upon Burgoyne's final word, the Indians, in unison, lifted the skulls tied to their bodies by bark twine. They swung each with a vivid movement and kissed each of the patriot's remnants with their sharp knives."

Jones's pencil lifted. He opened his mouth and then closed it, concerned if it was wise to go into such detail to the fair maiden – so sweet and innocent of life – the darkness David was learning that dwelled in each of us.

He stopped and looked at the spectacle before him.

He wrote, "When I heard Burgoyne prohibit the Indians from scalping their prisoners while alive but had full power to scalp the dead and destroy wherever opposition was made, I was stricken by this, but who was I to say different."

He knew he must be careful, very prudent, and write calmly.

"My dearest, fear not; I do not side with a monster. Many of our unhappy past friends may still reclaim their loyalty.

And maybe too wise not to see the fatal consequence of this usurpation and wish to resist it till a sufficient force shall appear to support them."

As he wrote, a scratch from the future lacerated the front door of his mind.

"General Burgoyne forbids bloodshed when they were not opposed in arms, my dear one. I stood up and saluted a young warrior with a scar on his left cheek, but he averted his eyes from me. As I continued to stare at His Majesty's Savages, my eyes came on the chest of a tall, muscular one that showed a wolf whose berry-stained teeth glistened like fresh blood."

David shook his head, focusing on the top rung of future battles. He had to; he was a soldier. Yet, he never could see the future of his beloved country. His convictions closed his eyes to the signs before him for telling these events to Jenny.

Never imagining what would come to be, a boat, the boat of humanity floating down the river of suffering, surrounded by a world ruled by the confusion of an insane person.

Striving to delude himself, who could command these painted warriors of the forest – to spare the innocent – a better chance in forbidding a wolf not to attack a helpless fawn was the truth.

"After the British General's speech," David wrote, "His Majesty's savages drank copious amounts of liquor supplied by the British, followed by a war dance and whooping to their heart's content."

He considered for a moment and recollected himself.

"My Jane, I am thankful I will not have to face them, for I fear I would fail as a soldier and succumb to a despicable fear." At Jeremy Bentham's residence in 1815, before he returned to America, his host told Burr that Edmond Burke, in late 1777, outlined in the House of Commons, "There's a riot on Tower Hill. The keeper of the zoo, before releasing the animals, says, 'My gentle lions, my human bears, my sentimental wolves, my tender-hearted hyenas, go forth, but I exhort you, as we are Christians and members of a civilized society, to take care not to hurt, man, woman or child."

This information much amused Burr's mind.

"What a fool he, Burgoyne was," said Bentham.

"I have known several like him in my life," Burr exclaimed.

"You have heard of Horace Walpole?"

"Yes."

"He told me," said Bentham with a grave face, "that the fat Lord North looked so amused that he almost suffocated with laughter when he heard of Burke's wit."

Burr's countenance was all smiles and good humor.

Jane McCrea put down a sheet of paper from David, rattled by his words, but held fast by her love for him; she knew he stood for principles. She remembered he welcomed all to friendship, but the rebellion ended this. It stole her love from her, his loyalty to the King outweighing her. The hostility to the King, he did not understand; she did not understand. Holding his words of love close to his heart, he knew she was unique and beautiful. When reading his words, tears swelled in her eyes. She learned to expose her feelings to others' notice, like her brother, was not a good idea. "Good heavens," she cried. "I miss him."

Jenny envisioned David, the causeway, and the bridge to a further shore. She longed to be touched by his sleek, expressive hands.

Nowhere before in her thoughts did the possibility that at any moment, life breaks its word and renders body, energy, possessions, and other goodly things useless. She was trembling with these very visions – the violence portrayed by his words – her mind could not bear the image of him with these. Yet, her heart tore as she gazed at her brother.

She looked down, hearing David's voice again tell her, "That on any particular day, my thoughts center on you, who lift my love and tug at my delight. Your mature buxom, the magnetic softness under your eyes, and delicate angel eyebrows resemble the Madonna."

Looking up into her brother John's eyes, she tilted her head and excused herself from her guardian. Torn, she felt her feet not touch the ground, so faint and beside herself with emotions divided between her love for her brother and David's passion. Knowing they would never speak again, she retired to the rooms he gave her a year ago when their father remarried. David engraved on an elm branch that he had flattened in his spare time, "Journey's End in Lovers Meeting." It was a gift for Jane. His fellow soldiers were envious; so young and unlucky, David did not know such love. It mystified them.

The McCrea and the Jones boys had remained friends since their childhood in New Jersey, and both, in time, repaired to the West side of the Hudson, a few miles from Fort Edward, which interrupted a continuous water route from Canada southward.

The Jones family lived on the Moreau side, west of the Hudson, opposite Fort Edward. A brother, John Jones, lived in Kingsbury, 3 miles north of Sandy Hill.

Built-in 1755, it housed six thousand troops under General Lyman, awaiting General Johnson's arrival, the commander-in-chief of an expedition against Ticonderoga and Crown Point. The fort, the scene of extensive military operations for many years due to its proximity to the French frontiers, was an army post of considerable importance during the French and Indian War. The locality, previous to the erection of the fortress, was called the first carrying place, being the first and nearest point on the Hudson where the troops, stores, &c. were landed while passing to or from the South end of Lake Champlain, a distance of about twenty-five miles. At first, called Fort Lyman, in honor of the General who superintended its erection, it was built of logs and earth, sixteen feet high and twenty-two feet thick, and stood at Fort Edward Creek's junction and the Hudson River. A deep fosse or ditch was from the creek around the fort to the river. An underground passage to the river from the fort existed, and an underground brick room with the date 1757.

The now dilapidated Fort Edward flats were populated and cultivated for 50 years, the hills above the valley later. Millers, shopkeepers, tavern keepers also farmed, and many loyalist families.

Hardwoods and conifers stretched for hundreds of miles at all points from the river, dwarfing the numerous near-like roads that served the needs of the inhabitants. Major Wilkinson described it as "A Fort at the end of nowhere."

Since the conclusion of the Seven Years' War in 1763, the farmers of northern New York replaced the rifle with the rusty ax and used its sharpened blade to create fields for their crops. Their devotion to the fertile land adjacent to the Hudson produced a harvest of plenty. The "Spirit" of America no longer needed to behave like a child: modest, timid, and guarded.

To those mines of happiness beyond the oceans of merit, they marched.

Liberated from war, they kept a heart and mind free from fear. The farmers' destiny existed through hard work and the port of refuge drawing near.

Jenny and David were unfazed by the fact that life never gets longer.

After her mother's death and her father's remarriage, the orphaned Jane removed a few miles north from Fort Edward to her brother, John

McCrae's home. A College of New Jersey graduate in 1766, John McCrea went to Albany to practice law but did not like it. He married one of "The" Beekmans of Albany and settled nearly opposite the mouth of the "Moses-kill" at Northumberland in 1773, near Fort Edward. It lay on the opposite side of the Hudson from the Jones'.

Jane and David found the love they carried since their youth. Their eyes were wide and fixed on one another with astonishment. At first, they knew not how to reconcile the lost past imposed by distance, but that soon passed.

David accompanied her, whether Jane sailed upon the Hudson, galloped on horseback along the great river's shores, or walked on the military roads to and from Fort Edward. John, could not have been more thrilled at the sight of his happy sister and that a welcome marriage would soon replace the weight of guardianship with his past friend, David.

His oars implanted many a path through the Hudson to the front door of the corpulent Mrs. Campbell's house near Fort Edward, where he would often find Jane visiting her friend, Miss Hunter, the granddaughter of Mrs. Campbell.

There, they made plans and dreamed dreams of their future.

John McCrea burst through the door of the home on one such occasion.

"Lake Champlain is in possession of the rebels."

David dropped the cup of tea he was holding.

"It is time to take sides."

Mrs. Campbell thought the wind of war was about to shatter the windows of the political horizon.

A hot, sticking mood struck the occupants of the tiny house.

The next day, John McCrea approached David Jones.

"Montgomery is leading an expedition to Canada. Come with me."

David hesitated. "Let me talk to Jane."

John wondered why David would not roll up his sleeves.

They parted as friends, but after two years passed, John McCrea realized the Jones family were prominent Tories in their hearts and remained loyal to the King. He wanted to shout and rant at Jane but withdrew when in her presence.

Sitting on a log by the Hudson River's shore, with amusement embalmed on their faces, David turned to Jane, "I must join General Burgoyne's army."

Her smile disappeared. "How will you get there?"

"We will claim to be patriots and proceed to St. John's and await

Burgoyne's arrival."

She brushed her hand through his hair, seeing the world through pink glasses.

# Chapter 39

# Burgoyne's Army

The English and German troops' varicoloured uniforms glowed against the blue water as General Burgoyne's army glided toward the enemy upon the 200-mile stretch of Lake Champlain's soft waters.

The General admired his redcoats, loyalists, 3000 Germans in gunboats and barges, and the two frigates, the *Inflexible* and the *Royal George*. From this state of elevation, elation overcame him for nearly a full minute. Standing tall, he switched off doubts of failure, envisioning victory due to the British strength and understanding of geography. He looked as graceful and lively as ever and talked to his aides.

At night, the wine flowed at his card table. Toasts of "Christmas in Albany" sprang from the lips of the young Lord Balcarres, commander of the Light Infantry, and Sir Francis-Carr, his aide-de-camp.

Leaning forward, Burgoyne poured another round of drinks into his ancestral crystal. His action brought on a loud and overpowering response, of which every part was sincere.

Meanwhile, the rebels inquired further and heard enough to know that Burgoyne was on his way.

Wilkinson smiled incredulously at Burr during the next morning's breakfast on the veranda at Richmond Hill. "St. John's lay at the northern extremity of Lake Champlain," exhorted Wilkinson. "He came from Canada, tall as a rock of ice, his army, the damned devil, his ego, the rising moon. He stood on the shore like mist on a mountain.

Theo and Washington Irving joined them, and Theo asked the General to go on.

"The road from Albany to Saratoga was good. From there to Fort Edward, tolerable, but from there to the head of Lake Champlain as bad as possible and nary a bridge over any of the small streams and brooks that filled Wood Creek."

Wilkinson flashed his listeners a smile before he continued his tale.

They said nothing as he stared at them, the morning overcast and cold, the Hudson a gray-blue.

The past suddenly opened. "Burgoyne's army," continued Wilkinson, "upon reaching land, following from its footsteps ruptured clods of soil, attacked grass and laid it to rest, and drew lines in its path without purpose. Then snatches of earth were further ground to dust by the oxen, the precious oxen which drew the carts filled with his supplies and much baggage.

From Major Kingston, I learned that the General's chain of command listened in pleasing silence to his strategy, passing praise, for everything had proceeded to plan. Stockpiles of supplies remained at St. John's, and Burgoyne set out with nearly 7500 conquerors and 130 brass guns. They began their trudge to their fate upon his hubris. It was not "if" we knew of his plans; he, himself, read them in a paper about publishing the whole campaign design almost as accurately as if copied from the Secretary of State's letter' in mid-May."

Wilkinson's face revealed a dash of freckles. His small dark eyes darted left and right, and his body emitted vitality as the father, daughter, and Irving cherished every word.

"By mid-June, Burgoyne rested at Crown Point, waiting for his entourage. Like a good soldier, he set up a military hospital.

The last night of his stay at St. John's, the poetical General penned a proclamation to the patriots promising a plague of Indian attacks."

> I will let loose the dogs of hell,
> Ten thousand Indians, who shall yell
> And foam and tear, and grin and roar,
> And drench their moccasins in gore:
> To these, I'll give full scope and play
> From Ticonderoga to Florida.

The proclamation brought a very sober look on Washington Irving, who felt an immediate dislike for him.

Dancing down the steps of the past, General Wilkinson said, "No one in his chain of command dared inform him of a favourite toast at our table.

> May every citizen
> be a soldier,
> and every soldier
> a citizen.

He would soon come to surmise the truth of this."

Theo shot Wilkinson a brief look as the sun made a feeble effort to appear.

"The sole purpose of his strategy was to effect a junction with General Howe about Albany and open the communication to New York." He raised his eyebrows, "But Howe had to cooperate."

Smiling like a summer morning, thought Irving, Burgoyne charged forward.

"Barry St. Leger," said Wilky, "and his force were to join him in Albany by Lake Ontario and the Oswego and the Mohawk River. We learned that St. Leger sailed at the end of June by way of St. Lawrence to Oswego with 700 regulars and loyalists. Upon landing at the great carrying place that separated the two waterways, 1000 Indians under the Mohawk chief, Joseph Brant, began harassing Fort Stanwix that stood between the Mohawk River and Wood Creek. After reducing the fort, the expedition was to proceed to Albany and flank our army."

Wilkinson sipped his morning tea and studied Burr, whose eyes were on Theo and the young Irving.

"He knew how to organize the details of an army."

Wilkinson turned to Burr and winked.

Getting the troops from point A to B is more than writing a paragraph, thought Burr.

"The British capture of Ticonderoga exhibited no excellent stratagem," said Burr.

"Pursuing the retreating rebels towards the forest exhibited no strategy; it was just a reaction."

"An overview of the geography was absent," Wilky said. "It required an understanding of the factors involved – roads – ravines – waterways – distances. Burgoyne scattered his resources over several areas and did not commit to a commonsense intended strategy."

For a few seconds, Wilkinson contemplated, then released a small, broken sigh.

"In early July at Fort Ticonderoga, in full view of my commander, General St. Clair, who stood by my side, we observed the enemy's varicolored uniforms contrasting with the green of the dense forest."

A few specks of rain fell upon the veranda's roof as Wilkinson steadied himself and looked back into elapsed days.

"The enemy was quick to agnise that Sugar Hill commanded a view of our works and buildings both of Ticonderoga and Mount Independence. The distance was about 1400 yards from the former and 1500 from the latter. The ground was ripe to be leveled to receive cannon and that the road to convey them, though difficult, might be made practicable. The British did so in twenty-four hours and thus commanded, in reverse, the bridge communication. They saw the exact situation of any of our vessels. Able to observe any material movement or preparation, they counted our numbers."

Wilkinson's eyes became wide and fixed on his audience. After a short pause, he said, "St. Clair recognized immediately we must be away from this, for our situation had become a desperate one."

# Chapter 40

# Politics

The water sparkled as the sun dove into the distant fast-flowing ribbon-like Hudson River.

"To the "spirit of 76," said the guests still on the veranda at Richmond Hill.

General Wilkinson stood refreshed by his medicinal herbs and enjoyed the occasion.

Wilkinson was again front and center for the next ten minutes, full of himself, but no one seemed to care. "I do not think," he said, "there was a moment where someone was not pointing the finger at someone else."

"Be careful," said General Willet, who caught Burr's eye, "or he will give you another rundown of the Battles of Saratoga."

Willet's words made Wilkinson laugh so hard that he feared spilling his drink. "It started," he said, "in the army when Schuyler, Gates, and Arnold had concurred on the retreat from Crown Point. A contingent of New England subordinate officers remonstrated to Washington, who rebuked the presiding officers without the fort's abandonment facts. As any man of honour would do, Schuyler asked for a court of inquiry from Congress, and upon it not being granted, he sent in his formal resignation."

General Willet, one of the many heroes who were under siege at Fort Stanwix, interjected, "The first of many because of his tinctured pride, that man possessed more vanity than leaves in the forest. If I recall, Congress appointed a committee to investigate the northern department's affairs, not with Schuyler in attendance but with his inferior, Gates, in command."

"Hamilton's future father-in-law," said Burr, "fumed about that."

Music did not come to Colonel Burr's ears when the name of Schuyler entered the conversation. He thought of his daughters, "Betsey" and Angelica, and John Church, Angelica's husband.

"The aristocratical Schuyler," said Willet, "thought in terms of social class, believing himself more equal, an octave above.

After considering the implications of this, Wilkinson shrugged.

Washington Irving's curiosity heightened, considering the conversation one of the most entraining of his life.

His mind in a different time, Colonel Burr sat quietly, a little off from the others, not hearing Wilkinson. He puffed his long seegar, thinking how Wilkinson could straddle the fence between Gates and Schuyler. This straddling between political parties plagued him throughout his political life. It dawned on him that the birth of political parties began with the battle between the Gates and Schuyler forces in Congress.

Gates, a Whig, personified the future Jeffersonian Republicanism. And Schuyler, the embodiment of the future Federalism of Alexander Hamilton. One committed to freedom from the hammer of authority, and the other believed the privileged should be the rulers.

The Colonel thought *politics, the jewelry of vanity*, sought out a point of access in Congress and, when found, impacted the lives of the innocent faithful soldiers.

His epaulets were highlighted by the light of several candles, and General Wilkinson's brow lifted.

Above, the black roof of heaven bejeweled by glittering stars, he scanned his fellow patriots and Congress's thought. Nausea entered his tone, "They were like a wandering compass, rotating in vain, trying to direct victory but endangering the revolution. Of course, they needed to organize a revolution. Fund it. Create an organization. But they feared the military."

Sighing, he walked the length of the veranda.

"These roaming elephants of ego nearly destroyed the revolution. The rising moon of their minds never full and the brilliant sun of ignorance never dispelling their mists of cloudy thought and behavior."

To his right, an owl in a maple tree chanted a steady chorus: hoo-hoo-hooooo, hoo-hoo-hooooo.

Taking notice of the recurrent sound, he picked up his glass, assuming he looked serious.

"Asleep to reality, drunk with power, their politics heedlessly spread the germ of defeat by confusing actions."

"Tin soldiers," said Burr, "who hoped to edge the sword to reap the glorious field but were without a file."

With a sound of disgust, Wilkinson returned to his chair and leaned back.

"Alas, from their politics came mighty plans and lofty schemes," he said. "They raided the dust and hoped to make a cover for their own mistakes. But for the battles of Saratoga, we would still be drinking tea."

A thought marched through Burr. The power of good is always weak, while the power of evil is vast and terrible.

# Chapter 41

# St. Clair to General Washington

"Colonel Wilkinson, I solicit your help," said General St. Clair. Xxxxxxxxxxxxxxxxxxxxxxxxxxxxxxxxxxxxxxx
"I am at your service, mon ami." xxxxxxxxxxxxxxxx
"A letter must be sent to General Washington explaining the details of the retreat from Ticonderoga." The nerve and speed of the request stunned Wilkinson. They talked, Wilkinson, drank, and then a letter was composed.

"Our force consisted of little more than two thousand effective. With these, I had lines and redoubts of more than a league in extent to defend. Judge how poorly these numbers could have defended them had they been perfected, which they were far from being. They were not defensible at all from the Ticonderoga side unless the enemy would have been so generous as to attack us in front of the old French lines and take no notice of the flanks of them, which were both open."

Frustrated, St. Clair turned away from Wilkinson his hands-on-hips. His predicament was annoying enough without having to justify it to his General. Wilkinson lifted a brow, waiting for St. Clair's nerve to settle.

"We had, last year, nine thousand men at these posts, and they were found barely sufficient for the defense of the works. This season, the system was slightly altered, not to make a smaller number answer, but to make a greater number necessary. The enemy had nearly invested us, nothing being wanted to complete it but they are occupying a narrow neck of land betwixt East Creek and the lake on the Mount Independence side. This, I had information, would certainly take place in the course of the next twenty-four hours, and had been left open so long only with a view to intercepting any cattle that we might bring in from the country, and then our communication would have been effectually cut off. We could have received neither supplies of provisions nor reinforcements."

Closing his eyes, St. Clair sat for a moment and considered resigning. Hearing his future filled with condescending voices, he shook his head as Wilky put quill to parchment.

"Sir, the militia of this country cannot yet be brought on to raise a siege. But it may be asked why I had not called in the militia to assist in the defense of the posts. For this plain reason—I had no provision for them and the minimal prospect of an adequate supply. When I first had notice of the approach of the enemy, there was no more than ten days' provisions in store for the troops then upon the ground. To have called in the militia in that situation would have been a certain ruin. So soon as a supply arrived, although but a scanty one, I did call for them, and about nine hundred joined me the day before the resolution to evacuate the posts was taken."

Heat and cold shot through St. Clair, his skin chilled by embarrassment, blood, and flaming at his situation. His future seemed to have fallen from his fingertips.

"They had come out in such a hurry and almost entirely without clothes they did not propose to remain but a very few days at the utmost. The term of Learned's and Wells' regiments, which made part of the garrison, also expired in two days. The commanding officers had acquainted me that they could not prevail upon the men to remain beyond the time they were engaged for. Your Excellency knows, but too well, the disposition of these people on such occasions. The batteries of the enemy were ready to open in three different quarters. Our whole camp, on the Ticonderoga side, was exposed to the fire of each, and, as soon as they did open, every man I had must have been constantly on duty, as, from our weakness, of which the enemy could not be ignorant, I had reason, every moment, to expect an assault."

The retreat raged in him. He desired to get away from it. He heard a mockingbird set a song in the trees behind him, the high, piercing notes mirroring his tension and anger.

"Judge, Sir, how long we could have sustained it, or whether our resistance must not have been a very feeble one indeed, especially when you take into the account that a great number were mere boys and that not more than a tenth part was furnished with bayonets. As the enemy was at least four times my numbers, the retreat was begun a little before day, on the 6th instant, unperceived by the enemy, after having embarked as much of the stores and provisions and as many of the cannon as was possible in the course of one very short night; and our march would probably have been unperceived for some time if General Fermoy's house had not been set on fire. How that happened, I know not. I had previously given orders against burning any of the buildings, that our march might be the longer concealed, but it served to the enemy as a signal of our leaving the place, and, in consequence, they were upon the Mount before our rear was clear of it, and fired a few times upon it, but without effect."

St. Claire drew away to think about what he said. He scribbled the information on a scrap of paper while observing men moving in and out of his sight. "I pressed the retreat as much as possible and reached Castleton that night, thirty miles from Ticonderoga, having, on our way, fallen in with and dispersed a party of the enemy, from whom we took twenty head of cattle, three British prisoners, and five Canadians."

A hard rain started to pound the ground, chirping birds finding shelter, and from the window of quarters, St. Clair observed a flock of Turkey Vultures perched on the tops of a tree with their wings spread. "I was at no loss to determine what part I ought to take, but I thought it prudent to take the sense of the other general officers."

St. Clair grunted in irritation. "A copy of the council has been transmitted to your Excellency by General Schuyler. They were unanimously of the opinion that the posts ought to be evacuated immediately; wisely, in my judgment, considering that a retreat, even with the loss of our cannon and stores, if it could be effected, would be of infinitely greater service to the country, and bring less disgrace upon our arms than an army, although a small one, taken prisoners, with their cannon and stores. I was fully in sentiment with them and believe I should have ordered the retreat if they had been of a contrary way of thinking. But here, again, it may be asked why, when I found myself in the situation I have described, I did not retreat sooner when everything might have been saved. I have only to answer that until the enemy sat down before the place, I believed the small garrison I had to be sufficient."

*He believes*! Thought Wilkinson. *We need commanders who know.*

"The intelligence that Congress had received, that no serious attempt in that quarter was intended, as it gained credit with them, I never doubted, and was unwilling, to be the occasion of drawing off any part of your army, as your operations might thereby be rendered less vigorous; and I knew, too, that you could ill spare them. Besides, until the case became so urgent that I had no alternative but the evacuation of my posts, or the loss of the army, it did not lie with me to determine upon."

With an increased heart rate and his jaw stiff, St. Clair stared at Wilkinson. "Colonel Long, with his regiment and a detachment from the other regiments, and the invalids with the hospital, were sent to Skenesborough by water, while I took the road to the same place, through Castleton, with the body of the army. As the enemy was at least four times my numbers, I had nothing for it but a forced march, and I pressed it as much as possible and reached Castleton that night, thirty miles: Repeating himself, he said, "From Ticonderoga, having, on our way, fallen in with and dispersed a party of the enemy, from whom we took twenty head of cattle, three British prisoners, and five Canadians."

At this moment in writing the letter, Wilkinson held the quill up. He thought, *Sometimes luck seems to fall from the sky.*

With quill to parchment, he continued, "The rear guard, under Colonel Warner, which, with those that had failed upon the march, amounted to a thousand, imprudently halted six miles short of Castleton and wasted so much time in the morning that they were overtaken and surprised by a strong detachment from Ticonderoga, which had been sent up the East Bay, which runs into the country very near the place where he was. They sustained the attack with great bravery but were finally obliged to give way, with the loss of about fifty killed and wounded. On the first of the firing, I sent orders to two regiments of militia, who had left me the night before, and were lodged within two miles of Colonel Warner's post, to move up to his assistance, which, had they done, that party would have been cut off. But, instead of that, they made all possible haste to rejoin me, and, at the same instant, I received the account of the enemy's being in possession of Skenesborough and having taken and destroyed everything that had been sent there."

Finding this information difficult to remember, St. Clair bore his teeth. "I was then constrained to change my route, both that I might avoid being put between two fires and that I might be able to bring off Colonel Warner. I, therefore, sent him orders to retire to Rutland, where he would find me to cover him. A considerable part of his detachment joined me at that place, and he, with about ninety more, two days afterward, at Manchester. A great many are still missing, though few, I believe, have fallen into the enemy's hands, as they did not pursue Colonel Warner but a minimal distance and, from all accounts, suffered much in the action."

*At least all was not lost*, thought St. Clair. "The Ninth Regiment followed Colonel Long towards Fort Ann and were almost entirely cut off. I have dispatched officers to Bennington and Four to pick up the stragglers, who, I suppose, have taken these routes to New England, and, on the 12th instant, I joined General Schuyler at this place after a very fatiguing march. Thus, Sir, I have laid before you, without the least reserve, everything I can recollect respecting Ticonderoga and the retreat from thence. Happy should I be if my conduct therein meets with your approbation, and I can, with the strictest truth, affirm no motives actuated me but what sprang from a sincere regard for the public welfare."

Shaken to the core St. Clair told Wilkinson, "My mother used to tell me optimism can turn rain into rainbows."

"We must turn this inside out," said Wilkinson, "and find the positive." Outside his quarters, heaven opened, and a rainbow dropped to earth.

# Chapter 42

# GW learns of the loss of Fort Ticonderoga

The time was nearly five in the humid afternoon as sweaty Colonel Hamilton rushed towards his commander, "Your excellency."

Seated, Washington tapped his foot and looked up at his aide-de-camp; *what now*, he thought.

"Fort Ticonderoga was lost to Burgoyne on July 5."

Washington shook his fist in the air. "General St. Clair abandoned Fort Ticonderoga without a fight?"

"He said he wanted to save his men as defeat was inevitable."

"When will the losses stop?" said Washington. The news circled through his head, whose face now sported a dark look. "How is this?"

"The fortress surrendered in a single day."

Washington slammed his hand on the desk, splintering its top.

Hamilton's gaze drifted over his shoulder. He sighed. "As recently as this past spring, we were told that it could never be carried without much loss of blood." The general stared vacantly, his nostrils flaring, his rage gripping him. "Albany," continued Hamilton, "might be taken before the northern army receives the reinforcements required to stop Burgoyne's powerful and well-equipped force."

*What is going to happen*? Thought Washington, whose blood rumbled in his head. Alex stayed awhile, penning a letter for his commander. "The evacuation of Ticonderoga is an event of chagrin and surprise not apprehended, nor within the compass of my reasoning."

Rage and disgust rising in his throat, Washington finished this dictation. "This stroke is severe indeed and has distressed us much!"

*****

John Adams, the book-read military expert, ranted to the delegates on the Continental Congress floor, "We shall never be able to defend a post until we shoot a general."

Samuel Adams turned to his fellow New Englanders, "Schuyler and

Major General Arthur St. Clair are traitors."

At Fort Edward, on July 14, 1777, Colonel Wilkinson briefed James Thatcher, "This event, apparently so calamity to us, will ultimately prove advantageous by drawing the British army into the heart of our country and thereby place them more immediately within our power."Wilkinson's words moved quickly, circling the room's walls, taking a turn with a graceful smile. The next hour passed with the former impressing the surgeon's mate attached to the provincial hospital at Cambridge, Massachusetts, who thought his pride in his self-worth stood front and center. In a letter to his wife, the surgeon wrote, "The claim that the enemy compensated the two generals for surrendering the fort without a fight is extravagantly ridiculous. Rumour actually circulates that they were paid in silver balls, shot from Burgoyne's guns into our camp, and that they were collected by order of General St. Clair and divided between him and General Schuyler."

*****

Colonel Wilkinson wrote to the Boston Gazette. "Believe me, sir, if virtue or justice has existence, the man who stands condemned for retreating from Ticonderoga, will, ere long, be thanked for the salvation of three thousand men, who, instead of being in captivity, are now opposing our enemy."

With the vision of a mirror, he displayed the details of the aftermath of Ticonderoga. "The British destroyed or captured 200 of our boats, seized more than 80 large cannon, five thousand tons of flour, a great quantity of meat and provisions, fifteen stands of arms, an enormous amount of ammunition, and two hundred oxen. And then there was our baggage and tents that we lost. But our retreat was by no means so disorderly as some have represented it." He stopped writing and grinned, managing to be both smug and cunning. "We retreated from Fort Ticonderoga like ants into the cracks of the celestial forest. As the worms of the Royal army followed, we maneuvered wearily along the treadless path of freedom under the heat of the unrelenting sun. Two of his Majesty's savages, Le Loup and the Panther wounded and scalped our men at the hospital at Ticonderoga and harassed our retreat. If one had listened closely, they would have heard our footsteps retreating towards Fort Edward, carrying our wounded in blankets, being that we were without carts." As the light was fading, he frowned and ran his fingers through his thick hair.

"Many marched by a circuitous route of about 150 miles thru the Green Mountains. Their hunger having not tasted food for three days. St.

Clair with some of his army arrived at Fort Edward on the 12th."

Concluding his message to the newspaper, he lowered his lip and told himself he needed another drink.

The depth of Wilkinson's memory would never equal the volume of liquor going into his brain. During his tenure on the earth, he added to the drama of life and polluted the sacred rites of truth. Not chaste, with a tongue the smoothness of polished bronze, he represented the cowardly dark colour of politics. Too often, his actions were like having a lawsuit with the wind – it blew back and gave him useless trouble. He was all in, like trying to paint two walls simultaneously with one set of hands. Yet, the General strode through the labyrinth of politics for 50 years. He knew the weaknesses of the players in the affairs of state of the times. He was an intelligent observer and always gathered information.

"The morning of the day after my arrival at Skenesborough on July 7," Wilkinson told the gathering at Richmond Hill, "General Burgoyne believed that our army at Ticonderoga was entirely annihilated. The greater part of our baggage and ammunition being in British possession."

Wilkinson raised his head as he recalled. "It was here that the British General committed his fatal mistake. By allowing Fraser to chase us towards Hubardton and himself sailing to Skenesborough in the hope of cutting off our soldiers and catching them between his own and Frasers', he lost his opportunity for victory when the comforts of Skene's house on the south bay of Lake Champlain seduced him. The former, a retired British officer, had spent many years axing the forest for his estate at Whitehall, 30 miles above Fort Edward." Colonel Burr shrugged, thinking he knew too many men who fit that description. Sitting back, Wilkinson stared at his drink of Madeira.

"The playwright felt at home." For a moment, Wilkinson sat still, caught up in memory of disbelief. "He blundered. By allowing us to carry off large Magazine of Flour & other Provision." With a ray of sunshine over his face Wilkinson said. "Had a large Corps of the enemy advanced to the Cross Roads near Fort Edward, or more properly the greater part of their Army leaving a Detachment at Skenesborough, they would have got an immense supply of our Provisions which they could have consumed on their route, and gained much time." After a quick scan, the General believed his audience wanted more. He stepped further inside his past, the melody, the voices, the lights of his times. "I later learned Gen'l Burgoyne had intelligence of our supplies. The Storekeeper of Fort George (originally in the British service & whose Son was with us) told him to advance, but he allowed us to make two or three trips with 40 or 50 Waggons. And having full time without enemy interference, we carried off or destroyed the minutest articles and also drove the Cattle belonging to the Inhabitants away from the enemy. His

Indians attacked one of the last Division of Waggons and Seized one Waggon which had broken down. They began to plunder it of the Horses &c, but could not be prevailed on to pursue the rest of our waggons."

"The price of the pact one makes with the devil," said General Willet, whose eyes flickered like a flame. General Wilkinson paused and surveyed his audience, stopping upon young Irving's dark eyes whose handsome face boasted a straight nose, which might perhaps be called large.

"This was the grim and truthful view of the situation at the time. But buried deep in the mystery of fate, a foreshadowing occurred on July 7 at the heavily wooded Hubbarton. The enemy under General Fraser came upon the rear guard of the retreating patriots under Seth Warner, who exuded courage but lacked discipline. He had been ordered to retreat but spent the night, for he did not like orders and itched for a fight. While having breakfast in the morn with the men, they were surprised by the enemy. A severe affair while it lasted. Among the injured were lord Balcarras, Burgoyne's card mate, and Major Ackland, the husband of Lady Harriet Ackland. When enemy re-enforcements under General Reidsel arrived, Warner's men intermingled with the wilderness."

Wilkinson shook his head, and his eyes dabbed at his listeners, "I learned," he said, "that Digby felt 'this eclaircisement should have taken place when something more than honor was to be gained.'"

With this statement, his words increased in number and meaning.

Appearing cheerfully unconcerned, he laughed, took another glass of spirits, and continued.

"Whatever footing the British might wish to put upon the Action near Hubbarton, they certainly discovered that neither they were invincible nor the Rebels all Poltroons. Many of Fraser's men acknowledged we had behaved well and looked upon General Riedesel's fortunate arrival as a matter absolutely necessary."

He gulped in the air. Outwardly composed, he continued, "Corporal Roger Lamb, who served in Burgoyne's army as senior corporal of Major Gordon Forbes's company, 9th Regiment of Foot, was a conscientious and shrewd observer. He commented, 'After the enemy retreated, we marched down to the works and were obliged to halt at the bridge of communication which had been broken down. In passing the bridge and possessing ourselves of the work, we found four men lying intoxicated with drinking, who had been left to fire the guns of a large battery on our approach. Had the men obeyed the commands they received, we must have suffered great injury, but they were allured by the opportunity of a cask of Madeira to forget their instructions and drown their cares in wine. It appeared evident they were left for the purpose alluded to, as matches were found lighted, the ground was strewed with powder, and the heads of some powder-casks were knocked off in order, no doubt, to injure our men on their gaining the works. An Indian did some mischief from his curiosity-holding a lighted match near one of the guns, it exploded, but being elevated, it discharged without harm.' "The enemy broke the great chain I had worked on for weeks in minutes by firing cannon from their gunboats, and within two hours, they were a chase upon the Lake; a precious two hours for us."

Theodosia knew if Irving were to say anything, it would beam forth from his eyes even before the words were spoken, but his eyes were dull.

Wilkinson lingered for a moment, savouring the social sweets like a man born to leisure and seemingly idle life conversations. His eyes turned to Theodosia and quizzically said, "In his grasp were 400 carts, 1600 horses, and piles of supplies guarded by 700 ill-equipped militia. Gates and I jested, on many a night, that the Playwright lacked the mettle of command; for he had left 400 men at Crown Point, 910 at Ticonderoga, and 3000 at Skenesboro."

Irving lifted his head, a beam in his eye, and looked straight at him. Wilky's eyes, animated with passion, amused him. "You tell a good story."

Wilkinson took the comment with a snort of laughter. "Worrying about an attack from Vermont on his left flank, he sent 2000 men to Castleton," said Willet.

"And his supplies were always so uncertain," added Wilkinson.

"He moved," said Willet, "across the terrain of the British invasion with easy strides, dragging the enemy after him."

"General Riedesel's march to Castleton," said Wilkinson, "caused great hardship, fatigue, and privation for the British soldiers who were without horses and had to carry heavy loads for several days. They were without tents, and many suffered from dysentery. Upon reaching Castleton, Major Skene took the oath of allegiance of many loyalists by promising them protection but rebel spies reported these partisans." Taking a deep breath, Wilkinson stood, his words waiting to spew forth. "By ordering Riedesel to return to headquarters at Skenesborough, Burgoyne allowed the plundering patriot parties to take the dwellings and cattle of those who adhered to England. Many were ruined and made prisoners because of his ill-sightedness."

General Willet, who membered it well, said. "Ain't that so."

Wilkinson's eyes narrowed and poured himself another drink before sitting.

"After the action at Fort Anne, the British 9th Regiment withdraw and joined the Army at Skenesborough, no other Detachment being sent out. William Digby, an officer in the invasion wrote, 'The Enemy tho.

not victorious were the real gainers by this affair, the advantage they made of it, was to Fell large Tree's across Wood Creek, and the Road leading by the side of it to Fort Anne.' The clearing of these felled trees by Schuyler's 1000 ax men cost Burgoyne much labour and time. It gave us spirits & leisure to wait for those reinforcements which enabled us to retire deliberately, always keeping near enough to prevent their sending out small Detachments. Our situation would have been perilous if the enemy had advanced to Fort Anne. It would have increased our Fears and prevented their delays. They had us on the run but they were the ones that slipped."

Idly, General Willet sipped his drink and stared back into the past. "A good General would have established a strong force at the crossroads leading to fort Edward and fort George, but instead Burgoyne sent General Riedesel to Castleton, as a "threat" towards Connecticut, calculating we would send re-enforcements." Burr discerned that there existed a large gap between Burgoyne's good and bad decisions, that he refused to make decisions rationally, failed to look into alternatives and comprehend the consequences, and was the lord of obtaining inadequate information.

"The playwright," Wilkinson said, "in the best of British snobbery appointed Governor Skene to act as Commissioner, to administer the Oaths of Allegiance, to grant certificates to such inhabitants as he thought proper and regulate all other matters relative to the supplies and assistance required from the Country or voluntarily brought in. Skene had previously built a direct path to Fort Edward. Many believed that he induced Burgoyne to turn it into a 22-mile road, thus avoiding the portage between the southern end of Lake Champlain and Lake George.

By the 10th, the British General was in want of everything. His men and equipment scattered from Three Mile point to Skenesborough with only 2 days provisions and wanting tents and baggage. With his army much fatigued, he found it necessary to stay his headlong advance for two weeks. His Indians losing attention, their eyes on plunder at Ticonderoga and the rum bottles in the British tents. They were mostly drunk & consequently very irregular. Bold with rum, they pushed on with the greatest rashness."

"And," said Willet, "he neglected to immediately take fort George, a strategic position, and gain a large supply of provisions: horses, wagons, cattle."

"Luckily for us," said Wilkinson, "he allowed our men to remove the supplies that Fort George contained. "A welcome present," said a smiling Willet.

"On July 18," continued Wilkinson, "the Playwright lacked enough horses to carry the tents of his soldiers. This was not a play where he could write them into a scene."

With a toss of his head, he lifted his drink. "The western Indians joined him with approximately 150 warriors at Skenesborough on the 19th under the command of the belligerent St. Luc and the King's superintendent, John Campbell. They harassed our guard and patrolled the outskirts of his camp. Since the fall of Ticonderoga, we were forced to regress further southward till in August, our army was at the junction of the Mohawk and Hudson rivers. In our retreat, we destroyed in days what took months to build."

Sporting a smirk as sly as Scaramouche, General Wilkinson, with Merlin's assurance, stopped speaking. The killing sounds of silence left young Irving, Theo, Burr, and Willet squirming.

Thoughts like bullets and projectiles whistled through the air: a remembrance of youth laid to dust – fighting fields overflowing with grief – weak, feeble hands – bleeding pieces of earth – ran into one another like light and shade.

"From the bowels of war the human flesh of freedom smoldered," said Wilkinson.

Willet eyed him for a moment, then laughed. "Not for long."

Since the dawn of the hard hand of authority," announced Wilkinson, "its flame waited to light the torch of liberty." He turned his head away, divided between history and reality, the thought exploding inside his mind like the blinding, brilliant war sounds.

"As summer descended northward on Crown Point," Wilkinson said to Irving and Theo, "a fort on a peninsula protruding into Lake Champlain that commanded the passage of the lake, General Riedesel's thirty-year-old wife with three children accompanied by their servants, cooks, and supplies arrived."

Wilkinson remembered the curves of Riedesel's wife's body for one who birthed three children.

"After our misfortunes, we soon set our ribs right again," said a proud Wilky. "Burgoyne elated in the heat of the chase skipped an act in the great drama as Gates was want to say. His sudden success had brought him too far too fast and to the wrong place."

With a great deal of pleasure on his face, General Wilkinson concluded, "Fate, irony, or the way of nature taking root allowed for a tragedy to occur that would circulate to Europe, and some would say rally thousands to the rebel cause, but that is another story."

# Chapter 43

# Burgoyne in Thought

The pulsating water of Woods Creek consorted with the usual chatter of croaking frogs, chirping crickets, and whizzing bats. This symphony of the thick gray-green forest helped soothe Gentleman Johnny's half-sleep. He was disappointed and vexed; a great deal weighed on his mind as he talked out loud, "Damn! I calculate a fortnight, 23 miles from Skenesboro to Fort Edward, along a winding, swampy track through the dense forest, unable to accommodate any wheeled carriage. On the other hand, we could march back to Ticonderoga, wait for the boats to transfer to Lake George, and then water down to Fort George. The easier, shorter route to Fort Edward is just sixteen miles via Glenns Falls. We would be less exposed to a flank attack. The horses, the horses where are the thousand of them hired in Montreal. 300, not enough."

At two in the morning that night, to be exact, a blood-curdling scream from a woman awoke him; his body was drenched with enough sweat to boil tea for two. At first, he thought it was his late wife, Charlotte, crying in agony, but he ruled it out. He knew her pain-induced wail, and this made that appear like a whisper. Since he was behind in his correspondence with his confidants in England, he preferred not to go back to sleep. Staring at the dark, he reflected. "The excellent food and drink provided by my host in the evening leave me little time to write."

He was not happy that he had put on several pounds. And besides, if he succumbed to slumber, that scream, mounted on a thunderbolt jockeying straight into his essence, might come back. He wrote two letters, but sleep overcame him during the third.

The next day, July 11, was long and very hot; he rose early, his mind still swimming indecisively. A walk to Wood Creek left him girted by luxuriant trees that stood up to the water's edge, the dawn filtering through the overhanging branches. The leaves were polished like a prism. He rested on a fallen tree, touching jagged branches that scratched his skin and sent pain through his body. Consistently, a Red-eyed Vireo sang while feeding in the treetops. Nonsense, blatant nonsense, he thought as he lifted his face, letting the light and shadow dance across its surface. Bees hummed in and out of an erect hairy branching herb having purple-blue flowers. The playwright inhaled its minty smell without delighting in its fragrance nor observing the sound of leaves falling from the trees. Sitting still like a statue in the British Museum, his mind weighing his options on how to proceed he downplayed that his Army of 9078 men slowed to a near standstill. There were not enough horses, carts, and oxen to pull the necessities of war, and the carts he possessed were made hastily and poorly. "That damn Guy Carleton, who did nothing during the winter of 1776-77 to prepare for the essential ingredients for the upcoming northern campaign," he muttered to a nearby Whip-poor-will's loud song that went on and on. Conveniently, he forgot to put off his requisition for 1400 horses and five hundred carts until June 7. *Not the best of planning*, Burgoyne thought. He tried to look nonchalant, his rapid advance and success leaving him loose and too comfortable. The General needed to determine whether to take the waterway from Lake Champlain to Lake George, then portage over the land to the northern Hudson or cut a road from Skenesborough (proposed by Colonel Skene, who owned the ground) and then portage to Fort Edward. His Army would have to retreat to Ticonderoga by the Lakes, and retreat was not what he wanted the loyalists to perceive. "Fort George," his aides later that day informed him, "is well fortified by the rebels. It stands 221 feet above Lake Champlain, a three-mile trek up with artillery, stores, and boats – through a gorge that separates the Lakes." He listened and then said, "What is the downside." "This would signal that New England is not threatened," said Francis-Carr Clerke, his Aide-de-Camp. "This irks me because I do not like the Bostonians, as the Indians called them." "The Rebels are retreating towards Fort Edward. If we pursue them, we must go east & south unless we are sure that by taking the Lake George route, we can cut off the traitors before they reach the Hudson." Contrary to his usual confidence, he was just not sure. "If the army comes to be south of the Rebels," said Lord Balcarras, "we would be between them, and our supply lines could do much harm." "But regardless of which route we choose," said Francis-Carr Clerke, "there would be a portage to the Hudson, either by Lake George or from Wood Creek to Fort Edward, but there would be two portages at Lake George." That afternoon at Woods Creek, he watched the light create new shadows and dark patches around him. From tree hollows, eyes glimmered as the wind wailed between distorted trunks, carrying the sickly stink of wood rot. He returned to the mansion of the wealthy Loyalist, whose hospitality so pleased the General. July 11, as the glowing golden orb set, signaling that the day is dead, Gen'l Burgoyne determined. "All the provisions, Stores, Artillery &c should pass over Lake George and Glenns Falls to the Right, under the escort of one

Regiment and the Corps of Royal Artillery." He decided that a sufficient number of the Gun Boats be kept armed and cleared for Action. The rest of the vessels were loaded with Stores and Provisions. The Army cut its way through nature on its way to Fort Edward by Fort Anne. They would carry with them, thru Wood Creek, as many Batteauxs as necessary to Transport their Provisions down the Hudson River. The evening was gay as Burgoyne played cards with his aides, and the party made numerous toasts, "Albany by winter." Comfortably occupied, the playwright enjoyed a full flow of confidence. On several occasions, he folded, knowing he held the winning hand. The following morning, the sky muttered with thunder, which made the hills and valleys ring. The bountiful rain flowed freely like from a pitcher full, causing the clay soil to turn into a slippery sludge. It required all his artillery horses to pull a single medium twelve-pounder. He felt it necessary to bring up to Fort Edward a "huge Train" of artillery consisting of 42 pieces, including four medium 12-pounders and two light 24-pounders. The delay in bringing up his guns gave the rebels time to recover, block the roads, and build defenses that would later require his artillery to batter down. Gates noticed the irony and chortled to Wilkinson, "A prophecy quite self-fulfilled to the man who delights in sweet, mindless gratification."

# Chapter 44

# Castleton

A quizzical brow sprung up on young Washington Irving as he turned to the General. "Why did some colonists side with the British?"

Burr noticed a grin spread across Willet's face, "General Willet, what say you?" asked Burr.

"Because men are easily seduced by complacency." Irving recalled his private school teacher, who suggested he fly to his pen and put his thoughts on paper. He thought of writing a whimsical essay on political juggling. "By ordering Riedesel," continued Wilkinson, "to return to headquarters at Skenesborough, Burgoyne allowed plundering patriot parties to take the dwellings and cattle of those who adhered to England. Many were ruined and made prisoners because of his ill-sightedness."

The words hit home, and Irving nodded, thinking that Burgoyne was the natural pest of society that lacked a gentleman's sincerity and justice.

"After the action at Fort Anne," said Wilkinson, "the mighty windmill, the British 9th Regiment, withdrew and joined the Army at Skenesborough, no other Detachment being sent out. William Digby, an officer in the army of invasion, later told me, 'The rebels tho not victorious were the real gainers by this affair, the advantage they made of it was to Fell large Tree's across Wood Creek, and the Road leading by the side of it to Fort Anne.'" Wilkinson appeared delighted by the memory. "Great minds have purposes; others have wishes."

Theo joined the group and plopped down on her father's lap.

Irving felt Burr's heart beat faster and watched as his eyes brightened.

The young man, two months older than Theodosia, tried to keep his eyes off her, and he did, but she bobbed up from beneath his thoughts.

When spending time in her company for the past few days, she brought out optimism, which gave him great pleasure.

He could get used to her by his side. He wanted her by his side. His heart swelled.

Knowing her from a distance was one thing, but upfront and personal put a different perspective on his life. His countenance was one of smiles and good humour.

Nothing is unattainable; he wanted to believe as he sat with his hands clapped into his side, his back slumped, and his eyes level.

She brought out a confidence in him that shot out rays from among the clouds. He knew their social difference, rolled away, and disappeared any hope, he being one of the youngest of 11 children of William Sr. and Sarah, Scottish-English immigrants.

He liked to call her Theo.

Descended from Jonathan Edwards, the theologian whose sermons shaped Protestant thought and asserted that nothing ever comes to pass without a cause stood as a stone curtain between them.

Was love a just cause that could penetrate the veneer of a girl who studied Greek, Latin, German, classical literature, arithmetic, French, music, and dancing?

She had a life that separated her from him—a moment of enmity molded his face into a solid, unyielding line.

No, his emptiness and hollowness would have to remain, the thought twisting inside him.

They could talk and walk and be friends, but the nucleus of life imposed complex fast rules.

Young Irving fell head over heels and felt secure in her company but knew his love would remain an obscure footnote in love's almanac.

Wanting her as a best friend, he scribbled in his journal, "A kind heart is a fountain of gladness, making everything in its vicinity freshen into smiles."

General Wilkinson broke the silence. "It gave us spirits and leisure," he continued, "to wait for those reinforcements which enabled us to retire deliberately, always keeping near enough to prevent their sending out small Detachments. Our situation would have been perilous if the enemy had advanced to Fort Anne. It would have increased our Fears and prevented their delays. They had us on the run, but they were the ones that slipped."

Willet shot Wilkinson a stern look.

"A good General would have established a strong force at the crossroads leading to Fort Edward and Fort George. He instead sent General Riedesel to Castleton as a "threat" towards Connecticut, calculating we would send re-enforcements." Willet hesitated, having promised not to tread on Wilkinson's story, yet he was drawn into every detail.

Wilkinson drew his eyebrows together. "Continue," he said, then made a sound of annoyance before pouring another glass of brandy.

"The playwright," said Willet, "then in the best of British snobbery appointed Governor Skene to act as Commissioner. His job to administer the Oaths of Allegiance, to grant certificates to such inhabitants, and regulate all other matters relative to the supplies and assistance required from the Country or voluntarily brought in." Willet stopped. The realization filled his eyes. "Previously, Skene built a direct path to Fort Edward. Many believed that he induced Burgoyne to turn it into a 22-mile road, thus avoiding the portage between the southern end of Lake Champlain and Lake George." Wilkinson listened, memories exploding inside his head like a thunderous storm

With his mind effectively intrigued, young Irving dangled as he continued to listen, thinking great minds have purposes; others have wishes.

Wilkinson was agitated as he remembered that they harassed their guard and patrolled their camp's outskirts as time marched on; he finished the bottle of brandy, frittering away his tale with impunity.

Irving detected a touch of humanity, perhaps an almost forgotten sense of humility.

"Since the dawn of the hard hand of authority, its flame has failed to light the torch of liberty."

Theo wanted to hug Wilkinson quickly, but his story charged forward.

"Summer descended. Northward on Crown Point, a fort on a peninsula that protruded into Lake Champlain and commanded the passage of the lake."

With a very proper degree of bygone times, Wilkinson repeated himself. "Fate, irony, or the way of nature took root. A tragedy was soon to occur that would circulate to Europe, and some would say falsely rally thousands to the rebel cause, but that is another story.

# Chapter 45

# The Wolf Le Loup, AKA the Wolf

From the beginning of his cycle
without smiling face,
always in frown
an untamed grimace

a path of belligerence.
Waring consumed his mind.
Under the command of Burgoyne,
his itch to kill and scalp tingles.
always on the prowl,
a minister of death.
a shattering thunderbolt
moves like the crane, the fox, or the thief;
quietly and lightly.
Many left in flight,
quaking in a hundred directions.
In lore, the son of Evil

heaped upon time
without a beginning.
Night and day, without respite,
pays no heed to what is done
and prefers the undone.
an extinguisher of existence.
Not known to have a friend
in the vaults of the sky.

In upstate New York in 1777, Le Loup, His Majesty's Foremost Savage," was disgusted by his new ally, the British, and their rules. He remembered well the bounteous rewards for years of service to the French in the war of 1757-63.

He resented the British's lack of promised pillage and yearned to be a "wild boar," the French's name given to the tribe. "Does not the British general know," said Le Loup, whose face was streaked with black and red paint, "that Hurons are robust and tall and require greater respect than any other Indians?" The braves said nothing as they stared at him, his eyes thunderbolts of hate, knowing that he needed to give misfortune to a person or persons.

By the end of the earlier war, he learned that he could sleep anywhere, whether in a swamp, a tree's foot, or a cave. Whether cold, hot, rainy, or windy, he welcomed any resting place along the plunder trail as his scent lingered in the forest.

When Burgoyne first met Le Loup, he stepped back from the warrior whose long black hair was greased from a bear's spleen and glowed from the hardened rising sun.

Burgoyne said to his aide Sir Francis-Carr Clerke, "What have we come to?"

"He goes by the wolf's name or the panther," said Clerke, "depending on whom you ask."

"There is no doubt," said Burgoyne, "his balance rests in derangement: passion and darkness."

"He takes pride in blackening goodness." Burgoyne frowned and then turned to Le Loup, staring at his blemished, grimy face, sensing he was as unconscious as cloth and could not cease from any evil deed. Looking up at the warrior, he told him through a translator, "No women, children, the old, and others should be scalped!"

Seeing Burgoyne's lip quiver, Le Loup smiled and set his foot firmly in front of him. He made a suspicious sound, his yellow-burgundy stained teeth visible as he nodded that he understood. Thinking he heard the sounds of footsteps, Burgoyne said nothing. The Huron laughed, then yelled, knowing he spoke with fork tongue because he was a slayer who scalped. He stretched his hands towards the general, dried blood visible beneath his long sharp nails.

He smiled and scratched his face, almost daring Burgoyne to comment.

Burgoyne moved around the camp for the next hour as Le Loup's scent lingered in the hot air.

The forest lit by the moon's rays' balm often calmed Le Loup, but not these past several days, temper springing into his eyes.

By the last weeks of July, no sword, poison, fire, or precipice could calm the passion of "His Majesty's Foremost Savage."

He thirsted to remove the skin that covers the top of any head.

With a near-naked, tattooed body that secreted stench so vile that even jackals would not slink near, he stalked the forest as moonlight danced on his skin.

On the flanks of a thunderbolt
aside the hand of death
with a soul grimaced in revolt
never out of breath

alienated by the wind
unstable like leaves on a tree
goodness unlined
destruction his decree

humanity torn asunder
glistening like ice in winter
itching for warfare's plunder
Survival's splinter
in lore, the son of evil twisted throughout
teeth clenched, waiting to shout.

# Chapter 46

# Jane at Fort Edward

The sun's penetrating rays reflected obtusely against the Hudson River's rippling green waves as Jane remembered the good old days when politics did not make a friend an enemy. Sitting on the river banks by Fort Edward, watching hummingbirds feeding on the flowers and eagles perched on old-growth branches, she wondered when Burgoyne's army would arrive. Startled by a 200-pound, 8-foot-long Atlantic sturgeon that jumped out of nowhere, she let loose a wild smile while admiring its olive-green to blue-black on its back and upper sides shading white on its belly.

Feed an army, she thought.

Free of patrolling the river bottom and eating shellfish, the sturgeon kept leaping into the air, much to the astonishment of the composed geese flying overhead.

She looked up to the few houses at the foot of a steep incline known as Fort Edward Hill, where she and David use to stand on the summer grass, their backs to the river, watching squirrels race betwixt field and tree.

A poem dropped into her head:

> Love rests on the canopy of the forest
> the earth bobs for distant galaxies to see
> forgotten identities look over creation's unrest
> I dream of things that shall be

Thinking David would come for her, she walked the road from the Fort to Sandy Hill, crossing East Street on her way to the top of the hill. There were two hills, one rising above the first.

She trekked to the top of the second hill, where the road forked toward Sandy Hill or south. As usual, the top view took her breath away, and she strained her eyes, looking out, hoping to see David coming for her. Not seeing David, she decided to proceed north to the Pitch Pine

Plains and continued to the small village of Sandy Hill but still no David. The British were expected, she learned.

She called his name for several moments before walking about the marshes and hills that predominated the terrain.

Shaking off her disappointment, she took a footpath back to the fort, stopping at the earthworks on top of the first hill, which ran along the high ground near the Hudson River's bank.

She remembered walking with David's hand in hand and looking, but the beauty and goodness were now absent. Dejected but brave, she had some thoughts of waiting for her love but joined the main road by a causeway a little north on the River Road's Westside.

Strolling to Mrs. McNeil's house, where she now resided, her eyes started to swell, and tears fell down her cheeks. *Is there a single person in the world who could be insensitive to her situation?* She thought. Entering the sixteen-by-twenty-foot square log house, built of round logs with one door, she eyed the hidden trap door to an unwalled cellar hole. "Remember, a place to hide," Mrs. McNeil informed her, "if an occasion calls for it."

Tired, she approached the fireplace at the North end, ascending the ladder-like stairs to a loft. Hot and cold shot through her as she realized her love for David was the point of her life. His essence remained with her for some time.

Half-awake, she heard and honored his presence through prayer and worship, it eased her mind. The next day she put an elm seed into the moist ground near the house, feeling free from danger or injury. She could only hope.

The following morning, she clutched a letter from Lieutenant David Jones delivered by Alexander Freel, employed by David to deliver messages to her.

"We will be united soon." He went on to narrate his adventures from the time he left her to join Burgoyne, describing the majesty of the army as it sailed up Lake Champlain, the entrance of the Indians on the Boquet, and of a particular Indian, Le Loup, who had the tattoo of a wolf on his chest.

The description of the war feast and dance and the demeanor and physical size of the newly arrived western Indians at Skenesboro excited her. She dropped down in a blood-red chair and read that section again.

Saint-Luc de Langdale, whom the Americans imprisoned, hated them, which gave her goosebumps. His motto is, "Il faut brutalized les affairs! It is necessary to brutalize. David concluded with the note, "Five hundred warriors from the Great Lakes arrived. Four hundred were "Ottawa," a formidable and belligerent nation but also harsh and mean.

They had been sworn enemies of the English up to this time and had frequently caused them grievous damage during the last war. Their leader is the sixty-six-year-old St. Luc de la Corne, dressed in green with silver fringe. He danced before Burgoyne and Sir Clerke, singing in the Indian tongue. An opened barrel of rum heightened the occasion until the Indians could not stand, let alone dance. Their warpath had to wait a full two days.

Beside the Ottawa stand the Mohawk on the side of England, physically more prominent than the Indians who accompanied Burgoyne from Canada. Mohawk translates to man-eater, and they delight in cruel torture.

Rumor circulates that Burgoyne's new allies tear to pieces with their teeth, their enemy's flesh, and they delight in taking scalps. Their scalping knives are wielded in England."

Jane stopped reading and shivered, praying that David would arrive soon.

"Their skill in throwing the tomahawk, with the utmost dexterity, is as deadly as an expert rifleman.

Not the 500 brave and tractable warriors we expected but barely 150, and they are a ragbag of disparate characters, adventurers, and outcasts who thirsted for the chance to murder and loot without risk."

She glanced down at the last line of the letter. "Send me another."

As the sun dropped below the horizon, Jane stood under the night's glittering idols as they appeared.

With the corpulent Mrs. McNeil and her granddaughter, Polly Hunter, they waited in anticipation for the invading British force back inside the cabin.

"I need not remind you," said Mrs. McNeil, "that Burgoyne is not my enemy, for General Fraser is my cousin."

Miss Polly Hunter and Jane were comforted by this fact, Jane dreaming David's mouth closing over hers, pleasant and simple. Fixed on Miss Hunter's bed lay a special dress stitched together by Jane's supple velvet hands. She noticed that Polly's hands were shaking.

"Help me assemble a few of my belongings and rest them on the table."

With wide-open eyes, Polly followed Jane. As the moon's pale light cast a subtle shadow over the roof, Miss Hunter prayed to the Almighty to protect Jane and to hasten the day when "nation shall not lift a sword against nation, neither shall they learn war anymore."

They slept in bed side by side as the night howled with the shrill sounds of wolves. In silence, their hands joined, listening. Miss Hunter said, "Please, God, pity her."

Upon waking in the morning, Mrs. McNeil handed Jane another letter left by Alexander Freel. A flow of energy thrust over her, a strength that hurled her beyond the moment.

"Dear Friend, I do not forget you. I hope you remember me as formerly. In a few days. we will march to Ft Edward. There I will join you. My dear Jenny, these are sad times, but I think the war will end this year, as the rebels cannot hold out and will see their error. By the blessing of Providence, I trust we shall yet pass many years together in peace. Shall write on every occasion that offers and I hope to find you at Mrs. Mc. No more at present:–but believe me, yours aff'tly till death. David Jones"

After watching Jenny re-read the note several times, Mrs. McNeil informed her, "Lieutenant Jones and his brother Solomon, who recently joined the royal army as Assistant Surgeon, are encamped near Moss Street four miles from Fort Edward."

"I want to go there," said Jane, who stopped and ran her hand through her hair. "I can take the old military road."

Standing next to Jenny, the very wide and short Mrs. McNeil said sternly, "It is a broad, well-beaten path." She hesitated. "But it connects Moss Street and Fort Edward."

"Then I will go," said Jane.

"It is not safe, my dear; spirited skirmishes between the rebels and British soldiers and Indians near Moss Street left several of the former without scalps."

Jane drew away, unnerved by the information. "I understand, but I must be by David's side. He will protect me."

"Those soldiers that escaped," said Mrs. McNeil, "are in asylum at the Fort."

Shaking off any fear, Jane walked outside to take a look. Mrs. McNeil pointed to the fort, "They are prepared to retreat and join the main army at Moses Kill."

Jane eyed her for a second or two, then laughed. "No one will cause us harm; General Burgoyne said so." She savored with avidness, aware her dearest was alive, and the anticipation of felicity forthcoming filled her with more warmth than a summer day. Concealing the correspondence in her clothing, she trembled for her brother and her lover's safety, should they ever meet on the floor of war.

"Accompany Polly, on a social visit to a Mr. Gilmer, a loyalist promised safety by Burgoyne."

"I want to be here when David arrives." She looked at Polly, "I will miss my dear friend."

Polly brushed her fingers through her dark brown hair. "I will miss you, too."

In the midmorning, when Polly arrived at the Gilmers, St. Luc's Indians massacred a family. (Mr. Allen, his wife, his sister-in-law, three children, and three slaves leaving their bodies to the hogs who tore their bodies.) They learned of the tragedy from friends, the Gilmers, and all fled towards Fort Edward under the guise of the woods. The playwright's pledge of refuge was as empty as a bird's nest in winter.

Spending the evening with Mrs. McNeil, awaiting the arrival of General Fraser, Jane thought she would go mad if David did not come soon. In the morning, she stepped outside, seeing the cherished sun, feeling its warmth, smelling the fragrance of life, envisioning Lieutenant Jones leaving his camp to get her, a stream of passion raining down on his surface, his eyes moist with love. Innocence is easy to find, but those who will cause harm are not.

The naive lamb dressed, unaware that Miss Hunter spent the night in the forest's darkest recesses enveloped in terror. She clutched a new note from David telling her to meet him at the home of William Griffin, a royalist whom Burgoyne promised to protect. Ignoring the civil war's verve and speed, she was determined to be united with her betrothed, never fearing that she would encounter a forest of razored leaves in the interval. Leaves swaying in the direction of a breeze cooled her. As she observed the sun emblazoning the surface surrounding Fort Edward and the canopy of the forest with its radiant hue, her long, tressed hair absorbed the weak sunlight that trickled through the ill-humored clouds.

Jane stood a few feet from the log cabin door, her head held high, Mrs. McNeil watching her. She stirred her memory over the safest way to the home of William Griffin, a stroll performed with David a hundred times. And the rebels, who now kept to the fort, she realized, would not stop her.

"The walk would be just a whistle in the breeze," she said as she managed Mrs. McNeil's smile.

A euphony of chattering birds resonated from every tree lit by the sun's rays, but they were drowned out by the war hoops of Indians and the firing of Rebel militia that echoed straight into her ears. Birds swooped overhead in the figure of an S. Described by Wilky as "A Country girl of honest family in circumstances of mediocrity without either beauty or accomplishments," she believed any threat, danger, or hurdle crumbles in the path of love.

## Chapter 47

## Journals, Dairies, Letters

July 24th, Lieutenant Thomas Blake's Journal, "All the troops left Fort Edward except about 600 who tarried as an advanced guard for the army. This day the Indians killed a captain and a lieutenant, as they were walking in the road between Fort Edward and the army."

July 24th, Diary of Reverend Enos Hitchcock, "Walked up to Genl Nixon's Brigade–two men killed a little above them towards Fort Edward by some Indians–dined on pig–. . ."

7/26/1777 Burgoyne to Simon Fraser fort Anne 8 at night, "The news I have just received of the savages having scalped a young lady, their prisoner fills me with horror. I shall visit their camp to-morrow morning. I beg you to desire Major Campbell to have them assembled–none absent–I would rather pit my commission in the fire then serve a day if I could suppose Government would blame me for discountenancing by some strong acts such unheard of barbarities."

7/26/1777, The Revolutionary Journal of Col. Jeduthan Baldwin, "Recd. orders to march with 30 Carpenters to head Quarters Moses Creek, 4 Men & one Woman killed near Fort Edward & cut to pieces in a most inhuman manr."

7/26/1777, Diary of Capt. Benjamin Warren. Saturday 26th. "This morning came an express informing Major Whiting was attacked. A reinforcement was immediately sent off and Gen. Larned with 500 men went around to come off the backs of them. But it rained hard and prevented this design. On their return we learnt that an advance guard of twenty men from Major Whiting being posted on a hill was attacked, in which a Lieutenant and seven were killed and a number wounded. They also took two women out of a house, killed and scalpt them; our people repaired to the fort defended it and drove them off."

Saturday, the 26th, Diary of Reverend Enos Hitchcock, "Six brass field pieces arrive in Camp–rained P.M.–we were alarmed about 2 O'clock by an attack at Fort Edward–The enemy, supposed near a 1000 crept up & surprize fired on the Picquet Guard killed & Scalped them, the Guard retreated & were pursued with 40 Rods of the fort took away two women from the House, Killed, scalped & mangled one in a most inhumane manner; four are missing."

July 26th, Lieutenant Thomas Blake's Journal, "The enemy made an attack upon the outguards at Fort Edward, who retreated into the fort, and the enemy pursued until they received a shot from the fort, and then retreated. The number of the enemy were supposed to be about 2000. After this alarm was over, our party moved down the river to the army, except 100, who still tarried as advance guard."

Sunday the 27th, Diary of Capt. Benjamin Warren, "This day the Lieutenant and Miss McCray was brought up and buried here four miles below, Fort Edward, the Lieutenant under arms his name was Van Vacken (Van Vechten) of Vandikes regiment."

Sunday, the 27th, Diary of Reverend Enos Hitchcock, "Divine Service at 11 o clock, A. M. Is: 57,21, at 5 P. M.Ps 53, 1. Some further accounts of what happened at Fort Edward yesterday–the Lieut: who commanded the Picquet, Van Vechten, was killed, scalped & cut his Hands off–& otherwise mangled–The two women, Mrs. Jenny McCray & Widow Campbell were going to meet the Enemy for protestion, when they came up to them were shot & Scalpt & most inhumanly boochered– the former found yesterday the other to Day–the advance Body of the men are on the flat about the Fort supposed about a 1000–"

July 27th, Lieutenant Thomas Blake's Journal, "In the evening the enemy sent a party in between the army and the fort, but the guard at the fort discovering them, forded the river and came off safe on the other side."

July 27th in the night, Diary of Joshus Pell, Junior, "The rebels abandoned Fort Edward."

Monday, the 28th, Diary of Reverend Enos Hitchcock, ". . . .A Scout returned towards eveng–who went out yesterday, who gave an account of a horrid murder of a Family about four N. E. of Gort Miller: the Father, Mother & six Children killed and left to be torn by the Hogs–"

## Chapter 48

## British Advance

"Burr," pronounced General Wilkinson, "anyone slightly familiar with the area knew the common sense, and the direct route from Ticonderoga to Fort Edward is by Lake George. Yet, the playwright-general ignored the obvious. Major Kingston, his aide, informed me, his general thought that it was a retrograde movement and he refused to retreat."

Burr shielded his eyes from the sun as the mighty Hudson flowed, silently but swiftly, saying, "Sometimes you have to go back so you can go forward."

The general grinned, relaxed by the brandy, good food, and secure company.

"As Gates often repeated," Wilkinson said, "when it comes to Burgoyne, 'Common sense is not necessarily common to a Baron.' His uncontested victory at Ticonderoga, thought to be the key strategic position by Congress and the British command, was taken beyond the most optimistic conception." Wilkinson greeted his teeth and shook his head. "He certainly possessed an eye for the unorthodox." His eyes widened as he looked at Burr. "Now was the time to end this act and take a brief intermission, but the playwright continued with his play's theme, pursue and never retreat."

Burr's laughter rang out as he threw his head back. "His first error."

"Victory outstripped his further advance capability. Lacking sufficient numbers of draft animals, vehicles, and conductors to move his stores, baggage, and artillery, his military advantage disappeared."

It ran through Burr's mind that Burgoyne possessed no idea how to general. "How could he be so deceived?" he asked.

Wilkinson shrugged, then suddenly smiled. Both brows vaulted high on his head.

"I learned from Major Kingston that with a glass of wine in one hand and his mistress in the other, Burgoyne complained he spent his time indulging the Indians, in all the caprices and humour of spoiled children.

He felt they were pretty good as their guards and patrols but amounted to precious little in battle."

Burr watched Wilkinson glow as he carefully arranged his tale, his shoulders square. "Colonel Hill of his army when reaching Fort Anne, an old timber fort on the South side of a small tributary stream running into Wood creek, 12 miles from Fort Edward, noted that it would take about six or seven days in making the road between Skenesborough and Fort Anne, and Fort Anne and Fort Edward."

'A general with wine in one hand," said Burr, "and a woman in the other moves slowly."

Wilkinson tried to suppress a grin but nodded, wasting no time as he continued.

"In one of my many conversations with Major Kinston, he informed me that his general always attended, when Ticonderoga fell, to go south, the accepted military route to the Hudson by going across Lake George and portage the ten miles from Fort George to the water highway of northern New York."

"What changed his mind?"

Almost too astonished to answer, Wilkinson, paused, unlocking the door of the past. "At Skenesborough, he took a great fancy to Colonel Skene, who persuaded him to lead the troops to the Hudson by a 28-mile trail up Wood Creek past Fort Anne to Fort Edward."

"Not the brightest star in the heavens," said Burr, who wore a bright grin.

Wilkinson managed a faint smile. "Though he did send a majority of artillery and supplies in Batteaux across Lake George."

"Deciding to start at one end of the forest," said Burr, "and find his way down to the other end. A curious way of generaling."

"Fortunately for us."

The words hit their mark, and Burr nodded cheerfully.

"He chose," said Wilkinson, "the trail of toil and trouble, a labyrinth upon a shallow, serpentine creek clogged with logs and debris and when on land a rugged wilderness road broken repeatedly by deep ravines, narrow bridges, overgrown brush, and swamps. His men worked to create a corridor for his European style army."

A breeze exhilarated Wilkinson as he said with a beam, "Schuyler's ax men cut and chopped, as Burgoyne cleared and constructed, as we moved southward."

Wilkinson looked lively. "During his stay with Colonel Skene, he failed to see the ominous clouds forming over his army as he naively proceeded to drink and sing to the brink of an abyss."

A quick smile spread on Burr's thin lips, "The hand of the Divine works in many ways."

"In a full, steady course, words fell from the lips of General Wilkinson, "By the 22nd of July the roads were completed, and the track cleared of the impediments caused by us. The arduous march thru the forest began with precious time being consumed."

*Wilkinson appeared all happy at this fact*, thought Burr. "From Skenesborough on the 23rd, believing that we were in considerable force at Fort Edward, he sent his newly arrived Indians ahead to gather intelligence. Within a quarter of a mile beyond Fort Anne, they captured a captain and eighteen soldiers, The rest were killed or scattered. We retreated through Fort Edward to Moses creek, leaving one regiment of 600 as a rear guard."

Burr thought *Burgoyne flattered himself that everything proceeded well*.

"Gates and I knew that his impatience would not allow him to come to a satisfactory strategy. The roads now clear and Wood creek navigable, Burgoyne would march his army into our grasp without considering alternatives – needs."

The General's voice altered; Burr heard the change. It was flat, now, absent of emotion.

Burr took it all in and steadied his head. "Know thy capabilities and limitations. You cannot stretch what you do not possess." "Their first morning out," said Wilkinson, "Burgoyne's new friends captured an American captain, nineteen of his men and scalped three others. Losing two of their warriors in the skirmish they requested to revenge this loss."

General Wilkinson sent a short, knowing look before he unbuttoned more of his tale. "The warriors wanted Burgoyne to give them three of the captured rebels. Their customs and rules purposed roasting and eating two of the men while the third viewed the ordeal. They would send the survivor back to his comrades to tell them what to expect." Wilky took a breath of air, Burr digesting the story.

"Civilized society in England," Burr interjected, "put those guilty of even minor infractions in stocks, to be jeered and spat at by women and stoned by men and boys."

Wilkinson raised his brows as Burr continued.

"In London, stealing food along with 165 other offenses could lead to a public hanging at the gallows in Tyburn. It was a form of popular entertainment."

Wilkinson let loose a lop-side smile, wanting to get back to his tale.

'"The age was brutal, and the Indians were not alone in practicing savagery," concluded Burr, who turned to Wilkinson, inviting him to continue.

"This movement of the Army," said Wilkinson, "was deferred until the day following, when it moved to Fort Anne 14 miles from Fort Edward, and Gen'l Frazers Corps proceeded to Jones's Farm (about 7 Miles farther) in the Pitch Pine Plains. His surgeon, Julius Friedrich Wasmus, wrote, "I pity the first Americans that fall into their power."

After several moments of silence to sip more wine, Wilkinson charged forward.

"As the enemy advanced to Fort Edward our citizens fled southward to Albany amongst carts piled with furniture, horses with 2 or 3 riders, and a caravan of straggling country people on foot. Bouts of sudden panic and screams of terror were heard when parties of Indians appeared out of the woods and opened fire. One unfortunate woman walked 20 miles, leading wagon horses, carrying an infant on one arm, and a club in her free hand. No one assisted her. 'Everyone for himself was the constant cry.' In the distance could be seen the smoke from burning cabins." Burr calculated for a moment, then displayed a flicker of dismay. "Try as you might, you cannot do anything about what people say when they are scared." "The King's army," informed Wilkinson, "broke camp at Skenesborough on the July 24 in high spirits and marched on a road that led over terrible cliffs and rocky mountains towards the Hudson."

The memory produced a giant smirk across Wilky's jowled face.

"Two days later Burgoyne's army reached the charred ruins of Fort Anne where decomposed bodies left a 'violent stench.'

That evening near the general's sleeping tent, he and his followers dined at a table set with linen, silver, and crystal under an ancient oak."

A sharp observer of others' behavior, Burr wondered about Burgoyne's motivations and if he ever considered a general's proper role in the wonderland of war.

"By July 25," said Wilkinson, "our rear guard retreated to Moses creek on the appearance of the Enemy leaving major Daniel Whiting with a picket guard of 150 men from his own 7th Massachusetts and the New York militia at Fort Edward. The Indians, within cannon shot of the fort, caused a severe but ineffectual firing to take place." Rain started to pound the roof of Burr's veranda, the steady sound oblivious to Wilkinson.

"Colonel Burr! A scouting party on the 26th of July reported to Schuyler's camp, a horrid murder of a family about four miles of Fort Miller: the father, mother & six children sculpted, gaping and expiring and left torn by the hogs." Burr opened his mouth but closed it before any indecorous words came forth. "Sometime before noon on the July 26, a large enemy force attacked Major Whiting's rearguard, a picket he had posted on a hill some distance from the fort. Lieutenant Tobias Van Veghten and his twenty New Yorkers fled toward the stockade with the enemy nipping at their heels. The warriors overtook and killed five of them, including the lieutenant, and captured 4 or 5 others. The rest made it into the fort dragging two wounded men. Shots commenced with the Indians 100 yards from the walls."

Burr heard a subtle change in Wilkinson's breathing, his bottom lip trembling.

"Burr, let me tell you the true story of the death of the fair maiden of Fort Edward, Jane McCrea."

"Her brother," said Burr went to the College of New Jersey."

"A fine man, a true patriot. Her death aged him, but he was not present at Mrs. McNeil's house on July 26. For mon general, I conducted an investigation into what happened to Jane McCrea on that fatal day."

Burr leaned back, ready, excited to hear a first-hand account. The popular myth of her death fascinated him.

"Soldiers scurried to the fort," Mrs. McNeil told me, "with the enemy in close pursuit. If the bullets that were buzzing like the bees of spring were not frightful enough, the rushing forth of a gigantic warrior, eyes wider than a beast, with scalping knife in hand, and boasting a hideously scarred face, produced in Jane a wail that startled a young warrior with a scar on his cheek. Before they realized it, Mrs. McNeil and Jane were taken captive by a band of Indians."

Burr leaned forward in his chair and allowed his eyes to fix on the General.

The General remained unruffled and winked at him.

"That evening, when Mrs. McNeil and the rest of the day's prisoners arrived at Brigadier Fraser's camp, Miss McCrae was not among them.

Unbeknownst to all concerned, her naked and mutilated corpse lay crumpled in the brush on Fort Edward Hill beside Lt. Van Veghten." How quickly the bloom fades from the face of existence, thought Burr. How soon the golden bowl breaks. The days of youth and romance wiped clean.

"Her long, luxuriant hair," said Wilkinson, later that day was displayed by a young warrior from one of the far western tribes."

Her aura returned to darkness, thought Burr. Her fate forever faded and passed away.

"Let me tell you, Burr, there is no evil greater than what happens to the innocent bystander who resides in the path of battle."

Burr found himself listening more than ever. The long, deranged story intrigued him.

"The details of this maiden's death are many," said the General, "hearsay having grown into myth, the one fact that is not in doubt is that she was killed on July 26th."

"Morgan Lewis of New York told me," said Burr, "that he examined the body and noticed three bullet wounds, but made no mention of the loss of her scalp." "This was implicit in the letters between Gates and Burgoyne," said Wilkinson. "I should know. I wrote the letters to Burgoyne for mon general."

"Well, General, you have my undivided attention."

Wilkinson was trying to discern if there was any sarcasm in Burr's voice and if so should he return the volley. Deciding to take Burr at his word, he said, "The warriors were content to take the "fair maiden" and Mrs. McNeil back to the British, but upon reaching the hill, where the earlier fighting occurred, a situation occurred."

Burr twisted and turned in his chair as numerous expressions raced across his face.

"Contrary to myth," said Wilkinson, "no Iroquois chief named Le Loup or a Wyandot chief called the Wyandot Panther killed Miss McCrea."

The general extended his arms to the ceiling of the veranda and collected himself.

"Caughnawages, who thrust for the gold Burgoyne offered for prisoners, approached the warriors who were taking the fair maiden to David Jones to claim the special reward offered by him. And more rival Indians approached, hoping to collect a bounty." "She had a high price on her head," said Burr.

"The truth," said Wilkinson, "is that provoked by the prospect of losing both honor and profit, the warriors who first laid hands on the fair maiden shot her to stop rival tribes from claiming the generous reward. Being informed that late-arriving rebel re-enforcements were near, the young warrior with the scar on his cheek scalped her, and the warriors mutilated the corpse before departing."

Burr noticed Wilkinson's lip quiver, but the General continued before he could say anything. "Burgoyne still at Fort Anne the next morning reprimanded the Indians in stringent terms for their late behaviour. He showed great resentment towards them, which led them to lose what little respect they had for him. They become ill of humour, displayed a mutinous disposition, and came to realize that the general did not lead but used them to fight and die so the redcoats could march safely through the woods. He did not reward them with honour but with scorn and public insults. The war chiefs resented control by European command and reluctantly continued to harass the retreating army of the Congress."

Wilkinson lifted an eyebrow, Burr expecting him to comment on European warfare. Then he would have an opening to give him the full force of his knowledge.

A smile pulled at Wilkinson's mouth. "Burgoyne's conscience clear, he proceeded to move his army towards Fort Edward, encamping on the height beyond it. Col. Burr found himself more curious than ever in a flash, listening to Burgoyne's exploits and surveying what not to do when in command. "The playwright-general," stated a wide-eyed Wilkinson, "regrouped his army at Fort Edward on the 31st of July. Encumbered with enormous amounts of superfluous baggage and 52 cannons, the march took 23 days to advance from Skenesborough, at the mouth of Wood Creek, to a position on the East side of the Hudson River, south of Fort Edward. He once again had to wait for his stores that just landed at Fort George. Amidst a paucity of oxen, 38 carts of the indulgent playwright's personal effects had been trudged towards Fort Edward."

Burr frowned with cold disapproval, thinking Burgoyne was deficient in the angles and details of war.

"The river was fordable at the fort," said Wilkinson. "an island lying in the center. From here the Hudson descended with a rapid current for six miles until Fort Miller where it came to be calm and free of movement. Here, at Stillwater on the 9th under the torch of August, the British army encamped on the East bank of the Hudson amongst the bright green of the forest. The only trace of civilization the narrow, winding roads following each side of the river." Wilkinson hesitated, half expecting Burr to comment on the Hudson, but the Colonel lifted a brow.

"At this point in his advance his losses did not exceed 200 killed or wounded and this due to his miscalculation of the strength of the force to be put forth by him, an error he would repeatedly make. With better judgment and command, he could have arrived two weeks earlier. This never dawned on him. 'I am invincible" rattled through his circuitry.'"

With scorn, Wilkinson said, "So invincible that security was lax at best, the officer's wives in Burgoyne's camp knew everything that was to happen.

Gates boasted such news flew like a bird to our nest at Rebel headquarters. During August, Burgoyne occupied Duers House" where he continued to entertain his "little" society." Burr gave what passed for a laugh at the mention of Duer. Knowing that the General would go off track and tell him about Lord Sterling's son-in-law, he let him. "Col Wm Duer came in 1768 with letters to Lord Sterling and Philip Schuyler.

Upon Schuyler's suggestion, he purchased land in the vicinity of Fort Miller, including the falls at that place, where he built a sawmill and, afterward a large grist mill. In 1770 he built a mansion at Fort Miller upon a bluff rising from the Hudson River, which was fifty-two feet square, two stories high, the lower level being eleven feet and the upper ten feet. A high basement contained a kitchen and other rooms. There was a wide hall through the centre of the house on each floor, and two large square rooms on either side and the staircase on one side of the lower hall, which it was said to have been elegantly finished. The windows on the upper story were all bow windows. The roof was nearly flat, built in four triangles, running each way. The house faced toward the west and on the rear, or east side, was a wide, two-story veranda, the entire length of the house. On each end was a wing, twenty-two feet square and one and one-half stories high. The frame of the house was a heavy oak timber, the walls were being lined with two-inch plank and filled in with brick, over which was lathing and plastering. The windows were all hung with chains and leaden weights. The main part had a cornice carved all around."

Wilkinson hesitated and poured himself another glass of wine before continuing. "In 1772, he was one of the commissioners of highways for the county of Charlotte, and one of his associates was Col. Philip Skene. In 1773, along with Schuyler, he was appointed associate Judge for the county of Charlotte. He married Catherine Alexander, daughter of Wm Alexander, Titular Earl of Sterling, and his wife was familiarly called Lady Kitty."

*Yet, another Kitty* thought Burr with big quiet eyes. "At the commencement of the Revolution, he erected a powder mill," said Wilkinson, who folded his hands in front of Burr, feeling foolish. "Of course, you know of Duer. He was Assistant Secretary of the Treasury under Hamilton."

"Died in 1790 at 43 years," said Burr. Down from the Veranda of Richmond Hill, the Hudson absorbed a traffic of boats as the steady fall of rain bent the view, but the general was too drunk to notice.

"At Fort Edward," said Wilkinson, "Burgoyne's officers were in want of everything but to the astonishment of Baroness Riedesel ate bear's meat and in the evening played cards. The *cards of war* thought Burr"The British General neglected to comprehend the ever-varying impediments placed in his path, which increased in magnitude and complication. His conduct was one of impulse for he had us, the rebels, retreating by his "coup de main." Thinking it was he who would write the final act, he underrated our ability to ensnare him. Once off the water, he needed to move his supplies on wheeled vehicles. This required 1200 horses. Unaware that his transport service was inadequate for the task at hand and would only get worse he blindly wrote to Germain at the end of July that success is near and that he wished to return to England in the winter."

"I presume," said Burr, "the easy victory at Ticonderoga swelled his vanity and invincibility."

"Yes, it produced bold, impetuous, and sometimes rash movements southward." "He thought he held all the right cards," said Burr.

"At Fort Edward," continued Wilkinson, "he was stalled for near a month by bringing the Bateaux, provisions, artillery, and ammunition forward from Fort Anne. He had preceded with too much baggage and too many guns thus expending too much time and great physical effort upon reaching the Hudson, and the countryside became inundated with continued rain. His demand for supplies always outweighed his supply." Wilkinson bit his lip to hold back a smile. "Our intelligence allowed us to know by late August that the thousand or more of his Majesty's savages were reduced to hardly more than 50. They felt he lacked the qualifications required of a war chief, only the ignorant or the gullible would follow him any longer."

Burr thought storytelling was more than a passion for the General, but his job.

"Thus, free of their constant harassment," said Wilkinson, "we ventured nearer their outposts; well knowing the cunning wild men, possessed of acute eyes and ears were gone. We freely molested their outposts and became very troublesome."

# Chapter 49

# Lt. Colonel Burr

Ordered to Philadelphia in the winter of 76-77, Major Burr accompanied General Putnam to shore up its defenses in preparation for a British siege.

While surveying the city, his eyes shifted to familiar places, remembering when he resided there after his parents' and grandparents' death.

Pain, at first, rose in his throat, but the memory of the kindness of William Shippen and his wife helped fight it off. A visit was required, and he made arrangements. For the first time, he grinned and seemed to relax.

While preparing to visit the Shippens, he heard that their niece, Margaret "Peggy" Shippen, who was entering her seventeenth year, collected men as a sugar bowl attracts flies.

Upon meeting her, he stared at her and blew out a breath. He thought her pretty, but not a precious stone, smooth and polished.

"I desire the latest fashions of the English court and detest American homespun."

'Why," queried Major Burr.

She caught a condescending tone but smiled. "They are elegant and graceful, the parasols of my dreams."

They did not bond like glue, Burr failing to sympathize with her dreams.

She narrowed her eyes, "People wearing fine lace make me feel at home."

By her tone, he realized she did not court change nor revolution and was indicative of many Philadelphia citizens. He told Putnam of his visit, "soothing and chilling."

For a moment, Putnam stood still, trapped in the topsy-turvy of the revolution.

"We face," said Putnam, "a dark and threatening task."

Burr took in the General's eyes. "All the emotions, needs, and wants of a population unsure of fighting England."

Putnam sent him a fatherly look.

"No matter," said Burr, "we must secure ammunition and necessary supplies, impose price controls to thwart rising prices, enforce a curfew, and tell Congress to find a new home."

While maintaining civil order, they watched as the population, sensing a British takeover, leaned more toward the loyalists.

The Major wrote William Patterson, "My stay with General Putnam separates me from the military gossip, and I am glad I am no epistolary politician or newsmonger. I serve as a clerk, adviser, and bureaucrat – any role to get the job done."

Patterson thought the stiffness in his writing did not match his character.

"I have become an able and loyal administrator through tempering my zeal and finding utilitarian answers as opposed to Utopian ones with a glowing pragmatism."

After leaving Philadelphia for Princeton in early March of 1777 with "Old Put," Major Burr received a letter from Matty Ogden.

"My closest friend, your rank in the army festers my soul."

A quick grimace came to Burr's face, but he shrugged it off, replying, "As to Expectations of promotion, I have not the least, either on the line or staff. You need not express any surprise at it, as I have never made any applications, and as you know me, you know I never shall."

He looked up and thought of his mother and father, hoping they were proud of him. He would not admit it, but he struggled with the disappointment surrounding him—his expectations a step behind.

"I should have been fond of a berth in a regiment, as we proposed when I last saw you. But, as I am happy in the esteem and entire confidence of my good old general, I shall be piqued at no neglect, unless particularly pointed, or where silence would want of spirit. Tis true; my former equals, and even inferiors in rank, have left me. Assurances from those in power I have had unasked and in abundance, but I shall never remind them of these. We are not to judge of our own merits, and I am content to contribute my mite in my station."

A little surprised by the tone of the letter, Matty laughed. He vowed to himself to keep a close eye on the situation.

"Major Burr," said General Putnam, "I need you to interview British deserters at Brunswick, New Jersey."

Shifting in his seat, Burr nodded.

The next day he wrote an account of the enemy's situation, strength, and staff intentions.

Putnam thought for a moment, then nodded. "Excellent, Major."

While at Peekskill in mid-July, Putnam told Burr, "Proceed to the Sound and transmit without delay the intelligence you shall occasionally receive of the movements of the enemy or any of their fleets."

Burr nodded, the knock of the door of war rousing him.

"I have been thinking about it; you possess the knack for discovering facts where others draw a blank."

Burr flashed Putnam a smile that radiated happiness before he turned away to prepare for his mission.

When Major Burr learned he was granted a commission as a lieutenant colonel in the Continental Army, he glanced around and hoisted his brow.

On July 21, 1777 from Peekskill, he wrote to General Washington, 'I was this morning favoured with your excellency's letter of the 29th ult. and my appointment to Colonel Malcolm's regiment. I am truly sensible of the honour done me and shall be studious that my deportment in that station be such as will ensure your future esteem. I am nevertheless, sir, constrained to observe, that the late date of my appointment subjects me to the command of many who were younger in the service and junior officers the last campaign."

For a moment, Burr wanted to pound out anger, but rationality took control. It made him see the humour of life and released the tension in his mind.

"With submission, and if there is no impropriety in requesting what so nearly concerns me, I would beg to know whether it was any misconduct in me, or any extraordinary merit or services in them, which entitled the gentlemen lately put over me to that preference? Or, if a uniform diligence and attention to duty has marked my conduct since the formation of the army, whether I may not expect to be restored to that rank of which I have been deprived, rather, I flatter myself, by accident than design? I would wish equally to avoid the character of turbulent or passive, and am unhappy to have troubled your excellency with a matter which concerns only myself. But, as a decent regard to rank is both proper and necessary, I hope it will be excused in one who regards his honour next to the welfare of his country."

Puzzled on how to conclude the letter, his eyebrows drew together, and his teeth flashed before he wrote, "I am not yet acquainted with the state of the regiment or the prospect of filling it, but shall immediately repair to rendezvous and receive Colonel Malcolm's directions."

Thus, after about a year with 'Old Put,' he became attached to

Malcolm's regiment as Lieutenant Colonel in his twenty-first year.

Malcolm, a wealthy merchant, informed him, 'You shall have the honor of disciplining and fighting the regiment while I will be its father." Genuinely surprised, Burr smirked. "Better late than never."

He gasped later that day, reeling from the statement, his mind probing and exploring as weak sunlight filtered through the morning haze. De facto, commander, he could see if his ideas of command held water.

The coming of command, finally at hand, he understood the prime object of his duty. He instilled the necessary military discipline to make the regiment fit to serve the cause of liberty.

Glad to be left to himself, he wrote Matty, "I welcome the challenge to superintend my quest for achievement."

Tilting his head backward and looking skyward, he took on the undermanned regiment and brought it up to five hundred men from its initial count of three hundred.

On September 11, 1777, Burr shook his head when he learned that General Washington suffered defeat at Brandywine, the British outmaneuvering the patriot's army, causing the rebels to lose 1000 men, twice that of the enemy, before retreating in their attempt to prevent the British from capturing the American seat of government, Philadelphia. He refused to grant Washington a compliment during his lifetime, believing the General possessed little wisdom or knowledge, a costly error to Burr's place in history. Informed by General Putnam that an enemy force of two thousand men was around Bergen and Hackensack, New Jersey, Burr marched the Malcolms to the Hackensack River, where they rested.

He went out by himself to survey the situation and discovered an advancing British guard.

Returning to his resting soldiers, they engaged, leaving 16 enemies dead.

"The "militia intractables" left camp," he reported to Malcolm, "the morning of the surprise attack. Not a man of the Militia with me, although some joined us last night but are gone."

His eyes tightened, and his face settled into an angry scowl, followed by his nose scrunching as he thought of the militia.

"The prisoners," said Burr, "consisted of twenty-seven privates, a corporal, and an officer."

He lifted his eyes, "They left most of their plunder."

When reading the report, Malcolm imagined Burr daring them to return.

"Upon preparing to attack more of the enemy," said Burr, "word arrived that the loyalists took off to New York City."

"The British," wrote Malcolm, "took and occupy Philadelphia, and Washington wants to surround the city."

Wondering what direction the Malcolms should take, Burr learned the was to march toward Philadelphia on Old Put orders to join General Washington.

"When not fighting the British," Burr wrote Matty, "I find myself at war with the rascal inhabitants who attempt to smuggle goods into the city." He paused for two moments. "I strive to find a system" to solve the day-to-day problems of low morale, petty crimes, and plundering."

"Colonel Burr," said Malcolm, "the regiment is ordered to Valley Forge to spend the winter there."

Something twisted in Burr's heart, but he stayed optimistic.

"The discipline is slack," Burr wrote to Matty, "the supplies and food scarce except at the table of Washington and his worshipers.

Half-naked men drink and fight with one another as the shadow of the cold winter light stretches slowly towards spring."

He stopped to take a moment to consider the situation. "At least," he told Matty, "Malcolm's regiment did not dissipate into a chorus of disgruntled soldiers, I made sure of that. We were frequently in battle and were considered among the best disciplined in the American army."

His upper lip curled into a scowl as he continued, "Because of many frequent false alarms that the redcoats were coming, the officers at Valley Forge unnecessarily prepared their troops at night."

He learned that General Alexander McDougall persuaded General Washington to send him as the commanding officer to the Gulf, a passageway the British would use if they left Philadelphia. "I vowed to impose rigourous discipline, night and day, some of the disgruntled men, slackers, and drunkards," he wrote Matty, "plotted to slay me, but upon being informed of the time, I made sure their guns were without bullets and approached the malcontents on a moonlit night. When the leader attempted to shoot me, I looked at the surprised man. I drew my sword and asked, 'Would you like your arm severed below the elbow. Quaking in his worn boots, the man shook his head from side to side. That was the last of the false alarms or mutinies."

In March of 1778, as president of a Court Martial, Burr was quite happy–quite fulfilled; the court needed work, and his experience provided a rational approach.

He pardoned two soldiers for wasting ammunition but promised to "show no lenity to any who quality of the same offense in the future."

As president of another court-martial, two soldiers who plundered a loyalist family were ordered whipped at the aggrieved party's residence and had to ask the victims for forgiveness.

"You might consider me foolish," he confessed to Matty, "for I considered putting a "p" on the front of their uniforms."

He laughed and added, "Honesty stands tall in my mind. I court-marshaled a servant for lying to my face."

Matty approved that Burr "particularized" men deserving censure for poor performance rather than punishing the entire unit, wanting to do justice to the vigilant men.

One of his soldiers said, "Every day afforded some lesson of instruction."

# Chapter 50

# At his Fort Edward House

In the Red House, an old and once lovely building, at his Fort Edward headquarters, Burgoyne awoke later than usual on Sunday, August 3. His breath smelled of liquor, and his eyes sagged like an old chair seat. The Red House stole a view of rushing water while calls of mockingbirds beyond its edges echoed through the woods' heart. With long, light strokes, the fingers of the playwright's whore rubbed his broad, shaped shoulders, which were not as smooth as her long fingers' tips. She embraced him and bit into his lips.

Dreaming of a sweet-smelling bathhouse, where canopies gleam with pearls over delightful pillars, brilliant with gems, rising from mosaic floors of bright, sparkling crystal, a knock at the door startled him.

She smiled; something was behind that smile--a certain amount of mischief.

"One minute!" he hollered.

Letting her breasts warm his chest, she put her tongue deep into his mouth, his eyes soft and moist.

He pulled back from her, saying, "It is not time that robs us of the zest for life; it is duty and disappointment."

She kissed him and hurried off to a side room, where Sir Francis-Carr Clerke, his aide, entered with his orderly book.

He read, "The Advanced Corps of the Army are encamped on Fort Edward's height. The Indians, Canadians, and such as the Provincials are in the front and upon the Left Flank of the Advanced Corps.

Riedesel Dragoons are encamped in the Plain. The Right Wing of the Line encamped on the rising ground on this side the Plain."

Behind schedule, he wrote quickly to his superiors in London, ignoring the fluttering in his belly. Work was work he reminded himself.

"The Transport of Provisions and Camp equipage of the Advanced Corps and the Right Wing, having been greatly impeded by want of punctuality in the arrival of the ox teams ordered from Skenesborough, it becomes necessary to halt the Left Wing at Fort Anne, till that Service is performed; during this halt, Major General Riedesel will order proper Detachments to convey to Skenesborough all the Batteaux from Fort Anne, and after delivering them there, those Detachments will rejoin their respective Corps."

Burgoyne's mind swum in indecision, so far victorious, a hero to himself, but meeting Howe at Albany, the critical element of his plan.

"Get me some coffee; the blacker, the better."

Dejected and humbled when his aide informed him that his two messengers to Howe were captured and hung, the gregarious General sensed he was on his own. The aroma of his coffee he ignored.

He sat like Buddha; his eyes closed, his soul experiencing freedom, the master of his fate without speaking. He washed the few lingering traces of liquor from his lips, thinking again, it is not time that robs us of the zest for life; it is duty and disappointment.

A British officer escorted in by Major Kingston brought him to the present.

A hollow silver bullet containing a message written on July 17 by Howe dropped into his hand.

His spirit rose momentarily as he read the message, the gamester wanting to see the cards turning in his favor.

"Congratulations on taking Fort Ticonderoga, a great event."

"Damn sure it is," he muttered.

"I lament the difficulty of communicating to the northern wilds; Washington keeps a keen eye on my movements, and in the interval, he ordered 2500 men under Sullivan to Albany."

Burgoyne's jaw tightened.

"My intention," Howe informed, "'is for Pennsylvania, where I expect to meet Washington."

Reality slapped Burgoyne's face. This information did not ease his mind. "No Howe at Albany," he said to his aide as he continued to read.

"After your arrival at Albany, the movements of the enemy will guide yours; but my wishes are, that the enemy be drove out of this province before any operation takes place in Connecticut. Sir Henry Clinton remains in command here, and will act as occurrences may direct. Putnam is in the highlands with about 4000 men. Success be ever with you."

"Damn, the son-of-a-bitch" mumbled the playwright, "my plans have gone awry by this idiot. No meeting in Albany, no opportunity to mount an expedition."

He glared at his aide, "No strike into the heart of New England. My plan of conquest. dismissed by a rebel sympathizer."

Clerke released a big, deprecating smile. "You will find a solution."

The rumour that Howe was the illegitimate uncle of King George marched forward in Burgoyne's mind, swelling his pride and arrogance. At first, he thought all his plans for knighthood rested by a cliff. "That bastard Whig, I will show him."

He turned to Clerke, "Our movements will depend on the enemy's deployment of Sullivan and Putnam's force."

"St. Leger is on his way," said Clerke, "but with only a small amount of men."

"It seems unlikely Howe will detach Clinton to act as occurrences may direct."

"Then we are on our own with no help in sight!"

Closing his eyes, Burgoyne rested momentarily, considering what to do. "My instructions are to force my way to Albany, and I will."

Clerke glanced down at the orderly book. He drudged up the words, "You will show friend and foe alike that you are equipped to serve our king and immobilize the serious trouble that portends."

"But first and foremost are our supply lines, replied Burgoyne. "The army's needs must be served."

The light from the sun filtered through the window, highlighting his mistress as she entered the room. For the first time that morning, he smiled and appeared to relax.

"Are you ready for your bath, mon general?"

# Chapter 51

# St. Leger

Theodosia sat with a quill, recording the evening's tales that long week in 1797. Her father sat across from her with a feeling of deep pleasure, General Willet and Washington Irving flanking her.

General Wilkinson, remembering the Great Catskill Mountain shadows, blue and misty in the far distance, standing out like the morning sun.

Dressed in an elaborate uniform with gold epaulets, gold braid, and buttons,

Wilky enjoyed the soft rays of the filtered sun, his left hand with drink, and his right with Seeger.

Full from his diet of insects, berries, and seeds, a mockingbird with spread wings rested on a branch that filtered the sun upon the General.

"General Willet, will you tell the story of St. Leger's siege?

Willet sent him a warm look, thinking his knowledge would greatly benefit him.

He nodded in approval, and the puffy red lips of Wilkinson were motionless.

"The woeful commander, Colonel Barry St. Leger, arrived at Fort Stanwix on the 3rd of August with too little force for the task at hand. The fort, an earthen, bastioned, and moated installation, linked the Mohawk River's headquarters with the water route to Lake Ontario.

St. Leger ascended the St. Lawrence from Montreal on flatboats for 150 miles. Then he proceeded slowly up Lake Ontario, now and then having to take the boats ashore and carry them around rapids or cataracts. His force crossed Lake Ontario to Fort Oswego, moved up the Onondaga River eastward, traversed Oneida Lake, and proceeded to Wood Creek, its feeder."

Irving lifted a brow. His eyes fixed on Willet, thinking he was a character that rivaled Robinson Crusoe and Sinbad the Sailor.

"From there," said Willet, "the troops had a laborious march overcoming natural difficulties and obstacles placed in the way by us Americans before reaching the head of the Mohawk where Fort Stanwix stood. With maybe 450 white troops, including loyalists but only 280 hardened regulars, two 6-pounders, two 3-pounders, and four small mortars, the "under" siege began."

Willet gave his friends a long searching look, but it missed Wilkinson, who turned away with no pleasure. A beat of silence chimed like a church bell in a heavy breeze.

"St. Leger, with 44 years and little combat experience except during the French & Indian war in North America, had entered the army as an ensign in 1756 and left it on half-pay in 1763 as a major. He campaigned in the upper Hudson in 1757, participated in the capture of Louisbourg in 1758, was with Wolfe's assault on Quebec in 1759, and at the surrender of Montreal in 1760."

Theodosia lifted her eyes. "You should be in the storytelling business."

Willet winked at her. "I enjoy stirring the soup."

Irving could not stop thinking of Theodosia, wanting to live out his fantasy.

Wilkinson ran a fingertip over the crystal glass's rim, admiring that it was smooth and flawless. He looked up at Willet but remained silent.

"On the 10th of July," Willet said, "the ruddy-faced, hard-drinking man who looked older than his years proclaimed himself a brigadier general to impress his troops and awe his foes.

Never holding an independent command and possessing no knowledge of the territory he was to traverse and knowing nothing about the Indians he would command, he forsook reality."

Wilkinson glanced over as a servant brought another bottle of wine. Burr poured him a glass.

Wilkinson tried to interrupt, but Willet charged on.

"Telling the Indians that the rebels were children and lacked guns and when shaken they would submit," Willet announced, "St. Leger underestimated the enemy they would encounter and the hurdles they needed to surmount.

Full of arrogance, he refused to listen to Sir John Johnson and Colonel Daniel Claus, who commanded his Majesty's savages. He miscalculated the size, determination, and efficiency of his enemy. The Indians were informed that they would never lack food or clothing and that rum would be as plentiful as the water of Lake Ontario. Each warrior received a suit of clothes, a brass kettle, a gun, a tomahawk, powder, and money."

Envy sprang into Wilkinson's eyes. He leaned back in his chair, not being the center of attraction.

"The "brigadier General" did not have a higher number of troops because he chose not to," continued Willet. "This, coupled with the lack of powerful artillery, made his siege a tissue of blunder. His three artillery batteries consisted of little firepower."

Willet paused and took a drink. He then put up his forefinger and began speaking, "1st three light guns," two fingers were now shown, "2nd, four small mortars," and finally, three fingers abreast, "3rd, three more small guns."

Burr gave a little laugh and then refilled his glass as General Willet resumed.

"Exclusive of his Indian allies, he scattered his forces between camp and his depot. The carriages of his two six-pounders were so rotten that when needed, they were still not yet repaired."

Wilkinson interjected, "With fourteen pieces of artillery mounted at Fort Stanwix and nearly 1000 Americans preparing for a month, we were in high spirits."

He looked at Willet, who half-smiled.

Burr recalled a conversation with the Indian Thayendanegea, Col. Joseph Brandt, who told him, "The Indians soon realized that St. Leger was incompetent and depended on wine and rum for military inspiration. They complained that he drank more than they did. With only one plan, a siege, he hoped for the best, and any doubts were soothed by intoxication."

Willet interrupted Burr's thoughts as he charged forth with his story.

"He diverted his forces so they could not act together and, during the last days of the siege, 'drank heavily.' He was in no condition to handle his duties responsibly during the final crisis."

General Wilkinson wanted to interject but said nothing as he stared at Willet, almost daring him to stop but to no avail.

"Upon hearing on the 5th of August that a re-enforcement under General Herkimer of upwards of a thousand men was near, he sent the Indians, 400 soldiers, and loyalists under Johnson and eighty Germans to surprise the Tyron County militia.

General Herkimer's subordinates blithely desired to march without taking precautions, neglecting that the woods were ripe for ambuscade. They accused their General of being a Tory because he acted prudently."

Willet's voice alerted somewhat, his audience hearing the change.

"Herkimer abandoned his plan and succumbed to these accusations. 'March on!' was his order. The men proceeded in a disorderly fashion. At a marshy, narrow ravine, semi-circular in form, surrounded by trees and shrubbery, Colonel Butler, with his Tory Rangers and Col. Brandt commanding the Indians surprised the naive, unprepared militia. The howling of" his Majesty's Savages" echoed through the forest and re-echoed along the declivity. They attacked with their faces, necks, and shoulders painted with a thick coat of vermillion. Their blood-curdling yells, along with the piercing whiz of bullets, paralysed the militia who fell like leaves, being completely surrounded by a whirl of lead."

Wilkinson turned and looked at Irving for the first time.

Irving's mouth opened as he dragged a hand through his thick hair.

"During the six-hour battle, the horrid yells of the Indians pierced the forest while the ringing bullets of battle clapped like thunder from all sides. The occurrence of a severe deluge from a thunderstorm curbed the ambuscade and saved the militia. The enemy sought shelter among the trees while the militia regrouped at an advantageous piece of ground and formed groups of men in a circle. To counter-act the mode of fighting by the Indians who, when the Americans fired a shot from behind a tree, would run out and tomahawk them before they had a chance to reload, two men now stood behind a tree, and only one fired, the other waiting for the charging Indian."

Wilkinson focused on Theodosia, who lifted a brow and angled her head. Envious of the bloom of youth, he released her as she continued to listen and write.

"This battle, called Oriskany, found hostile men bursting upon each other with bayonets and spears. The personal bitterness of neighbor opposing neighbor and the deep-felt hatred of loyalist refugees facing those who had driven them from their homes exacerbated the situation. Neighbors grappling and combating with herculean fury as the clashing of sword and bayonet echoed through the chimes of steel. A chorus of Indians persistently screaming added to this opera of death."

To Willet's dismay, Wilkinson, his patience fray, cut in.

"Brother fought, brother. Lt. Bernard Frey accompanied Butler's Indian department of Officers while John Frey marched with Klock's regiment and acted as Herkimer's major of brigade. In time, the battle evolved into a hand-to-hand combat."

Wilkinson hesitated and looked at Willet, who refilled his glass.

"Men born on the banks of the Mohawk left their hands clenched in each other's hair, the right grasping in a gripe of death, the knife plunged in each other's bosom; thus they lay frowning."

"For an old veteran, you remember the facts quite well," remarked Burr.

"I was told first hand."

Wilkinson refilled his glass, letting Willet continue.

"According to the Indian Blacksnake, 'I have seen the most dead bodies all at once that I never did see, and never will again, I thought at that time the bloodshed a stream running down on the descending ground during that afternoon, and yet some living crying for help.'"

Quietly, Willet sat until the memory passed.

"The Indian losses were 'sorely felt.' Some of their favourite chiefs and confidential warriors were killed; in total, 33. Thirty-two were wounded, many badly. Senecas suffered the most and became bitter enemies to the rebels, and they resented St Leger sending them."

Seeing Theodosia's lip quiver, Irving wanted to hold her hand, love having no bounds.

"A few days after the battle, a soldier reported," said Willet, "he beheld the most shocking sight he ever witnessed. The Indians and white men were mingled with one another, just as they had been left when death had first completed his work. Many bodies had also been torn to pieces by wild beasts."

General Wilkinson turned to Theo, inhaled, and with measured words volunteered, "Yes, war, the breathing out of life, took its toll at the battle of Oriskany where nature and the follies of man were combined into terror."

He stopped and turned to General Willet as Burr asked. "Please, sir, recount your role at Fort Stanwix while the struggle at Oriskany raged."

The older man took a deep breath; his eyes were dreamy. He recollected softly, "I led a party of men towards the enemy's camp. There was no opposition at all to our sortie. We plundered the enemy camp entirely denuded of their defenders. Three times we loaded seven wagons and sent them back to the fort without the loss of a man. St. Leger's "under" siege." He smiled at Wilky and went on. "But the Indians "no liked it" and were mad about the loss of the finery given them by the superintendent. Since my sortie, they had nothing to cover themselves at night."

Willet's pulse pounded like the hammer of a blacksmith.

"It was St. Leger, not the Indians," he said, "who first deserted the field of combat, and he did so in shameful confusion. The "Brigadier General's" retreat, as he called it, was a downright flight . . . nor do I find that it was owing to the cowardice or bad Dispositions of the Indians that they came away."

Willet paused and peered into the past. A smile lit his face.

"Burgoyne later claimed, 'the Chiefs insisted that he should retreat or they would be obliged to abandon him. He had no choice as the Indians began looting his stores and equipment before they could be properly packed. His Majesty's savages referred to St. Leger as 'the man whose words are big with danger.'"

Wilkinson interjected, "Luckily for St. Leger, the war hawks in Parliament did not go after him because it would have cast light on their incompetence."

A pause occurred, and Irving interjected, "The sunset, that glowing golden red, announcing that the day is dead, now loomed over Burgoyne's army."

General Wilkinson shrugged his shoulders with a grin as wild as the fabled Cheshire cat—the three soldiers, with Theo and Irving, clanked glasses.

A bullfrog croaked as a mockingbird chortled in rapid succession as the soldiers drank in remembrance of the War of the Revolution.

## Chapter 52

## JW Rambles

General Wilkinson announced, "Lady and gentlemen, on August 19, Gates arrived at General Schuyler's camp and took command to many a despondent soldier. Many felt that without reinforcements, they might as well give up the matter and go home. That night a shooting star streaked through the sky, and the next day came news of Stark's victory at Bennington. 1200 killed & taken, plus a large amount of baggage & 4 brass field pieces. Four days later, news arrived that the enemy's attempt to storm Fort Stanwix had been repulsed, and St. Leger met with considerable loss. John Glover best personified the new feeling of the army of the Congress, 'we will compel Burgoyne to return back to Ticonderoga, if not to Canada.' Arnold arrived on August 26 at Gates' headquarters from Fort Stanwix with more troops, itching for battle."

Wilky refilled his glass, studying the veranda's walls, ceiling, and floor, thinking "nice space."

"For the next two months, I was Gates' shadow. I, the bee, who takes the nectar from the flower."

Till the fall of 1806, Burr was shadowed by Wilky and failed to see his friend's enrollment in the war of the revolution and afterward let him drink on the foibles of men, regardless if they were military or private.

A fool is a friend to no one unless his purpose is served, and "Wilky" came to serve the purposes of Arnold, Gates, Washington, Adams, Hamilton, Jefferson, and Burr. And in return, he was to be General James Wilkinson, commander of the American army.

"Early September, in a conversation with General Gates," continued Wilkinson, "I advanced the proposition that our position was not defensible because it was too flat & open. My General agreed fully. From the junction of the two rivers, our army moved to Stillwater, but it was found less suitable than thought. Again, we marched 3 miles north and I recommended to my commander that he send Thaddeus Kosciuszko, the young engineer, forward to find a defensive position. Upon my suggestion, the high ground of Bemis Heights, which stood on the West side of the Hudson, a bottleneck in the path of Burgoyne's advance, was to be the spot where the army of the Congress would make its stand."

Wilkinson put more wine into his glass, glanced up and around at his audience, and bore down with his story.

"On the right ran the Hudson; on the left rose rugged, wooded bluffs, in front marshy, rolling, tree-covered terrain, unbroken but for a few scattered clearings and wagon roads. We took a position on the 12th and began fortifications. It brought a smile to our faces. I was everywhere directing for my General and did a reconnaissance with a detachment of men, and determined the precise position of Burgoyne's army. His whole army of 7000 arrived by the morning of September 13, the same day Burgoyne crossed the Hudson. The enemy, on the evening of the 15$^{th}$, pitched camp at Coveville and began planning their battle strategy at Sword's house."

With a strained calm, Wilky curled his mind around the past that clung in his memory, failing to camouflage a chortle with a cough.

"Burr! We entrenched our strong position on Bemis Heights. As you know, the road to Albany was squeezed through a narrow passage between the hills and the Hudson River.

Previous to this, on the ninth, General Stark arrived with his brigade.

The forest soon came to resound with the strokes of the axe as the British and American Armies fortified their respective camps in the early autumn of 1777."

Irving stared at Wilkinson who swallowed a chuckle.

"We gave Burgoyne three alternatives: to progress along the road below our fortifications, retreat, or remove us from Bemis Heights. Regardless of his decision, we were well prepared. Gates knew he would attack, even under unfavourable circumstances. On September 9, the weather was charming, and our hearts soared like eagles."

Armed with his memories, he never missed a beat, magic-less and more potent than his words.

"Unfortunately, we heard that the grand army under Washington was ever retreating further from the advance of General Howe. He wrote to Gates for Colonel Morgan's riflemen, but we could not spare him."

Burr lifted his head and looked up at Wilkinson, whose eyes were wide and fixed. Both men turned to the past, knowing the noise of politics too often pierces the hull of a man's character.

"During this time, I served," said Wilkinson, who repeated himself, "as Gates' eyes, ears, and tongue as the General did not visit his pickets. It was then that I came to be affectionately called Wilky."

Irving eyed him warily as he spoke, thinking of a bullfrog.

"I had more admirers than fall leaves." Burr stared at him.

"Just let me go on record that St. Clair said, "I possessed great merit – and what is, in his opinion more valuable, a warm, honest heart.""

Burr recalled that Matthew Lyons, an Irish-born American soldier, printer, farmer, and politician, said of him, "He seemed to be the life and soul of the headquarters of the army: he, in the capacity of Adjutant general, governed at headquarters. He was a standing correction of the follies and irregularities occasioned by the weakness and intemperance of the commanding General."

"Gates observed me," said Wilky, "Jocose, volatile, convivial."

Wilky knew how to disguise his motives and provide the ultimate blindfold. *Talk about power. Talk about wonder*, thought Irving.

## Chapter 53

## Reflections AB

After returning from exile in mid-1812 Burr sat with Matthew Davis, a friend, and admirer, ruminating on two brothers and how they produced a strange military strategy during the American Revolution.

"The Tory governments chose Whigs, the Howe brothers, General "Billy," and Admiral, "Black Dick" Richard, to foster a semiofficial peace with the patriot rebels, which delayed the British from immediate action, and when their peace overtures came to naught, the Howes' only choice became military, though they always took their good time."

"*The path to victory,*" he thought, "*can take the strangest twists and turns.*"

"Washington's psyche compelled him to resist Howe's capture of New York, and Howe's psyche required him to proceed with circumspection."

Relaxing in an armchair, a dim light gleamed over Davis's shoulder.

"Military genius, to Father Washington, meant that the patriot army must maintain a fighting reputation. Military genius to Howe meant promoting reconciliation."

Davis sensed Burr was not in good spirits as Burr tossed his head back. His belief that you respect yourself and deserve to be respected by others skipped a beat when it came to Washington, never realizing how his pride affected his military career.

"Being defeated would have ended Washington's purpose, and allowing victory defeated Howe's mandate. Both men failed to accomplish their objectives, but Washington's reputation survived, despite his actions."

Davis recalled when "beset with failure at every encounter, under Washington, the rebel army retired to Morristown."

He stepped back, felt his pant's back pocket, pulled out a bandanna dotted with colors, and dried his moist lips; admiring neatness, he smiled.

"Yes," Burr said in an animated tone, "Our soldiers beyond fatigue collapsed to the ground in the woods and fell asleep despite the cold weather waiting for the British army in New Jersey, numbering at least 10,000 waiting for orders to march to New York."

He stiffened as he remembered Washington's worn-out army might have numbered 4,000, yet Howe again did not attempt to end the rebellion. With Cornwallis at Brunswick and Vaughn at Amboy and both in a fighting spirit, no order came from their Commander-in-Chief who continued to lounge in New York: feasting, gunning, banqueting, and in the arms of one of many lovers.

"The 3,000 soldiers of Washington," recalled Burr, "delved deeper into New Jersey, and confidence in the Supreme leader sank lower than sea level. His "fatal indecision of mind" bantered from one town to the next." Davis closed his eyes for a moment; upon opening them they showed great curiosity.

"With losses at Brooklyn, Kip's Bay, White Plains, Fort Washington, and Fort Lee (without engaging the enemy)," said Burr, "his trusted aid Joseph Reed now preferred General Charles Lee and urged Lee to go to Congress with a new plan for the army."

A memory twisted in Burr's heart. The meager revolutionary army, many without shoes, proceeded on mud ankle-deep roads and arrived at Newark on November 22 amid heavy rain, cold weather, and no tents.

"The dogged British army, in hot pursuit, arrived at Newark on November 28, 1776," he mumbled, "only to learn, "the fox" pushed on to Brunswick and Raritan."

The wide-eyed Burr leaned back, and one could see how it still pained him; shaking his head, he chuckled as Davis gave ear to him.

"As their enlistment ended on December 1, 1776, 2,000 men from the New Jersey and Maryland militia headed for home as hostile forces were within two hours of Washington's depleted remnants. The American army with maybe 3,000 men withdrew to Trenton and the West bank of the Delaware expecting General Lee's reinforcements."

"That was when you were ordered to Philadelphia in December of 1776," said Davis.

The memory swam in the mists of Burr's existence. Which Philadelphia is it that I recall? He thought. When, as an orphan at William Shippen's house on 4th street, or was it his brothers' (father of Margaret or Peggy who married Benedict Arnold)?

Davis noticed a look of confusion surrounding Burr's face, not realizing that Philadelphia blended into one omelet, teasing his palette, spicing his senses, and challenging him. A highly dull town of one-colored brick houses, a dull red, so much like one another & all but a similar size that its regularity dulled his senses. Being built on the West side of the low banked, murky, watered Delaware River, Philadelphia rested about 150 miles from the sea. Ships could cuddle the wharves along the River's edge, the water being deep enough for 700 tons burthen.

When the orphan Burr walked down some of the most extensive streets, nary a person could be seen. The straight, wide & bountiful streets were designed to run parallel to the water and were named first, second, third, etc., as they distanced themselves from the River.

Market Street divided the streets running parallel to the water, that is to say, first, second, and so on, into two parts from which division commences the names North first, South first, North second, South second, and so on. The other streets are parallel to Market and at right angles to the water and are named after trees, such as Chestnut, Mulberry, &, &.Davis thought the Colonel squinted but knew his hunger for history required feeding.

"With orders to fortify Philadelphia, the city was put under martial law, citizens drafted, except the Quakers, into military service, and the arduous task of setting up a defense took place."

When not performing military duties, he visited William Shippen. His sister, Sally, and he lived here for two years after their parents and grandparents' sequential death.

It sported a vast formal garden and orchard that took up nearly a block. The large spacious red and black brick house features classical pediments above its doors and windows. Its family's roots went as far back as the Penns', and they lived very close to the founding family of Pennsylvania.

Burr remembered turning and smelling the subtly of flowers in a vase on a square table by a small open window.

The war had bound Edward Shippen; he was not a revolutionary. (William Shippen, his brother, served as surgeon general to the Continental Army.) Edward wanted to continue his life as it had always been and remained neutral. The Shippens traveled back and forth between a farm outside Philadelphia so as not to have to take sides; Burr never had much of an opportunity to speak with the family who tendered him in his hour of need.

With his chin up and his eyes level, Burr remembered just missing a common occurrence of seeing Benjamin Franklin, Thomas Paine, and Benjamin Rush walking together in the streets.

"There," children cried out, "goes Poor Richard, Common Sense, and the Doctor."

He heard that Franklin made suggestions to <u>Common Sense</u>, as Paine penned it, and that Doctor Rush titled the work.

"I could never understand," Burr said, "why Philadelphia was considered of strategic importance, and to make matters worse, a strong Tory sentiment existed in half the city."

A somber look draped Burr's continence as Washington came into his mind recalling that in New Jersey, the hand of fate sprinkled fairy dust upon the commander-in-chief. The British under Cornwallis had lingered for six days, allowing the beleaguered Continentals to regain their composure. On December 7, the British marched towards Trenton, and Washington decided to cross the Delaware to the Pennsylvania shore's waiting bonfires. Washington watched the enemy from his headquarters, a brick house directly across from Trenton. Camping in the underbrush and woods out of sight from the river, his forces camped within ten miles of headquarters.

"A general I respected was Charles Lee, who felt the best way to stop the enemy was by attacking their rear." Davis"Lee had moved from Peekskill, New York, to Morristown, New Jersey, where he made his new headquarters," said Burr. "With his corps of 900 men, he assaulted the rear of the British army. Davis's lips curved, his eyebrows lifted as he listened to the tale of history.

While reorganizing on the Delaware River's Pennsylvania side, Washington sent for General Lee and his troops but waited and waited for the alleged slow-moving Lee.

"The capture of General Charles Lee brought overwhelming joy to the hearts of the British," said Burr. "He made things unsafe behind their lines, and they needed to deploy extra troops to guard against his raids. He disturbed their support line and often captured small escorted and baggage wagons. Two days before his seizure, he managed to appropriate 1,000 sheep and hogs from their commissariat and captured several patrols and individual dragoons. From these captured soldiers, he gleamed crucial military information."

Davis, thinking not the reckless and thunderous man I learned about in school.

"Rumours spread of Lee's capture, but only later did I learn the facts of Lee being made a prisoner by the British. Historians have not been kind to Lee. Their official story is that he carelessly left himself exposed and that a Loyalist informed the British of his whereabouts.

Burr grinned, and a shower of wrinkles appeared on his face.

Davis shook his head. His attention stopped momentarily as he stared at the cracks in history.

Slipping into the past thrilled Davis.

"General Sullivan marched Lee's troops into Washington's camp a few days after this incident. The ragged army, now together, shivering by the icy river, huddled near their campfires." The cold ran through Davis like a cheetah

"Before leaving New Jersey, British General Howe established a net of posts in New Jersey to maintain his victorious ground. Usually adequate at intelligence, Washington possessed no idea that Howe and Cornwallis left the vicinity. Only 1,500 Hessians remained, under the command of Johann Rall." Burr tensed, then relaxed. Thinking nothing for a few moments.

"Washington moved his headquarters north about ten miles to Buckingham's township, where Generals Greene, Stirling, and Knox also dwelled. General Gates arrived with 600 men, and Washington's rebel army now consisted of about 7,500, of which 1,500 were unfit for duty."

The Colonel recalled that his comfort and pleasure were more important than continuing the fox hunt in the dark, depressing coming months, "Billy" retired to New York on December 13 to the arms of "his little whore," Mrs. Elizabeth Loring, attending ball upon ball complete with fireworks.

As was his custom, the British General wined, gamed, danced, and dreamed away the dull gray winter months engaged in festivity. A spark entered Burr's eyes.

"With his generals at his side, General Washington decided to attack Trenton on the eve of Christmas and strike he did. Crossing the Delaware at night in flatboats, the insurgent rebels advanced from all sides while a swirling blizzard of snow added to the enemy's confusion. Within 45 minutes, the Hessians surrendered, their commander, Rall, dead and 900 prisoners taken, with only four Americans wounded, James Monroe being one. Finally, victorious, for if not, no <u>Father of Our Country</u>."

Davis remembered confidence returning to the American army and the country's morale soaring like leaves in the winter wind. Rising from the ashes of humiliation, Washington now wore the laurels of victory.

The point that remained in Burr's mind was, "Due to the formidable pro-British sentiment at Philadelphia, "Old Put's" forces could not assist Washington in Trenton and Princeton's engagements. If they did not tally in non-strategic Philadelphia but instead joined with Washington, the entire Hessian retreat would probably have been entirely cut off, and their men captured or destroyed.

Upon learning of the defeat at Trenton, Billy's head had lain asleep in the lap of his amour. Upon waking, General "Billy" sent Cornwallis with 8000 men after the resurrected hero and Virginia planter.

As 1776 ended, Cornwallis and his army approached Trenton after the fox again. Burr tasted the new year, the exotic flavor of the revolution.

"Washington avoided a head-on attack (yes, he could learn) and circled by back roads to attack the enemy's rear at Princeton a la Lee," he informed Davis, "dividing his men into two forces under Greene to the left and Sullivan to the right, the battle began at sunrise, Friday, January 3."

The story all but mesmerized Davis.

"The surprised British were dumbstruck, thinking the rebel army was at Trenton. The out-numbered enemy lost more men than the victorious rebels, Washington notching another unexpected victory against an overconfident absent General who preferred the silken tables of New York City to the homespun field of winter warfare."

Though Trenton and Princeton were, in actuality, skirmishes, not full-blown battles, the psychological advantage bestowed on the American insurgents can only be explained as the difference between the sun and a pebble. From August to December, bleakness had reigned on the American cause, and these two incidents lit the landscape like a full moon does the ground below..

Both sides wintered in their quarters, waiting for the birds of spring to serenade their future engagements amid the aroma of bloom. For some time, Burr stayed with "Old Put" in Philadelphia and spent some of the winter in his college town of Princeton.

Before embarking for the upcoming campaign of '77, the British General and his brother, Lord Admiral Richard Howe (or "Black Dick" as affectionately labeled by his sailors), were the honored guests on May 20 aboard the ship Fanny. Several other guests, including Mrs. Loring, danced on the upper deck until three in the morning. Races between boats amused the party, and the Admiral gave "handsome presents" to the best craft. To think that a curtsy, bow, and or a twist helped determine the failure or success of a revolutionary struggle is not something the courtesans of history enunciate. Burr turned his head as if he was looking into the past.

"In June 1777, while I was in Peekskill, New York, General Howe entered Amboy, New Jersey, left a small garrison there, and then marched with some 30,000 troops on the main road through New Brunswick towards Philadelphia. Instead of attacking the beleaguered patriot army, Howe marched back through New Brunswick, settled at Amboy, divided his forces, and attempted to encircle Washington. Having learned of this strategy, Washington marched his men back to the heights at Middlebrook. Howe then returned his entire army to Staten Island, where they boarded his brother's ships. The lovelorn "Billy" hurried to New York and spent two weeks coquetry with Mrs. Loring while his troops sweltered on the crowded ships, waiting to depart."

Burr tried to smile, but his leathered lips refused to obey, thinking Moliere could not have concocted a more absurd farce regarding the egregious blunders committed by the opposing generals in the ensuing Campaign of 1777. No matter how ridiculous an error one General committed, the opposing General brushed it off and gave the advantage back to his opponent.

"General "Billy" should have advanced north up the Hudson to meet John Burgoyne, coming south from Canada," said Burr. "This maneuver would have challenged Washington. But, when Howe proceeded south towards Philadelphia, Washington should have marched north to join forces with Gates and finish off Burgoyne earlier than his actual defeat by Gates." "Jamie" Wilkinson, who then served under General Gates, entered his consciousness. "According to Gates," 'I have not met with a more promising military genius than Colonel Wilkinson, whose services have been of the last importance to this army.' "Due to his General's urging on November 6, 1777," said Burr, "Congress conferred the honor of brevet (a document entitling a commissioned officer to hold a higher rank temporarily but without higher pay) of Brigadier General on the young puffed-up Wilkinson."

Realizing he had strayed from his subject, he returned to his story, having worked it out in his mind. "The enemy's guns, artillery, stores, and other prizes would have replenished the meager means of Washington. He and Gates could have returned to New York to contend with the depleted forces of Clinton. Then and only then, Washington could have been in a check position. Instead, the simple Virginia farmer (and please know I cast no aspersions on farming) followed Howe towards Philadelphia, which possessed no strategic value. Yes, Congress presided there, but the town lacked value militarily. "Brandywine came, and Washington stood on the brink of capture again, but General "Billy" let him go. Freed from defeat, Washington achieved a quick hit-and-run victory at Germantown and regained some esteem."

Burr took a slow swallow of brandy. For one untamed second, the earth stood still.

"Meanwhile, back in the New York area, General Putnam ordered me to interview British deserters at Brunswick. I pieced together an account of the enemy's situation, strength, and Intentions for staff use."

While at Peekskill in mid-July, Putnam ordered Burr to proceed to the Sound and 'transmit . . . without delay the intelligence you shall from time to time receive of the enemy's movements or any of their fleets. He had a knack for discovering facts where others found noise. Davis leaned forward, intending to stand at attention, but his legs trumped him.

"In late June 1777, I received a promotion. (Long overdue, I believed) Washington granted him a commission as a lieutenant colonel in the Continental Army, yet he was not pleased.

"What made me dislike Washington?" he asked.

I thought, *him unfit for his situation.*

"Yes, he wanted military skill, but he was only fit to command a regiment and was not 'first in war.' His ignorance resulted from his having only read but little, and even less on military affairs, maybe Sime's *Military Guide* but not John Muller, a German-born professor at the Royal Military Academy, a renowned authority on fortifications, who also wrote a treatise on the artillery."

Davis watched Burr's hand squeezing the arm of his chair, asking, "Was I either blind or stupid to his qualities? His esteem would have opened many doors for me. I knew how to flatter my fellow man's ego, and I knew that this General bathed in the words of praise, yet when in his presence, I felt as depressed as the future winter sky of Valley Forge. A stiff, cold statue spoke with more feeling than this surveyor from Virginia. No one excelled more in the chasm of vanity than the old pale-faced Washington, with his harsh-lined mouth and a slow mind to rise. No rhyme of mental absorption beat in his large hollow frame. General Washington subsisted as a dull mirror needing the reflection of another's intelligence. Since my youth, I knew no medicine existed to cure a stupid person. Unfortunately for me, Washington never forgave my insolence to him and eventually blocked prestigious appointments for me. He possessed an allergy to my criticism." Nearly half asleep Davis stood up and opened a near by window, the cold air waking him. "My advice is, Be kind to everybody. You never know who might appear on the jury at your trial."

In his mind Burr wanted to reach for his sword and swipe the past.

"In September, I was informed by General Putnam that an enemy force of two thousand men was creating chaos around Bergen and Hackensack, New Jersey. I marched a regiment to the Hackensack River, where I gave them some rest, surveying the situation, and discovered an enemy picket of thirty men." Davis's head rose as Burr continued, "I returned to my resting soldiers and captured the entire picket minus one sentinel he shot. The prisoners consisted of twenty-seven privates, a corporal, and an officer. Upon preparing to attack more of the enemy, word arrived that the loyalists returned to New York City, leaving most of their plunder."

Burr smiled and looked up, but something rushed through him – his Pride.

"Old Put then sent orders for the Malcolms to join General Washington in his failed attempt to free Philadelphia from British control. A few months later, the Malcolms were at Valley Forge, spending the winter that 'tried men's souls.' Once again, the discipline was slack, the supplies and food scarce, except at the table of Washington and his worshipers. Half-naked men drank and fought with one another as the cold winter light's shadow stretched slowly toward spring. At least Malcolm's regiment did not dissipate into a chorus of disgruntled soldiers; Burr ensured that. They were frequently in battle and were considered among the best disciplined in the American army."

Burr's mind went blank for a moment, absent of any thought. Collecting himself he said,

"Because of frequent false alarms that the redcoats were coming, General Alexander McDougall persuaded General Washington to send Burr as the commanding officer to the Gulf, a passageway the British would use if they left Philadelphia. These false alarms made the officers at Valley Forge unnecessarily prepare their troops at night. He imposed rigorous discipline, night and day. Some of the disgruntled men, slackers, and drunkards plotted to slay me, but upon being informed of the time, he made sure their guns were without bullets and approached the malcontents on a moonlit night. When the leader attempted to shoot me, he drew his sword and severed the man's arm below the elbow; that was the last of the false alarms or mutinies." Late into the night they played themselves but not before Burr said, "Never leave the coals of the fire unattended; you never know what your enemy might do."

## Chapter 54

## Left Alone

His room at the Red House stole a view of rushing water while calls of mockingbirds beyond its edges echoed through the heart of the woods. Sir Francis-Carr Clerke entered and said, "Sir, it has come to my attention that collecting horses, cows, and oxen is paramount."

Burgoyne stared at his aide, then released a slight, broken grimace, Clerke waiting for him to comment, but silence reigned.

"Without the procurement of food," Clerke declared, "the strength of the horses cannot be sustained."

"What does Major Kingston say?"

"We need provisions and forage, Sir."

Burgoyne's eyes arched from one side to the other.

"Have Colonel Baum lead an expedition to the Connecticut River country."

"May I suggest General?"

'Yes."

"We need more men for our Loyalist corps."

"How many?"

"General Riedesel, who knows the terrain, says three thousand men are necessary.

Burgoyne rose quickly, leaving his aide blinking in bewilderment.

"Enlist them and have Colonel Baum rejoin the army at Albany in about two weeks."

As ordered, Colonel Baum left on August 9, his men marching with heavy jackboots with immense spurs, thick leather breeches, gauntlets, and enormous hats topped with large feathers. The next day Clerke rushed to the Red House, saying to Burgoyne with speed and force, "Sir, information just arrived that a large supply depot at Bennington in Vermont possesses what we need, and it is much nearer than Connecticut."

Failing to tell his general that the road from Bennington to the Hudson was in poor condition and passed through thick woods, Burgoyne flew out the door, grabbed Colonel Skene, a local loyalist, and rode after Baum to change the objective.

Seeing the sunlight reflect off the heavy cavalry swords hanging down from each soldier's side, he told Baum. "Change of plans, Colonel."

Baum's jaw dropped.

With a beam on his face, Burgoyne said, "Take the men to Bennington."

"Where is it, General?"

Burgoyne looked at Colonel Skene.

"It is situated at the Hoosic River forks, about 24 miles from the Hudson, southeast of Batten Kill. I will show you the way."

They marched off under the playwright's eye and orders, Burgoyne wanting to jump for joy as he watched large pigtails swinging around the surface of each soldier's back and each soldier carrying a short carbine along with his rations.

Watching the men, guided by Colonel Skene, as they progressed under an unrelenting throbbing sun, Burgoyne rode off comfortably erect, unaware that Skene's military acumen waited for testing, for he could not distinguish a rebel from a loyalist.

Through the thickets of the torturing thorns of the sword-leaved forest, afflicted by August's heat, Baum's men dreamed of calm waters, wishing for glades of delight, lakes scented by splendid and delightful spring, heavy rains hindering their passage, and a dozen oxen needed to draw a single bateau.

Colonel Baum sent a message to Burgoyne, "I cannot ascertain the number of cattle, carts, and wagons taken here, as they have not yet been collected. A few horses have also been brought in, but I am sorry to acquaint your Excellency that the savages either destroy or drive away what is not paid for with ready money. If your excellency would allow me to purchase the horses from the savages, stipulating the price, I think they might be procured cheaply; otherwise, they ruin all they meet with, their officers and interpreters not having it in their power to control them."

On the 13th, he wrote his General, "The enemy numbers 1800 men and could not carry out the projected plan. Send reinforcements, as I expect to be under attack."

Upon receiving the information, Burgoyne's teeth ground.

"What is wrong, Sir," said Clerke.

Burgoyne tried to erase the thought that an enemy triumph would cause discouragement.

"Have General Rieshel send re-enforcements to Baum."

Clerke's eyes were wide and fixed on Burgoyne.

"Any other orders, Sir."

'Tell General Rieshel that any animals or wagons secured by Baum must remain in our possession!"

On the 14th, Baum sent a messenger to Burgoyne. "By five prisoners taken here, they agree that 1500 to 1800 men are in Bennington, but they will run on our approach; I will proceed so far today as to fall on the enemy tomorrow early and make such disposition as I think necessary from the intelligence I may receive."

Burgoyne's eyes gleamed like the sun in midsummer.

"People are flocking in hourly," continued Baum, "but want to be armed. The savages cannot be controlled; they ruin and take everything they please."

In an instant, Burgoyne's eyes showed agitation. He cursed the Indians, then tightened his hands into fists by his side,

Clerke interrupted his General with the news, "The legislature of New Hampshire called into combat General John Stark who agreed to leave his farm and serve with 1500 militiamen under his command but only on the condition that he be accountable to them. Not Congress!"

The General lifted his head and looked up at him, scratching his chin. "I see no problem, do you?"

The question twisted inside Clerke.

"Amateurs against professionals," said Burgoyne, who glanced up and smiled, seeing himself dancing with his lover.

On the 15th, Stark's men's detachment at Van Schaick's mill on the Wallcomsac River taunted Baum's corps. Under the guidance of Major Skene, Baum allowed proclaimed loyalists but, in truth, rebels enter his lines.

The Germans, outnumbered 2 to 1, went forward in pursuit.

Temper sprang into Baum's eyes as Stark's troops surrounded the British a few miles west of Bennington, several bullets bursting Baum's chest. Only seven of his corps regained the British camp. At two o'clock on the morning of August 17, the playwright heard a knock on his door.

"General," said Clerke, Baum is dead, and the re-enforcements under Breyman, close to reaching Baum, became engaged in their own battle."

The news surged in him hatefully as he shook his head, determined not to show emotion to a subordinate.

"With their ammunition gone," continued Clerke, "their artillery horses dead or wounded, Breyman ordered his heavy guns to be left behind while his men carried off their wounded."

Without a word, Burgoyne dropped his eyes as he moved about the room.

"529 to 907 killed or wounded," said Clerke, "depending on the source."

The General began organizing his thoughts. "Get on with your business."

He wrote home angrily, "The reinforcements sent for marched too slowly, at the rate of two miles an hour."

Returning to bed, he told his whore, "What is a general to do?"

Under her breath, she said, "The Germans are idiots."

The next day, the General's aide-de-camp informed him of General Riedesel's request for liquor.

Clerke observed him flush with embarrassment.

"Give him four dozen bottles of port and the same quantity of Madeira," Burgoyne read the astonishment on his aide's face.

"A better spirit is just out of the question for the Germans," he informed Clerke. "I must consider the present condition of my wine cellar and my staff's well-being." Later that day, the light from the sun filtered through the window, highlighting his mistress as she entered the room.

"Are you ready for your bath, mon general?" Said his lady of the evening.

For the first time that evening, he smiled and appeared to relax.

## Chapter 55

## 1st Battle of Saratoga 9/19/1777

"Did you know, Burr, the Hudson River traverses 315 miles in length?" Said Wilkinson on his second night's stay at Richmond Hill in 1797, Irving, Willet, and Theodosia having retired.

Burr glanced at the blue water meandering like a snake from the Veranda of Richmond Hill, sounding and looking peaceful in the wee hours of the morn.

"No. Why do you ask?"

"I thought of when Gates arrived at General Schuyler's camp on August 19, 1777, and took command of the despondent soldiers, who felt that without reinforcements, they might as well give up the matter and go home."

Burr sensing a story, tilted his head back, his eyes firmly focused on Wilkinson.

"That night, a shooting star streaked through the sky, and news of Stark's victory came the next day. 1200 killed & taken prisoner plus a large amount of baggage & 4 brass field pieces."

Wilkinson, his excitement almost unbearable, said, "The feared British," he smirked, "were no longer dreaded as invincible."

Not at Brandywine in September or Germantown in October, remembered Burr.

"Hundreds of prisoners, arms, dress, accouterments, and cannon," Gates said to me, "encourages the seekers of liberty."

The belief in the indomitability of the British troops," I responded, "wilts like un-watered lettuce."

Burr surprised him by grinning.

Wilky's memory solidified in his mind. A quick boyish grin covered his face as he took in Burr.

"Yes," said Gates, "the heavy summer air dissipates, and the struggle for independence floats."

"I interjected. On liberated, sparkling particles of hope."

"As we stood on the summer grass, our backs to the Hudson," Wilkinson paused, thinking of his words. "Well, Major, said Gates, the patriot army will now grow in numbers."

*The sprint to freedom gathering steam* thought Burr,

"The British lack any military strategy," said Gates.

"And as a matter of fact, it lacks intelligence," I added.

Burr sent him an amused look.

"I remember chortling," said Wilky, "This playwright, this dreamer, this fictional general sent an inadequate force."

"I am not amazed," Gates told me, "my former colleague in arms continues to direct his fantasy play in such a predictable way and proves to be a parody of military intelligence and not the genius of a superior general."

"He is a greater clown than Shakespeare's Feste," Wilky said.

"Shortsighted," responded Gates, "glory caving inside his head."

"Contrary to the usual course of Generaling," said Burr, "Burgoyne invited defeat."

"He is not nor has he the mental traits," Gates said to me, "to profit from random success or the prescience to calculate consequences from his actions."

"Not against mon General," Wilkinson replied.

Burr imagined their eyes connecting like a bridge across a ravine.

"Much is lacking in King George's prescience," Gates said to me." How little do Kings know, Wilky said, "of the power of the melody of freedom."

Wilkinson stopped unbuttoning his words and puffed on a Havana cigar.

"I learned," Wilky recalled, "from Alexander Hamilton that when Washington heard the news of this first reverse, he said, "Poor judgment" and lifted his head and looked down on Hamilton, "And it will be repeated!"

"Little did Burgoyne imagine," Wilky said to Burr as he looked him in the eyes, "that it was all but over."

Unknown to Burr or Wilkinson, on August 22, when Ticonderoga's news reached the King, he ran into the Queen's room whooping, "I have beat them all the Americans." This scene would later distress the King, and when alone in the evening, it haunted him till his death.

"Four days later, on August 25, Wilkinson said to Burr, "news arrived that the enemy's attempt to storm Fort Stanwix failed and St. Leger met with considerable loss."

"I remember," said Burr, "that John Glover, who went to upstate New York, best personified the new feeling of the army of the Congress, "we will compel Burgoyne to return to Ticonderoga, if not to Canada."

Wilkinson laughed and started to light another cigar before announcing, "The playwright General, left with only quill, parchment, and willing mistress, determined on an advance once they obtained thirty days of provision. Ironically, Burr, his lover, was the commissary's wife."

Wilkinson pulled back to weigh his words.

"Like Rome, he was lying in sleep dreaming the impossible, and his eternal blight would soon arrive.

Burr listened and decided that Wilkinson should try writing an account of the first battle of Saratoga.

"Arnold arrived," said Wilkinson, "at Gates' headquarters on August 26 from Fort Stanwix with more troops."

Burr, saw Arnold's bulging neck muscles twitching for battle.

"For the next two months, I was Gates' shadow. I, the bee, who takes the nectar from the flower."

Burr would not learn till the fall of 1806 that Wilkinson drank on the foibles of each man he addressed since his enrollment in the War of the Revolution, regardless if they were military or private.

"A fool is a friend to no one unless his purpose stands served," said Wilky under the veranda at Richmond Hill as the Hudson River, a tidal estuary, ebbed and flowed with the ocean tide

In time Burr would feel the truth of those words.

"Early September, in a conversation with my General," said Wilkinson, "I advanced the proposition that our position was not defensible because it was too flat & open. My General agreed. From the two rivers' junction, our army moved to Stillwater, but it was found less suitable than thought. Again, we marched 3 miles north. I recommended that my General send Thaddeus Kosciuszko, the young engineer, to find a defensive position."

Burr did not remind him he was repeating his suggestion from an earlier tale. "Upon my suggestion, the high ground of Bemis Heights, which stood on the west side of the Hudson, a bottleneck in the path of Burgoyne's advance, was to be the spot where the army of the congress would make its stand. On the right ran a river; on the left rose rugged, wooded bluffs, in front marshy, rolling, tree-covered terrain, unbroken but for a few scattered clearings and wagon roads."

Seeing the dimples on Wilkinson's face flush, Burr lifted a brow.

"On the ninth, re-enforcements arrived. We took a position on the 12th and began fortifications. It brought a smile to the men's faces. I was everywhere directing for my general, did a reconnaissance with a detachment of men, and determined the precise position of Burgoyne's army. His army of 7000 arrived by the morning of September 13, the same day Burgoyne crossed the Hudson. The enemy pitched camp at Coveville on the evening of the 15th and began planning their battle strategy at Sword's house."

Comfortably occupied, General Wilkinson continued a full flow of thoughts and happy memories with Burr.

"Burr! We entrenched our strong position on Bemis Heights. As you know, the road to Albany squeezed through a narrow passage between the hills and the Hudson River."

Burr imagined the forest resounding with the ax's strokes as the British and American Armies fortified their camps.

"Our position gave Burgoyne three alternatives: to progress along the road below our fortifications, retreat, or remove us from Bemis Heights. Regardless of his choice, we were well prepared. We knew he would attack, even under unfavorable circumstances, our hearts soaring like an eagle."

Upon the whole, Wilkinson instilled in Burr soft, obliging feelings. He stirred the past with his vivid imagination.

"Unfortunately, we heard that after the battle of Brandywine, the grand army was retreating from the advance of General Howe. Washington wrote to Gates for Colonel Morgan's riflemen, but I told Gates not to answer."

Stepping back, Burr brushed a hand through his hair, seeing the flowers and blooms of the coming battle.

"I served as Gates' eyes, ears, and tongue as the General did not visit his pickets."

At this time, he became affectionately called "Wilky," having more admirers than fall leaves.

Burr recalled St. Clair telling him that Wilkinson "has great merit - and what is, in my opinion, more valuable, he has a warm, honest heart."

Matthew Lyons told Burr that Wilkinson "seemed to be the life and soul of the headquarters of the army: he, in the capacity of Adjutant general, governed at headquarters. He was a standing correction of the follies and irregularities occasioned by the weakness and intemperance of the commanding general."

"That was before their fallout," Burr recollected. Lyons said, "Yes, he called him jocose, volatile, and convivial."

Unlike an owl in an oak who hooted steadily, "Wilky" knew how to camouflage his motives and was the ultimate blindfold.

Wilkinson looked out from the veranda as white clouds began to block Hudson's blue sky.

Burr turned to Wilkinson.

"Did you hear a distant rumble of thunder?"

"No, you imagined it," Wilkinson breathing in the pleasant warm afternoon.

The rumbling grew louder and louder, and the sky turned black.

Wilkinson raised his eyebrows, "The speed by which the black clouds appear always amazes me."

Burr said nothing as he stared at him, watching the cool wind blow and the whole sky engulfed by dark swirling puffs.

As the wind increased and the trees in Burr's garden bent to one side as though they were going to fall over or get blown away like feathers, he asked, "Think it is going to rain, General?"

In a flat tone, devoid of emotion, Wilkinson swallowed hard, the rumbling of thunder and the howling of wind impressing him.

The pouring rain crashed down upon the roof of the veranda.

"Proof is in the pudding," said the General

Flashes of lightning lit up the darkened sky.

A rain blur cut the Hudson's visibility to a few feet.

The storm raged for about an hour but did not drown Wilkinson's story.

"Slowly, the British General came south with boats, baggage, and artillery. Immediately upon learning that he moved his entire force across the Hudson on boat bridges, therefore cutting his communications with Ticonderoga, Gates ordered General Lincoln to march directly upon the ground over which the British army had passed and attack that Part of the Enemy's Force, yet upon the East Side of the River. Five days afterward, he took 100 prisoners, nearly 300 royalists, and retook Mount Defiance, Mount Hope, the French lines, the Block House, the landing, and 200 Bateau."

A silence overcame him for a moment, then he shot forward and paced, releasing whatever ran through him.

"Upon Burgoyne's evacuation of Skenesborough, we attacked Forts George and Edward, and Col. John Brown led a military march towards Ticonderoga. Of utmost importance, Burgoyne's communication and supply lines were evaporating like the morning mist. By the 15th, we were sure Burgoyne was ready to risque a battle. That day the British General adhered to our intuition advancing with drums beating and colors flying. He encamped near Sword's House, four miles from our lines. On the 18th, after skirmishing, the bulldog, Arnold, with 1500 men, probed Burgoyne's strength. He wanted to attack and confront his commander-in-chief, who did not take kindly to Arnold's aggressiveness. Gates adhered to the chain of command. My general and I discussed the situation and were willing to let the enemy come forward. The commander put Arnold on a hill about a mile from the Hudson, General Ebenezer Learned in the center on a fortified plateau near Neilson's Barn, and Gates took the bluff, overlooking the River in command of the right wing."

Wilkinson took a deep breath as his hands clenched into fists. "With fog over the River on the morn of the 19th, Burgoyne stood at the door of Sword's house, 3 miles from Bemis Heights. He knew he must act on our terms. A doable hundred miles was the distance of retreat to Ticonderoga, but it never crossed his mind."

Burr listened, amazed by his friend's memory.

Wilkinson continued, "The enemy, near full force, with eight artillery pieces, marched southward on a fury of fulfilled determination. Their strategy was to turn our left wing. They approached Freeman's farm at noon, the only open land in a forest riddled with hills and ravines. After 2 PM, heavy fire commenced from both sides. At 3 PM under a hard sun, the British General marched across the open space three regiments in line with two others on our flanks against our 7,000 well-fortified men, spread west and south surrounded by abatis, fallen trees with sharpened branches, cannon sighted to the river road, sharpshooters and militia."

Burr held his eyes steady as he drifted over the battle.

"We had something more at stake than fighting for sixpence, said Wilkinson, "a four-hour battle flowed like waves of a stormy sea. Bullets and projectiles whistled through the air creating gaps in human flesh. The battle swung back and forth; gaining ground took a long time. Colonel Morgan's sharpshooters picked off "Kingbirds."

Burr, aware of their deadly accuracy at 250 yards, thought they needed to step back.

"Arnold directed a spirited charge of the American left, but no American general was on the battlefield. The killing sounds of war left life squirming on the ground–men with limbs limp as water.

Both armies returned to their fortified positions when the first star lifted its head. The dark gray-green woods of the Alder-leaf Buckthorn forest and all its wilds serenaded the groans of sorrow with an intermittent uttering of frogs, crickets & bats. Nature's sounds eternalizing as the starless sky muttered with thunder."

As General Wilkinson paced, an involuntary smirk danced on his lips; inside his core, pride soared.

"The light from the East rose upon the bed of darkness the following morn. The sounds from the trees commingled with an aura of grief upon the fighting field. Courage treads to dust upon one's path of fate. The siren of freedom alive and well."

Glancing up, Burr laughed. "I like you, General. Shakespeare would have called you a fabler."

The General lifted a brow. "Is that praise?"

"The highest."

"The Brits," continued Wilkinson, "believed the field of battle remained in their possession, an outright act of arrogance. They lost 600-800 men killed and wounded. Twenty taken prisoner, nearly a third of Burgoyne's regimental strength and three-quarters of his artillery paid their debt to his hubris. We had 100 killed, 250 wounded 20 taken prisoner.

That night, I remember it so well; the stars shone ever so bright as we learned of the attack on Fort Ticonderoga and the release of our prisoners."

General Wilkinson stretched his limbs and torso. With a look of bewilderment, he recalled in satisfaction, "The Playwright General chose not to hold the ground he gained but decided to push southward recklessly.

Fort Edward was just nineteen miles from the first battle on Freeman's farm but retreat he would not. His rationale was his orders to a junction with Howe at Albany. He failed to comprehend that he would stand surrounded, and his communication with Canada gone."

Wilkinson laughed and shook his head at Burgoyne's arrogance.

"According to Major Kingston, on the 20th, the day after the battle, he still believed he could force his way to Albany but was becoming unsure about supplies. He wanted to know if Clinton could open communications and supply him from the South. He still had The opportunity to fight his way back to safety, but he exhibited leadership far below mediocrity. His conceit refused to allow him to recognize his weaknesses; it placed all under his command as pawns on a chessboard. As long as he remained on the board as the winner, so be the sacrifice of his pieces. His vanity and delusion resulted in a disservice to the King and the lives of several of his friends. There would be no Christmas in Albany."

"He could fool himself," said Burr. "He could fool his aides, but he could not fool reality."

"For the next twenty days," said Wilky, "both sides strengthened their positions."

The General turned to Burr and held his nostrils with thumb and forefinger, "The enemy's camp stunk from decaying corpses, and the heavy rains dissolved the shallow graves, which led to more stink."

Proud as a farmer after harvest, Wilkinson looked out to the vault of the universe, which is now shown with a million speckles of light, saying, "Late September, the Army of the Congress was reinforced with a least 3000 militia in high spirits. Burgoyne's hopes sank back to reality as he waited for nonexistent reinforcements from New York."

The mockingbird spread its wings, and the bullfrog exhaled a croak followed by a chorus from the songbirds gathered on an adjacent tree.

> "the hero, not always he
> who wins the throne
> tis often he
> who, fighting
> dies unknown"

# Chapter 56

# Charles Lee's Plan

"I know General Howe that my life is in great danger as an alleged deserter."

At this moment, Howe sensed he could use Lee to his advantage.

"Let me tell you, General Howe, I disapprove of the Declaration of Independence. I could but seek an interview with a committee from Congress that could open the way to a satisfactory adjustment of all disagreements between Great Britain and the colonies.

The idea startled Howe, who tilted his head to study Lee's face.

"I know, as a bit of a pacifist," Lee said, "you should try to sanction such an interview."

"Congress refused the request," said Howe. "What can you do for me?"

"I will prepare for General Howe a campaign plan against the Americans in which I sincerely and zealously profess will enter into the British interests."

Howe, playing his cards close to his chest, said, "Anything else?"

"I can outline an expedition to the Chesapeake Bay."

Howe's secretary, Sir Henry Strachey, wrote, "Mr. Lee's plan was dictated on March 29, 1777.

An expedition commenced the following summer.

With the plan before them, on the night of the 29th, Howe and Strachey discussed the idea.

"On the supposition then," said Strachey, "that your Army, including every species of Troops, amounts to twenty or even eighteen thousand men."

"Over twenty thousand," said Howe

Strachey continued. "You are at liberty to move to any part of the Continent, as fourteen thousand will be sufficient to clear the Jerseys and take possession of Philadelphia."

Howe thought for a minute, feeling his chin with his thumb and forefinger.

"Go on, but stick to the key points; I have a meeting."

Thinking of Mrs. Loring, he moistened his lips and shook his glass.

"I would propose," said Lee in his letter, "that four thousand men be immediately embarked in transports. One half of which should proceed up the Potomac and take post at Alexandria, the other half up Chesapeake Bay and possess themselves of Annapolis."

Howe's face softened, and he looked like the man he was in the carefree days before his coming to command the King's army.

"They will probably meet with no opposition in taking possession of these Posts.

When possessed, they are so firmly situated that a few hours of preparation and some trifling artillery will secure you. You need not worry against attacks of a much greater force than can be brought down against them."

Howe heard victory on the battlefield, a steady murmur of conquest.

Strachey observed a slight smile spread on his General's lips.

Lee's paragraphs continued at a clipped pace.

"All the Inhabitants of that great tract southward of the Patapsco and lying between the Potomac and Chesapeake Bay and those on the Eastern Shore of Maryland will immediately lay down their arms."

Howe remained silent at this grand scenario, thinking of Lee with astonishment,

"But this is not all. I am much mistaken if those potent and populous German districts of Frederick County in Maryland and York in Pennsylvania do not follow their example."

Strachey smirked, "Brilliant," he said and went on reading.

"The submission of the whole Province of Maryland will prevent or intimidate Virginia from sending aids to Philadelphia."

Howe spared Strachey a glance as he looked at his watch.

"One paragraph left, Sir."

"Go on," said Howe

"If any force is assembled at Alexandria sufficient to oppose the Troops sent against it getting possession of it, it must be at the expense of the more Northern Army."

## Chapter 57

# In-between

In between the Battle of Bennington (August 16) and the first battle of Saratoga (September 19) was the battle at Brandywine (September 11, 1777). Sir William was no longer interested in a crushing military victory than he had been at Brooklyn, in New York, at White Plains, or during the chase after Washington across New Jersey.

Conciliation stood front and center in his mind.

"There are hosts of floral friends in Pennsylvania," uttered Howe, "enough to furnish the necessary nucleus for conciliation."

"Armies on the defensive can quell no rebellion," said Clinton.

"Take Philadelphia, and Jersey will fall," said Howe.

"You said the same thing about New Jersey," Clinton said.

"The current plan seems on false principles," responded Howe, "that if conquered, which I doubt more and more every day, we must afterward keep, which is impossible."

October 4, the Battle of Germantown transpired, the last obstruction to Philadelphia. One thousand rebels posted in the woods suffered defeat. The two armies were four miles apart, but nothing occurred. The following day Washington took a position on the heights east of Brandywine.

The British under Cornwallis swung around in a side-enveloping movement. General Sullivan discovered the enemy behind and before him, similar to what happened at Long Island.

Washington misunderstood the situation and ordered Sullivan to push across the Brandywine and cut off the enemy.

Long Island all over again, the hammer poised to the anvil, and Howe needed to strike the blow by saying, "Push on the attack!"

Thinking of his hungry men who had marched since daybreak covering seventeen miles of rough country with arms and heavy packs, he gave orders to halt for dinner.

The rebels, having time to regroup, rushed off in the direction of Chester, Billy letting them go and allowing Washington's army to speak another day.

Washington left Brandywine in haste and confusion. He received a note from Howe regarding the left behind wounded men. "As we are not situated to give them the necessary relief, I suggest you send surgeons to attend to them."

Itching for a fight, Washington planned a surprise attack on Howe's rear, but his attacking party surpassed in the night and punished the encounter called the Paoli Massacre.

In the middle of the night, Congress tumbled out of bed and escaped from Philadelphia to Trenton and then to Lancaster, and finally to York.

## Chapter 58

## General Burgoyne Sends Message to Foreign Secretary

General Burgoyne was quiet momentarily and then began to pace as though possessed by a devil who refused to keep still.

He called for his aide de camp, Sir Francis Carr Clerke, who, upon entering, twisted and turned under his glare.

"Sir."

Burgoyne's eyes narrowed, "Have a seat."

Sensing anxiety and wanting to soothe it, Clerke shot him a smile as warm as the logs burning in a fireplace.

"I need to send a message to the Foreign Secretary."

His aide-de-camp took a seat and, with quill in hand, wrote.

"Provisions for about thirty days having been brought forward, the other necessary stores prepared, and the bridge of boats completed. I passed the Hudson's River to force a passage to Albany and moved forward and encamped in a good position in Dovacote. On the 13th and 14th of September, my army encamped on the heights and in the plains of Saratoga. The enemy camped in the neighborhood of Stillwater. I did not think myself authorized to call any men into the council when the peremptory tenor of my orders and the season of the year admitted no alternative." Burgoyne sipped some champagne Mrs. Loring's husband provided and studied his situation, never feeling insecure. "It is found that there were several bridges to repair, that work was begun under 16th, covered by strong detachments, and the opportunity was taken to reconnoiter the country.

The army renewed their march, repaired other bridges, and encamped upon the advantageous ground about four-mile from the enemy."

Clerke glanced at Burgoyne, thinking the stiffness in his voice suited the situation.

Armed with his notebook, organized earlier and divided into

sections, the General continued.

"The enemy appeared in considerable force to obstruct. Further repair of bridges occurred on the 18th with a view, as it was conceived, to draw on an action where artillery could not be employed. A small loss was sustained in skirmishing, but the work of the bridges was affected."

September 19, the passages of a great ravine and other roads towards the enemy having been explored, the army advanced in the following order."

Burgoyne took a deep breath and picked up the events leading to the battle.

"Brigadier General Fraser's corps, sustained by Lieutenant Colonel Breyman's corps, made a circuit to pass the ravine commodiously, without quitting the heights, and afterward to cover the march of the line to the right. These corps moved in three columns and had the Indians, Canadians, and Provincials upon their fronts and flanks. The British line, led by me in person, passed the ravine in a direct line south. It formed in order of battle as fast as they gained the summit, where they waited to give time to Fraser's corps and left-wing and artillery under the commands of Major General Phillips to make the circuit. Major General Riedesel, with two columns, repaired bridges by the great road and meadows near the river. The 47th regiment guarded the Bateaux."

Clerke watched Burgoyne, seeing a quiet, introspective man who wanted to do the right thing. He waited for a beat before Burgoyne continued.

"The signal guns, which had been previously settled to give notice of all the columns being ready to advance, having been fired between one and two o'clock, the march continued. The scouts and flankers of the column of the British line were soon fired upon from small parties but with no effect. After about an hour's march, the picquets, which made the advanced guard of that column, were attacked in force and obliged to give ground, but they soon rallied and were sustained.

On the first opening of the wood, I formed the troops. A few cannon-shot dislodged the enemy at a house from whence the picquets had been attacked. Brigadier General Fraser's corps had arrived with such precision in time as to be found upon a very advantageous height on the right of the British."

Clerke watched as Burgoyne strolled over to an arrangement of flowers and smelled: intoxicating, stifling, aromatic, the general thinking of his mistress. He stopped for a moment to gather himself.

"In the meantime, the enemy, not acquainted with the combination of the march, moved in great force out of their entrenchments, with a view of turning the line upon the right, and being checked by the disposition of

Brigadier General Fraser, counter-marched, to direct their great effort to the left of the British."

Burgoyne looked at Clerke, found his eyes understanding, and sighed.

"Off the record, Sir Francis. In war, urgency can be exciting, even contagious. You and I know how long it takes to build and secure victory. Politics reverse, governments do an about-face, but history will stand firm."

Clerke looked at him, solemn-faced, no flush on his cheeks. He would damn well lead us to victory.

"From the nature of the country, movements were effected without a possibility of there being discovered," Burgoyne dictated to the Foreign Secretary.

Burgoyne paused, weighing his following words carefully.

"About three o'clock," Clerke wrote, "action began with a very vigorous attack on the British line and continued with great obstinacy until sunset. The enemy is continually supplied with fresh troops; the stress lay upon the 20th, 21st: and 62d regiments, most parts of which were engaged nearly four hours without intermission; the 9th had been ordered early in the day to form in reserve. The grenadiers and 24th regiment were some part of the time brought into action, as were part of the light infantry, and all these corps charged with their usual spirit."

Burgoyne leaned back in his seat. A slight frown appeared when he thought of his strategy.

"The riflemen, and other parts of Breyman's corps, were also of service; but it was not thought advisable to evacuate the heights where Brigadier General Fraser was posted otherwise than partially and occasionally."

As he recorded the narrow, winding story, Clerke admired his general, realizing the dangers of his trade. He grinned at him, the Hudson rumbling in his ears.

"Major General Phillips, upon first hearing the firing, found his way through a difficult part of the wood to the scene of action and brought up with him Major Williams and four pieces of artillery, and from that moment, I stood indebted to that gallant and judicious second, for incessant and most material services, particularly for restoring the action in a point which was critically pressed by a great superiority of fire, and to which he led up the 20th regiment at the utmost personal hazard."

Again, he felt proud of his tactics, thinking he need not force himself to rationalize.

"Major-General Riedesel exerted himself to bring up a part of the left wing and arrived in time to charge the enemy with regularity and bravery."

Looking up, Burgoyne put on a smile that flew in the face of probability. He shook his head, remembering the first thing he learned about soldiering was that the winner seizes the opportunity.

"Just as the light closed, the enemy gave ground on all sides and left us completely masters of the field of battle, with the loss of about five hundred men on their side, and, as supposed, thrice that number wounded."

It annoyed him that darkness prevented a pursuit, and the prisoners were few.

"The behavior of the officers and men, in general, was exemplary. Brigadier General Fraser took his position at the beginning of the day with excellent judgment and sustained the action with constant presence of mind and vigor. Brigadier-General Hamilton was the whole time engaged and acquitted himself with great honor, activity, and good conduct.

The general artillery was distinguished, and the brigade under Captain Jones, who was killed in the action, was conspicuously so."

Burgoyne's eyes narrowed. For a moment, he sat still, caught in a deluge of disbelief that he did not extinguish the rebel's will to fight.

"The army lay upon their arms the night of the 19th, and the next day took a position nearly within cannon shot of the enemy, fortifying their right, and extending their left to the brow of the heights, to cover the meadows through which the great river runs, and where their bateaux and hospitals were placed.

The 7th regiment of the Hesse Hanau and a corps of Provincials encamped in the meadows as further security.

It was soon found that no fruits, honor excepted, was attained by the preceding victory, the enemy working with a redoubled ardor to strengthen their left; their right was already unattackable."

Clerke shivered, making him realize that war, chilled him to the bone. He rubbed his hands over his face, thinking the impossible is cut and dried on the battlefield,

## Chapter 59

## War of Words

During the long weekend at Richmond Hill, General Wilkinson, in answer to a question by Colonel Burr regarding the relationship between Gates and Arnold, said, "Oh, that there I could lift the curtain upon a beautiful perspective, instead of the dark and dismal scenes, where the light is lost, and memory can no longer look on the form of hope."

Burr's lips twitched, but he managed to control a snicker. "A few days after the first battle of Saratoga," said Wilkinson, "Gates and Arnold's personalities ran into one another like bright light and deep shade. A dispute arose between these gentlemen. The slightest spark of collision sufficed to light up the flames of discord between the two men. Arnold protested that he was not mentioned in Gates's report to Congress on Freeman's farm battle. Now bold and impatient, Arnold refused to linger under Gates's trepidation."

Burr wondered if Arnold ever was not annoyed when he failed to get his way.

"Previous to the battle, I had served as a link between the ready-to-fight Arnold and the reluctant-to-battle Gates. I sided with my General. One did not have to be in the room when the two Generals were together to hear their conversation."

Wilky parroted the two men's voices while using hand gestures and body movements to depict Arnold as shrewish and Gates as pedantic.

Arnold demanded, "We must march boldly against Burgoyne's army."

Gates replied, "Sir, what will be gained?"

"Attack the enemy on our terms rather than wait for them to assault us from their lines," said Arnold, "Why allow the enemy to move at their will in front of our position? Perhaps use their heavy artillery to our disadvantage against our defenses."

"No, Sir," our best course of action is waiting for the old gamester, Burgoyne, to make the first move," said Gates. "Attack is more costly than defense. Our troops should not be forced into linear formations. That is the strength of the British and German regulars. Sir, What good would be Morgan's sharpshooting riflemen when withdrawn from their concealed positions? They are deadly effective when sniping from behind trees but in open battle would lose every advantage they possess."

The attack is the way to defeat the British," said Arnold.

"No! You will lead the left wing from a hill above the Hudson," said Gates, "Brigadier General Ebenezer Learned in the center on the fortified plateau near Neilson's barn. I will take command of the right-wing on the bluff overlooking the river."

You are wrong! The enemy will flank our position on the left," said Arnold, "unless engaged outside our defenses."

"Then I will send," said Gates, "Morgan's corps and Dearborn's men into the thick woods north of our line to oppose the British advance."

"Who will re-enforce Dearborn if his men get into trouble?"

"Sir, you will," said Gates. "That should make you happy."

"Attack makes me happy, General."

"My faith in Morgan and his men's battle skills gives me confidence.

"I trust," said Arnold, "that I give you the same confidence."

Wilky's voice sounded somewhat husky as he poured brandy into his glass. He took a long swallow from half of the glass and then drank more, which he gargled before it eased down his gullet. With a swashbuckling demeanor, he boasted, "After the battle, I was discussing with my General what to do with General Arnold when the hot-brained Arnold entered the room. Gates jumped up immediately as a snake was in his lap. The latter snarled like a dog and glowed with fire. His eyes fixed on me, telling me to leave the room. I rose and saluted both generals, 'Excuse me, I'm going out to reconnoiter."

Wilkinson paused and swallowed another glass of spirits.

"While walking from the tent, I heard Arnold."

"You prevented a glorious day for America. If you had given me the reinforcements I requested, I would have exploited the weakness in the center between Burgoyne and Fraser's right-wing. Their defenses would have been crushed, and the battle ended then and there. Then you ignored my advice on a general advance against Burgoyne. You, General Gates, prevented the destruction of the enemy. Why wasn't my division mentioned to Congress? You steal my honor and belittle my rank. It is an affront to my honor, Sir. Morgan's corps are part of my division, which is an independent unit. I am responsible to you. How dare you insult me!"

"Sir, you have fantasies of adequacy. I had my reasons for leaving your name off the Praise List.

"Your reasons! Damn, your vanity! You are jealous of me," said Arnold. "I am a fighting general. You were a mile from the battle, sheltered from the fury of war, a coward."

"Sir, need I remain you of the chain of command? You are addressing a superior. I once believed you had good instincts and proper diligence, but your overbearing ego has swept them away like the outgoing tide."

"Damn, you! Your chain of command and your insults."

"General Arnold, I told you when you arrived in camp that my sole intention was to hold Burgoyne and allow his impetuous nature to destroy himself. You are dismissed, Sir."

"I shall leave this department."

"Feel free to file out when Gen Lincoln arrives."

"I want a pass to join Washington, and I am not a deliverer of letters to John Hancock."

"It will be granted, and don't bluff me, Sir, better men than you have tried. General Arnold, some men bring felicity wherever they go and others whenever they go. You are dismissed!"

# Chapter 60

# Burgoyne and the 2nd Battle of Saratoga

He was deaf to the rain that slapped against the thin roof of the Red House. The constant pitter-patter, pitter-patter, pitter-patter, pitter-patter buried his thought. Will he ever be happy at the moment as opposed to waiting for his happy moment? He knew the winning odds on a winning bet were against those who wait for their happy moment and wager it will never come to be.

While resting in his room, the fire warmed him. He looked outside, feeling the chill in the air.

Oblivious to the thunder rolling across the sky, he thought someone was hammering on the clouds' top. His mind clicked, his spine straightened, and he noticed the continuous downpour that drenched the ground, forming, he thought, a pool of tears.

He writhed under the unblinking memory of his past performance.

Outside, the sky, a thousand shades of gray, painted its pictures in the clouds.

Major Kingston entered. "Sir, you called for me."

"How is my private secretary?"

"The wounded Sir Francis-Carr was captured by American soldiers and taken to their headquarters where General Gates ordered he be placed on his bed."

Burgoyne shook his head in disbelief.

"Have a seat, Major. What happened?"

"Wounded by a rebel sharpshooter as he was attempting to deliver your order to withdraw the artillery, Sir."

"Had the order been delivered," said Burgoyne, "the outcome of that battle, and perhaps the entire conflict itself, might have been different."

Major Kingston nodded, but from the expression in his gray eyes, he disagreed.

"I need you to record my thoughts."

As he studied Burgoyne's chiseled face, his quill paused on its journey to the parchment.

"I thought it advisable on the 3rd of October to diminish the soldiers' ration to lengthen out the provisions, to which measure the army submitted with the utmost cheerfulness. The difficulties of a retreat to Canada were foreseen, as was the dilemma, should the retreat be effected, of leaving at liberty such an army as General Gates's to operate against Sir William Howe.

This consideration operated forcibly to determine me to abide by events as long as possible, and I reasoned thus. The expedition I commanded was evidently meant at first to be hazarded."

Hazard never entered his mind.

"Circumstances might require it should be devoted. A critical junction of Mr. Gates's force with Mr. Washington might possibly decide the fate of the war; the failure of my junction with Sir Harry Clinton or the loss of my retreat to Canada could only be a partial misfortune."

Burgoyne broke his thought by stepping back—disgust and fury in his throat.

Major Kingston failed to move a muscle.

"In this situation, things continued till the seventh when no intelligence having been received of the expected co-operation, and four or five days for our limited stay in the camp only remained, it was judged advisable to make a move to the enemy's left, not only to discover whether there were any possible means of forcing a passage should it be necessary to advance, or of dislodging him for the convenience of a retreat, but also to cover a forage of the army which was in the greatest distress on account of the scarcity.

A detachment of fifteen hundred regular troops with two twelve-pounders, two howitzers, and six six-pounders were ordered to move and were commanded by myself, having with me Major-General Phillips, Major-General Riedesel, and Brigadier-General Fraser."

Still standing, Burgoyne looked down into Kingston's face. "I need a drink."

The Major poured him a glass of brandy.

Burgoyne took a long, slow gulp.

"The guard of the camp upon the heights was left to Brigadier-General Hamilton and Specht, the redoubts and the plain to Brigadier General Gall; and as the force of the enemy immediately in their front consisted of more than double their numbers, it was not possible to augment the corps that marched, beyond the numbers above stated.

I formed the troops within three-quarters of a mile of the enemy's left, and Captain Fraser's rangers, with Indians and Provincials, had orders to go by secret paths in the woods to gain the enemy's rear and by showing themselves there to keep them in a check."

Burgoyne poured himself another drink and dragged his hand through his hair before he took a sip, watching Kingston over the glass's rim.

Kingston sat as stiff as a mummy in the British Museum.

"The further operations intended were prevented by a very sudden and rapid attack of the enemy on our left, where the British grenadiers were ported to support the left wing of the line. Major Ackland, at the head of them, sustained the attack with great resolution, but the enemy's great numbers enabled them in a few minutes to extend the attack along the front of the Germans, which were immediately on the right of the grenadiers, no part of that body could be removed to make a second line to the flank, where the stress of the fire lay. The right was at this time engaged, but it was soon observed that the enemy was marching a large corps around their flank to endeavor to cut off their retreat. The light infantry and part of the 24th regiment, which were at that post, were therefore ordered to form a second line and secure the troops' return into camp. While this movement was proceeding, the enemy pushed a fresh and strong reinforcement to renew the action upon the left, which, overpowered by a great superiority, gave way, and the light infantry and 24th regiment were obliged to make a quick movement to save that point from being entirely carried, in doing which, Brigadier-General Fraser was mortally wounded."

His attention diverted, Burgoyne turned to the sizzling logs, wondering what he did wrong.

In silence, his thoughts linked; he watched the past weeks' streak in front of him, senseless that a trap was closing around him.

The Major put another log on the fire, bringing his general into the present.

"The danger to which the lines were exposed becoming at this moment of the most serious nature, orders were given to Major General Phillips and Riedesel to cover the retreat, while such troops as were most ready for the purpose returned for the defense of them. The troops retreated hard pressed, but in good order; they were obliged to leave six pieces of cannon, all the horses having been killed, and most of the artillery-men, who had behaved as usual with the utmost bravery under the command of Major Williams, being either killed or wounded.

The troops had scarcely entered the camp when it was stormed with great fury, the enemy rushing to the lines under a severe fire of grape-shot and small arms."

In the darkness of his night, Burgoyne stirred his memory, frowning down on it.

Frustrated, he rose, wondering how he would continue in life. Curiously, he seemed content to Kingston, who gave him a puzzled look.

Burgoyne met the challenge in his eyes while large waves from the Hudson lashed the coastline with a mighty force.

"The post of the light infantry under Lord Balcarras assisted by some of the line, which threw themselves by order into the entrenchments, was defended with great spirit, and the enemy led on by General Arnold was finally repulsed, and the General wounded, but unhappily the entrenchments of the German reserve, commanded by Lieutenant-Colonel Breymann, who was killed, were carried, and although ordered to be recovered, they never were so, and the enemy by that misfortune gained an opening on our right and rear. The night put an end to the action.

Under the disadvantages thus apparent in our situation, the army was ordered to quit the present position during the night and take post upon the heights above the hospital."

Glancing up, Kingston noticed Burgoyne was admiring a Royal Albert tea set with a floral bouquet. He studied his general with wide, astonished eyes.

"Thus by an entire change of front, to reduce the enemy to form a new disposition, a movement was effected in great order and without loss, though all the artillery and camp were removed simultaneously. The army continued offering battle to the enemy in their new position the whole day of the 8th.

We labored under a series of hard toil, incessant effort, and stubborn action; till disabled in the collateral branches of the army by the total defection of the Indians, the desertion or timidity of the Canadians and Provincials, some individuals excepted; disappointed in the last hope of any timely co-operation from other armies; the regular troops reduced by loses from the best part to 3500 fighting men, not 2000 of which were British; only three days provisions upon short allowance in-store; invested by an army of 16,000 men, and no apparent means of retreat remaining."

Burgoyne checked his watch, finding himself impatient that three hours remained before his meeting with Gates.

After a toss of his head, he downed another drink.

"Intelligence was now received that the enemy was marching to turn the right, and no means could prevent that measure but retire towards Saratoga. The army began to move at nine o'clock at night, Major-General Riedesel commanding the vanguard and Major-General Phillips at the rear.

This retreat, though within musket shot of the enemy and encumbered with all the baggage of the army, was made without loss, but very heavy rain and the difficulties of guarding the Bateaux, which contained all the provisions, occasioned delays that prevented the army reaching Saratoga till the night of the 9th, and the artillery could not pass the fords of the Fish-kill till the morning of the 10th.

At our arrival near Saratoga, a corps of the enemy, between five and six hundred, were discovered throwing up entrenchments on the heights but retired over a ford of the Hudson's River at our approach and joined a body posted to oppose our passage there."

A log tapped out of the hearth, crumbling in a shower of sparks, his life personified.

He gave what passed for a snicker before continuing his dictation.

"It was judged proper to send a detachment of artificers under a strong escort to repair the bridges and open a road to Fort Edward on the west side of the river. The 47th regiment, Captain Fraser's marksmen, and Mackoy's Provincials were ordered for that service, but the enemy appeared on the heights of the Fish-kill in great force and making a disposition to pass and give us battle: the 47th regiment and Fraser's marksmen were recalled; the Provincials left to cover the workmen at the first bridge run away upon a very slight attack of a small party of the enemy, and left the artificers to escape as they could, without a possibility of their performing any work.

During these different movements, the bateaux with provisions were frequently fired upon from the opposite side of the river, and some of them were lost, and several men were killed and wounded in those that remained.

The attacks upon the bateaux were continued; several were taken and retaken, but their situation being much nearer to the main force of the enemy than to ours, it was found impossible to secure the provisions any otherwise than by landing them and carrying them upon the hill: this was effected under fire and with great difficulty."

The image tore at his past grief; he wanted to kneel at his late wife Charlotte's grave. His eyes shifted to the window at his side.

Panic filled him at the thought of facing his critics.

"The possible means of further retreat was now considered in councils of war, composed of the general officers, minutes of which will be transmitted to your Lordship.

The only one that seemed at all practicable was, by a night march to gain Fort Edward with the troops carrying their provision upon their backs; the impossibility of repairing bridges, putting a conveyance of artillery and carriages out of the question, it was proposed to force the ford at Fort-Edward, or the ford above it.

Before this attempt could be made, scouts returned with the intelligence that the enemy was entrenched opposite these fords and possessed a camp in force on the high ground between Fort Edward and Fort George with cannon. They also had parties down the whole shore to watch our motions and posts so near to us, upon our own side of the water as must prevent the army moving a single mile undiscovered."

Kingston noticed the tightness in Burgoyne's voice never wavered, knowing there was enough pride left in him to repair his reputation, but the sound of defeat echoed in the latter's ears.

"The bulk of the enemy's army was hourly joined by new corps of militia and volunteers, and their numbers together amounted to upwards of 16,000 men. Their position, which extended three parts in four of a circle around us, was, from the nature of the ground, unattackable in all parts.

In this situation, the army took the best position possible and fortified, waiting till the 13th at night, in the anxious hope of succors from our friends or the next desirable expectation, an attack from our enemy.

During this time, the men lay continually upon their arms and were cannonaded in every part; even rifle shot and grape shot came into all parts of the line, though without any considerable effect.

At this period, an exact account of the provisions was taken, and the circumstances stated in the opening of this letter became complete.

The scouts, on their return, reported that the rebel's position on the right was such, and they had so many small parties out, that it would be impossible to move without our march being immediately discovered."

Burgoyne's blue eyes were hard and glittery, his seasoned face white with fury. He leaned against the wall and let his mind travel over his defeat from head to toe.

"We were a defeated army hoping to retreat from an enemy flushed with success, much superior in front, and occupying strong posts in the country behind. We were equally liable upon that march to be attacked in the front, flank, or rear. My army was entirely boxed between 4000 rebels behind him and 12000 in front of him. I had fewer than 5,800 men.

I called into council all the generals, field officers, and captains commanding corps of the army, and the event ensued which I am sure was inevitable, and which, I trust, in that situation was honorable, but which it would be superfluous and melancholy to repeat. By their unanimous concurrence and advice, I was induced to open a treaty with Major General Gates."

The quiet of the room was beginning to disturb him even more than the storm outside. After quickly circling the room, he rested in a chair by the window. At once, the playwright caught the scent of defeat, wanting to write another act.

Postscript
10/20/77 to George Germaine

"I well remembered that a preference of exertions was the only latitude given me and that to force a junction with Sir William Howe, or at least a passage to Albany, was the principle, the letter, and the spirit of my orders.

I then made a supposition that anything like what has happened might have happened and remained cautiously posted, no exertion attempted, my conduct would have been held indefensible by every class and distinction of men in government, in the army, and in the public, in the jaws of famine, and inverted by quadruple numbers, a treaty which saves the army to the state, for the next campaign, was not more than could have been expected?

I call it saving the army because if sent home, the state is thereby enabled to send forth the troops now destined for her internal defense; if exchanged, they become a force to Sir William Howe, as effectually as if any other junction had been made.

My conjectures were very different after the affair of Ticonderoga, but I am convinced they were delusive, and it is a duty as a soldier to confess it.

I grew to see the panic of the rebel troops is confined and of short duration; their enthusiasm is extensive and permanent.

In regard to myself, I am sunk in mind and body."

## Chapter 61

# JW relates 2nd Battle of Saratoga

The evening of the third night, still young at Richmond Hill, Wilkinson and Burr relaxed under the Veranda that sheltered them from a *thin fog hovering on the ground.* The sky's shades changed as Wilkinson talked, and Burr listened as the black blanket of velvet of the vault above sprinkled with shining gems.

"For ten days, from the 22nd of September to the 1st of October," said the general, "Gates and Arnold fired incriminations back and forth. The outcome left the latter excluded from headquarters and denied command of the right-wing, assigned to Major-general Lincoln. Arnold stayed in camp without command, and the command of Colonel Morgan's riflemen was put under the authority of headquarters as they were neither brigaded nor encamped in the line." Joy and contentment towered beside Burr when he began to hear a first-hand account of the events leading up to the battle. He intended to write a history of the War of the Revolution, the General continuing to entertain and inform him.

"Before the battle at Bemis Heights on the 4th or the second battle of Freeman's Farm, I, Major Wilkinson, found myself doing my general's bidding. That scalawag Richard Varrick who served on Arnold's staff at the time blamed me as being 'at the bottom of the dispute' and labeled me 'fundamentally a sycophant.' Wilkinson continued to shove the past out of his mind as Burr slanted a look at him with bold black eyes, both wary and clinical. "If I had known, I would have challenged him on the spot. Varrick and Brockworth Livingston were the instigators of this conflict. They hated Gates because he took over command from their benefactor, Schuyler. They believed Victory had been taken from Schuyler's hands when he was relieved of command. They had been writing letters to Schuyler criticising Gates since his arrival. Burr! Varrick opened a letter to Gates and sent a facsimile to Schuyler. After the first battle, they claimed that Arnold saved the day and that he would have defeated Burgoyne if Gates had followed his direction to attack. The hothead could not understand that Burgoyne would come to us under our terms, and his defeat was inevitable."

His tone, matter-of-fact, and a smile pulled at his mouth as he said, "The Battle of Saratoga, should not it be Saratogas? There were two of them."

Burr bent his head in a short, quick downward movement, smiling. After thinking and a heartfelt sigh, he said, "I like the plural." "I wrote, for my beloved Gates, a letter to Governor Clinton," the general hesitated before bringing forth, "Despair may dictate to him, to risque all upon one Throw; he is an old gamester & in his time has seen all chances."

Feeling a stiff breeze whipping in from the west, sending leaves scattering across the Hudson's starlight view, Burr watched a hawk swoop to the roof of the veranda, voicing a hoarse, screaming kee-me-arr unnoticed by Wilkinson, who continued talking.

"On the 5th of October, General Riedesel recommended to Burgoyne to withdraw to Battenkill where communications with the lakes could be established and await news from Clinton." "But it sounded like a retreat to his General. I've often wondered, Burr, Did it dawn on the playwright that retreat rhymed with defeat."

"The colorful sight of the German Dragoons, the advance guard, and a rear Guard composed of one Captain and Company from the Rear Regiment; the Provincials in the Rear of the British; the artillery between the main body and the rear Guard, and the Provost Guard a Quarter of a Mile in the rear of the whole marched from the British General's camp on the 7th hoping to escape entrapment."

For a moment, Wilkinson stared at Burr vacantly. Then, as though the devil burst onto the Veranda, the past continued to race before his eyes.

"He chose not to pause but to rush into danger, putting forth 1723 men and leaving 5423 to man the fortifications without a clue regarding the terrain or our strength.

Having just returned from a reconnoiter of the enemy, Gates asked me "what appeared to be the intentions of the enemy." "They are foraging and endeavoring to reconnoiter your left; and I think Sir, they offer you battle."

"What is the nature of the ground and your opinion?"

"Their front is open, and their flanks rest on woods, under cover of which they may be attacked; their right is skirted by a lofty height. I would indulge them."

"Well, then, order Morgan to begin the game."

Wilkinson's lips drew back, his teeth showing, and dimples deepened. "The battle began against 1500 British regulars and 600 Loyalists and Indians about the same hour & near the same spot of the ground as the first battle. Under cover of the woods, Morgan gained the height on the enemy's right. Poor's brigade of New Hampshire and New York troops attacked the flank and front of the British grenadiers. Morgan poured down like a torrent from the hill, attacking the enemy right in front and flank. Dearborn, at a precipitous moment, then pressed forward with ardour and delivered a close fire."

Burr gave Wilkinson a sufficient nod, much more than the General expected. With all smiles, he charged on - the war of words closest to his heart.

"Soon, we fell upon the enemy's right flank & partly in their rear, which soon obliged Burgoyne in person to quit. 'He gave way and made a precipitate and disorderly retreat, leaving two twelve and six six-pounders of their heavy artillery & a considerable number of waggons with ammunition and other stores. More than 400 officers and men were killed, wounded, or captured. And the flower of his officers destroyed."

A quick smirk was Burr's response. "Well, war can be rude when it wants. A child is lost and will do anything to get home."

"By nightfall, Burgoyne had retired to his original position behind a great fortified ravine. By leaving his remaining baggage and guns, he could have placed himself in a position to fight another campaign by retreating to fort Edward. But it was to defeat that Burgoyne proceeded. Out of delusion to his desire for military notoriety, he destroyed his own happiness like an enemy."

A British officer, Lieutenant Digby, described the battle in his journal. "The men and horses were all killed – which gave additional spirits, and they rushed on with loud shouts – we drove them back a little way, with so great loss to ourselves that it evidently appeared a retreat was the only thing left for us.

The force and abundance of this battle burned like fire. Bullets of burning coals, heated rocks, and daggers made men lie prostrate forever. Their flesh fallen away, bones the colour of a white rose. Comrades wailing in agony with feelings of grief, vexation, and despair. Their bodies inflicted with lacerations and waiting for amputations. Lives drowned in an ocean of misery, unending and savage, courtesy to Mr. Burgoyne."

The night at Richmond Hill aged, weak moonlight filtered through the bad-tempered fog as a rattling on the trees grew stronger. Were the animals listening to the general thought Burr?

"The next morning, I observed a sight that still haunts me."

Burr leaned forward. Wilkinson rose and walked around him.

"An artillery captain who distinguished himself as a commander staggered between hundreds of dead on the battlefield talking to some whom I presumed were his friends."

Burr showed no emotion, but Wilkinson noticed a sadness in his eyes.

"He broke his sword into pieces and wandered off into the woods."

Wilkinson yawned as the Hudson flowed rapidly from an earlier downpour, hissing and moaning as it cascaded below Burr's home.

"Gates noted in his report 'the gallant Major Genl. Arnold's leg was fractured by a Musket Ball as he was forcing the Enemies Breastwork.' He was observed on the field of battle serving his country unable to restrain himself, though without command yet barking out orders. The same knee injured at Quebec received a crippling shot."

Burr glanced back at Quebec's siege, looking over the field, realizing war glorifies killing rather than condemning it.

"At dusk," said Wilkinson, "a shower of song sprang from gray geese, ducks, black swans, and other exotic water birds that flew over the battlefield, paying no attention to men without limbs. Their throats parched and gazes wretched from feverish horror. Many silent like an axed log."

> like a dewdrop
> on a blade of grass,
> here one instant
> gone the next

"Yet, the playwright still longed for another act in which to achieve his brilliance. But the curtain touched the floor, the final battle occurred, and his army passed pointlessly to surrender by their fruitless association with a fool."

Wilkinson drew closer to Burr, not in friendship but as a comrade in arms.

"On the ninth, the enemy evacuated the whole of their lines, leaving 500 sick & wounded on the ground & a considerable quantity of provisions.

At Saratoga on the tenth Burgoyne was cannonaded by Gen Fellows while the main army marched towards him. We found everything in great confusion, baggage scattered along the road. One brass 12-pounder is buried in the ground. The cannonading was kept up all day, accompanied by a scattering fire of musketry.

By the 12th the enemy retreated to a better defensive position, but their line of march was now cut off. Further retreat from the high ground of the Hudson was prevented by the New England militia to the East side of the Hudson and northward by volunteers under General Benjamin Lincoln. In the evening his army came to rest at Saratoga."

The morning light was dim as the sun shot through the vines hanging on the sides of the Veranda. Catching Burr's attention, Wilkinson winked and patted him on the shoulder.

"Our force," said Wilkinson, "according to the best intelligence obtained amounted of upwards of 14,000 men, and a considerable quantity of artillery were on this side the Fish-kill, and threatened an attack. On the other side of the Hudson River, between our army and Fort Edward were more of our forces. According to Major Kingston, the numbers unknown to Burgoyne but one corps, which there had been an opportunity of observing, was reported to be about 1500 men, and cannon on the other side the Hudson's River was observed.

They were aware as stated by Kingston that we had a bridge below Saratoga church, by which our two armies could communicate." Wilkinson's eyes lit, and narrowed.

"The only means of retreat for Burgoyne's army therefore, was by the ford at Fort Edward, or by traversing the mountains in order to pass the river higher up by rafts, or by any other ford which was reported to be practicable with difficulty, or by keeping the mountains, to pass the head of Hudson's River, and continue to the westward of Lake George all the way to Ticonderoga. Very unlikely, this last passage was never made but by Indians, or very small bodies of men."

Wilkinson shook his head, and then a smile from ear to ear appeared. "The first thing he learned about a battle was that position was a powerhouse."

Burr smirked at Wilkinson's observation but said nothing, knowing the General was heading into his tale's far end.

"In order for the British to pass cannon or any wheel carriages from hence to Fort Edward, some bridges needed to be repaired, under fire by our men from the opposite side of the river. The principal bridge needed the work of fourteen or fifteen hours. There was no good position for Burgoyne's men to take to sustain that work, and if there were, the time stated as necessary would give our soldiers on the other side the Hudson's River an opportunity to take post on the strong ground above Fort Edward, or to dispute the ford while General Gates's main army followed in the rear."

With a strained calm, General Wilkinson continued.

"The next several days were engulfed by a thick London fog, and I saved General Learned from advancing into the enemy without the aid of our brethren who had retired." Wilkinson looked over his shoulder as if sensing a past event.

"We fortified our positions with Morgan's corps on the enemy's left and extended to their rear, and Glover and Nixon waited on the heights west of the great road. Even Burgoyne could now see the inside of a box with no way out.

Before he assembled his council of war, every part of his camp was exposed to grape and rifle shot, without power to counter our volley of disrespect."

Wilkinson reflected, smirking, thinking how well he performed and how indispensable he was.

Burr thought he was peeping rearward.

"On the night of the 15th of October, Burgoyne sent General Gates a letter stating a request to meet with both armies at a matter of high moment. The next morning, I met Major Kingston, his emissary, a well-informed, ruddy, handsome man who was brought blindfolded to General Gate's headquarters about a mile in the distance. Always willing to exhibit friendship, I listened as Kingston extolled with taste and eloquence to the beautiful scenery of the Hudson's River and the charm of the season."

Wilkinson swirled his drink without drinking, sending Burr a calm, direct stare, Burr considering it too early in the morning for wine.

"Several letters passed between Gates and Burgoyne. The latter hearing that Henry Clinton was approaching Albany. He proposed to forego surrender and spoke of resuming combat. His two aides were far less sanguine. I appealed to their sense of honour through artful logic and guise.

The interactions between the General's aides led me to pursue a course that would convince Sutherland that Burgoyne violated his word, to surrender, something Gentleman do not do."

Laughing, Burr squeezed his hand. "I know you know about the code of being a gentleman."

The General winked at him.

"Gates, tired of delays, commanded that the negotiations be broken off, too many deadlines had passed but I persisted with Sutherland. Another thirty minutes, I asked the messenger to tell why General Burgoyne did indeed finally sign the surrender documents, referred to as a Convention, before Gates ordered a return to the field of battle.

The next day dawned and what a glorious one, clear and cool with the forest in color. I escorted the defeated General to the American camp. Gates in an unadorned blue coat stood with Burgoyne with gold-braided scarlet coat and the Hessian commander General Friedrich Von Riedesel with dark coat adorned with gilded epaulets."

Burr tried to imagine his friend standing beside the dignified trio of generals. It did not add up.

Wilkinson, giddy over the prospect of bragging about his role in the surrender.

"I, a youth in plain blue frock without military insignia than a cockade and a sword, stood in the presence of three experienced European generals, soldiers before my birth–yet the consciousness of my independence did not shake my purpose. I, the unadorned young soldier, went on to introduce the generals. Burgoyne doffed his hat to Gates, 'The fortune of war, General Gates, has made me a prisoner.' Gates responded I shall always be ready to testify that it was not through any fault of your excellency. An hour later, the British marched out of our camp to the beat of their drums while piling up their muskets. Lieutenant Digby observed that the drums seemed almost ashamed to be heard on such an occasion."

Burr opened his mouth to speak but only uttered a muted breath.

The notoriously lavish Wilkinson shelled out the last act of Burgoyne's defeat. "Yes, Burr, the British General fell upon the wrong path in the wilderness. He became a slave to weariness and, in his mind, fearful of thieves, bears, and other predators. Soon, unconscious as space, he came to live in emptiness, for the delusion of what had to be done remained an illusion. As strategy was beyond his conception he dwelled in the inconceivable. Finally, he gave up hope that he may still get his own way. He had longed for the impossible and found torment in the fact that all his hopes were shattered. He did not realize that life is like a dream and he could dream anew. But fame and honour generated so much pride in him that he destroyed his own path as well as others."

"Yet," said Burr, "we owe our freedom to him. He defeated our enemy."

"When the people heard," said Wilkinson, "he was crushed, the great one became the object of everyone's ridicule."

Wilkinson looking down at his empty glass, poured himself another glass of Madeira as he said, "From his defeat, burst the bell of liberty, chiming upon American soil." A soft breeze drifted through the land, refreshing the air, ruffling the leaves of liberty. "He did not know it then, but the King stopped running into the Queen's room with a swaggering show of superiority."

The General studied his glass and said nothing for a moment or two

"I remember reading in a newspaper," said Burr, "a true account of Britons loss in the northern department in America 1777 at Huberton, Fort Anne, Bennington, Fort Stanwix, Still Water & Saratoga in kill'd wounded & taken in the whole 10,250 men & 47 pieces of brass artillery besides a vast quantity of stores baggage &c."

"The autumn sky after Burgoyne's surrender," said General Wilkinson, "belched with thunder as a dark storm released tears of compassion from the bowels of heaven. Droplets of hard rain swelled the streams to rivers, producing a roar, loud and rough. It continued from the 27th until the 29th. So heavy, the rain was never known before. The ground, needing a cleansing of the blood of war for the men gone to that sleep which knows no waking."

'All the world's a stage,
And all the men and women merely players
They have their exits and their entrances'
-the Bard

# Chapter 62

# Loss of Burgoyne

The following appeared in newspapers:

Here followeth the direful fate
Of Burgoyne and his army great
Who so proudly did display
The terrors of despotic sway.
His power and pride and many threats
Have been brought low by fort'nate Gates
To bend to the United States.

British prisoners by Convention, 2442
Foreigners—by Contravention, 2198
Tories sent across the Lake, 100
Burgoyne and his suite, in state,
Sick and wounded, bruised and pounded, 12
Ne'er so much before confounded, 528
Prisoners of war before Convention, 400
Deserters come with kind intention, 300
They lost at Bennington's great battle,
Where Starke's glorious arms did rattle, 1220
Kill'd in September and October, 600
Ta'en by brave Brown*, some drunk, some sober. 413
Slain by high-famed Herkerman**
On both flanks, on rear and van, 300
Indians, settlers, butchers, drovers,
Enough to crowd large plains all over,
And those whom grim Death did prevent
From fighting against our continent;
And also those who stole away,

Lest they down their arms should lay.
Abhorring that obnoxious day;
The whole make fourteen thousand men, 4413
Who may not with us fight again.
This is a pretty just account
Of Burgoyne's legion's whole amount,
Who came across the Northern Lakes
To desolate our happy States.
Their brass cannons we have got all—
Fifty-six—both great and small;
And ten thousand stand of arms,
To prevent all future harms;
Stores and Implements complete.
Of workmanship exceeding neat;
Cover'd wagons in great plenty,
And proper harness, no way scanty.
Among our prisoners there are
Six generals, of fame most rare;
Six members of their Parliament—
Reluctantly they seem content;
Three British lords, and Lord Belcarras,
Who came, our country free to harass.
Two baronets, of high extraction,
were sorely wounded in the action.
    *Col. John Brown, of Mass. **
    Gen. Herkimer, of New York

## Chapter 63

## At Monticello

While imprisoned at Charlottesville, Virginia, after the British defeat at Saratoga, General Riedesel and his wife found themselves as a guest of Thomas Jefferson at Monticello. They walked the grounds with Jefferson, whose head tilted back slightly and a baby smile adoring his tanned face; he told them, "I grow 330 vegetable varieties in this 1000-foot-long garden terrace." He failed to mention that "i" consisted of slaves of every size and shape. Mrs. Riedesel noticed a pasted shyness on his face as Jefferson pointed at his orchards, "There are 170 fruit varieties of apples, peaches, grapes."

She thought there was joy and righteousness here. A pause occurred, a language one. Fumbling, Mrs. Riedesel tried to fill it. A pale light from the cloudy sky draped over them as they crossed the lawn and returned to the unpainted plaster dining room; Mrs. Riedesel looking at the high, crisp walls. Jefferson's curiosity about the Battles of Saratoga charged forward, and he maneuvered Mrs. Riedesel to talk of Burgoyne.

"Having settled into the comforts of the home of Colonel Skene at Whitehall," she told her host, "General Burgoyne invited General Riedesel and me to dinner."

Jefferson stared at General Riedesel, then back at Mrs. Riedesel. "You should write an account of your time in America," he said in thoughtfully spaced words.

Her mind opened to the swift suggestion. She turned off the present and onto the private past. All she knew, in her gut, tumbled from her lips." It is very true," claimed Mrs. Riedesel, "that General Burgoyne liked to make himself easy and spent half his nights in singing and drinking and diverting himself."

With a reluctant smile tugging at Jefferson's mouth, he whispered, "That is disgusting."

"General Riedesel would say to him, 'There are only a few dozen ambitious people who direct this whole affair and who make the land unhappy. As for the others, they do not know why they fight.'"

Jefferson cocked his head and rolled his eyes, proud he was among the few dozen.

"Every night, General Burgoyne raised his glass several times," said General Riedesel, "We must find some good hemp and a tall tree."

Jefferson choked on his wine, the image unsettling him. He blushed and laughed at his regression and then regained a sober countenance.

Wishing she could capture the look on his face, Mrs. Riedesel studied his gaze, thinking he drinks like a camel. Jefferson then drank another glass of wine to elevate his spirits.

"Mr. Jefferson, let me tell you of the éclat of the aristocracy and kindness towards the foe. A few days after the defeat, I drew near the tents; a good-looking man advanced towards me, helped my children from the clash, and kissed and caressed them. He then offered me his arm, and tears swelled in his eyes. 'You tremble,' he said, 'do not be alarmed, I will pray for you.' 'Sir,' I cried, 'a countenance so expressive of benevolence, and the kindness you have displayed towards my children, are sufficient to dispel all apprehension.' He then ushered me into the tent of General Gates."

She breathed, drew in another, and tasted goodwill, sweet and genuine. "The gentleman who had received me with so much kindness said to me, 'You may find it embarrassing to be the only lady in such a large company of gentlemen; will you come with your children to my tent and partake of a frugal dinner, offered with the best will?' 'By the kindness you show to me,' I returned, 'you induce me to believe you have a wife and children.'"

Eyebrows lifting, Jefferson studied her, admiring the curves of her body.

"He informed me that he was General Schuyler and regaled me with smoked tongues, which were excellent, with beef steaks, potatoes, fresh butter, and bread. Never did a dinner give me so much pleasure as this. After many months of anxiety, I was easy and read the same happy change in the countenances of those around me."

The evening with Jefferson continued quiet and convertible. She learned that he was elected Governor of the Commonwealth of Virginia by joint ballot (sixty-seven to sixty-one) by the two houses of the Assembly over his close friend, John Page, on the second ballot. None of the original three candidates having a majority in the contest, Mr. Jefferson took up residence at the Governor's Palace in Williamsburg in the summer of 1779.

## Chapter 64

## PH Another Term

Nominated by Richard Henry Lee for a second term as governor, no other candidate put forward. Jefferson reiterated allegations about Patrick's aspirations for a dictatorship, but they only existed in Jefferson's jealous mind. Insecure of Henry, he smelled rot and mildew when Henry was re-elected by acclamation on May 29, 1777, making a flourishing bow as glasses clinked later that night.

As governor, Henry's heart pounded like a blacksmith's hammer, recruitment problems foremost on his mind. "Although it seems impossible," Henry informed Washington. "To enlist continental recruits here, yet the zeal of our countrymen is great and general in the public cause."

A few days later, his daughter burst into his office in tears. "Your uncle Patrick died."

Patrick stood rooted for a moment, then rushed off to Hanover, his sadness mitigated by the marriage of his sister, Elizabeth. At the wedding, he observed the eighteen-year-old Dorothea Dandridge, Martha Washington's first cousin and the grown-up daughter of his friend, Nathaniel West Dandridge. Remembering holding her in his arms seventeen years earlier, he wanted to run his hand through her black hair.

Slightly older than his daughter, the forty-year-old Patrick fell in love with Dolly, her nickname since her youth. Unknown to Patrick, his son, John, who served as an artillery captain in the northern campaign against Burgoyne, asked Dolly's father for her hand.

Dolly rumbled in his mind in early July after returning to Williamsburg, but the British haunted his every moment, having received intelligence that a large fleet carrying 15,000 men was sailing towards Chesapeake. Governor Henry called up troops to meet the enemy if they attempted to land. Learning that General Howe was not interested in Virginia but in Philadelphia, Henry rode back to Hanover and asked his friend for permission to marry his daughter. The forty-one-year-old man married Dolly on October 19, 1777, and with her came twelve slaves, increasing his bound workers to forty-two.

"Husband," said Dolly, "the Governor's mansion is a homecoming for me." She drew his hand through her arm and led him upstairs. "My grandfather, Alexander Spotswood, directed the building of the mansion, and my mother was born here."

"Well, my love, you should be at ease directing the social and other obligations of the governor's wife."

"I can do it with tact and grace and take care of your five children." Smiling, she led him to their bedroom, his essence falling into a void when she looked him in the eye, forgetting everything but that he was finally alone with her.

Henry jumped from his desk the next morning when news of Burgoyne's defeat reached Virginia. After informing Dolly, who asked if he had received a letter from his son, "No."

Later that day, he ordered discharges from the cannon, three volleys of musket fire, and three huzzahs from all present. On Gloucester Street or at the Raleigh Tavern, he participated in the joy and satisfaction upon the occasion. In the evening, he ordered a gill of rum for each soldier amidst ringing bells and illuminations, declaring to Williamsburg's patriots, "God save the British colonies the United States."

Confidently, he walked from his past and sold his Scotchtown plantation. He bought ten thousand acres in Henry County, a new jurisdiction in southern Virginia, and named his estate Leatherwood.

Governor Henry wanted Washington's permission to direct military affairs in Virginia, but they were not always on the same page regarding Congress and Virginia's interests. Receiving an anonymous letter that implored him to destroy it, the addressee asked Henry to spread the word that Washington needed a replacement as commander-in-chief. Henry forwarded the letter to the General with a note.

"You will no doubt be surprised at seeing the enclosed letter, which the accolades bestowed on me are as underserved as the censures aimed at you are unjust. I am sorry, there should be one man who counts himself as my friend who is not yours."

Five weeks later, Washington responded, "Your friendship, Sir, in transmitting me the anonymous letter you received lays me under the most grateful obligations." Washington noted on the cover of the letter, "The Superscription on the Back (from its Similarity) proves that Doctr Rush was the Author of the Letter to Govr Henry and for that purpose is filed with it." The General told Henry, "I am disgusted with Rush's hypocrisy, for Rush recently spoke kindly of me."

Wrongly judging Henry's feelings towards Washington, Rush's actions towards the Commander might have gained momentum if Henry sided with a group in Congress who wanted to replace the General. Henry learned that Washington had miscalculated his strength after Howe's army landed on the northern shore near Philadelphia. Centering the Patriot lines along the East bank of Brandywine Creek, which blocked Philadelphia's road, he erred, allowing Lord Cornwallis, the British General, to sneak 8,000 troops to the Northeast and circle behind Washington's lines. From being closed in from three directions, Washington's army lost 900-1000 men during the retreat.

Benjamin Rush, a signer of the Declaration of Independence, a close friend of J. Adams, B. Franklin, and T. Jefferson, who served as the Continental Army's middle department's medical director, plotted to relieve Washington of command as his military acumen was gone like yesterday. Because of his deep and steadfast belief in Washington, History turned on Henry's loyalty to his fellow Virginian.

# Chapter 65

# The Bastard Confers with the Butler

Hamilton, set to dine with Lafayette and Laurens the third week of October 1777, was summoned to Emlen House, Washington's headquarters near White Marsh, Maryland. Washington informed him, "There is news of Burgoyne's defeat but no official word from General Gates."

His excellency paused his head jutted forward in a steady gaze as Hamilton noticed his displeasure at not being informed.

"Good heaven!" exclaimed Washington, "what can be the meaning of this?"

"I could bring the news in four days," said Alex, who took this neglect as an arrogant slight and an insult to his commander.

Washington gave Alex an absent nod and said, "Clear my schedule and notify the necessary major generals and brigadiers that there is a meeting in an hour, and you draft the minutes."

Too angry to utter another word, he dismissed Hamilton.

Alex, concerned about Washington's distress, knew those in Congress wanted to have control over the war and were dismayed over his generalship; he refused to accept this fate.

Samuel Adams and his cousin, John, and Henry Lee, were prominent among this group. They bought the Gates line, "You generaled a Road Builder," his victory at Saratoga cementing their ire.

With the general's chin resting on his clenched hand, Alex reentered and said, "Congress does not know a weed from a daisy."

Washington delighted his aide with a smile.

Stepping outside into the cool evening air, Alex listened to John Laurens tell him about the politics of Philadelphia.

"I just finished reading a letter," said Laurens, "that stated that the radical Benjamin Rush of Pennsylvania, a member of the Continental Congress, gossips that General Greene governs Washington, General Knox, and me." He stopped and looked Alex in the eye and said in French for the benefit of Lafayette, "Colonel Hamilton, one of his top aides, is a young man of twenty-one years."

Alex grimaced very broadly, puffing out his chest, and then informed his best friends that Washington's command was in jeopardy."

"I was thinking the same thing," said Laurens.

"You should write to your father," said Alex.

His father, Henry Laurens, resided as president of the Continental Congress.

"At the war council that night, Alex sat aside, taking notes for his general.

"It is necessary to strengthen our position," said General Wayne.

"Gates must relinquish a good number of his troops," said General Greene, vexation inching up his spine.

"The British threat in New York is considerably diminished," said General Knox, who thought he heard rain drumming on the ground.

Washington looked around at the war council members, all nodding in accord.

Turning to Hamilton, Washington said, "Colonel Hamilton make haste to Albany and inform General Gates of our decision."

Hamilton galloped off the following day carrying a letter, but not before Laurens and Lafayette instructed him to delve into his core and bring forth – cunning and diplomacy.

The letter:

"Head Quarters near White Marsh,

15 Miles from Philadelphia, October 30, 1777.

Sir: By this Opportunity, I do myself the pleasure to congratulate you on the signal success of the Army under your command in compelling Genl. Burgoyne and his whole force surrender themselves as prisoners of war. An Event that does the highest honor to the American Arms and which, I hope, will be attended with the most extensive and happy consequences. At the same time, I cannot but regret that a matter of such magnitude and so interesting to our General Operations should have reached me by report only or thru the Channel of Letters, not bearing that authenticity, which the importance of it required, and which it would have received by a line under your signature, stating the simple fact."

Washington paused then walked toward the south wall of his headquarters before continuing. "Our affairs having happily terminated at the Northward, I have, by the advice of my Gen'l Officers, sent Colo. Hamilton, one of my aids, to lay before you a full state of our situation and that of the Enemy in this Quarter. He is well-informed on the subject and will deliver my Sentiments on the plan of operations that is now necessary to be pursued. I think it improper to enter into a particular detail, not being well advised how matters are circumstanced on the North River and fearing that by some accident, my Letter might miscarry. From Colo. Hamilton, you will have a clear and comprehensive view of things, and I persuade myself you will do all in your power to facilitate the objects I have in contemplation."

To Albany, three-hundred miles distant, Hamilton rode sixty miles a day, thinking how he would deal with Gates, who stood as a hero to the people.

Stopping at Fishkill on the Hudson's eastern shore, he sought an audience with General Israel Putnam, whom he informed, "His Excellency needs more men."

Putnam listened to the young pup because of protocol.

"How many?"

"You must shift two brigades southward to help General Washington."

Putnam swallowed, hard thinking 500-800 men.

Writing to Washington that night, November 2, "I induced Putnam to promise an additional seven hundred men of a New Jersey militia. I concluded you would not disapprove of a measure calculated to strengthen you, though not but for a short time, and have ventured to adopt it on that presumption."

While studying the letter, Washington smiled more than a little, a rare thing for him, thinking how lucky he was to have Hamilton on his staff.

Upon further reading, Washington read that Alex was "Eager to move on and that a quartermaster was pressing some fresh horses for me. The moment they are ready, I shall recross the River in order to fall in with the troops on the other side and make all haste to Albany to get the three brigades there sent forth."

Arriving in Albany on November 5, he met with Gates, who struck him as vain and inept. Staring at his gray hair and glasses on his long, pointed nose, Alex later derided him in a note to Laurens as "Granny Gates.

"I am," said Gates, "reluctant to cede any of my brigades."

"General Washington must have the men!"

"Sir Henry still might march up the Hudson and threaten New England."

"The likelihood of that happening, sir, is.

Gates cut him off, wishing he possessed the power to put a hex on him.

"I will send a single brigade commanded by General Patterson."

Before retiring for a needed sleep, Alex met with Robert Troup, who informed him that Patterson's brigade was "lacking."

Later that evening, he wrote to Gates, "These six hundred men are by far the weakest of the brigade now here."

Stopping momentarily, he uttered, "What a puffed, ridiculous, imprudent, conniving turncoat."

Continuing his note, "Under these circumstances, I cannot consider it either compatible with the good of the service or any instructions from His Excellency, General Washington, to consent that that brigade be selected from the three to go to him."

Alex managed one muted groan, then lost himself in writing another letter before sleep captured his eyes. "I used every argument in my power to convince him," he wrote to Washington, "of the propriety of sending troops, but he was inflexible in the opinion that two brigades, at least of Continental troops, should remain in and near this place."

Letting the issue rest with Gates, Alex spent the next day with Robert Troup, who told him, "General Schuyler preceded Gates as head of the Northern Department and laid the groundwork for the triumph at Saratoga."

Alex, picturing the slime Gates jumping up and down like a four-legged weasel.

"Gates," said Troup, "is a child of fortune."

Alex vowed to knock him down. *You attack my general; you strike me*, was his thought.

Dining at General Schuyler's mansion with Troup, Alex met the twenty-year-old daughter of the general, Eliza, whose figure left a lasting impression. He kept his face blank, her eyes reminding him of a Greek goddess.

Not able to get any further concessions from Gates, he rushed off down the Hudson.

Stopping at the residence in New Windsor of George Clinton, governor of New York, he learned that the two brigades promised by Putnam never appeared.

Before retiring, he wrote to General Putnam.

Head Quarters New Windsor [New York]

Novr. 9th. 1777

Sir, I cannot forbear Confessing that I am astonished. And Alarmed beyond measure to find that all his Excellency's Views have been hitherto frustrated and that no single step of those I mentioned to you has been taken to afford him the aid he absolutely stands in Need of, and by Delaying which the Cause of America is put to the Utmost conceivable Hazard."

Fearing he exceeded his authority, Alex wrote to Washington that he told Putnam, "I now, Sir, in the most explicit terms, by his Excellency's Authority, give it as a positive Order from him, that all the Continental Troops under your Command may be Immediately marched to Kings Ferry, there to Cross the River and hasten to Reinforce the Army under him."

Washington responded, "I approve entirely of all the steps you have taken and have only to wish that the exertions of those you have had to deal with had kept pace with your zeal and good intentions."

Alex spent two extra days at New Windsor, "Delayed," he wrote Washington on November 12, "by a fever and violent rheumatic pains throughout my body."

Despite his sickness, he rode south, directing troop's movement to join Washington, and he put pressure on Putnam for the brigades.

In Putnam's defense, he learned that the brigades' men refused to obey orders until they received paid. It pained him that money proceeded liberty.

At Peekskill, in late November, Alex collapsed in a bed in the home of Dennis Kennedy.

Captain I. Gibb reported that Hamilton "seemed to have all the appearance of drawing nigh his last, being seized with a coolness in his extremities, and he remained so for a space of two hours."

The next day his legs from feet to knees were chilled, and this, combined with a fever that lasted for four hours, left his attending physician to pronounce, *he is a goner.*

Little did he know Hamilton, who remembered speaking to his mother during his coma when they both were at death's door back in 1768 in St. Croix.

Rachael's boy did not fully recover until January 20, 1778, when he joined his general at the winter quarters in Valley Forge, near Philadelphia.

"The general is well but much worn with fatigue and anxiety," Martha Washington told Alex, "I never knew him to be so anxious as now."

Hamilton looked around the camp, seeing mud and log huts, men shivering by campfires, snow stained from the blood of bare, bruised feet, carcasses of scores of decomposing horses, and troops ravaged by smallpox, typhus, and scurvy.

For breakfast, he joined his fellow officers eating cornmeal mush, the talk that for some days past, there had been little less than a famine in the camp.

"Your Excellency," said Alex, "to bolster morale, let me stage a play.

For a second, Washington thought him mad. "Suffering requires stoicism." Washington listened. "The ancient Romans are a good example of self-sacrificing statesmen."

The play took second fiddle to Alex helping plan with Washington the military campaign for the next year in the stone house of Isaac Potts, whose iron gorge gave the area its name of Valley Forge.

Day and night, he recorded for his general, "Some 2,500 men, almost a quarter of the army, perished from disease, famine, or the cold."

Before sleep ambushed his eyes, he read Addison's *Cato*, "A man must be both stupid and uncharitable who believes there is no virtue or truth but on his own side."

## Chapter 66

## Wilky Stirs the Pot

On the last day of the long weekend in 1796, Wilky, still the young Cain, and Burr "not yet exiled" by the God, Jefferson, sat in chairs with slightly angled seats and a back-rest facing an open westerly window at Richmond Hill.

They exhaled concentric rings of rich, pervading, and aromatic cigar smoke. Taking note of the "rings," the record stood at nine; Wilky frowned, watching his 7th ring fail to perform its intended result, the night still in its puberty. Tired of losing, he took to pacing, his arms whirling in motion; his inhibitions gone like a child's innocence.

Colonel Burr, the cagey one, sat quickly for a moment, reflecting, deliberating, and then directed the general with a question, and off to the bombastic went the indomitable Wilky.

"Is it true you almost died after Burgoyne's surrender?"

The alluring and attractive Theo entered and sat, leaning beside her father.

"Burr! My belly screamed with pain. I could not mount a horse. Convulsive colic brought on by the campaign. On a bed in a wagon by the side of Colonel Philip Van Courtland of the New York troops, we were conveyed to Albany, where I nearly expired the next night."

Theo observed that the general pressed his lips into a thin line and thought them inoffensive (little did she know), complete and sharply sculpted.

"On October 20, 1777, freed from death, a surgeon of the hospital, Doctor Hagan, accompanied me with "Dispatches, from my General of the "treaty convention," to the president of Congress. I was still enfeebled, but duty required me to go forth. The first days and nights of my journey were painful in the extreme, but moderate exercise and climate change gave me strength, yet I was extremely sensitive to fatigue. On the 24th, I achieved Easton."

In true Wilkinsonian fashion, he lingered, remembering he spent two days with his "Nancy" and fell in with Doctor William Shippen, whose anatomical lectures he had attended in 1774-5.

"Relentless torrents of rain detained my news to Congress."

Burr and his daughter observed sweat on his brow as he worked hard to recall an incident. After a few seconds, he continued, "Upon the invitation of Lord Alexander Sterling, who was confined to the village at Reading due to a fall from his horse, I consented to take a potluck dinner with him."

Something in his tone, a hint of anxiety, made Theo want to comfort him, thinking her father was lucky to have such a good friend. Ha Ha

"I learned from Lord Sterling that the new Board of War, composed of leading men, intended to throw obstacles and difficulties in General Washington's way. They wanted to force him to resign."

Burr could not but smile and sighed out an approving inward chuckle.

Wilky's eyes were open like a cave, with much mystery in the background. He looked straight at Burr, whose black eyes locked on his.

If anything could be more, it was always the grasp of politics wanting power, thought Burr.

"Dr. James Craik, the General's physician," said Wilky, who winked, "had connections at Congress and made sure Washington was informed of the threat to his authority." General Wilkinson paused and took a deep breath; his cheeks indented briefly. Carefully, he said, "One faction was tired of another blunder by General Washington."

He smiled at Theo, who sneezed and took a handkerchief Wilkinson handed her.

"After defeating Washington at Brandywine on September 11," said Wilkinson, "and General Wayne's encampment near the Paoli Tavern on September 20, General Howe outfoxed Washington, seizing Philadelphia, our newly proclaimed capital."

Burr withheld a smile and picked up his glass of water, sipping slowly to soothe his dry throat.

"The other faction in Congress," said Wilkinson, "understood Gates pursued the correct strategy in entrapping Burgoyne."

"Factions," said Burr, "each perfectly knowing the correct path and protesting against the other's path as most injurious."

"Sides are always drawn," said Wilkinson.

He frowned at this knowledge, remembering only one person (he) brought the anti-Washington forces to the foreground. Making the issue public, he birthed the Conway Cabal, the censure of Washington, and his handling of the war, ending up to the ears of the Second Continental Congress.

"I was waiting for the rain, hail, and snow with a gale so piercing to let up," said Wilky, "that no matter how warmly wrapped, it penetrated to the very marrow."

The statement sent Burr into a fresh memory, recalling Valley Forge. The cold was one thing, but the most dangerous threat was disease. After six months, 2,000 men—about one in six—died.

"That night, I dined with Major General Sterling."

Wilky stopped, recalling Sterling, "A vain man, extremely well satisfied with himself."

The pot calling the kettle black thought Burr.

Wilky gave Burr an awkward smile.

"Yes, we dined with his two aides, James Monroe and William McWilliams."

Burr, finding Wilky so determined upon telling his tale, remained silent.

"A brandy or several landed upon the table at Sterling's headquarters that evening," related Wilky. "Serenaded by the continuing rain, the conversation too copious and diffuse to remember."

The liquor led the twenty-year-old to utter private words of his general, Gates. The imbibed tongue of the cunning Wilky spat forth a quote from a letter of General Conway to his friend Gates. "Heaven has determined to save your country, or a weak General and bad counselors would have ruined it."

"The next day with the rain abated," said Wilky, "I put spurs to my horse and continued with Gates' papers for the waiting Congress in York, Pennsylvania. A deluge that would have impressed Noah caused the Schuylkill to overflow its banks, thus delaying my arrival until October 31."

Burr lifted a brow. "I suppose you notice it rains a lot when you travel?"

Wilky ignored the retort.

"Upon arriving at York, I met the delegates, giving them relief. I informed them that the letters needed arranging, and I was granted till the following morn to present the papers in their proper order. The delegates did, indeed, revel in the official news. Things had not been going well."

Burr recalled hearing that Dr. Witherspoon, in Congress, opposed giving a sword to Wilky for bringing official news of Burgoyne's surrender. He suggested, "Ye'll better give the lad a pair of spurs."

There was a pause, an unexpected one, but Wilkinson filled it.

"I took leave to Valley Forge where I learned from Dr. Craik that 47

Colonels opposed my promotion to brigadier General by brevet of Congress."

Burr could see that this memory was still a thorn in his pride. He knew that after learning of the statement by Conway, General Washington, on November 4, wrote him regarding the line in his letter to General Gates, "a weak General or bad counselors" and asked for an explanation." The matter became public, Burr recalled, when Conway sent to Henry Laurens, president of Congress, his original letter to Gates and his recent communication with Washington.

Becoming informed of Washington's communication to Conway, Gates became obsessed with finding "the wretch who betrayed him." He investigated the issue but to no avail.

When his Wilky returned, after stopping to see "Nancy" Biddle again, General Gates questioned his young aide, who professed innocence.

The General failed to see that something wary, like a frown, tugged at Wilky's mouth.

"Perhaps," said Wilky, "Robert Troup."

"My aide," said Gates, "who delivered the letter from Conway?"

'Maybe he incautiously conversed on the substance of Conway's letter with Colonel Hamilton, who was at our camp?"

Gates sat down to think and was downcast, thinking it a wretched business.

"You should write Washington," said Wilky, "that your private correspondence has been illicitly purveyed!"

Gates smiled, pleasing Wilky.

General Washington wrote back, informing Gates that Colonel Wilkinson communicated the information to Major McWilliams in a "friendly view to forewarn, and consequently forearm me, against a secret enemy."

Thus the Conway Cabal was born and died in its infancy.

As Wilky selectively gave his account of his indiscretion, Burr recalled a conversation at a tavern with Robert Troup. They would later study law together for twelve hours a day.

"As part of the prisoner exchange after the loss of Long Island," said Troup. "I ended up serving on the staff of Gates during the fall of 1777."

"Another round," said Burr to the friendly barmaid, who subtly flirted with him.

"He tore the General's heart," said Troup, "when he learned that his "Wilky" was the leak. His very aide stood surefooted as a young god and spoke with soft and slow sentences stemming from passion, crystal in substance, and pleasing to one's senses."

Burr remembered observing Troup's eyes narrowing, wondering where the truth lay.

"Colonel Wilkinson's reaction," said Troup, "to his indiscretion was to challenge Gates to a duel,"

Burr recalled that Troup paused and shivered, the incident still chilling him.

"Burr," he said after another round. I still recall Wilkinson's words, "In spite of every consideration, you have wounded my honor and must make acknowledgment or satisfaction for the injury."

Burr's sunny look and bearing turned severe. He suspected that Wilky bathed in mud.

"The farce continued," said Troup, "as the young colonel also challenged Sterling, but through the efforts of Clement Biddle, an accord was reached."

"Burr!" said General Wilkinson later in the evening of '96, "Lord Sterling informed me that General Conway told him that I denied the reported words of the letter in question. He possessed the nerve to ask me if Conway made such an inquiry and, if so, my response. I informed Sterling that I could not recapitulate particulars and that I disdain low craft, subtlety, and evasion and will acknowledge it is possible, in the warmth of social intercourse, when the mind is relaxed. The heart is unguarded, that observations may have elapsed which have not since occurred to me." Burr suspected that the ambidextrous Wilky played both sides, something he would learn firsthand in the future

"I further went on to inform his Lordship," said Wilky, "I can scarce credit my senses when I read the paragraph in which you request an extract from a private letter which had fallen under my observation. I have been discreet, my lord, but be assured I will not be dishonorable."

Pleased with himself and Burr's smile, Wilky decided to tell him more.

"At the Board of War, my reception from Gates did not correspond with his recent professions; he was civil, but barely so, and I was at a loss to account for his coolness but had no suspicion of his insincerity."

Burr thought Wilky looked more pleased than he cared to express.

"Always sensitive to my wounded honor, I wrote a moderated letter to Lord Sterling."

Burr shot him a curious look. "Honour fascinates you."

General Wilkinson looked through him. "It is the only true path."

The General drew closer to Burr as he spoke, "My Lord, I said in the letter – the propriety or impropriety of communicating to his Excellency any circumstance which passed at your lordship's board at Reading; I leave it to be determined by your own feeling and the judgment of the public. But as the affair has eventually induced reflections on my integrity, the sacred duty I owe my honor obliges me to request from your lordship's hand that the conversation which you published passed in a private company during a social hour."

Seeing Burr's lip quiver, Wilkinson set his eyes firmly on his. Their eyes met but died away as Wilky continued, "Sterling replied that words passed under such circumstances, but they passed without any injunction of secrecy. Pacified, I gave up the idea of issuing a challenge."

Burr knew through the efforts of Clement Biddle that Wilky met with General Washington, who came to believe that Colonel Wilkinson "was rather doing an act of justice than committing an act of infidelity" when he quoted from Conway's letter.

"Washington said to me," exclaimed Wilkinson, "I beg leave to receive the grateful homage of a sensible mind for your admission in exposing to me General Gate's letters, which unmask his artifices and efforts to ruin me."

"The authenticity of the information," I replied to Washington, "received through Lord Sterling I cannot confirm, as I solemnly assure your Excellency I do not remember the conversation which passed on that occasion, nor can I recollect particular passages of that letter, as I had but a cursory view of it at a late hour. However, I so well remember its general tenor that, although General Gates had pledged his word it was a wicked and malicious forgery, I will stake my reputation if the genuine letter is produced, that words to the same effect will appear."

Burr drew in a breath, then let it out with a wink. "Go on."

"When in White Plains, New York, to give testimony in Arthur St. Clair's court-martial for the loss of Ticonderoga, I encountered Gates."

Burr knew what was coming and let him undress the incident.

"I once again challenged him to a duel for alleged remarks concerning his conduct at the duel at York the preceding February. We met September 4 with Colonel Tadeusz Kosciuszko as Gates' second and John Barker Church as mine."

Giddy over retelling the story, Wilkinson was determined not to leave out any detail and straightened his shoulders.

"At the first order, Gates' pistol flashed in the pan, and mine fired in the air. On the second order, I fired, and Gates withheld his fire. On the third command, I fired, and Gates' pistol flashed in the pan. No more firing occurred as Gates pronounced that I acted as a gentleman in the duel at York."

Wilkinson laughed and picked up his glass of spirits, his tale whispering from his drink.

"A statement to this effect was signed by Kosciuszko and given to Church," he said to Burr. "The former requested the document back so he could make a copy of it. He then refused to give it back until I signed a similar statement."

Wilkinson picked up a pencil on the table and snapped it, his lip quivering.

"The next day, I exploded at Gates, calling him a rascal and coward, and again challenged him, but Gates at the "field of honor" ignored me and walked away."

Burr envisioned Wilky glowing and telling him to go to hell.

"The seconds," said Wilky, "brandished their swords at the entrance to the court-martial later that week and needed to be restrained by the guards."

Burr observed a smug consideration on his face.

The rattling surrounding Wilkinson rang as it would for the next forty years.

## Chapter 67

## Lee's Treason

Since arriving at the Council Chamber of City Hall in December 1776, the sentry brought wood and candles to Lee's "confinement." Sensible to his plight, the long, slim-legged Lee began devising a letter to "Billy" Howe.

On March 29, 1777, a gloomy rainy evening, he concluded that the colonies could never achieve victory and that continuing the conflict would only weaken America and Britain.

His letter to General Howe read, "As on the one hand it appears to me that the continuance of the War, America has no chance of obtaining the ends desired by the combatants."

A log dropped from the guard's hand to the maple floor ending Lee's thought. He turned and snarled like a bulldog and soon continued his address to Lord Howe thirty minutes later, receiving a note from General Gates. He guffawed ferociously at Gates's description of Burgoyne, but his eyes glared. His nostrils dilated as he continued to Howe, "the object of the scheme which I now take the liberty of offering to the consideration of his Lordship and the General, and if it is adopted, I am so confident of the success that I would stake my life on the issue."

The prisoner of war leaned back and poured himself a glass of port, continuing his draft, but inside, he missed his dogs, wanting to rub his cheek against their snouts.

"Fourteen thousand will be sufficient to clear the Jerseys and take possession of Philadelphia. I propose that four thousand men be immediately embarked in transports.

One half of which should proceed up the Potomac and take post at Alexandria, the other which should go up the Chesapeake Bay and possess themselves of Annapolis."

Smirking the way a bully glared at an innocent victim, he closed with, "I am so confident of the event that I will venture to assert with the penalty of my life if the plan is fully adopted, and no accidents (such as a rupture betwixt the Powers of Europe intervenes that in less than two months from the date of the proclamation not a spark of this desolating war remains unextinguished in any part of the Continent."

Howe liked the Philadelphia part of Lee's plan, and in taking it, he embarrassed Washington at Brandywine.

Howe spent the winter of 77-78 in the city of brotherly love with Mrs. Loring, worrying that he, Lee, was about to sail to England for trial; word came from General Washington, "Five Hessian officers held by me as hostages for Lee's safe return."

The British commander was glad to trade for the Hessians and avoid angering the German troops and the governments that had hired them out to the British.

Nothing was known in the American camp about Lee's treachery.

He ventured to the rebel army at Valley Forge in May 1778, hoping to supplant Washington and emerge as America's savior.

Hope sprang eternal for the brilliant, imperious, liberal-minded but narrow-minded officer, vain to the verge of insanity, an acid of the tongue, talented yet unbalanced, brave yet treacherous, a lover of animals but quarrelsome with men, a spirited man. A strange jumble of good and evil Washington would learn, and Hamilton experience.

## Chapter 68

## Franklin Makes a General

At his temporary home in the Parisian suburb of Passy, Benjamin Franklin, as one of the Commissioners of America to France, entertained de Vergennes, the French Foreign Minister, and Pierre Beaumarchais, a Frenchman of many talents: a playwright, musician, diplomat, spy, publisher, watchmaker, inventor, horticulturist, and an arms dealer. Franklin notably led the two Frenchmen to continue to give valuable aid to the rebellious American Colonies.

Recent news informed him that Philadelphia and New York were securely in British hands, and he was trying to imagine what it was like to be in Washington's shoes; realizing he would never know, he poured his guests another glass of Chardonnay.

Beaumarchais left the bottom of the wine glass firmly planted on the table. He made a few circles with the base while de Vergennes picked up the wine glass and slightly flicked his wrist, making little circles in the air.

Turning his head, Franklin was overly showy with his swirling, making grandiose motions like he was getting ready to lasso a steer. The Frenchmen rewarded his gesture by narrowing their eyes and letting out a slight snicker.

"My friends," said Franklin, "it is not like you to be quiet and shy."

"It is a story of Eighteenth-Century intrigue," said Beaumarchais.

"Not because of the French ministers," said de Vergennes, "who desire to promote the cause of democracy."

"I understand," said Franklin, "you desire to embarrass your neighbor and ancient enemy, his Britannic Majesty."

"Yes," pronounced de Vergennes, "but still preserving all of the forms and proprieties of strict neutrality."

Franklin opened his lips. "You enjoy working behind the scenes."

"As it is necessary to camouflage our American operations, I turned to the ingenuity of Pierre-Augustin Caron de Beaumarchais, one of the arch intriguers of the Eighteenth Century."

"We formed," said Beaumarchais, "a commercial corporation known as Hortalex & Company that entered into the business of shipping arms and munitions to America."

Franklin grimaced, "But some were lost at sea, and the British captured some."

"More serious losses occur in the Continental Army itself. It lacks organization, discipline, and administrative experience," said Beaumarchais.

"To such a man as Count St. Germain," said de Vergennes. "The American crisis diagnosis is simple. The American commander needs competent technical advice."

"Washington is an able and forceful leader, but he was not a trained soldier," added Beaumarchais. "He needs a staff officer trained in the practical business methods of conducting war."

"It was just while St. Germain was considering this need with me," said de Vergennes, "that his old acquaintance, Baron von Steuben, came to Paris in quest of employment." Looking at Franklin, "Here was the man Hortalez & Company should send to Washington. The Baron was not an officer of high rank, but Comte de-Saint Germain had known him for years."

"But the American commissioners are not empowered to make any contract on behalf of the Continental Congress or promise him suitable rank or pay."

"When the front door is closed," said Beaumarchais, "one must find another alternative."

"So many European adventurers have gone to America that Congress has become disgusted and has instructed the commissioners not to encourage any others," said Franklin.

De Vergennes winked, "The Baron should not seek to make any terms with the American commissioners."

"He should go as a distinguished foreigner who desires to serve as a volunteer with Washington's army," said Beaumarchais. "As such, he would travel to America ostensibly at his own expense."

"You and Silas Deane can supply letters of introduction and nothing more, telling of St. Germain's high estimate of Steuben's abilities to Washington and Congress's leaders."

"There is one flaw in this plan," said Beaumarchais, "the Baron is only a captain."

"Simple," said the author of Poor Richard's Almanac.

"If the Baron's American embassy's success depends on his wearing a general's coat, the problem is purely sartorial."

"Any good military tailor can solve it," replied Franklin.

Captain von Steuben remained in Europe and disappeared from history. His Excellency, Lieutenant General von Steuben, picked up a military secretary and two aides-de-camp, procured brilliant uniforms for himself and his staff, and sailed for America with a letter.

"Sir, The Gentleman who will have the Honour of waiting upon you with this letter is the Baron de Steuben, Lieutenant General in the King of Prussia's Service, whom he attended in all his Campaigns his Aide-de-Camp, Quartermaster General, etc. He goes to America with a real Zeal for our Cause and a View of engaging in it and rendering it all the Service in his power."

Franklin wanted to explode in glee but settled for a light smile. "He is recommended to us by two of the best Judges of Military Merit in this country, M. de Vergennes and M. de St. Germain. They have long been personally acquainted with him and interest themselves in promoting his Voyage from the full Persuasion that the Knowledge and Experience he has acquired by 20 Years' Study and Practice in the Prussian School may be of great use in our Armies. Therefore, I cannot recommend him warmly to your Excellency, wishing our "Service may be made agreeable to him."

At the seat of Congress at York, the Baron told a committee through his translator, "I come solely as an officer of high rank desiring to serve a campaign under General Washington as a volunteer. I seek no rank or commission in the American Service, nor do I seek any pay. I only asked that my actual expenses while serving be reimbursed as is customary under such circumstances in Europe." Thrilled by the thought, the committee continued to listen, "I will stake my future fortunes upon the success of the American cause. If my services lead to the eventual independence of the colonies, I should be reimbursed for my sacrifices for leaving Europe and to reward me as you should consider fitting."

A perfectly reasonable request, thought the committee, who were grinning at each other like a child eating ice cream, the Baron rubbing his fingers on his chin.

*****

On a cold February afternoon in 1778, General Washington and his staff rode out from the rows of dilapidated tents and huts at Valley Forge. A stockily built man was riding toward them wearing a Prussian general uniform and accompanied by an aide, a French valet, and a Russian greyhound. Grasping the Prussian's hand, Washington said, "Baron von

Steuben, in the name of the Continental Army, I welcome you." His cheerful look and manner made him a welcomed volunteer for the American cause. Not wanting to offend the American generals, Washington made him his "inspector general" without a line command.

Walking around the camp, von Steuben observed men naked, some of them to the fullest extent of the word. The officers who wore coats had them of every color and make, and officers mounted guard in a sort of dressing gown made of a blanket. "About regard to the military discipline," he said to Washington, "I may say safely no such a thing exists."

"Draw a plan for a better organization of the army."

The next day von Stuben informed Washington, "From what I have learned, the army of 17,000 has shrunk to 5,012 nondescript troops. Some regiments have only a handful. Desertions are frequent and usually ignored. There is no uniform manual of arms or drill. Each officer gives his soldiers any maneuvering he has learned. Muskets are neglected and rusty. There are no forms to account for military property; no uniform rolls for muster or commissary accounts."

"You are extremely honest," replied Washington.

Highly gratified, von Steuben said, "Your praise gives me much pleasure."

He went to work. From various regiments, he selected 120 men, ostensibly to form a guard of honor for General Washington but actually to serve as a demonstration of military training for all the rest. He showed the men how to aim and fire a gun in his high, shiny boots.

Hamilton, Laurens, and Lafayette listened as he told them in broken English, "In Europe, a man drilled for three months is still a recruit. I must make finished soldiers in two months." The inspector general rose at three o'clock every morning, drank coffee with his valet, brushed his hair, gulped a hurried breakfast, and mounted his horse, eager to begin the long day's work on the parade ground. An officer reminded him that drilling troops were the work of sergeants. Looking at the American in the eye coldly, he retorted: "I was a sergeant already!" Sharing the privation of Valley Forge, he stomped about in the snow with the men, squatted around the campfires, and illustrated his infantry tactics by marks with a sharp stick. The men chuckled merrily at his outbursts of temper. Exasperated at an incredibly clumsy squad, he would call, "Mein captain, kom und at dem swear fur me in English!"

In less than three months, the man with shrewd but friendly eyes, graying hair plaited in a pigtail, and aquiline nose taught every soldier at Valley Forge the manual of arms.

"Learning how to load and fire in unison," said Lafayette, "the ranks execute the facings and evolutions with true military precision." "More importantly," said Alex, "he has kindled an esprit de corps never before known by the colonial troops."

"Officers vie for the best units at inspections," added Laurens. "Platoons and companies compete for the resounding "Goot! of General Steuben."

# Chapter 69

# France Makes a Treaty

There was no resisting the news, no possibility of avoiding the consequences for England when France announced its treaty of amity with the American colonies on the thirteenth of March 1778. A complete change of military plans became desirable in London as the Cabinet took a different view of the whole nature of the struggle on the American seaboard.

No longer were their past actions the top priority as March ticked forward to April

The King's hair stood curled on his head, and the Queen admired the beginnings of his somewhat decent-looking beard, rubbed her hand over his chin, wondering if he should give growing one a fair shot but noticed his mind was elsewhere.

"Keeping Pennsylvania is a joke."

She desired to comfort him but thought better of it.

"The decisions for England have become global."

Her mind tightened on the days previous to the war with the colonies before England lost control of its supremacy.

"The English navy patrols India and Africa's coasts and now must consider making the Caribbean the main focus of the war in the Western Hemisphere," said the King.

She could feel the heat of his anger. It sizzled through her to her core.

"Patience," she told him.

His gaze scanned over the Queen and lingered as his eyes narrowed. He looked away with a conspicuous frown and focused on his crown that rested on a gilded table, thinking it was in a poor state of repair.

"For the first time in a hundred and fifty years, England will be fighting France singlehandedly."

With one brow arched, she studied his face.

"With Spain ready to join France, the British navy will be hard put to hold off the Bourbon powers."

"What say the various Lords that run the government?" she asked.

"Lord Sandwich frets over potential danger in the Channel."

She rolled her eyes. "Oh, please."

"He wants to know the direction the Comte d' Estaing, who commands the ships at Toulon, is preparing to sail."

For an hour, she tried, really tried to understand, fatigue leaving her eyes shadowed, she rubbed them.

"Until he does, no ships can sail to the Mediterranean."

Comprehending his train of thought, she held up both hands. "You have convinced me."

He snagged his temper and looked at her elegant neck, slim and graceful, wanting to nibble on it.

"The political picture of England stood in a state of vexation." For a moment his focus wavered,"Germain argued long and hard to stop the French in the Mediterranean; I agreed, and Lord North tended to side with them." She wanted to hypnotize him and remove his trouble.

"Admiral Kepple, the new commander of the home fleet, disagreed and sided with Lord Sandwich and delayed sending any home fleets to check the French in the Mediterranean."

I think we have little to fear at home," bantered Germain, who was trying to ease the King's mind, but Lord Sandwich refused to risk the country upon any account; the words were more to Germain than to King George III.

"There was a bottomless conceit about him," said the King, who found it easier to avoid meeting his eyes, afraid to weaken the defense of the Channel; the Cabinet let the Comte d'Estaing aim for Clinton's army.

"Admiral Howe's small fleet left the door open to an end of the American war, then and there," said the King

Finally, the Admiralty produced some proof of the Compte d'Estaing's direction, sent out a detachment of the home fleet, and hoped for the best, rarely, the road to victory.

King George III confessed to the Queen, "The war effort, feeble in all its parts and consequently unsuccessful." With a shake of her head, he collapsed into a chair saying, "The Cabinet wants to give the rebels everything they want short of Independence."

"Nothing but a name without any substance," said the Queen, "a more visionary title of subordination."

"One jot more substantially, King of America than King of France," said the King.

The Queen's blood started to boil, infuriated that the colonies might be lost under her husband's reign.

"And then there is General Sir Henry Clinton, who is anxious to separate himself from the military as far as possible. He fidgets in New York, waiting for his transfer to London, unhappy being second-in-command to General Lord William Howe."

Howe thought much of the evils of politics, not a little of his military career's fatigues, but his concerns were needless.

Unbeknownst to him and the population, Mrs. Loring shed tears for him several months earlier when he sent a letter to London requesting to resign. Sir Henry was most agreeably surprised to learn that he was assigned command at Philadelphia.

Lieutenant General Lord Charles Cornwallis was his second in command, a squat, gentleman-like, and ambitious man.

Clinton learned, "You are instructed to evacuate Philadelphia by sea and reestablish your headquarters in New York, and if need be, abandon New York and retreat as far as Nova Scotia," his fighting spirit ruffled.

He thought of the evils of his orders. He neglected little of the consequences for the loyalists in Philadelphia: his situation, the subject of hours of discussion with his aides.

"I suffer a moral dilemma – What to do with the fate of Philadelphia's loyalist citizens."

"Let those that want to leave come with us to New York."

"This means that much of the limited shipping space available to the army would be used for nonmilitary purposes."

"Do you write your instructions," said Cornwallis, who thought Clinton not bright, "and move the army overland to New York, carrying along all the supplies and munitions that could not be sent by ship?"

"The two American armies represent the greatest threat to our march," said an aide.

Clinton made no answer and tried to look cheerful.

"Fourteen thousand men under Washington are at Valley Forge," said Cornwallis,

"And another four thousand," said Clinton, "commanded by Horatio Gates covering New York."

"I have calculated," said another aide, "to get from here to there requires provisions and military baggage to fill a train of fifteen hundred wagons."

"And it must be protected," said Cornwallis.

Clinton was conflicted, wanting the moral dilemma very much gone.

"What do our scouts say?" he asked.

"For some distance, the primitive American road network should allow us to march in two columns."

As Clinton came to understand the problem better, other issues arose.

"To negotiate the here to there," he said, "we must divide our ten-thousand-man army – half leading the procession, half trailing it."

"You choose to adopt a risky expedient," said Cornwallis.

Clinton's decisions increased in number and meaning, his cheerful look gone.

*****

In the spring of 1778, Hamilton noticed a slight smile tilting the corners of General Washington's mouth.

"The army's improvement," Alex said to his General, resolving to tell him his opinion, "is greater than I could have imagined in the darkest winter days at Valley Forge."

Washington remained silent, trying to look cheerfully unconcerned about the past.

"Despite," said Alex, "all the terrible suffering, the sickness, starvation, privation, desertions, and intrigues your army endured, General.

"To be sure," said Washington, who was not in a humour to value the truth of Alex's words.

"Thanks to the opportune arrival this past winter," said Alex, "of the determined drillmaster Lt. General Baron Friedrich Wilhelm Augustus von Steuben, the Continental Army is the best trained it has ever been."

Washington rose, knowing he would only have made it through the winter of 1777 with Hamilton.

Despite himself, George put on a happy expression, "France is now in the war, and Franklin says assistance should be coming."

With a half-smile, Alex said, "Let Congress carp over our failures to defend Philadelphia; the past is the past."

Washington agreed to it, but with so quiet a "Yes," Alex wondered at his sincerity.

Regardless, Alex thought, his duty was to promote the General's leadership in any method possible. He should talk of encouragement and be aware of his views, accepting his attention but steering him in the proper course.

"The dogged circulation of forged correspondence," said Alex, "purporting to represent your unflattering views on the war and your leadership of the army is subtly challenged."

The statement renewed his failures as Commander.

"With several successors waiting in the wings," Alex said with a wink.

Washington bore the intelligence well.

"And that damn, indiscreet second-in-command, Maj. Gen. Charles Lee."

"You seem determined to think ill of him."

"Not at all, but I wonder," said Alex, "if he suffers from fatal jealousy of mind."

Washington did not make a direct reply to this, choosing to store it in the back of his mind.

Alex understood better than most the symbolic value of specific military actions, explaining, "The British movement from Philadelphia represents a chance to score the kind of low-risk success that could reap important morale benefits with both the Congress and the army, as well as improve your influence."

Pausing for a breath, Alex realized how stern-looking the man facing him was.

At night, Washington weighed the danger in such a move, for a severe reversal might damage Continental prestige well out of proportion to its strategic value. Wrestling with the problem of finding the right balance between potential jeopardy and possible advantage, he failed to see any similarities of Burgoyne's march to Albany.

The following day Hamilton saw that his General was in a happy mood.

"Sir, what brings a smile to your face."

"Intelligence informed me the British are marching east into New Jersey."

"That will make Brig. Gen. Anthony Wayne's day," said Hamilton. "He wants to punish them as much as possible."

"I like his aggressive tactics," said Washington.

"What are your orders?" asked Alex.

Washington hesitated. Time, he knew, must be allocated for being prepared.

"Sir, I suggest immediately dispatching a force under Maj. Gen. Benedict Arnold to occupy Philadelphia."

"And the rest of the army?"

"Move on a northeastern track and cross the Delaware River at Coryell's Ferry."

Hamilton's proposals restored Washington's comfort.

On the twentieth of June, the Continentals, unimpeded by a large baggage train, marched in three parallel columns.

The plan is to be determined by Clinton's movement.

"Any news," asked Washington, "whether Clinton pushed north to New Brunswick and Amboy before crossing over to Staten Island, or did he angle to the Northeast to reach Raritan Bay, near Sandy Hook, and complete the journey by naval transports."

"Either way, Your Excellency, we must commit to a course of action."

Gathering near Hopewell, New Jersey, for a council of war at 9 AM on the twenty-fourth of June, an eclipse of the sun took place.

The officers rushed out, observing the gloomy darkness and the army's soldiers, who were anxious about the event that lasted more than four minutes.

"It is midnight in the morning," uttered Washington.

"In 1715 was the great eclipse of the sun, and was presently followed by the rebellion at Preston, and in 1745," said Alexander, "the rebellion in Scotland occurred presently after the eclipse of the sun."

"Then the sun," said Lt. Colonel John Laurens, "is on our side."

"I fear," Anthony Wayne said, "the eclipse will cause general consternation and frighten the men who know not the cause."

"As long as the religion of the army," said Sterling, "augur it good, it is fine with me."

"I enjoy the idea of people being spooked," barked Charles Lee, whose dogs were howling.

The return of the sun brought a return of the men's good sense and brighter hope.

Alex took notes of the meeting, believing that Washington needed to engage the British before arriving in New York.

Success was rare since he came to the army.

Major General Marie Joseph Paul Yves Roch Gilbert du Motier, the Marquis de Lafayette, said, "It would be disgraceful and humiliating to allow the enemy to cross the Jerseys in tranquility."

"People expect something from us," argued Maj. Gen. Nathanael Greene.

"I think we can make a partial attack without suffering them to bring us to a general action," said Lord Sterling.

Looking at Wayne, Washington asked, "Your opinion."

"Fight, Sir!"

"To preserve our reputation," said Greene.

"And not allow the enemy to march in tranquility," said Wayne.

"The thought of embarking on an all-out attack on the British," countered General Lee, "is highly absurd. The advantages to be gained by victory are not to be put in competition with the evils that might result from defeat."

"It would be humiliating to do nothing," said Hamilton.

"Better alive and fight another day," said Lee.

Lee saw a change in General Washington's eyes, ready to test his army.

"How many soldiers are you willing to lose?" asked Lee, who looked down upon him, so well understanding the gradation of rank above him.

"One at a time," barked Wayne, "if that is what it takes to bring liberty to the people."

"You take the flower of the British army lightly and are blind to what faces you."

"It is a law of the universe that flowers wilt," mumbled Alexander, who was sorry to have to pay respect to the man he did not like.

Lee smiled, knowing, as bright and pretty as a picture, from his minions in Congress that another misstep would allow him to replace Washington as commander-in-chief.

With a toss of his head, Wayne rejected Lee's remark.

"We must at least," said Washington, "continue to harry the British column if fair opportunity offers."

Alex withheld before saying, "That the council of war would have done honor to the most honorable body of midwives and them only."

The meeting ended, and Alex accompanied Washington back to his quarters.

Observing his anxiety, Alex wanted to appease and said with sincerity, "General Lee is an inelegant creature that one must keep their eyes on."

"I am always on the lookout and pity him from my heart."

Washington noticed a change in his expression and was sorry for it.

"Perhaps it is not fair," said Alex, "to expect him to know how very much he is your inferior in courage and all the energies of command,"

The next day Lee wrote to Gates, "Washington's hesitations and evolving strategy before the battle indicate that he still has things to learn about leading an army and effectively communicating with subordinates. While understandable, his predilection for composite units made up of picked men will also create problems he does not foresee."

"Do you think," Washington said to Hamilton, "we should engage the British?"

"After the difficult winter encampment at Valley Forge," said

Hamilton, "God knows we are hardened and better disciplined."

Washington's pulse galloped.

"An opportunity we should exploit," said Alex, who itched for battle.

"I want the point of my sword," said Washington, "to be as sharp as possible."

Hamilton gave a little laugh unseen by his commander.

"A good time for the Continental Army to enter the stage of history, General."

"Let us harass the long British column already being plagued by the New Jersey militia," said Washington, "and send a detail of six hundred select riflemen commanded by Colonel Daniel Morgan."

Later, he ordered Alex to send a second detachment of 1,440 picked men under Brig. Gen. Charles Scott.

Hamilton's eyes glittered, capturing the substance and shadow of the coming battle.

Twenty-four hours later, Hamilton said to his general, "Send a third force of a thousand men (like the others, drawn from the best soldiers in various units) under Wayne and place all under the command of Lafayette. A posting, Sir, that Lee declined."

Washington was too astonished to comment.

An hour later, Alex informed his general, "Your Excellency, on second thought, Lee has decided to invoke his seniority and demands to be placed in charge." Washington sighed deeply, "I must agree."

"And to prevent any embarrassment to Lafayette," Alex whispered in his commander's ear, "enlarge the advance party with six hundred additional soldiers to justify Lee's assumption of command and have Lafayette remain attached to the operation as a supernumerary."

Lafayette, the liaison for General Washington, rode back and forth, surveying the enemy lines, and reported the officers' information.

As the echoes of hoofbeats faded, Washington's mind groaned after much thinking, but determined nothing better than waiting on Clinton's next move.

Believing he would battle the combined armies of Washington and Gates, Sir Henry halted his long columns around the small village of Monmouth Courthouse on the afternoon of the twenty-sixth of June. He anticipated a severe attack the next day; a subtle but refreshing thought entered his mind concerning Washington – victory.

The twenty-seventh of June, a hot, calm, and peaceful day, left Clinton's military mind with an inspiring image. He reconnoitered the area, alert to the relatively open plains northwest and south of the village, observing the area west of Monmouth Courthouse.

More undulating and creased by several ravines, he noted the deserted road that wriggled between the gorges west of the village that ended at a boggy morass spanned by a small bridge.

His aides told him, "Should the enemy attack him at Monmouth Courthouse, the best course would be to press the Americans against the swampy barrier."

"However pleasant the prospect," said Clinton, "the careful and cautious Washington would never jeopardize his army in such terrain. Certainly, he is not a fool."

On the afternoon of the twenty-seventh of June, 1778, after advancing the main Continental Army to within four miles of Englishtown, Washington again called his generals to a war council.

Clearing his throat deliberately to bring the meeting to order, "Your opinions are requested, gentlemen. Do we wish to court a general engagement?"

"Attack the enemy on their march, at all events," said General Wayne, dressed in a ruffled shirt under an immaculate blue uniform coat with white facings."

Lee thought *does he have nothing better to say?*

"We must engage Clinton," said Major General Nathaniel Greene, "before he can reach the safety of New York."

"The French alliance means victory in the long run," said Lee, "and it is foolish to commit the army to battle unless we have overwhelming superiority."

"My men," said Wayne, "can stand up to the attacks of any British regulars."

"You are mad," said Lee.

"If you lead from the front," said General Knox, "the men will follow."

"Did you read that in a book when you were a bookseller?" asked Lee. Knox whipped around, wanting to drive a fist into his face.

"An advance force," said the Marquis de Lafayette, should seek contact with the British."

Later that day, a violent thunderstorm turned the dirt roads into mud and slowed the armies to a crawl.

"General Lee," said Washington, "I suggest you hold a strategy session with your subordinates to attack the enemy's rearguard."

"I must say, General, I strenuously object to this plan."

"Your objection is noted, Sir!"

Lee realized there was no resisting his decision, no possibility of avoiding the command of his dour face.

After Washington departed for the main army, he sent a pair of couriers to Lee with some of his afterthoughts.

"I worry that the British might launch a spoiling attack. You must alert the militia, then watch the enemy."

The second message to Lee read, "Send forward a strong (six-hundred-to eight-hundred-man) observation force to fix the British rear guard in place come morning."

Lee convened the requested meeting, but nothing was accomplished, having satisfied himself with the thought that his usual incompetence would conquer Washington.

Anthony Wayne recollected, "Lee had nothing further to say on the subject since the position of the enemy might render any previous plan invalid."

In a letter to General Gates, Lee noted, "If the country is overlooked, and the force, disposition, and situation of the enemy doubtful, I must profess that I cannot persuade myself that a precise plan can be attended with any good consequences, but that it must distract, lead astray, and in effect be ruinous."

Gates knew the trap was set for General Washington's command to be vilified, to promote Lee to commander.

Within a few hours of midnight of the 27th, Clinton's army was encamped near Monmouth Court House in Freehold, New Jersey.

Lee and his men rested six miles away, Lee making little effort to rectify any intelligence gaps.

He instructed Brig. Gen. Philemon Dickinson, whose eight hundred New Jersey militia were shadowing the enemy, to alert him when the British column began moving. Traveling with the main body some three miles west of Englishtown, Washington, late on the night of the 27th, dispatched an order drafted to Lee. He let him know that support would be close at hand and to "skirmish so as to produce some delay and give time for the rest of the troops to come up."

Lee and his soldiers were six miles from Monmouth Court House in Freehold, where the British encamped.

The general paid more attention to his dogs than the situation at hand. He knew Washington's instructions allowed him to refrain "Unless there should be very powerful reasons to the contrary."

Lee interrupted his orders to have high discretionary power, knowing neither geography nor tranquility could upset his plans.

Attempting to coordinate with the expert riflemen under Colonel Morgan was a clerical error. The note's imprecise wording resulted in

Morgan's experienced fighters missing the start of the next day's action.

Initially, they could have operated against the British right flank. Clinton, who looked a tad tired, a tad concerned but very much in charge, recorded.

"The patriot militia remained busy filling up the wells and breaking down and destroying the bridges and causeways before us."

His aides predicted the likelihood of a run-in with Washington's regulars at a choke point near Mount Holly.

When no serious opposition appeared, the English commander became convinced that Washington "feared to risk a general action." Protecting his exposed wagon train was foremost on his mind, but even in his defensive stance, he itched for a chance to strike. His experience would undoubtedly support him.

One hour after the predetermined time of 3 AM, Clinton sent forth his forward division and the long wagon train to Middletown's safety.

As the twenty-eighth of June progressed, sweat dripped from my every pore of the soldiers, and the temperature, ninety-six degrees.

As Lee surmised, Washington mixed and matched commands and officers to the degree that confused all involved, releasing a ripple of anxiety.

"His blending of units posed a serious challenge to effective control," Lee wrote to Gates.

Hours later, when Lee was in the midst of a desperate effort to choreograph this "admixture," he commented, "What a shocking situation. I hardly know a single man or officer under my command."

Several of Lee's unit commanders sought him out to discuss the matter.

"Contradictory intelligence prevails, Sir."

"There is no clear sense of the enemy's design."

Lee advanced to the other side of the lone bridge spanning the swampy passage of Spottswood Middle Brook, referred to as the West Morass.

With several of his dogs, he noticed General Dickinson and by his side William Grayson, approaching with their heads held high.

"In the morning General Lee," said Dickinson, a militia commander, "we engaged in a sharp scrap with a small British detachment."

Lee made a noncommittal sound. "What choices do we have?"

"General Lee," they said.

Lee's lips formed a down-open curve.

Dickinson continued, "If you march your party beyond the ravine now in your rear, which has only one passage over it, you are in a perilous situation."

"I decline your advice, though I will take the precaution of grouping my three leading regiments (perhaps one thousand men) plus Lt. Col. Eleazar Oswald's four cannons under the command of Anthony Wayne, and at the same time will place Lafayette in charge of what had been Wayne's detachment."

Dickinson and Grayson stood silently at the foot of the bridge.

"I will advance on and ascertain with my own eyes the enemy's number, order, and disposition and conduct myself accordingly."

Marching in fits and starts, evaluating each new piece of information, Lee scouted ahead toward the courthouse.

He observed British cavalry and infantry shielding the Middletown Road just north of the village.

Clinton ordered his trailing division, now four hours away, to march towards his wagons. This left a small detachment, maybe thirteen hundred cavalries and infantry; Lee decided to target this rear screening force.

He re-joined his column and instructed Wayne, "Push ahead with your three regiments and engage the enemy."

The thought of battle put a smile on Wayne's face. "By all means."

As his units approached Monmouth Courthouse, he met a local guide who told him, "Use the little-used road that will take him around the right flank of the British line."

While carrying out his flanking maneuver, Wayne needed to advise Lee.

Overlooking Monmouth Courthouse, Lee observed that Wayne took the path he intended and that there needed to be a Continental presence in the village.

He then saw a small detail of the 16th Light Dragoons riders push out from the rear guard to counter Wayne's threat.

Understanding that the British cavalry was fooled into thinking their opposition was only a small party of mounted militia, Lee grinned. He ordered the guns of the line of Pennsylvania Continental foot soldiers to scatter them with a volley.

Lee knew his plan needed modification, but confusion reigned within his mind. He felt a bad taste in his mouth but let it pass with a "so be it."

Noticing Lafayette guiding his command into a line just on the village outskirts, he rode to him, "My dear Marquis, I think these people are ours."

In response to one of his sub-commanders who had ridden forward for instructions, he exclaimed, "By God, he would take them all."

To an aide sent ahead by Washington, Lee explained, "I am going to order some troops to march below the enemy and cut off their retreat."

Unfortunately for Lee, the bulk of Clinton's trailing division was just out of sight, waiting for instructions.

He ordered the whole rear guard to face about and return. Clinton flashed a toothy smile at his chance to flog the Americans so they would forget about his vulnerable wagon train.

The 2nd Grenadiers poured out of their concealed position. The British line began moving toward Monmouth Courthouse; Clinton correctly judged Lee's right flank as his weakest point.

Lee's commanders acted in cross purposes, and the units began falling back.

By about 11:30 AM, a withdrawal was in full swing.

An enemy force advancing on him numbered, Lee thought, perhaps six thousand.

Agitated by the events, General Lee should have kept Washington informed of changing circumstances and, more importantly, his plans to deal with them.

Sucked into the whirlwind of chaos everywhere, chaos, Lee was content to retreat and retreat with more haste.

He informed his aides, who were virtually afoot, "Retreat with more haste."

Their horses were severely wounded, and the animals carrying his acting adjutant general and French adviser were all useless from heat and fatigue.

He screamed, "The enemy has too much cavalry for us."

Pressed by an aide of Washington for a situation report, Lee answered, "I really do not know what to say."

Hearing the sounds of battle, Washington sent Hamilton to scout Lee's movements.

Riding up to Lee, Hamilton observed soldiers fleeing.

He shouted, "I will stay here with you, my dear General, and die with you! Let us all die rather than retreat."

Herding the patriots toward the West Morass, Clinton hoped Washington would send reinforcements to assist them; telling his aides, "If Washington is blockhead enough to sustain Lee, I should have caught him between two defiles; and it is easy to see what must happen."

The heat made the men's clothes cling to them like a newborn baby to her mother's breast. The dust infiltrated their eyes and scratched their pupils, tongues as coarse as a barren field, and breathing was near impossible in the ravines.

Lee was content to let the retreat continue since it answered his purpose by keeping his units away from the British and putting more pressure on Washington. Smiling, he knew Congress would end Washington's command.

When Washington heard Lee's troops were in retreat, he galloped off on his white charger, a gift to him by William Livingston, in honor of re-crossing the Delaware. Reaching the Tennent Meetinghouse area, a civilian appeared, confirming that Lee's troops were departing, citing a nearby fifer as his source.

Not believing the thing to be correct, Washington let loose a cannon shot of profanities–that dame, asshole, bastard.

The General approached his soldiers and asked, "Men, will you fight?"

They answered him with three cheers.

A foot soldier thought that Washington seemed at the instant to be in a great passion; his looks, if not his words, seemed to indicate as much.

Finding Lee on a hill just east of the lane leading to the Rhea farmhouse, Washington demanded, "What is its meaning, Sir? I desire to know the meaning of this disorder and confusion!"

Either because of the noise about them or his feigned confusion, Lee remained silent for several seconds.

His first reply was a hesitant, "Sir."

"Why the retreat? Asked Washington.

Lee thought his tone had much bitterness and fury and that the retreat was in good order.

"By the time I made contact with the rear of the British column, my men crossed three ravines that cut through the sandy pine barrens at right angles to my line of march. This rugged terrain behind me prevented either quick retreat or quick support from you."

"You damned poltroon, you never tried them!"

"If I was thrown back, my men ran the grave danger of being cut to pieces. The troops cannot stand the British bayonets."

Hamilton observed that Washington continued swearing until the leaves shook on the trees.

With his back straightened, Washington said, "We are facing only a strong covering party of the enemy."

"The British are in greater numbers than you imagine, and I do not think it is proper to risk so much."

With his nostrils flaring and his eyes flashing, Washington replied, "I am very sorry that General Lee undertook the command unless he meant to fight the enemy."

Lee lifted his eyes and mumbled, "Do me a favor, general, and let me general."

Spotting some retreating units, Washington broke off the exchange and hurried over to them.

His horse dropped dead from the heat, and he jumped on a chestnut mare, screaming to the running soldiers, "Stand fast, my boys, and receive the enemy."

Lee stood silent for a few minutes, content within, knowing Washington's armies were divided by the ravines.

"The southern troops," shouted Washington. "Are advancing to support you."

Once on the field in sight of the enemy, Hamilton later told Laurens, "Washington's personal leadership came to the fore. His forceful will and determination infused the escaping American soldiers with a fighting spirit."

Lee began to issue orders, only to be stopped by one of his aides, who reminded him that Washington was now on the field and issuing commands.

He sought out Washington, who asked, "Are you prepared to hold the ground to buy time for the main body to form behind them along Perrine Ridge."

"I undoubtedly will, and I should see that I should be one of the last to leave the field."

The pair parted, each to his task. Washington met Lafayette, who had two detachments, Colonel William Stewart's and Lt. Col. Nathaniel Ramsey's.

Lafayette told his men, "Never have we beheld so superb a man."

Hamilton thought he never saw the general to so much advantage. That night he told Laurens, "His coolness and firmness admirable as he took maneuvers to check the enemy's advance and giving time for the army, which was near, to form and make a proper disposition, directing the men with the skill of a master workman."

Aware that the enemy firmly pressed the rear of the strike force, Washington asked the officers to delay the British advance, and they agreed to try.

Just after Washington left, Wayne rode up, took charge, and directed the pair to an ambush position in a nearby wood.

Lee, meanwhile, was organizing a defensive line along the northeast-southwest running hedgerow, dividing the Rhea and Parsonage farms.

Hastily, Hamilton positioned two cannons on a nearby knoll.

This allowed Lee to assemble pieces of two commands, Colonel Henry Beekman Livingston's battalion and portions of Brig. Gen. James Mitchell Varnum's brigade to confront the British. The British cavalry led by General Clinton charged.

Steady American musketry fired at them.

"This fire," Clinton wrote, "called the cavalry so much as to oblige us to retreat with precipitation upon our infantry."

The British commander rushed over to the first columns he encountered, shouting. "Charge, Grenadiers. Never heed forming."

It was face-to-face combat for a few terrible minutes as the two sides exchanged close volleys. One British veteran said, "The heaviest fire I have yet felt."

Continental cannons brought by Hamilton arrived in time to fire several rounds that rattled over the narrow bridge across Spottswood Middle Brook.

Lt. Col. Henry Monckton, the highest-ranking officer in the field, commanding the 2nd Grenadiers, died in the battle.

General Lee, the last American officer to fall back across the span, reported to Washington, who told him to reorganize his temporary division, most of which were streaming toward Englishtown.

Knowing his strike force of picked men never operated together, Lee needed to provide energetic leadership. He wanted to show Washington as a fallen commander.

Making no effort to share his thinking with his subordinates, he let control of the battle slip from his fingers.

Washington was left with no means to salvage the day.

After departing to accomplish another task, Washington removed Lee from all his responsibilities. He sent Baron von Steuben to replace him. Choosing to make his stand with the West Morass to his front rather than his rear, not at a disadvantage as Clinton hoped.

Clinton himself, raving mad from the heat, assembled his artillery of ten guns along the hedgerow's western side, his men overpowered with fatigue.

The rebels engaged with cannons along Perrine Ridge. The smoke from the cannonade filled the air while the grasping foot soldiers rested, and their officers looked for openings, the edge of survival meeting the brink of war.

Mary Hayes, the wife of a Pennsylvania cannoneer, replaced her husband on one of the gun crews, crediting the story of Molly Pitcher.

In a frenzy of courage, according to Lee, Hamilton came upon a brigade in retreat.

Fearing its artillery's loss, he organized the men along a fence and led them in a charge with fixed bayonets.

Hatless and exhausted by the scorching sun, his horse was shot from under him; injured, he was forced to retire from the battle.

Nearby, the conflict raged around Burr, who fought in the thick of it.

The Malcolms, serving under Major General William Alexander, Lord Stirling, were part of the American left wing. Their engagement had started in the morning, and the action was continuous.

In the afternoon, Burr noticed enemy troops below a ravine and directed his men to change course toward these isolated redcoats.

An aide to Washington, Colonel Barber, rode up with orders. "Hold your position."

"This leaves my men in a very precarious stead," said Burr.

The order resulted in the death of his second in command, Lieutenant Colonel Dummer.

Because of this command, the Malcolms occupied the dangerous, muddy ravine for the rest of the afternoon.

Burr, splitting his time between rallying his men and calming their fears, his horse shot from under him.

He believed the regiment would have captured their foes and left the rebels in an advantageous position, "a blunder on Washington's part," he later wrote Matty.

At this time in history, both Hamilton and Burr courted death under the battle's heat and effervescence, displaying proof of bravery and doing what soldiers dream of at the moment.

As the tempest concluded in the early evening, Colonel Burr remained up like he did the previous night, visiting his pickets and avoiding surprises.

He looked at his men as if wanting to read their thoughts.

His appeal to duty gained him the respect of his regiment members, and the idea of wanting gratitude and consideration never entered his mind.

Clinton realized that the American army fought the British to a standstill after the grueling all-day fight, assembled at the Monmouth Courthouse.

The battle was as much as he could bear. Without being downtrodden by his conscience, he refrained from any reproofs. After a brief respite and to Washington's surprise, he snuck out at night and, by sunrise, reunited with the wagon train and his other division.

His supplies were cleared from Sandy Hook for New York on the first of July, followed by his infantry on the fifth of July.

Washington chose not to pursue this, and his army rested at Monmouth for a few days.

Exhausted with fatigue and worn out from lack of sleep, Burr collapsed under a tree's shade for some time. Awaking the next morning, exposed to the brutal sun, he could not walk without great difficulty and fell to the ground, experiencing a rocking, swaying sensation.

Both generals downplayed the casualties.

Clinton reported 358. Probably above 1,100, and not recognizing the six hundred or more desertions.

Washington reported 362 killed, wounded, or missing; the figure five to six hundred.

Reports from Congress relayed, "Every lip dwells on his Praise."

Alexander Hamilton declared, "America owes a great deal to General Washington for this day's work."

Washington's stature rose accordingly. He knew his command had taken a bold leap after the previous setbacks.

With Washington a few days after the battle, Hamilton exclaimed, "Our troops, after the first impulse from mismanagement, behaved with more spirit and moved with greater order than the British troops."

"I assure you," said Washington, "I never was pleased with them before this day."

With a nod, Alex smiled at his General.

"But that son of a bitch, Lee, lost the opportunity to deliver a severe blow to the enemy."

"His failure to seriously challenge the enemy," said Washington, "at any point in the engagement is proof that his services are no longer required."

"Sir cast off the driveler in the business of soldiership for disobeying orders and making a shameful retreat or for something much worse."

"All this disgraceful fleeing without the firing of a musket."

He paused, shaking his head.

"Overground which might have been disputed inch by inch."

Hesitating momentarily, he was particularly struck by his dislike of Lee.

"Lee let the enemy convey ten thousand soldiers and a tremendous quantity of baggage through the arduous country, in the face of adequate numbers, without losing a wagon."

"I want the vile son of a bitch out of my life!" said Washington.

"I must admit, Sir, that you always acted with common civility toward Lee. His temper and plans are too volatile and violent to attract any gentleman's admiration."

"His conduct was monstrous and unpardonable on the battlefield."

His anger not yet drained, Washington continued, "His willful temper turned from one of promise to one of disappointment, if not of disgrace."

With a malicious grin, Alex said, "Convene a court-martial."

Washington stood for a bit, reflecting on how to proceed., an unbending, scorching, cancerous tumor gnawing at his soul.

Two days later, Lee was charged with disobeying positive orders to attack on the twenty-eighth of June.

Retreating before the enemy and disrespecting the Commander in chief irked him.

The court assembled at New Brunswick, New Jersey, on the fourth of July, 1778.

Lee's face tightened and trying not to lose his temper, he stood up and barked, "It is absurd to accuse me of doing something wrong!" Disobedience of orders, misbehavior before the enemy, and disrespect to the commander-in-chief were the charges.

"Have a seat," said the presiding judge, William Alexander.

The first witness, Lieutenant Colonel Hamilton, was sworn in.

The trial lasted for five weeks, from July 4-August 12, 1778.

The Verdict: Guilty.

The Sentence: Suspension from the army for one year.

As the Continental Army marched from New Brunswick toward the Hudson Highlands, Washington made arrangements to make his headquarters at the Paramus home of Lydia Watkins.

He received a note on the route, "Mrs. Prevost Presents her best respects to his Excellency Gen'l Washington. Requests the Honour of his Company as she flatters herself the accommodations will be more Commodious than those procured in the Neighborhood. Mrs. Prevost will be happy to make her House Agreeable to His Excellency."

## Chapter 70

## Wilky Saves Washington

His future brother-in-law, Clement Biddle, one of Washington's staff officers, asked Wilkinson, "Did you know you were instrumental in George Washington's career?" James Wilkinson shrugged, unsure of how to answer the question, and then straightened, hoping for a skyful of understanding.

"It turned into an act of justice," said Biddle, "than an act of infidelity as declared by your critics."

"I recall," said Wilky, "after rejecting my promotion by Gates to brigadier general I met the commander-in-chief through your effort and observed a bemused expression on his face." Biddle knew that look and stared at Wilkinson.

"I was rather doing," I said to Washington, "an act of justice than committing an act of infidelity in quoting Conway's letter."

"Sir, you did not quote it accurately."

Wilky's mouth collapsed like a house of cards, "I did not?"

"Let me show you the entire correspondence."

Washington's eyes rolled into the back of his sockets as Wilky's face twisted, learning that "Conway acknowledged writing the letter and had since said much harsher things to Washington's face, but his excellency weathered the storm surrounding him due to Wilky's loose tongue.

"It leaves me nothing else to explain," Wilkinson said to Washington, "it is satisfactory beyond satisfaction and renders me more than content. I am flattered and pleased." Washington gave Wilky an impatient glance, digging back, his mind clear; he saw the incident as a grab for power.

"I can only recall that Gates asked me to become the secretary of the Board of War." Washington held his head still and maintained a firm eye contact as his face turned to stone.

"After a few seconds, Gates nodded," said Wilky, and I did the same, and an uneasy truce settled in like a squatter without title."

Through the efforts of Clement Biddle, Sterling affirmed that Wilky spoke under no injunction of secrecy and that the passing of the letter's contents was justified.

While on his way to Valley Forge in February of 1778, Wilkinson visited Nancy Biddle in Reading and, for two weeks, flitted away time. Before his marriage to Ms. Biddle, Wilky confessed to Clement, "When in White Plains, New York, to give testimony in Arthur St. Clair's court-martial for the loss of Ticonderoga, I encountered Gates who acted with condescension toward me."

Feeling his self-control rumble, Clement Biddle knew what was coming. He realized that days passed in a blur of innuendoes on Wilky's character, and Clement grasped he was at a boiling point.

Biddle let him undress the incident, and he did, not for the first time, and then said, "All the charges against St. Clair failed to gain ground."

*A problem now existed for Colonel Wilkinson,* thought Biddle; there was only one general of higher rank for him to charm, General Washington. Having neither command nor a patron, he was too proud to seek one or the other. Like a cat with a piece of bony carp between its sharp teeth, afraid to swallow but unable to release it, Wilky's career in the army came to a standstill.

He studied his situation and resigned from the army, never stopping to blush and laugh at his vanity.

Failing to recognize what had been, might have been, and must be, he wrote the president of Congress.

"Sir - While I make my acknowledges to Congress for the appointment of Secretary to the Board of War and Ordnance, I am sorry I should be constrained to resign that office, but after the acts of treachery and falsehood in which I have detected Major general Gates, the president of the board, it is impossible for me to reconcile it to my honor to serve with him."

Congress returned his letter as "improper to remain in the files of Congress."

His resignation became official on the 31st of March, 1778.

"To youth and natural cheerfulness like yours," Biddle said to Wilky the day after his resignation, "though, under the temporary gloom of night, the return of day will hardly fail to bring a return of spirits."

Wilkinson laughed and picked up a glass of spirits.

Clement imagined his vanity relaxing and saw a smug consideration on his face.

On the 12th of November 1778, Wilky married his precious "Nancy" (Ann Biddle), becoming attached to one of the most prominent Philadelphia families, moving in the most sophisticated circles, and the populace gravitated to him by his sweet tongue. No one who knew him had ever seen him so satisfied.

Due to his command as a compelling orator, the aspiring adventurer animated ideas in friends and foes.

The evil of his situation was his awareness that he needed to pursue "riches." His disposition to think too little of others was a disadvantage that threatened him throughout his life.

In his years in exile in Europe, Burr often pondered if Wilky, in the recess of his Machiavellian mind, betrayed his "beloved" Gates for a "shot" with austere Washington. What existed between the three of them, Burr wondered to his grave.

*****

As the weekend soirée concluded at Richmond Hill, and Wilkinson mounted his horse, he said to Burr, "Our victory at Saratoga assured Victory."

Burr acknowledged, "You were there, stamping freedom for future generations."

Who could disagree?

# Chapter 71

# Love Enters

After the Battle of Monmouth, Colonel Burr rested with the troops north of the Paramus Dutch Reformed Church and was summoned to the temporary headquarters of Washington by Lord Alexander, who informed Burr that Washington, when learning that a French fleet appeared off the coast of Maryland, was disposed to partake in action against the British. Burr withheld a chuckle, realizing the British failed to keep the French navy in the Mediterranean.

They lingered but for a few minutes together, as General Washington kept them waiting,

"Colonel Burr," said General Washington, "I need you to gather information on British movements in preparation for a possible attack by combined French and Continental Army troops and the French fleet off Sandy Hook."

"Gladly, sir, I know the area quite well."

"Good," said his commander, "what are their preparations of shipping for embarkation of foot or horse?"

A hint of desperation in Washington's voice made Burr want to comfort him.

"And what expeditions are on hand?" continued Washington.

In Washington's eyes, Burr observed the clouds of decision-making and the lights of angst.

"Whether up the North River, Connecticut, or West Indies?"

"Yes, Sir!"

One thing Washington was good at, Burr knew, was obtaining information.

He accepted the secret mission to contact patriot spies and obtain the facts regarding British plans.

After Lord Alexander and Burr met with Washington, Mrs. Prevost, with a smiling face, came over to the Lord and Burr.

"Lord Alexander, who is this handsome young man."

Burr smiled but cautiously.

"Colonel Burr, may I introduce you to our hostess, Mrs. Prevost."

His cynical side thought she was a very plain woman.

"Please call me Theodosia."

Her hazel eyes and natural graces reminded him of his sister, Sally. He focused his eyes on hers, absorbed by what he glimpsed in them. Dreams, sadness, hope?

'Mrs. Prevost."

She frowned at him; "Call me Theodosia."

"Theodosia, fate prevented us from meeting earlier. My regiment was stationed to the north of the Hermitage in Suffern, New York, and after a successful attack on a British picket outside of Hackensack, we stopped in Paramus. Your cousin, Capt. John Watkins, a member of my regiment, suggested I stop by and introduce myself."

Pleased with this information, she inched closer, hoping to hold his hands someday.

"But my stay in Suffern was short as I and my regiment were ordered to winter at Valley Forge."

"The whats and ifs of life," she replied.

He wanted to take her arm, but her sister whisked her off.

Needing to rest, Burr sat by a window, letting the sun warm him, observing the thirty-two-year wife of James Prevost, a British army officer, interact with members of Washington's staff: Monroe, McHenry, Greene, Lafayette, and Hamilton. Later that evening, Lafayette and Hamilton were ordered to meet with Vice Admiral d'Estaing, whose fleet was now anchored off Sandy Hook.

Before leaving for his assignment, Burr was struck by her witty conversation. He found her engaging and liked that she was not inconveniently shy nor unwilling to express her opinion.

Busy admiring her soft eyes and listening to the talk and laughter, time flew away at an exceptional rate.

Until that day, he wondered if he would ever meet the woman of his prayers.

His heart quivered, and he let out a quick laugh. "Steady," he said to himself.

Watching her walk, laugh, and dance away the time, he wanted to know her and have a genuine friendship.

Wandering back to camp, he squinted at the sun, pleased, very pleased, recalling something in her eyes. His heart raced up to his throat and clanged like the College of New Jersey bell.

When it was decided that the French would attack a smaller British force in Rhode Island instead, Burr's spying assignment was terminated. He was ordered to rejoin his regiment in the Highlands, which marched to West Point in late July.

General Washington selected him to convey by sloop three highly placed Loyalists—William Smith, Cadwallader Colden, and Roeliff Eltinge—under a white flag down the Hudson River to the enemy. The Colonel welcomed the task of gaining information from Washington's informers. Mrs. Prevost, anxious to visit relatives in New York City, obtained permission from General Alexander to take passage on the ship with her half-sister Caty and a male servant.

"When I learned from General Alexander," said Colonel Burr, you wished to voyage south, in a blink of an eye, I added your names to the passenger list."

She stepped forward; he stepped back slightly.

'How long will the trip take."

"Depending on the number of stops, maybe five days." (August 5–10),

"That should provide," she said, "a considerable amount of time for us to become acquainted."

Burr gave her a serious nod, much more than she had hoped.

Full of confidence and smiling, she winked at the confident Aaron, who took her arm in his, and they strolled about the ship.

Burr spent some months on orders from Washington and, when the occasion allowed, enjoyed Mrs. Prevost's company at the Hermitage, though she was not in good health.

Writing from the Hermitage to his sister, "Believe me, Sally, she has an honest and affectionate heart. We talk of you very often; her highest happiness will be to see you and love you. I have given her the nickname "sister P," and think of her as our lovely sister."

The Colonel wrote General Washington from Elizabethtown on the twenty-fourth of October 1778, "The excessive heat and occasional fatigues of the preceding campaign have so impaired my health and constitution as to render me incapable of immediate service. For three months, I have taken every advisable step for my recovery but have the mortification to find a return of sickness upon my return to duty and that every relapse is more dangerous than the former."

He ran his fingertip over the surface of the side of his quill. It was baby-smooth and unsullied.

"I have consulted several physicians; they all assure me that a few months of retirement and attention to my health are the only probable means to restore it. A conviction of this truth and of my present inability to discharge the duties of my office induce me to beg your excellency's permission to retire from pay and duty till my health will permit. The nature of service shall more particularly require my attention, provided such permission can be given without subjecting me to any disadvantage in point of my present rank and command or any I might acquire during the interval of my absence."

Calculating his words for a moment, he continued writing.

"I shall still feel and hold myself liable to be called into service at your excellency's pleasure, precisely as if in full pay, and barely on furlough; reserving to myself only the privilege of judging of the sufficiency of my health during the present appearance of inactivity. My anxiety to be out of pay arises in no measure from intention or wish to avoid any requisite service. But too great a regard to malicious surmises, and a delicacy perhaps censurable, might otherwise hurry me unnecessarily into service, to the prejudice of my health, and without any advantage to the public, as I have had the misfortune already to experience."

Embarrassed and annoyed, he hesitated again, telling himself he was doing the right thing.

"I am encouraged in this proposal by the opinion of Lord Stirling, who has been pleased to express the justice of my request—the sense your excellency must entertain of the weak state of the corps in which I have the honour to command and the present sufficiency of its respective officers. I purpose to keep my quarters at this place until I have the honour of your excellency's answer, which I wait impatiently."

General Washington received his letter at his Fredericksburg headquarters and replied to Lieutenant-colonel Burr on the twenty-sixth of October, "I have your favour of the 24th. You, in my opinion, carry your ideas of delicacy too far when you propose to drop your pay while the recovery of your health necessarily requires your absence from the service. It is not customary, and it would be unjust. You therefore have leave to retire until your health is so far re-established as to enable you to do your duty. Be pleased to give the colonel notice of this, that he may know where to call upon you should any unforeseen exigency require it."

An attitude sprang into Burr's eyes, and his propriety and stubbornness refused to allow him to accept leave with pay. He stayed in the military.

By the beginning of January of 1779, he received orders to take command and patrol the "Neutral Ground."

It was an area of land between the upper limits of Westchester to somewhat below Peekskill, New York, where American and British soldiers plundered the inhabitants regardless of politics.

Thrust out of the active war, he was determined to solve the problem.

Protecting the farmers from the pillaging of the enemy and the patriots became his duty.

Upon arriving at White Plains, he discovered in the American camp stolen goods and animals and that the men were "infatuated with the itch for scouting."

Around him, bare trees circled in the dull glory of winter. The wind caught brown leaves, whisked by, and carried off.

After some small talk with the men, he steered the conversation toward his assignment.

"My first official act is to return all stolen property to their rightful owner regardless of the politics of the owner, be they Tory or Patriot."

Throughout his life, he never believed that politics determined right or wrong. The deed itself was what should be judged. This belief he maintained throughout his years, much to his determent, but more on that later. He made a complete list of all the inhabitants of this "no man's land" and an accurate map of this area. Ever since the Quebec march, maps fascinated him, and he understood their military value.

He set up an intelligence corps by recruiting trusted men in the area.

They informed him of the movements of the enemy.

He learned of those who claimed to be patriotic and of the plundering activities. This diligence on his part put an end to this looting and allowed the inhabitants to sleep at night, knowing that their property was safe from nefarious pillage.

By March, he informed General Washington, "I have walked all the way around my decision and no longer ponder it. My health is, and it is necessary to retire from the army. The British punched holes in the command of the men who succeeded him on the Westchester lines. The British captured Colonel Thompson, and his headquarters was destroyed.

Colonel Green, who replaced Thompson, was surprised by the British, and he and most of his men were killed.

William Hull, an officer under Burr's command, wrote in late May.

"The ground you so long defended is now left to the depredation of the Enemy, and our friends in distressing circumstances."

After his discharge, his friends saw his anxiety and wished to appease it. He did some work for Generals McDougall and Arthur St. Clair and engaged in some more espionage against the British.

His sister, Sally, said, "You look as if you were more pleased than you care to express.

A smile shifted towards a smirk as he acknowledged her words.

While in New Haven, still attempting to recuperate, in July of 1779,

British soldiers attacked.

He led some Yale students to obstruct the enemy while the women and children evacuated the town but his thoughts centered on Mrs. Prevost. His Theodosia.

    love is a bud looking for a tree
    the sun and rain give shape and form
    the seasons are constantly on furlough
    the persona of summer and winter transform

    the shears of life prune all too often
    nature's evolution can take a twisted turn
    deformity can be the regimen
    what could have been is left with no return

    love erupts upon the scene
    from shade to shine ready to apply
    a sheen waiting to be seen
    a spark that may never die

    love can hurdle both ocean and continent
    striking the chord of nourishment

## Chapter 72

## The Gone Man

After the Battle of Monmouth, the British concentrated their forces upon Lee's suggestions in the southern colonies, as Mr. Jefferson experienced.

The following year, Washington and his staff spent winter headquarters (December 1779 to June 1780) at Morristown, New Jersey, in the stately white house with green trim of the deceased Judge Jacob Ford. *How could it be so cold?* Thought Alex?

Snowstorm after snowstorm created snowdrifts six feet deep. The winter is more frigid than at Valley Forge and cold beyond all enduring, the ice forming a natural bridge that allowed the British to transport heavy artillery across the New York Bay, the lack of food–soldiers eating every kind of horse food but hay, and sickness and desertions in every direction.

On January 5, 1780, Alex penned a letter for Washington to Congress.

"Many of the men have been without meat for four or five days entirely and short of bread and none but on very scanty supplies. Some, for their preservation, have been compelled to maraud and rob from the inhabitants, and I have no power to punish or repress the practice."

Alex looked up at His Excellency, "These problems are caused by Congress's inability to tax the states or establish public credit."

So often hearing this sentiment uttered, the general had no reason to hope things would change. He tried to respond, but his voice took a hike.

"You must ask the magistrates of every county in New Jersey for their cooperation in a "requisition" of grain and beef provisions for the army."

*How contemptible,* thought Alex. Of all things in the world, he found Congress the most unworthy.

"Order the field officers into every county to supervise the collection of supplies."

Watching the soldiers mutiny and desert in large numbers depressed Alex.

His request to join John Laurens in a combat unit in the South left him drowning in a sea of despair. "I am chagrined and unhappy, but I submit," he wrote his friend. "In short, Laurens, I am disgusted with everything in this world but yourself and very few more honest fellows, and I have no other wish than as soon as possible to make a brilliant exit."

Alex tried to recollect himself but wrote, "Tis a weakness, but I feel I am not fit for this terrestrial country."

At the end of January, General Washington reported to Samuel Huntington, president of Congress.

"The army at Morristown is comfortable and easy in regard to provisions, in spite of a January blizzard of three days that left snow six-foot-high."

Though under the winter gloom of night, Alex's natural cheerfulness returned with the day's sunlight, and so did his spirits.

During the day, he worked in a log cabin attached to the mansion, his vast administrative burden tying him to his desk, but at night, Alex attended receptions with pretty young women who sled across the snowdrifts for "dancing assemblies."

In a black velvet suit with Washington, Steuben adorned with medals and fancy-dressed officers at a nearby storehouse; they exchanged pleasantries.

At a dinner with Washington, Alex acted as a waiter, serving food, refilling glasses, and offering a toast.

Here's to the men who are wisest and best
Here's to the men who with judgment are blest,
Here's to the men who are smart as can be –
I drink to the men who agree with me!

At another gathering, Washington and his staff were entertained seeing Alex smitten with a pretty, young female named Cornelia Lott.

Colonel Samuel B. Webb's fellow officer sang, "Now the conqueror feels the inexorable dart and yields a young woman to his heart."

Overpowered to reply, and after several moments of silence by Alex, he raised his glass, exclaiming, "My dear Colonel! Allow me to interpret my silence. I confess you have long known me better than I."

After Cornelia came Polly, but in early February, Elizabeth Schuyler arrived, staying with relatives at a house a quarter-mile from

Washington's headquarters.

When Miss Schuyler presented letters to Washington, the twenty-five-year-old Alex looked at her and never forgot having met her.

His view opened to sensations of tempered pain and glowing hope.

Tench Tilghman, a fellow aide, commented, "Hamilton is a gone man."

He addressed a sonnet to her entitled "Answer to the Inquiry Why I sighed."

> Before no mortal ever knew
> A love like mine so tender, true,
> Completely wretched—you away,
> And but half blessed e' en while you stay.
> If present love [illegible] 's soft? face
> Deny you to my fond embrace
> No joy unmixed my bosom warms
> But when my angel's in my arms.

Before he left Morristown for Amboy, New Jersey, at the beginning of March to negotiate a prisoner exchange for Washington, Alex, the poor West Indian youth, and "Eliza" Schuyler, the daughter of a prominent New York family, decided to marry.

Philip Schuyler accepted Alex's marriage proposal to his daughter, and Colonel Hamilton became part of New York's most prodigious families.

The Schuylers took a temporary house in Morristown and resided there until the Continental Army left in June, Alex visiting every evening. They were delighted that the "clerk" chose them.

Mr. Schuyler was only too happy to converse with Alex. Mrs. Schuyler listened, and Eliza smiled in peace. Schuyler seemed convinced as Alex continued. "The quantity of money in circulation is certainly a chief cause of the Continental's decline."

"It is depreciated," said Schuyler, "more than five times as much as it ought to be."

"The excess is derived from opinion, a want of confidence."

"What can be done?"

"Congress must create a central bank similar to the Bank of England to issue money to finance the war."

Schuyler sat back and listened.

"Taxes and domestic loans cannot finance the war alone."

Schuyler struck speechless, admiring Alex.

"The necessity of a foreign loan is now greater than ever. Nothing else will retrieve our affairs."

The following day, Schuyler told Eliza, "Colonel Hamilton affords me happiness too exquisite for expression. I daily experience the pleasure of hearing encomiums on his virtue and abilities from those capable of distinguishing between real and pretended merit. He is considered, as he certainly is, the ornament of his country."

Eliza lifted her shoulders and smiled. "And he is very handsome."

## Chapter 73

## Burr Enters Law

Middletown, Connecticut, a busy sailing port that sported boats sailing in the slow-moving Connecticut River, was Burr's temporary home while he had read law for the past few weeks.

While approaching the law office of Titus Hosmer, a delegate for Connecticut to the Continental Congress in 1778, he noticed two men carrying the body of Hosmer. In disbelief about what he observed, a throbbing headache hit him like a ton of bricks.

"Colonel Burr," said an astonished Robert Troup, "What are you doing in Raritan? I thought you were reading law with Titus Hosmer in Middletown."

"He died suddenly."

"What are your plans?"

"To ask Judge Paterson for his opinion."

The pain of Hosmer's death throbbed in Burr's heart. Hesitating, he said, "Join me under the guidance of our college friend and mentor, William Paterson."

Grinding his teeth, Troup responded, "Yes."

"I want to gain admission to the bar quickly so I can marry Theodosia."

"Judge Paterson rules against our period of study." Troup knew Patteron's decision was like a fire burning in his friend's soul.

"I have contracted," Burr said to Troup, "with a lawyer, named Thomas Smith, at Haverstraw, New York, for six months starting in April of 1781 for a "fee" to make us fit as soon as possible for submission to the bar."

Troup felt light-headed, and his heart seemed to swell in his chest.

"Why are you giggling, Robert?"

"The sight of being a lawyer in six months fills my mind with hope for the future."

The Colonel read and took notes sixteen hours and more a day, spurred on by two great incentives: love and no money. With a letter of introduction from General McDougall to Philip Schuyler, he rode to Albany in October 1781 to solicit his license to practice law in New York courts.

"Colonel Burr," said Schuyler, General McDougall compliments you as a "soldier, an officer, and a worthy citizen, who commanded the advanced corps of the army in the southernmost part of the state in the winter of 1779, during which you discharged your duty with uncommon vigilance."

Burr, with a backward head tilt, looked skyward, his eyes sparkling. "Please be our guest, Colonel."

"Thank you, General, for your kindness."

"You have only studied law for six months?" Burr chuckled, wanting to press his lips to the center of Theo's neck. "The law requires three years of instruction under a suitable teacher before one can be admitted to the practice of law." Burr's lip twitched, knowing no limitations of his powers. A slow smile spread on Burr's thin lips.

"Precedent exists," he said, "to waive this requirement,"

"But one," said Schuyler, "has to have the unanimous consent of the judges of the state Supreme Court."

"I plan on petitioning the three judges: Chief Justice Richard Morris and Justices John Sloss Hobart and Robert Yates, and will wait patiently in Albany." He waited and waited for three months. The last judge, Robert Yate was too busy to see him.

While in Albany," he wrote Theodosia, "Philip Van Rensselaer compelled me to stay in more elegant quarters, and I reside in the two upper rooms at his maiden aunts' home." He stopped writing, carefully weighing his words. "These two obliging ladies are incredibly good-natured and the very paragon of neatness. Not an article of furniture, even to a teakettle that would soil a muslin handkerchief."

A little after the new year of 1782, the state supreme court published a blanket edict open to all. He informed Theodosia, "The three-year training period will be waived for applicants who had marched to the patriotic trumpet and could muster the required scrutiny."

At twenty-six, the Colonel received a license as an attorney in the Supreme Court on January 19, 1782, in April, having passed the examination that qualified him to practice as a counsel-at-law without remaining for two years under a practicing solicitor's guidance. Telling Theodosia the excellent news, he added, "I received no favor from Judge Yates nor the other Judges as some jealous persons have suggested." He ended the letter by telling her, "When I first met you, it was like a visit from the sun; you warmed my soul and spirits. Up to then, love for me had been in total eclipse." Opening a law office in Albany's small but busy town on April 18, he discerned glimpses of her in his office.

"Marriage," he said, "as soon as possible."

On July 2, 1782, the love-struck Colonel made a quick jaunt to Paramus, New Jersey, to marry Theodosia Prevost, ten years his senior, not in the best of health, with little money, and the recent widow of a British officer, Colonel Prevost, with four children: Augustine James Frederick, John Bartow, Anne Louisa, and Mary Elizabeth. The brilliant and elegant Theodosia described the wedding to his sister, Sally, ". . . A simple ceremony at the home of my sister, Caty, Mrs. Thomas Brown. . . It cost us nothing. The fates led Aaron on in his old coat. My gauze gown, ribbons, gloves, etc., were gifts from Caty, and the parson's fee took the only half joe (a Portuguese gold coin) Burr was master of. . . the want of money is the only grievance we have." Not deemed beautiful by her contemporaries, her cultivated mind, and graceful winning etiquette drew her further to him. She corrected and sympathized with him upon the famous authors of the day, Chesterfield, Rousseau, Voltaire, and others.

"The wit of Voltaire, I cherish," she told him, "without being stained by his ridicule."

"Do you have a favourite line?"

"Justice is often extremely unjust." She noticed his face exhibited a questioning expression.

"You inspire me," said the Colonel, "with respect for that of your sex."

Half-smiling, she said, "Chesterfield, I relish except his indulgence."

His lips curved in a wistful tenderness. "My favourite, though, is Rousseau, but his sentimentality does not beguile me, and I enjoy Gibbon."

Without stumbling at his fifteenth and sixteenth chapters," he added.

She laughed. "I must confess," he said, "that my ideas in favor of female intellectual power had been founded in what I had imagined more than in what I had seen, except for my true love, Theodosia Prevost Burr."

## Chapter 74

# Wilky Does Arnold

Two men were settled comfortably on the front porch, enjoying the quiet of the summer evening." Would you like to buy one of the finest estates in Pennsylvania?" asked Joseph Reed, an ally of the Biddle family and president of the Pennsylvania Supreme Executive Council.

Wilky's chin at a sloping angle, and without hesitating said, "Do Indians carry arrows?

"I take that as a yes."

Wilkinson smiled widely. "Tell me more."

"It is a hundred-year-old mansion with large stables, a substantial farmhouse with barns, and five thousand well-cultivated acres spread across Bucks County."

The light of riches played in Wilky's eyes. "How is this possible?"

"Joseph Galloway once owned it."

"He was president of the colonial assembly."

"Correct, but he chose to side with our enemy when they occupied Philadelphia, and he withdrew with them in June 1778; his property was confiscated."

Reed noticed Wilky calculating, seeing that his face was excited, that a storm was brewing.

"I have served my country but have little in monetary holdings."

Reed darted a glance at Wilky. "The price can be forty-six hundred pounds."

"A bargain, I believe, but."

Reed cut him off. "Payable in installments."

Exhaling a deep breath, Wilky's face brightened and sent Reed a sparkling smile.

"With paper money rather than coins?" said Reed.

The stocky soldier ran fast fingers through his thick, black hair, thinking the outlay was reduced by one-third.

A thunderous hush ensued, and Wilky gave him a wry grin.

"Yes, the excessive printing of paper money by the state and central governments takes its toll," said Wilky.

Reed reached for his colleague's shoulder. But it slipped away.

"What is required of me?"

Reed hesitated, then rubbed his chin.

Wilky observed his face screwed with concentration.

"What do you know about your old commander, Benedict Arnold?"

Wilky swore, pacing the floor in a frenzy of contempt.

"He is fond of display and ostentatious indulgence."

Another long silence.

"And his influence, never that of a peace-maker, will stimulate existing animosities."

He sat. His face lined with confidence.

"He uses army resources to aid his business interests."

"He borrowed," said Reed, "a sum of money of the commissaries which he discounted on a contract for rum at a higher price than paid.'

"No doubt pocketing the difference."

Reed bit excitedly at his lip.

"His profits," said Wilky, "from these black markets help to refurbish his residence and headquarters at the Penn Mansion."

Reed's cool, cultured control intrigued and fascinated Wilky." His modus operandi is to make quick money," said Wilky, "through his back-room deals."

Wilky turned his head very slowly, very deliberately. "As early as the 23rd of June, four days after taking command, he entered into a very suspicious partnership," said Reed, "The goods not wanted by the public were to be purchased with the public money and sold to benefit himself and his partners.

Wilky's elevated expression grew wider." In Canada, he involved himself in all sorts of illegitimate speculations."

Reed's spectacles nearly slide off the end of his nose in his excitement.

"He unites himself," I've heard said Wilky, "with the City's leading families, in rank, wealth, and fashion, and with those who were almost without exception connected by sympathy with the Royal cause."

Reed looked at him and blinked, sending him a slow grin.

"His first appointment," continued Reed, "Major David Solebury Franks, a Philadelphia merchant rumored to have questionable ties to a wealthy family in British-occupied New York City who had worked with the General since the Battle of Saratoga.

His second appointment, Mathew Clarkson, whose loyalist daughter is close friends with a Miss Peggy Shippen."

Wilky blew out a breath and lifted his eyebrows. "His honour always flees like chaff before the wind."

Reed looked at Wilky. "He claims he is following his direct orders from Washington of giving "security to individuals of every class and description.""

As Reed continued, Wilky observed his eyes widen.

"Will you not think," said Reed, "it extraordinary that General Arnold made a public entertainment the night before last, of which not only familiar Tory ladies, but the wives and daughters of persons banished by the State, and now with the enemy at New York, formed a very considerable number."

It took a second to understand; Wilky stared angrily at the news.

The fact is correct," said Reed.

"He has," said Wilky, "no other aim than to gratify his ill-regulated passion for luxurious indulgence and display."

Reed stood and drew himself to his full height, thrusting his chin out aggressively. His face jumped to anger

"Yes," he said, "when the footsteps of the invader are still fresh upon the soil."

"Intoxicated," said Wilky, "by the attentions paid him by the fashionable and aristocratic portions of society."

Purple with rage, Reed said, "He seems to have borne himself as the military master of a conquered city rather than as a subordinate officer in command."

Stiffly, Wilky jerked as if a bolt of lightning jolted through him.

"He treats the local authorities," said Reed, "with ill-disguised disrespect."

What is wrong with the man, Reed thought before he said, "While life for many civilians grows worse on the streets, Arnold lives luxuriously in a manner that even Washington would not approve of."

Wilky raced to answer. "Arnold is overstepping the rights of the people and the Pennsylvania civil government. You should ruin him!"

He paused, thinking he would make the little man jump as if a burning log approached that portion of his uniform designed for sitting. "He is as fit to command Philadelphia as a dog is a judge on the bench."

Knowing that helping Reed bring down Arnold, Wilkinson's hopes increased in number and meaning. He took his wife from the "society" of

Philadelphia north to the town of Trevose, near Bristol, on the Delaware River.

There, he fell miserably short of his bold goals.

He worked his hardest to turn a diamond into coal. He could not produce enough revenue to meet the expenses created by his wife and his self-indulgence.

In late July of 1779, a realization came to him.

It was in his best interest to accept Congress's offer to the post of Clothier General of the army at an annual salary of $5,000.

Trying to burn the candle at both ends, Wilky burnt both hands.

He preferred the confines of his new estate to headquarters at Morristown, New Jersey.

It gave his critics great satisfaction to know the new clothier general was taxing the patience of General Washington.

And tax he did, preferring to ignore Washington's growing impatience, letting it fester like a sore, harmful to his future.

## Chapter 75

## Sir Henry's Plight

After the Battle of Monmouth on June 28, 1778, the Brits and rebels in the northern theater marked time as summer's warm, humid weather colored the sky and water to a crystal clear blue.

Without the French fleet, Washington only made forays, and Sir Henry Clinton contemplated bold moves that resulted in bluffs but put no money on the table.

With a shake of his head to those in earshot, his moderately styled hair swept back from his weathered face, Sir Henry elaborated, "The reality of the British situation in America lay in the power of the Cabinet. Having too much of their way, they think too well of their policies." He demanded to Whitehall, "Approve my plans on policy or relieve me of command," but his voice drowned in the waves of the Atlantic Ocean.

"You have taken from me ten thousand men and expect me to press on as everything was the same." He waved his hand in the air. "You cannot expect success without the means of securing it."

"Your Majesty," said Germain to the King, "we have to consider more than one general's discontent."

"Why did he assume command?" The monarch asked. "And why does he complain?"

"Lord Cornwallis told me earlier this morning that he needs to share his frustration and his anger but trusts no one under his command."

The sovereign's attention never dropped, and he listened with bated breath.

"British officers," continued Germain, "are deserting America in droves: Lord Howe, Generals Pigot, and Grey. "I wonder why?" The King said.

"They are not happy men." The King glanced up, meeting the shrewd eyes of Germain, the British secretary of state.

"Cornwallis believes that Clinton needs comfort, a kind word, and someone to bounce his ideas off. It is hard for him to accept; look at things as they really are."

"The King and his ministers," Germain wrote to Clinton, "promise you all possible reinforcements and you have the entire freedom of action."

Clinton read the letter and hated his helplessness more than anything else, thinking a man could fall out of love with his dream when reality triumphs.

"Can you think of coming home?" continued Germain, "at this critical time when the country looks upon you as the only chance of saving America?"

"This is not good," Germain informed the King, "it strengthens the arguments of the opposition that the war is madness."

In the spring of 1779, the Cabinet promised to send sixty-six hundred troops to America, and more by summer. They hoped this would permit Clinton to attack the coast and bring Washington to a decisive battle. Newcastle wrote his cousin, Sir Henry Clinton, "Your duty is to serve not on your own conditions but as the King commands."

Clinton wheezed a sound of disagreement. In a separate communication, Sir Henry learned, "The realities in England disallowed sending the necessary requisites for carrying on an active summer campaign."

"I want results," Sir Henry told his aides, not lamentations. I want a field army of thirty thousand men!" *Damn it*, he thought.

"With the small inadequate force at my disposal, I will do my best," he promised the Cabinet, "I wish I had been left to do it exactly in my own way; I will, however, do it." A humorless smirk spread on his plump lips.

While waiting for reinforcements, Sir Henry ordered troops to the Chesapeake and Albemarle Sound, meeting minor resistance, and his soldiers destroyed a large number of supplies and shipping before returning to New York laden with the booty.

"The prospects are so bright," he told William Smith, "I expect to be presented with the heads of some of the rebel leaders."

"Rest assured," wrote General Cornwallis to Clinton from England in early April. "I do not want to succeed you but come to share fortunes with you, but I will not let you desert me."

Sir Henry discerned jealousy and suspicion marching across his bow.

A month later, Lord Cornwallis wrote to his brother, "I have many friends in the American army. I love that army and flatter myself that I am not quite indifferent to them. I hope Sir Henry will stay; my returning to him will likely induce him to do so. If he insists on coming away, I cannot decline to take the command and must make the most of it. And I trust that good intentions and plain dealing will carry me through."

His wife had died, and the grieved Cornwallis craved a change of scene. On July 21, he landed in New York and returned to his old position as second in command.

"I must warn you, Sir Henry, a French squadron is bound across the Atlantic, designation unknown."

'I surmise," said Clinton, "that British forces will be kept in the West Indies as long as a French attack is dangerous.

Clinton knew that Cornwallis wished to bathe his thirsty limbs in the glory of victory.

"Once Admiral Arbuthnot arrives," said Sir Henry, "I want to aim at South Carolina. Speed is the essence as Washington can send reinforcements."

Caught between his ambition and his feelings for Clinton, Cornwallis sat by the window and let the morning light warm his skin.

"I do have concerns," said Clinton. "I received news that the Admiral is a bit of a proser and not so young as he has been."

The Admiral's fleet arrived on August 25, the day in full bloom, observed Clinton.

Without a word, Sir Henry watched Cornwallis beside him as the Admiral and his men began to disembark.

"He looks a great deal older than seventy," said Sir Henry later in the day.

"Looks can deceive," said Cornwallis.

"I am annoyed that the Admiralty ignored my suggestion of names put forward."

Cornwallis knew that selecting the older man to collaborate with Sir Henry was plain outright stupid.

"Admiral," said Sir Henry, "how many men did you bring?"

"Only half of the sixty-six hundred men promised by the government, and most are sick with a fever."

His words produced a stab of pain as shock draped Clinton's face. The disease spread through the town, and military operations faltered, leaving Sir Henry gnawing on his lip.

"The Admiral," Sir Henry said to Cornwallis, "is quick to take offense and slow to take responsibility."

Lord Cornwallis held his words, hoping Sir Henry would resign and return to England.

Clinton turned away from Cornwallis, prepared to face the day, thinking, Ah! There is nothing like the heads of the British army and navy in America at loggerheads for a real disaster.

For two years, trouble followed Sir Henry Clinton and Admiral Arbuthnot, and Cornwallis used it to alienate Sir Henry.

"My plan," said Clinton to the Admiral and Cornwallis,

"Is to move to the South."

"No," said the Admiral. "The Governor of Jamaica fears a French squadron under d'Estaing."

"Governor Haldimand wants two thousand men for the defense of Canada," said Cornwallis.

Sir Henry mumbled, "What do you know about the day-to-day frustrations of command."

Four thousand men under Cornwallis's command sailed to Jamaica but returned to New York when he learned from a ship that d'Estaing was heading for North America.

Sir Henry, the Admiral, and Cornwallis worried about Halifax, Rhode Island, and New York. A plan was made one day and another the next day. Clinton smirked and lifted his head to look down on the two men. On September 1, 1779, he learned that Spain had entered the war.

"The drain on England's resources would now be greater than ever," he said to Cornwallis.

"The support of the loyalists," replied Cornwallis, "is not to be counted on."

'I am not to expect," said Sir Henry, "that we shall be thought of, at least for a time."

On the other side of the Atlantic, the King assented to meet with Germain.

"I must suppose," said Germain with a straight face, "that the news from America assures me of there being a conclusion to the war."

The King clasped his hands together, palm pressed hard to palm, letting himself touch victory's bright idea.

"There is reason to think that the campaign of 1781 will be the last of the resistance."

"What is this based on?"

"Our spies tell us the rebel army lacks cash or credit and mutinies are common among the hungry, unpaid troops."

Germain observed a sense of delight on the King's face.

"Tell me more," demanded the King.

"They have no magazines nor money, and in a little time, they shall have no men if they have no money."

The King licked his lips. "Victory is at hand."

"They have lived upon expedients till they can live no longer," said

Germain.

"Three years of French alliance," said the King, looking down his nose at Germain, "and almost a year of military support from the French have been utterly inconclusive."

The King was unaware that feuds in the British army in America paralyzed sound planning.

"A great pity for the British, I assure you."

It would be as much as the King could bear without becoming impolite. He restrained himself from giving any reproofs to St. Germain and thanked him instead with a chilly air.

The circumstances in America allowed Sir Henry to attack the South, leaving the army in the North on the defensive and the military in the South on the offensive, depending totally upon the sea for supplies and support. Knowing it was dangerous that the two armies were not integrated, he allowed each to march down the war's rough road, knowing the British Navy covered their backs.

Cornwallis invaded Charleston and North Carolina while Sir Henry established a significant post on the Chesapeake, the former assuming a large degree of independence due to the division of command.

Upon Clinton's return to New York, contact with Benedict Arnold started through the auspicious of Major Andre. Clinton refrained from giving a puzzled look but did let loose a skeptical glance at a view of the Hudson River from a multi-paned window that let natural light flood the room.

## Chapter 76

## Love, Hate and Treason

Edward Shippen wanted his daughter, Margaret "Peggy" Shippen, to receive "the most useful and best education that America afforded at that time."

His family glanced up, saw he was serious, and then applauded. As a youth, she was not idle, becoming an expert with her needle and instructed in drawing, dancing, and music by her father. To show her off, in 1774, Edward Shippen brought to dinner a tall, grave provincial officer who was a delegate from Virginia.

In her fifteenth year, Mistress Peggy first met the Road Builder. Engaging in conversation, the youth in the bloom of womanhood caught the notice of George Washington at Wednesday's meal of the day. She considered him plain, remarkably plain, not British enough. Her grace and loveliness made an impression on the Virginian.

On parting, Washington told Peggy, "I hope someday I can serve you."

Little did either know a fire waited in the distance. After the British took control of Philadelphia in 1777, Peggy met John André, a charming, well-educated British officer who occupied Benjamin Franklin's house. André enchanted her when visiting Edward Shippen's large spacious house built of red and black brick that featured classical pediments above its doors and windows.

Dropping down beside him, her fingers brushed through her hair, and she glowed like a full moon. As beginnings went, André was thrilled, her eyes admiring his handsome face.

"Mademoiselle, would you allow me to sketch you?"

Her voice asked subtly. "You are an artist?"

"I have been known to give art lessons."

Lifting a hand to touch his shoulder, she stopped, focusing on his eyes. She wanted to lean over and rest her cheek against his. He sketched her and wrote poetry for her, closing the distance between them.

Peggy's social scene was filled with parties and balls with numerous

British officers and Tory sympathizers. As one of the belles of Philadelphia, she attracted the admiration of every beholder, and the British officers declared she was the most beautiful woman in England or America. André excelled at entertaining the otherwise boring days and planned an extravaganza in tribute to Howe.

"My dearest Peggy," said Andre, "will you partake in my Mischianza this coming May 18, 1778, in honor of Howe's impending departure?"

"What is a Mischianza?"

"A fete given by the British officers to General Howe."

Her mind so bound upon his, her eyes burned, shot out of a blazing hearth; it could have melted winter ice. It took her a split second to agree.

"I want you and your sisters to participate in my performance as Ladies of the Blended Hose and Burning Mountain. You will be the center of attraction." Observing her happiness leap toward his face, a tingling sensation overcame him. Their names appeared on their dresses, and Peggy talked about nothing but dancing.

At the last moment, Edward Shippen received a visit from some of his companions, prominent members of the Society of Friends, who persuaded him that his daughters should not appear in public in the Turkish dresses designed for the occasion. Taking heed, Shippen forbade their attendance. With an absent frown, Peggy lifted her eyes and wondered what it would have been like.

Before leaving Philadelphia, her hero was ordered by General Grey to pack books, musical instruments, scientific apparatus, and a portrait of Franklin from Ben's home. He never hesitated for a minute; orders are orders, and advancement depended on it. Before departing, André and Peggy sat on a bench watching small waves on the surface of the Delaware River. Sitting back in her simple handmade cotton dress, Peggy steered the conversation over her growing love for him. André lit a cigar, then narrowed his eyes against the smoke.

"Take me with you."

André beamed a smile. "You deserve a better life than tramping around with a soldier."

With a bright look, she leaned her head on his shoulder. "I hope I will see you again."

*****

*CONGRESS* .June 5, 1778.

*RESOLVED,* That, should the city of Philadelphia be evacuated by the enemy, it will be expedient and proper for the commander in chief to take effectual care that no insult, plunder or injury of kind may be offered to the inhabitants of the said city;—That, in order to prevent public or private injury, from the operations of ill disposed persons, the general be directed to take early and proper care to prevent the removal, transfer or sale of any goods, wares of merchandize in possession of the inhabitants of the said city, until the property of the same shall be ascertained by a joint committee, consisting of persons appointed by congress, and of persons appointed by the supreme executive council of the state of Pennsylvania; to wit, so far as to determine whether any, or what part thereof, may belong to the king of Great-Britain, or to any of his subjects.

When the British withdrew from Philadelphia in June of 1778, Washington wrote Arnold,

'Sir,

YOU are immediately to proceed to Philadelphia, and take the command of the troops there. You will find the objects of your command specified in the enclosed copy of a resolution of congress of the 5th instant. The means of executing the powers vested in you, I leave to your own judgment, not doubting that you will exercise them in the manner which shall be found most effectual, and at the same time, most consistent with the rights of the citizens.

I have directed the quarter master general, commissary general and clothier general to send proper persons in their respective departments into the city, to take possession, for the use of the army, of all public stores lest in the city by the enemy, which may not properly fall under the description of the enclosed resolve. In the execution of this duty, they will act under your directions and with your assistance."

*Given at bead-quarter,* this 18th day of June, 1778.

Considered by Washington as one of the bravest and most daring of the American generals, General George Washington wrote Benedict the IV on May 4, 1778:

"A gentleman in France having very obligingly sent me three sets of epaulettes and sword-knots, two of which, professedly, to be disposed of to any friends I should choose, I take the liberty of presenting them to you and General Lincoln." Taking it for granted, Benedict said, "Well, this is God's reward." Washington appointed Benedict Arnold on the 19th of June 1778 as military commander of Philadelphia, the second-most populous city in North America after New York—it consisted of neutral Quakers, along with many Patriots, former Loyalists, or Tories remaining in the town waiting for the outcome of the war to determine their loyalty. The slight murmuring of support for King George III evoked strong responses from the partisans.

A cauldron waited to overflow.

*****

Upon first seeing Benedict Arnold IV, Peggy Shippen thought there wasn't any wasted timber in him and soon learned he was blessed with almost superhuman energy and endurance. She considered him handsome and charismatic, his black hair, gray eyes, and an aquiline nose prominent in her mind.

His blood boiled when looking at her, and he found it difficult to swallow. *A delicate flower*, he thought. After a minute, she said, "I want to know about you." He grinned, thinking she was a fairy princess and wanted to impress her. "I rose from colonel to major general, but at a much slower rise than should have, and others with less experience and capabilities gained promotions instead of me."

He tried to avert his eyes from her firm breasts.

Together, they walked the streets of Philadelphia. Peggy noticed the sweat on his forehead and debated if it would be good to be in the company of a man twice her age who was in charge of Philadelphia. Her uncertainty vanished like a receding hill when he wrote her.

"My hand held my pen twenty times, frozen.

Fearing of giving malfeasance

Your charms are superior to time, absence, misfortune

Spare me a cruel indifference

Show me my progress

My affection for you is abundant.

Consult your happiness

Whatever my fate may be,

my most ardent wish is for your contentment

My last breath will be to implore the

blessing of heaven on you, my idol

The only wish of my heart is to hold your hand with devotion

You light a flame in me too deep ever to be untrue

You inspire me with pure and holy passion

Expand your heavenly bosom with a sensation finer

And more inviting than sunshine."

She let out a sound of pleasure, and they met the following afternoon amidst houses being built and, in the distance, open fields turning to farms." Why have I heard unkind words about you?"

"My troubles began with Joseph Reed of the Executive Council of Pennsylvania, whose house was adjacent to mine and took offense, I guess, when I failed to introduce myself."

Welcome to the pettiness of life, she thought. Close enough to touch her, Arnold turned and laid his hand on her shoulder, her demeanor asking him to continue. With warmth in his eyes, he continued, "The Executive Council resented the Continental Congress, the military, and I, and on June 19, established martial law. British and Loyalist property was documented for use by the army." It took a week to sort out the problem, Arnold's arrogance and avarice compounding the situation.

Meanwhile, he dipped his hand into the former goods of British loyalists and drew the criticism of Timothy Matlack, Secretary of the Executive Council, and Joseph Reed.

The press jumped over the story and exposed the secret agreement between Arnold and Gideon Olmsted on Arnold receiving money from selling the ship, the *Active*, and its goods.

You were a Whig or an enemy of the state; no in-between existed.

Though Arnold, the soldier, tried to remain above the politics, his enemies dragged him down.

Francis Lewis of NY wrote Governor George Clinton of "animosities run high, between Genl. Arnold and the executive branch of this state, in so much, that I fear it may form parties in the Congress,

"Reed and his colleague, Timothy Matlack, hated Pennsylvania's Loyalist residents, and Reed advocated on the floor of Congress the seizure of their properties and treason charges for those aligned with Great Britain. When President of Pennsylvania, he presided over trials of alleged Loyalists." The memory produced a scowl but then Arnold gave a half chuckle. "Reed and his family lived in a confiscated Loyalist home." Glancing at her ringless hand, he realized his life jumped from one focus, the command of Philadelphia then realigned with two dominating forces, Reed and Peggy. "Congress," he told Peggy, "benignly looked at the Loyalists citizens, but after James Wilson defended 23 people accused of treason, Reed stirred up a mob by his speeches and the mob's love of liquor." Outside, the wind bent the gusty trees, and inside, his eyes were dark and stormy. "This attack on Wilson came to be known as the "Battle of Fort Wilson" ; if not for the arrival of the cavalry, Wilson and his friends faced death. Following the cavalry's handling of the conflict, Reed felt it necessary to pardon and free the remaining rioters."

Anger now shifted into his voice. "Reed, vice-president of the council and elected president in December," said Arnold, "assembled names of Tory sympathizers for prosecution and punishment. I stood in the way of retribution, which earned me a rebuke because I did not hold a grudge against the Tories. This led Reed and his henchmen to bring eight corruption charges against me, most of them based on rumors spread by his doormats."

1. Issuing a pass to a known smuggler
2. Closing the city shops while making private purchases and sales
3. Forcing militia to do menial jobs (one of his aids used a militia sergeant to get a barber)
4. Interfering with Pennsylvania court ruling on profiteers
5. Using government wagons for personal business
6. Issuing passes without signatures from the Pennsylvania committee
7. Failure to report his use of government wagons for personal use
8. Supporting loyalists rather than patriots

"I demanded a court martial to clear my name, and a special committee of Congress investigated my finances." Arnold's eyes cast down, wishing he could make a joke out of this." Reed lacked the evidence to make a credible case against me, but he wanted to delay the court-martial for as long as possible, hoping to find more hearsay evidence." Peggy sighed and stretched, Arnold, wanting to draw her close to his side." General Washington urged me to remain patient, and my reputation would be restored." "I meet the General at a gathering at my father's house," said Peggy, who filled her lungs with air. "Tell me more of this Council."

"The Supreme Executive Council failed to provide evidence—because it had none. In December 1779, the court-martial did not charge me on any account, but this was the final slight to my honor, and I refused to tolerate it." Wearily, she dropped a hand to her side.

"In January 1780, the serious charges were dropped, but my reputation was smeared 'by a set of wretches beneath the notice of a gentleman and a man of honour." A rebel general commented that Arnold was "served up as a constant dish of scandal to the breakfast of every table on the continent."

Elizabeth Tilghman, Peggy's cousin, said, "What demon has possessed the people with respect to General Arnold? He is certainly much abused, ungrateful monster, to attack a character that has been looked up to, in more instances than one, since this war commenced."

Arnold sacrificed his health and most of his savings for the American Revolution and felt the men in power failed to treat him with honour. Pocketing a goodly sum from the sale of linens, glass, sugar, tea, and nails taken from the ship, the Charming Nancy, docked in Egg Harbor, Benedict IV bought up merchandise such as expensive food, wine, and wheels of cheese, the army did not need. He rationalized that these private dealings were payback the country owed him when the British abandoned Philadelphia. Resigning from his military command in April 1780, Peggy knew his pride hurt was hurt, and he clung to her like a dog to a bone.

"I told Washington on May 5, 1780, having made every sacrifice of fortune and blood, and become a cripple in the service of my country, I little expected to meet the ungrateful returns I have received of my countrymen, but as Congress have stamped ingratitude as a current coin I must take it. I wish your Excellency for your long and eminent services may not be paid off in the same coin."

His court-martial was delayed because of British threats in the area and absurd excuses from Reed. The prolonged court martial kicked off on December 19, 1779, in Morristown, New Jersey.

"A judgment exonerated and acquitted me, but the Pennsylvania commission said I issued "irregular" passes and was also guilty of improper use of government wagons." Peggy chuckled, "I gather your enemies kept you up all night."

Unable to resist, he smiled before continuing. "Taking months to act because he feared as did Congress that Reed's Pennsylvania would be less helpful toward the revolution, General Washington issued a reprimand on April 6, 1780."

"A gentle rebuke, my father informed me," said Peggy.

Arnold's ego kept him from comprehending he lacked the skills necessary to navigate Philadelphia's complex political theatre, specifically with the Pennsylvania Supreme Executive Council headed by Reed. (In England in 1801, he admitted his temperament had been ill-suited to the task.) When with her, he found her most charming, more than enough, and knew he was in love. She tittered and walked her eyes across his eyes. Parties and balls with her exploding in his head, she played on his vanity, shooting him a glance under her thick, brown lashes. She calculated for the moment by lowering her head and staring at him, knowing she could have him begging on his knees.

He took her, he thought, on a wild surge of urgency and delight, but he was just putty in her hands. After their marriage on April 8, 1779, they lived at his house, Mount Pleasant, in Philadelphia in such a style of ostentation that the rebel authorities claimed he violated military regulations.

"Benedict, I miss my British friends," said Peggy, who wished to separate him from his patriotic beliefs as far as she could. She advised him, "You deserve a higher command."

"And higher pay, too, and not in depreciated currency, he said."

"Your enemies bring corruption or other malfeasance charges against you."

He tried to fight off the hate that rushed through him. "I have spent much of my money on the war effort, and Congress claims I owe them money!"

"I know you are frustrated and bitter at this."

A silence settled instantly and stiffly over him. "Have you ever considered changing sides?" He stared at her unblinkingly, watching her pucker and mouth contract her eyelids a little, looking beautiful. She lowered her head.

"Forget what I said."

"I must admit that Joseph Reed and the Supreme Executive Council of Pennsylvania are working to my disadvantage."

"Congress refuses to shield you from your opponents in political office?"

Unamused, he glanced around, thinking that he could not have risen from obscurity as quickly as he did in any other army in an established nation. "The rebels want to confiscate the property of men of means,"

"They will drive luxury from the feet under us," said Peggy, "that is why I dream of a British victory."

"Feeling his way, he declared carefully, "Before I take any drastic step, the British must promise me the equivalent of all I hold and hope for."

"I have a friend who can help."

Admiring her hair tied back in a plain bow, Arnold wanted her to be happy as the day was long.

"Congress should have accepted," she said, "Britain's proposal to grant full self-governance in the colonies." Patriotism hinged on treason in the blink of an eye. He wanted to touch and feel her soft skin on his fingers. It was strange; he thought that he felt safe talking about treason. "When the fraction-torn colonies return to a firm class structure under the equitable rule of a humble Crown, everyone will be grateful to you as the creator of peace and prosperity."

Caution, he thought, caution. His anxiety hanging over his head, unable to relax or enjoy himself. "I will give the army one last chance to clear my name."

Little did he know that in front of him was an inferno of oppressive venom. His opponents in Pennsylvania threatened never again to supply the army with wagons for transport.

"I find myself," wrote General Washington, "working on a command for you."

Hearing a voice behind him, he ignored it as he contacted Peggy's friend André. "I can provide information to help the British win the war."

"As my mother says, the proof of the pudding is in the eating."

The words slammed at his ego. "My accomplishments will speak for themselves, yanking the door open to treason. "And I will want the British to pay me a large sum of money and give me command in war."

On June 29, 1780, he was awarded not only command of West Point but also the area from Fishkill to King's Ferry, the infantry and cavalry on the east side of the river down to British lines, and the forts at Stoney Point and Verplanck Point.

In a letter dated July 15, Arnold offered to surrender West Point for 20,000 pounds. He did not know until August 24, 1780, that his offer to surrender West Point had been accepted. According to Robert Morris, Washington offered Arnold the position of the left wing of the army, which earlier in Arnold's career would have been a coup. But now, he used his crippled leg as an excuse to take command of West Point. While he attended to his duties, Mrs. Arnold stayed in Philadelphia, communicating with André in Manhattan, and spent her time dreaming back and forth between her past and future. Not departing Philadelphia until Thursday, September 6, 1780, she followed the route sent to her by Benedict the IV and stopped at the Hermitage but missed Theodosia Prevost, who was at Sharon, Connecticut. Reaching West Point safely, she took up her abode in the Robinson House, situated on a knoll on the eastern side of the Hudson overlooking the river. With her in his arms, he enjoyed how her lips rubbed warm over his, treason a foregone conclusion.

Benedict Arnold
His way or the highway
The hero left in the cold
Traitor to his country's dismay

## Chapter 77

## West Point and the Chesapeake Bay

In Admiral Arbuthnot, Sir Henry Clinton saw a man who could smile and be a villain, but in truth, just a fool, a wild boar easier to pin down.

He wrote to friends in London, "The Admiral rarely holds to a course for long, and his memory fails, and he will not commit to writing, and he forgets all he says and does and talks nonsense by the hour."

With Cornwallis by his side, Sir Henry said, "William Green, Arbuthnot's secretary, is dishonest and he blows the coals of trouble between the admiral and me."

Later that day, after bickering with Arbuthnot, he said, "You fail to understand Washington's strength as a commander.:"And that is?" "He learns from his mistakes."

Really.

"I have it on good authority he believes he ought not to look back unless it is to derive useful lessons from past errors and for the purpose of profiting by dear bought experience." Arbuthnot said nothing and started to walk away but turned back saying, "You fail to steer clear of the shelves and rocks that one strikes upon the trail of command." Soon, he was striking them when dealing with Cornwallis, whom he was forced to consult on every step because he might succeed him.

His mind became so rattled that he believed that after dinner, when a violent illness with convulsive spasms and other intense symptoms of poison appeared, it was an attempt at murder, according to Dr. Morris, the Physician General of the army. "The bottle of wine is the culprit. It was sternly impregnated with arsenic," said Morris.

"I believe it is the work of William Livingston, the rebel Governor of New Jersey, who took offense at my barbed contempt for him a year earlier."

Clinton noted to Cornwallis, "Arbuthnot patrolled the waters off the bay of Rhode Island for sixteen days, not realizing he had been there before and not gaining any idea of the terrain or the enemy's disposition."

Each man blamed the other, and eventually, Arbuthnot objected to all of Clinton's plans, and Cornwallis turned on his commander. When Admiral Sir George Rodney arrived at the Hook with ten sail of the line, replacing Arbuthnot, the Royal Navy controlled the American waters. His victory at Gibraltar made him the most celebrated officer in the service, and he possessed a fighting spirit. Shrewd and aggressive, Rodney and Sir Henry brewed up bold ideas, thinking of attacking Newport and sending an expedition to the Chesapeake.

When hearing rumors of military action, some Americans descended into consternation, and the French home office received a communication, "We give ourselves up for lost on the arrival of Rodney."

Admiral Rodney wrote to Whitehall, "Sir Henry wants to join forces for an attack on Rhode Island and then an expedition to the Chesapeake; the next week, he throws his weight against it."

For a moment, Rodney held his quill in bewilderment. He wanted to tell the ministry he was joking but forced himself to take a deep breath and continued writing.

The next day, a new plan more attractive than taking Newport or destroying the French came to Sir Henry – Take West Point.

"Even more," he refrained, writing, "Sir Henry annoys me."

He stopped and stared at the letter with an unsatisfied nod.

"As the senior officer on the station," he told Whitehall, "I took over command, Sir Henry was delighted, Arbuthnot furious, and he complained he was doing the hard work of blockade while Sir Henry and I transacted business in New York without taking notice of him."

Vexation tugged at the corners of his mouth.

"The attack on Newport vanished because of squabbling," His eyes narrowed, "When commanders in chief differ, how much do nations suffer?"

Finding himself on Pearl Street on the way to Fraunces Tavern, Clinton spotted Major Andre.

"Major," said Sir Henry, "I need your help."

The Major waited for him to explain, studying his changing face and angry eyes.

"With New York safeguarded by our fleet, I want to move troops upriver to take West Point. For three years, I have believed the Hudson to be the key to the war."

"What does Admiral Rodney say?"

"He most handsomely promises to give me every naval assistance in his power."

Andre said nothing as he focused on him, almost afraid to comment—Sir Henry, fidgeted about the table at the tavern.

"We have been in negotiations for fifteen months with General Arnold."

Andre shot him a stern look.

"He approached us," said Sir Henry

" Can he be trusted?"

"That is why I need your assistance. Is there a true willingness to surrender West Point for a price?"

"It would be my honour, General."

"I need to know if the enemy is concocting a ruse."

Sir Henry paused to get his thoughts under control.

"Are you still carrying on correspondence with Peggy Shippen Arnold?"

"Yes, I can get a reply from my new post in New York to Philadelphia and back the same day."

"Most excellent, before risking my troops on the Hudson, I need to know my pseudonymous correspondent is General Arnold and coordinate with him precise plans for seizing the complex of forts."

"You want me to be your liaison?"

"Exactly, I trust you implicitly."

"I am honored to be your friend and confidant."

"Listen to me carefully," said Sir Henry, "do not take off your uniform, do not go behind enemy lines, and do not carry any papers on your person."

Sir Henry opened the door to espionage for Major Andre, expecting him to help take the Highlands above the Hudson.

Sir Henry's plots were furious. If he moved fast, he could attack Narragansett Bay in Rhode Island, return for West Point, and then sprint to the Chesapeake.

He vacillated between Rhode Island, which Rodney's arrival made feasible, setting up a compound on the Chesapeake and sending Major Andre off to talk with Arnold.

"If Arnold is aboard, I will make a feint for the Chesapeake and then turn northward as I advised Howe in 1777."

"Well, if Admiral Rodney puts up no resistance, I handsomely promise you," said Andre, "to give you every assistance in my power."

Seeing no obstacles to his success. Sir Henry put out his hand to grasp his big goal of controlling the Highlands.

"Contact must be made," he said to Andre. "We must know if this is real."

"My dossier on Arnold," replied Andre, "says he exhibits the morals and manners of a pirate."

On the evening of September 20, 1780, Andre went up the Hudson on the British sloop-of-war, the *Vulture*, to conclude negotiations with Arnold, the latter indicating a willingness to surrender West Point for a price.

Near midnight on September 21, a boat with Joshua Hett Smith, a landowner and attorney from Haverstraw, from the West side of the Hudson was afloat. Two of his farm renters, Samuel and Joseph Cahoon, paddled to the *Vulture* to get a "John Anderson" and take him to Long Clove, where Arnold awaited.

When Smith called out his pseudonym, the tone left a smile tugging at Andre's mouth.

After speaking with Arnold in the woods near shore for some time, Andre thought the conversation had little or no consequence. They rode to Smith's house, behind American lines, where Arnold steered the conversation toward the work at hand.

"I want a good price for committing treason," he said.

"Rest assured, Sir Henry is willing to pay."

"And I will throw in the great valley for which Burgoyne had fought and lost."

Andre studied him with wide, astonished eyes.

"Sir Henry will see to it that you are reimbursed for the property you are losing."

"Good," said Benedict IV, who stopped, turning a little to stare at him, "I expect nothing more than indemnification and equal rank in the army."

"I believe you."

Before leaving Smith's late in the morning, Arnold handed Andre six documents about the works at West Point. The Adjutant-General of the British Army and head of British North American Intelligence put them between his stockings and feet.

When he departed, he wondered what it would be like to serve under Arnold; now, with a plan and with effort, everything was in place.

At dawn that day, American artillery cannonaded the *Vulture*, which retreated downriver. Irritable and desperate he was forced to return to New York City by land.

Exchanging his military surtout for a civilian overcoat of Smith's, he set out with him and his black servant at sundown on the 22nd. They crossed to the Eastern shore of the Hudson at King's Ferry and spent the night at a farmhouse near Yorktown.

Sitting on the porch, Andre studied the imposing mountains and the menacing sky, then sketched it as a gift for the black servant.

The following day, Smith, fearing an encounter with a band of British cow thieves rumored to be in the Neutral Ground (the area between the lines extending from New York City to the Hudson Highlands), parted company with Andre several miles above Pine's Bridge. Andre's attempt to ease his way south was interrupted when he approached Tarrytown. Stopped by three men (Paulding, Van Wart, and Williams), who were on the lookout for suspicious persons heading for New York City, Andre had blundered.

Paulding, who had escaped from prison in New York four days earlier, was still wearing a German Yager's uniform given him by one of his captors.

Thinking he was among the British friends, Andre said, "I hope you belong to the "lower" party."

They nodded in the affirmative.

"I am a British officer."

They watched him pull out his gold watch to demonstrate this fact.

"Sir, tell us where you're going and whence you came?"

I bear the British flag, sir; I have a pass to go this way; I'm on an expedition and have no time to stay."

The three men surrounded him.

"Dismount," said Paulding.

"Come, tell us where you're going, Give us a strict account, for we are now resolved That you shall ne're pass by."

With his heart rate increasing, he realized he had made a mistake and changed his story, and pulled out Arnold's pass.

The three men looked at each other, suspecting something was amiss.

"Search him," said Paulding.

"Look what I found," said Van Wart.

Williams, the only one who could read, scanned the incriminating papers.

He looked up at Paulding, "Make him a prisoner."

"Set me at large."

They looked at him, Paulding giving Vav Wart a proud nod.

"Here's all the gold and silver I have laid up in-store, but when I reach the city, I'll give you ten times more."

"I scorn the gold and silver You have laid up in-store," said Van Wart

Andre repeated himself. "How much money do you want to buy my freedom?"

"No, by God, if you would give us ten thousand guineas, you should not stir a step," Paulding uttered.

Andre shrugged; any glint disappeared from his eyes. Whatever he wished would have to wait. He realized he should have produced Arnold's pass, for if captured by the British, the truth of whose side he was on would have prevailed.

Taking him to Lieutenant Colonel John Jameson, commander of the nearest American outpost at North Castle, Andre was later escorted to Camp Tappan.

Hoping Sir Henry could arrange his release through a prisoner exchange, he soon realized the severity of his situation.

He sat straight up, looking at the American military tribunal members, thinking he could not have dreamed it. No one would have imagined it. While rubbing his hand through his coarse hair, his Peggy Shippen strolled before him.

During the days before his execution on October 2, 1780, Hamilton and Lafayette watched Andre perform a sentimental hero's romance as he orchestrated his final days with consummate skill.

He bowed and spoke to Hamilton and Lafayette on the way to the scaffold.

They watched him on the gallows cart adjust his blindfold. (that he brought with him)

He declared to the vast assemblage, "I pray you to bear witness that I meet my fate like a brave man."

Hamilton turned to Lafayette, saying in French, "Would we have the elegance of mind and manners and his elevated sentiments, and his easy, polite, and insinuating elocution if we were in his place?

Lafayette glanced down at the ground and then looked up at Andre, who lost consciousness in about 8 seconds, although his body movements continued for two to three minutes.

"I will leave that question to you."

## Chapter 78

## The Road to Yorktown

"Maintain patience and never stop trying," said the lovely five-foot Martha Washington, who had just arrived from Mount Vernon in Morristown, New Jersey.

"I do not know if I have any resilience left in me," George said while pacing. "It has been six months since our treaty with our illustrious ally, France."

Paling some, her eyes widened as she cut him off. She took hold of his wrist, her grip firm enough to show him she was serious. "George, for five years, you have bounced back again and again from shattered hopes and bitter disappointment."

"Too many defeats, too few victories." He stopped pacing, his love for Martha increasing beyond his core.

"You will overcome the hardest of circumstances. I know it in my heart."

From narrowed eyes, General Washington looked out the window, recalling Surgeon James Thacher's words regarding the January 3 blizzard of 1781, "so terrible, that no man could endure its violence many minutes without danger of his life."

He remembered four feet of snow piled up in as many days, covering the tents and burying the men like sheep.

Twenty-seven more snowstorms ravaged the surrounding area that winter, the temperature so frigid that the Hudson River froze from Manhattan to Paulus Hook, and the snow did not melt till May.

"This is going to be your time," continued Martha. He shrugged, thinking *time will tell*.

"Some of my infantry companies can muster only four or five men; the average is about fifteen."

Trying to rid himself of great fear and worry, he let out a breath, still knowing his situation was dire.

"One of my generals reported that his officers are embarrassed to leave their huts."

"Why?" Asked Martha.

"Because they were almost naked, and to make matters worse, the men are suffering from hunger."

Martha shook her head, the horror of war curling in her stomach.

She remembered hearing that Private Joseph Plumb Martin, a Connecticut Yankee, was without food for four days, except for some black birch bark he gnawed off a wood stick.

"Men roast their old shoes," George said, "and eat them."

Recalling a servant telling her, "Officers killed a favourite dog for a meal, she watched as George sat back drumming his fingers.

"Some officers live on a diet of bread and water," he said, "so their men can eat what little meat there is."

Watching his fingers tighten, "Okay, you are right," she said, "but this war is a prelude, the symbolic and formal beginning of freedom and independence for the people."

George caught between feelings and common sense, walked to an open window and let the cool air massage his uncertainty.

A few weeks later, after returning from France, Lafayette rejoined his commander at Morristown.

He informed them of the meeting with Washington and Hamilton

"Seven French ships of the line, ten to twelve thousand experienced troops led by Comte de Rochambeau, and 6 million livres were to arrive in Rhode Island in June."

Extinguishing his cigarette on the tip of his boot, Washington swung around and let loose his first full smile since Martha joined him.

"Mon General," said Lafayette in broken English, "the army is reduced to nothing, that wants provisions, that has not one of the necessary means to make war. I must confess I had no idea of such an extremity."

Washington stood mortified, thinking the French would observe America's helplessness and sail away when they arrived.

"Congress is an assembly of rattling noise with opinions of no value," Alex said. "It is incapable of providing the army with the bare necessities."

*Good God!* thought the commander, trying to compose himself.

"The history of the war," continued Alex, "is the history of false hopes and temporary expedients."

Unintentionally, Washington's gaze swept down.

"Mon General, the glue of patriotism will hold your army together."

Washington made no answer, trying to look cheerful, but felt uncomfortable and desired the war to be gone. He sighed and then half-grinned at his two officers. In late April 1780, the circumstances were so dire that General Nathanael Greene observed, "A Country, once overflowing with plenty, are now suffering an Army employed for the defense of everything dear and valuable, to perish for want of food." By May, Washington was informed, "The troops of the 4th and 8th regiments of the Connecticut regulars mutinied, not having been paid for five months and having not eaten meat or bread for ten days."

The General, imagining their anger and suffering, shook his head at Hamilton.

"The worthless Continental currency," Hamilton said, "is the root evil."

There was tension in his voice, something Washington never witnessed before.

"Urge the Commissary General Ephraim Blaine," he replied, "to find some meat."

Hamilton observed his commander's grave look; stepping back, he did not move a muscle.

"The record of Congress's command," he said, "is a catalog of misstep after misstep."

From the South, Washington received word in May of 1780 of the fall of Charleston by Sir Henry Clinton and that Benjamin Lincoln's entire command of fifty-five hundred men and enormous quantities of supplies were lost.

White as a surrender flag, his temper kept him standing erect.

He heard that Sir Henry was greeted by Admiral Thomas Graves's six ships of the line at Sandy Hook after returning to New York. Gaining a thirteen-to-eight superiority over the French Navy, Washington realized that capturing New York was out of the question. From the corner of his eye, Hamilton noticed that his commander shut his eyes for a second, then drew a deep gasp.

Washington's aides observed a frustration in their commander but not the bitterness in him that existed in Sir Henry Clinton, whose aides knew he lamented that Admiral Arbuthnot's fleet did not crush the French reinforcements upon their arrival at Rhode Island and establish themselves. "It gave," Sir Henry wrote home, "additional animation to the spirit of rebellion, whose expiring embers began to blaze up afresh upon its appearance."

Learning of Horatio Gates' army's rout on August 1780, at Camden, South Carolina, by Lieutenant General Charles Cornwallis, Clinton wrote him, "There are two underlining necessities for our success in the south, sea power and loyalist support. If you are out of touch with the sea, then you will be chronically short of supplies, having to move to search for them or starve. Not being able to stay long in one place means you cannot call out, protect, and organize the loyalists; therefore, not being able to hold territory."

Cornwallis growled, "What does the son of a bitch know?" as he finished reading the letter.

A smirk spread on his full mouth, "I am smarter than him and know what I am up against."

As hope springs eternal, it fails to flower any signs of optimism for Washington, who sighed and hardened when informed of Gates' defeat. Sitting where he was, as shocked by the news as he ever had been surprised by anything, he leaned back at his desk and eyed a somber Hamilton.

Keeping his hands folded, the General asked, "Who should command the Southern army?"

Without debating the question, Hamilton's grin returned, fast, bold, and sure, "General Greene."

A fresh smile returned to Washington's face.

After Benedict Arnold deserted in September 1780, Greene was placed in command of West Point. Washington and Hamilton were impressed by how he quickly strengthened the location to prepare for a British attack.

Planning on seeing his wife, Greene stood taut. His face resolved into hard lines as he wrote her, "I am at this moment setting off southward, having kept expresses flying all night to see if I could hear anything of you. I have been distracted. I wanted to see you so much before I set out."

After stopping at Philadelphia and conferring with Washington, Greene spun around to face the situation. Heading to his assignment, he possessed the feeling of going to his doom, so dire was the news from the south.

A fury rippled under the calm Hamilton's surface as he wrote to the secretary of the French ambassador, "The want of money makes us want everything else, even intelligence. I confess I view our affairs in dim light."

Greene took command at Hillsborough, North Carolina, on December 3, 1780, over all the troops from Delaware to Georgia; unintentionally, his gaze swept down at his newborn responsibility.

At Charlotte, he observed the ghost of Gates's army. He said nothing, peered off into the distance, and wrote a friend, "The troops are wretched beyond appearance and suffer from an appalling lack of food and clothing."

With an aide making some notes on a separate sheet of parchment, he continued his letter, "The public credit is lost, and every man excusing himself from giving the least aid to Government. From an apprehension that they would get no return for any advance."

After a few moments, Greene realized the situation was what it was, and a steadfastness flung up like a sunrise.

"General, may I ask you a question?"

"Yes, Major," said Greene.

"How did the son of a well-to-do Quaker preacher become a general?"

Greene hesitated a few beats before replying. "My father owned an ironworks, and I read little as a youth. He was prejudiced against book learning."

He turned away, his face drained of color at the memory. "My mother died when I was eleven, and I grew up on the family farm, schooled by an itinerant tutor."

The Major felt the atmosphere going into space as Greene managed to continue his story.

"I stumbled upon the world of books at eighteen, and from then on, I have seldom been without one."

Letting out a breath, Greene rolled his eyes up, then brushed his hand through his full head of deep black hair. "My father died in 1770, and my brothers and I continued to operate the ironworks, which became one of the state's biggest enterprises."

The Major looked at the near six-foot, husky general's friendly face with somewhat narrow, penetrating eyes, admiring his desire to improve his life.

"How did you resolve your belief in the pacifist teachings of the Society of Friends in the quarrel with Britain."

"That was easy," replied the thin-nosed, sensuous-mouthed man. "They expelled me from the church for failing to abide by its principles."

Nodding, Greene flipped over to a past chapter in his life. "Having a pronounced limp from a stiff knee since childhood, I was forced to begin my military career as a private, but the state assembly put me on a committee to revise the military laws of Rhode Island. Traveling to Boston, I watched the British soldiers drill on the Common and examined their fortification at Boston Neck. Taking a wrong turn while looking for a tavern, I discovered Henry Knox's London Bookstore, purchased military manuals, and discussed military strategy with Knox, who became a friend."

"What was your role in the siege of Boston in 1775-1776?"

"I organized the raw troops, and when Washington arrived, we related to each other."

Greene's face turned a dull pink. "The General considered my soldiers the best disciplined of all those around Boston."

"And the highest in morale, I imagine," said the Major, who refrained from saying that Henry Knox regarded Greene as nothing short of a military genius.

"Within a year, I was given command of the troops on Long Island in 1776."

"Alexander Hamilton, I heard," said the Major, "that General Washington immediately had confidence in you."

"I would like to think I gained it amidst all the checkered varieties of military vicissitude."

He gave the Major a small, approving smile, opened his mouth, and then closed it before continuing.

"Though outnumbered in the South, I want," the General said, "to split our small army, knowing we cannot stand up to Cornwallis in a head-on battle."

He watched his aide's eyebrows scrunch together as his head tipped to the side. "I want," said Greene, "to protect and encourage the local inhabitants."

Pride galloped through Greene like a racehorse. "I am informed," he said, "that Daniel Morgan is in the area of the Broad River with his small and quick, flying army, while Colonel William Washington, who prefers the heat of the action and not the tedious calculation of strategy, is not far from Morgan."

The Major let loose a grin from ear to ear, "The Colonel, who trained for the ministry, defeated a Tories party."

The news struck a chord. "I have plans for both officers. They are bold, collected, and persistent."

"What do we do now?" Asked the Major.

"For our position here, I would describe it as a camp of repose to repair our wagons, recruit our horses, and discipline the troops."

With his brow lifted, Greene continued, "I want to divide our paltry army. In no way can we stand up to Cornwallis in a pitched battle. We must keep rivers and streams between our army and the enemy as the season allows the rivers and streams to rise rapidly."

His eyes, a deep blue-green, seemed to lighten.

"These conditions will be beneficial to us."

Greened hesitated, then said, "We must lure Cornwallis to Guilford Court House, North Carolina, thus distant him from his main base of supplies at Wilmington."

"But are we not giving the impression of retreat?"

"We must battle Cornwallis on the ground of our own choosing."

Greene turned to the window; the sun was high and bright.

"You want to bewilder Cornwallis?"

"Exactly; by sending the left-wing west of the Catawba River, we improve our chances of provisioning both wings of the army while their presence will protect and encourage the local inhabitants."

"Who will command the left wing of light infantry?"

"Daniel Morgan," He dropped into a chair,

"We will let Cornwallis learn that the rebels eye the British post called Ninety-Six, and he will make plans." When hearing shots, sweat pearled on Greene's forehead as he ordered an advance upon the enemy's left, then right.

General Greene laughed before he wrote Morgan, "I have just received information that Colonel Tarleton is on his way to pay you a visit with 750 men and a pair of three-pounders to engage you to the utmost, forcing you to fight or withdraw. I doubt not, but he will have a decent reception and a proper dismission."

Morgan's anger seared upon reading the letter; he sneered at the forthcoming stocky redhead whose name was abhorrent to him. He was known as the "Bloody Tarleton" for his primitive attacks.

Rebel scouts tracked the "Butcher."

The rebel leader, Morgan, moved to Thicketty Creek on the raw and cold evening of January 16, 1781.

He recollected himself, guzzled some whiskey, and reflected on the situation like the Roman commander, Scipio Africanus.

"This is where we will stand and fight," he informed Greene. "It provides security in case the battle proves unfortunate."

A volunteer recollected, "He went among the volunteers, helped them fix their swords, joked about their sweethearts, and told them to keep in good spirits, and the day would be ours. Long after I laid down, he was going about among the soldiers, encouraging them and telling them that the "Old Wagoner" would crack his whip over Ben in the morning, as sure as he lived. "Just hold up your heads, boys," he would say, "three fires, and you are free! And then, when you return to your homes, how the old folks will bless you, and the girls kiss you for your gallant conduct." Morgan turned, determined to let the door of victory open wider.

"Get up, boys," Morgan bellowed at dawn, "Benny is coming. Move the wagons to the rear of the encampment, eat heartily, and have the horses of the mounted militia tied to the rear."

With the details and precision required, he further ordered, "Have Picken's men take shelter in or behind trees and shoot for the epaulets, boys! Shoot for the epaulets!"

He thought there was no better job in the world for a flash, but then the responsibility of command took hold; his shoulders slumped, but only for a moment.

"On the rising ground," he pointed, "have three hundred Maryland and Delaware Continentals with fixed bayonets reinforced by militiamen from Virginia and Georgia. Do not fire until I give the word."

He laughed, "I hope they appreciate my reception."

"On the hillock behind," he pointed again, "have Colonel Washington's cavalry and some mounted infantry under Lieutenant Colonel James McCall assemble."

He then rode through the lines and visited every unit of his thousand-man force, urging his troops to sit down, "Ease your joints."

"We are going to tear "Benny" Tarleton to threads."

Thomas Young, a sixteen-year-old Private from the South Carolina backcountry, said after the enemy came into sight, "It was the most beautiful line I ever saw."

Morgan yelled to his soldiers, "They give us the British halloo, boys. Give them the Indian halloo, by God!"

Loud war hoops echoed in the dawn light.

Morgan rode back and forth, telling his men, "Do not fire" as the enemy approached.

When the British were a hundred yards away, Morgan gave the command.

The Patriots fired, reloaded, and fired again and again, killing many of the enemy soldiers.

By order, Picken's troops ran across the rebel left, fifty British dragoons bearing down on them. Then Colonel Washington's and McCall's horsemen appeared as if by magic, sabers in hand, and charged Tarleton's outnumbered cavalry three to one.

Tarleton, seeking glory, thought the rebels vulnerable and ordered his infantry to charge. The men followed his orders, and three hundred Continentals aimed low, exchanging volley after volley for thirty minutes.

Calling on his reserves, Tarleton directed them forward with bagpipes blaring.

"Colonel Howard, what is going on," said Morgan. "Why are the men retreating to the rear?"

"They are not. They misunderstood an order."

"I will pick a new place," said Morgan, "where we can establish a new line."

William Washington observed Tarleton's cavalry from a knoll and sent a message to Morgan. "The enemy are racing up the slope in complete disorder and look confused and are behaving like a mob. Give them fire, and I will charge them."

Morgan turned to his right as Picken's riflemen appeared.

"Face about," he told the Continentals. "Give them one fire, and the day is ours!"

"Give them the bayonets!" Howard yelled.

Morgan watched as the confused British broke ranks, dropping their weapons and running for the wagon road.

"The prettiest sort of running," said Thomas Young.

With Tarleton's defeat on January 17, 1781, at the Battle of Cowpens, about nine-tenths of the entire British force were killed or captured by Morgan.

The portrait of the British defeat was inviting to Washington, who thought of Marta's words, "Victory will come."

When receiving news of the battle, Cornwallis abandoned reason and stopped playing with a full deck. "I will attack them everywhere they go."

Wanting to free over 800 prisoners and capture the rebel commanders, he left Charleston and destroyed all of his fortifications while pursuing Morgan, who wrote Greene, "Cornwallis wanting speed destroyed his baggage, burnt his men's tents and is marching north to engage our army."

He knew the news would bring delight to Greene's face.

A day after the battle, Greene and Morgan met.

"Cornwallis journeyed 40 miles in 16 hours and destroyed all on his march."

"His is a mad scheme," said Greene, "of pushing through the country."

"Moving further from his supply bases," said Morgan, who fancied Greene's sparkling eyes.

Greene continued to listen with astonishment and replied: "Then he is ours as long as we stay just far ahead of him to tempt him to follow and force a fight."

"It is a huge risk," wrote Morgan. "I will not answer for the consequences if the plan falters."

"You will not have to," replied Greene, "for I shall take the measure upon myself."

Morgan shrugged. "Fine by me."

"Be off to the Catawba River, cross it, and make haste to Yadkin, thirty miles away."

Here, the conversation closed; the war's demands now needed their full attention.

Greene rode alone to Salisbury and dismounted at Steele's Tavern.

"What? Alone?" Asked an acquaintance.

"Yes, tired, hungry, and penniless."

"Would you like some breakfast?" Asked Mrs. Steele, the innkeeper.

"Gladly." He closed his eyes and dozed off for a few minutes.

Awaking at the food aroma, he noticed she was holding two small bags.

"Here is some hard currency. You need it more than I."

She watched as a deluge of energy surged through his body.

"Indeed, I do. Thank you."

He chose to keep it to himself that those bags contained all the money hoarded just then by the army's southern department.

From northward, Washington sent Lafayette and men south to reinforce the Southern army, much to Hamilton's chagrin, who craved active duty.

A rain began, fast but not heavy, as Cornwallis marched into Virginia towards Yorktown to pursue Morgan and Greene, ignoring that Yorktown was surrounded by water on three sides.

At their shared lodgings near Washington's headquarters, the recently married Eliza watched her husband, Alex, who stood stiff as a soldier at attention. "He does not respect me. He is a testy boss."

She felt his pride spill over. "The hardships of the revolutionary struggle twist upon your heart, husband."

"He no longer chokes down his anger over the officers on his staff."

Her eyes saddened slowly as Alex spoke. "Thinking of her father, Phillipe Schuyler, Eliza said, "Be less proud, bow to the greater cause. You are gifted, my dearest one."

Rigid with fury, Alex said. "I suffer not infrequently from the renowned commander's irritable temper."

Eliza studied her husband, surveying his hurt feelings.

"I am eager to advance in rank. For four years, I have subordinated myself with a smile."

He leaned back and looked upward. "I hunger for a field command."

She watched as a hint of color blossomed on his cheeks. "I yearn for fluttering flags, booming cannon, bayonet charges, and no longer being a clerk."

Eliza recognized his ambition and understood it but feared for his safety.

"Lafayette asked him to allow me," he vented to Eliza, "to lead a battalion for a raid on Long Island, but he declined, saying he could not afford to give me up."

Gone was the beam in her eyes.

He took her hand. "Mrs. Hamilton, the sky might mutter with thunder, the dark storms of winter might pour forth, the streams might swell to rivers, but I will return to your arms."

These were charming words, but she was on the point of tears, so she stopped them.

"Last fall, I reminded him about going southward and explained my feelings for my military reputation and how much it was my object to act a conspicuous part in some enterprise that might raise my character as a soldier above mediocrity, but he spurned me."

"Go forward," she said; I will not raise any outcry. I will keep my anxiety and fear to myself."

On February 15, at headquarters at a Dutch farmhouse on the Hudson River at New Windsor, Hamilton and Washington remained for some time, till midnight, on dispatches for French officers at Newport.

The next morning, he stood at the head of the stairs and was met by Hamilton, who had just delivered a letter to Tench Tilghman for him and had a brief conversation with Lafayette.

He was surprised the General was not in his room.

When locating him, he thought his eyes were like a weapon, the incisive view in then waiting to cause severe destruction.

"You have kept me waiting at the head of the stairs these ten minutes. I must tell you, sir, you treat me with disrespect."

Without petulancy but with a decision, Hamilton said, "I am not conscious of it, sir, but since you have thought it necessary to tell me so, we part."

"Very well, sir," Washington said, "if it be your choice."

The drama concluded, and the curtain fell; they separated.

Hamilton thought his absence, which gave so much umbrage, did not last two minutes.

The next day, Alex was missing from his usual desk.

The following day, he received Tilghman with a message from

Washington. "The General regrets his fleeting temper and encourages you to come and patch things up."

"No thanks! His temper has done violence to my feelings."

Later that afternoon, Alex wrote to James McHenry, "The great man and I have come to an open rupture."

"The war," he told Eliza several days later after stewing over the incident, "is too crucial to be threatened by frivolous frustrations."

She admired Alex carefully as he spoke. When he concluded, she put her hand on his shoulder. "That is the man I love."

Admiring the soft lines on her face, he shot back, "But I still want one last chance for battlefield honor not to be shackled to a desk for the duration of the war, a degrading form of drudgery."

This information did not ease her mind. She fixed on his face and put her left hand on her stomach. "You have to promise to return, not just for me."

He leaned over and put the side of his head on her stomach. Listening, realizing, he heard a heart thumping.

His hands shook as he jumped and squealed. "I hope I can be a good father to our child. I fear I will make the same mistakes as my father."

Embracing him in a loving hug, she said, "Worry not, my dearest one."

A week or so later, news arrived at Washington's headquarters.

Under the command of Admiral de Grasse, a French fleet was to be at the Chesapeake, not New York, with three thousand soldiers on board and to remain until October, no later.

Forced to abandon any hope of recapturing Manhattan Island, General Washington lifted his head. His eyes were wide and fixed on developing a new strategy.

"General," said Colonel Hamilton, "Lafayette informs us that General Cornwallis is now entrenched at Yorktown, surrounded by water on three sides."

"A perfect fortress."

"Or a perfect trap," replied Alex.

Washington fought to control a grin.

When their strategy finished, Alex came to say, "General, have you decided on my desire for a combat role?"

"I have the highest esteem for you."

"I must consider resigning if I fail to get my desired command."

Washington nodded and smiled.

"July 31, 1781, Dearest Eliza, "Tench Tilghman visited me today with the news the General will give me a command. I finally have achieved my chance for battlefield laurels. I shall have charge of a New York light infantry battalion."

The plan finally settled; the commander of the rebel forces and the French army in the North set off for Virginia, some by boat, the others marching,

"I must go without seeing you," Alex wrote to Eliza, "Without embracing you. Alas, I must go." His ambition awakened; an idea of glory swiftly darted into his mind.

When the combined forces crossed the Delaware, they knew it was too late for Sir Henry Clinton to stop them.

Foolishly, Clinton assumed the armies intended to strike Staten Island to cover a French fleet entrance into New York harbor.

General Washington stopped off at Mount Vernon, spending three nights with the French plotting, planning, and envisioning the enemy's action.

"Cornwallis will be left dangling in the wind," said Rochambeau, "it being tough to subsist if not in control of the Chesapeake."

Washington wrote Lafayette, "I hope you will keep Lord Cornwallis safe, without Provisions or Forage until we arrive. Adieu."

"Well, General," said Rochambeau a day later, "the French fleet and both the American and French troops have rendezvoused at the same time at the same place at the Chesapeake with more than thirty ships."

Washington heard the bell of victory, finding joy in the process of the rebellion ending. Rochambeau started to smirk as he looked at the general, seeing something rush through him.

"Our fleet will establish a presence on the James River, blocking Cornwallis from slipping away to the south and being cornered at the York River."

The besiegement of Yorktown commenced on October 9, and Cornwallis found himself in the teeth of defeat, the British Navy unable to come to his rescue.

Hamilton's light infantry stormed the British redoubt on the right; the French attacked the one on the left.

Acknowledging the power of glory, Alex vaulted over a kneeling soldier's shoulders and rushed forward, his men following.

They captured the enemy soldiers in less than ten minutes, ending the battle of Yorktown.

Pleading an indisposition, Cornwallis sent General Charles O'Hare, to handle his surrender on October 17, the British band playing . . . .

It took well over a year before hostilities terminated, and then the light of freedom danced on the face of insurrection—the hearts of America, more united than ever.

When Alexander Hamilton learned that King George III, on February 14, 1783, issued a proclamation notifying the world that hostilities had ceased between Great Britain, France, Spain, Holland, and the United States of America, he shook his head. His thoughts on his close friend, John Laurens, who was ambushed and killed on August 27, 1782, at the age of 27, only a few weeks before the British finally withdrew from Charleston.

'What is wrong? Asked Elizabeth. "Peace is finally here."

'I thought of John."

She observed his hollow, pained face, his heart mired in a bottomless abyss, the sadness that couched in his eyes, knowing that he was drowning inside again.

'"Try to keep your head high; John would want that."

With John Adams, Benjamin Franklin, and John Jay representing America, the British dragged on negotiations for eighteen months until September 3, 1783, when it was resolved that the United States was free, sovereign, and independent.

## Chapter 79

## Wilky Goes West

Bold and brilliant light blasted through the thick gray sky onto Wilkinson's face in late March 1781.
Learning that General Washington required him to resign as Clothier General due to his "lack of aptitude for the job," he was touched and trampled as the information spread over his profile and washed it. His countenance clouded into a pout, and his breath drew in, but he refused to let the shards of misfortune pierce him.

Whipping around, he decided to run for the Pennsylvania State Assembly from Bucks County and was elected in October of 1781 and re-elected the following October.

Bored with plucking a phrase out of his thoughts to self-serving delegates, his attention lurched to England's forthcoming peace.

Smiling, the dimples on his face stood at attention as he resettled his family in Philadelphia, his eyes here, there, and everywhere for opportunity.

No one who knew him had ever seen him so satisfied.

The real evil of his situation was his awareness that he needed to pursue "riches." As he followed this path, he grinned, and his disposition to think too well of himself took hold, a disadvantage that threatened him throughout his life.

With his "House" growing in arrears, he could not long enjoy the repose of the city of brotherly love.

After selling Trevose in the spring of 1783, a connection to the Province of Louisiana came to the eager businessman through his wife, Ann, who brought goods shipped from New Orleans to their home.

Quickly realizing the commercial possibilities, he moved to Lexington, Kentucky, in the late summer of 1783 to secure his "riches." He left his two infants and Nancy at her father's house and the Society of Philadelphia.

He congratulated himself as soon as he settled in Kentucky, his smirk riveting on Lexington's dirt.

"It would be very shocking, would it not?" he said, "not to have heard the clinking of the Spanish doubloons." While sitting inside the stockade, his hands folded, he dreamed of a dive into the Spanish mines, a lifelong goal from that time forward.

## Chapter 80

## Lest not Forget Jefferson

Jefferson recalled strolling towards the gate and turning to his wife Martha, whom he affectionately called Patty. She raised her eyebrows. "Are you thinking of pulling a Henry on me?'

Observing his mystified expression, she said. "Serve three one-year terms."

"Oh, the maximum allowed by Virginia law," he said.

"Well, "said Patty, replacing a slight frown with a big smile that showed her love for Thomas.

"I can live with that," he said.

"Can I?" said Patty.

"The legislature shackles the governor. It is more a figurehead position."

At first, she made no answer, trying to look cheerful. "Dash it," she exclaimed, "another perfect, fully good mind gone to waste."

Slightly, he swayed his head to one side, the way a dog does when looking confused. Talking of Henry, he just sent a note from his Leatherwood farm, lamenting the inflation inflicting the state and the indulgence of Loyalists whose actions hindered the war effort."

She made no answer and tried to look cheerful, hopelessly lowering her eyes. "He plans to introduce a bill to grant the chief executive's office with sweeping powers in raising and supplying troops and apportioning punishments to those who hinder the war effort."

"You must give that some thought," she said. "While Henry lives, more legislation will be formed and saddled forever on us. We need to devoutly pray for his death and prepare the minds of our young men."

He stepped aside, and Patty saw the look of contentment on his countenance. Jefferson then remembered walking in the gardens of the old governor's house, talking, listening, and dining twenty years earlier with his friend, Governor Francis Fauquier. Hearing the music he played with the Governor while attending school at the College of William and Mary, he remained silent momentarily, stirring the past like a stew in his head. Papa's Boy then went inside, where he embarked on a series of sketches aimed at remaking his house.

Two days later, the Virginia assembly passed a bill moving the government to Richmond. Anxious to prepare herself for the move, Patty returned to Monticello with a beam that graced her face, expecting significant accomplishments awaited her husband. With his thoughts curling towards his wife at Monticello, he heard her long, quiet sighs and felt her hand on his face. But he did not feel the threat and reality of a British invasion. The British attacked Savannah and controlled Georgia and South Carolina within a year while Virginia waited for the enemy.

Then in May of 1780, the Brits attacked Charleston. Lord Cornwallis defeated General Horatio Gates at Camden, South Carolina, leaving the Maryland, Delaware, North Carolina, and Virginia militias in disarray at the end of August. Governor Jefferson stopped unbuttoning philosophical thoughts and asked the Virginia council to help him execute "an immediate and great exertion to stop the progress of the enemy." Glaring at the intelligence that Sir Henry Clinton sent 600 British troops under Benedict Arnold from New York to Virginia, he did nothing.

Under gloom day and night, his thoughts centered on pressing his hands on Patty's shoulders as she attempted to get up from bed, nibbling at the base of her neck. The naval squadron that transported the enemy reached Old Point Comfort on December 29, 1780; about one-half of Arnold's forces, American Loyalists under Lieutenant Colonels Dundas and Simcoe. Afraid to move a muscle, Governor Jefferson declined to summon the militia until the invading forces quickly approached the capital. Indecision overcame him in coordinating a plan to stop Arnold on his march to Richmond. He turned his eyes from the waves of war, taking Virginia on a wild surge of fear and desperation. He ignored the shadow of the reality that waited over his shoulder. Annoyed with himself, he strolled back into the Governor's house and shut the door.

On January 5, 1781, the British marched into Richmond, formed a line, and bombarded the city; not a white person remained in ten minutes.

His distractors said, "He bore the matter poorly, blamed others with a deceitful disposition and lowly opinion of the facts."

He swallowed hard, sitting beside his indecision. "Go to purgatory," he muttered, trying to move past his actions.

At the end of May 1781, he relinquished the governorship "to abler hands with an entire extinction of all hope." His sadness fell abundantly, "but his grief was artless," said his critics. He prepared to snarl at them but thought better of it.

Back at Monticello, it was dark as he awoke. Having no idea of responsibility or the times, only a deep inner serenity and security beside

Patty, he inched towards composure.

An inquiry, on June 12, 1781, moved by George Nicholas in the House of Delegates with the backing of Patrick Henry into the conduct during the last twelve months of the executive (members of the council), passed the same day. When hearing of the inquest, heat and cold shot through him, his pride chilled, and his blood flamed by the accusation.

"I take it personally," he told Patty as he shook his head, the colour drained from his cheeks.

She looked up quickly into his misty eyes. "Prepare a defense." Her words restored his comfort as temper sprang into his eyes. Though reeling from the impact, he wanted her small round breasts pressed into his bare chest. Later that week, Patty informed him, "A member of the House of Delegates resigned.

"I must become a representative from Albemarle County."

"Words are important; if not said, they leave holes."

Absently, running his fingers through his hair, he said, "I suppose you are right."

She kept her eyes on his face, happy he was composed again. Reaching out, her fingers stroked his red hair; as he started to walk to the garden, Patty stepped in front of him to bar his way. She stretched her hand to his chin, and he noticed her eyes glittering with love and awe.

At the Assembly on December 12, 1781, the date of the inquiry, he sat pretending to be shy and polite but taking much interest in the circumstance. With the surrender of Cornwallis at Yorktown and George Nicolas absent, the matter fell by the wayside when no delegate moved to initiate the inquiry. Leaping up from his seat, he said, "It is very unjust to judge one's management without an intimate grasp of their situation."

He read from a list the expected charges he imagined and the ones sent to him by Nicholas, answering each in turn. The delegates glanced up, discovering he was serious, and suppressed their laughter. Relaxed and at ease, words rolled off his tongue, trying to charm the delegates. His attempts to stop were in vain.

He wrote Patty, "After finishing, the House unanimously passed a resolution thanking me for my service, and the Senate thanked me for my impartial, upright, and attentive administration while in office."

She wanted to rush to his side but strode to a window and studied the view. At Richmond, there could barely be a more satisfied creature in the world, but the accusations were still so bound up in his mind. It took him a few seconds to realize the ordeal left a bitter taste in his palette and animus towards Henry. That evening after the great event, he dined out at the Raleigh Tavern with friends but failed to realize the times required more, not fewer, leadership skills.

After a year of being back at Monticello, a perverse turn occurred as Thomas watched Martha. In ten years of marriage, she bore six children, three dying in infancy or early childhood; she now bordered on a serious illness.

Frantic that she must escape her sickness, he said, "Promise me not to venture into such hazard."

Martha made no answer, looking unconcerned but waiting to be gone. She watched him try to laugh it off.

"We must look to our future," but Martha knew there was no putting an end to her situation. That instant, she stepped outside of life and slipped away on September 6, 1782. Doomed to silence, unable to share any joy in his heart. his grief was stacked everywhere. The stupor of his mind rendered him as dead to the world as Martha was, mourning until the middle of October 1783.

"I am very much obliged to you," Thomas said to James Madison in late November."

"You are a very exceptional friend," replied James. "Through your efforts at the Continental Congress, I am glad to be one of the ministers plenipotentiary to France for negotiating peace with England."

Silently, Madison sat observing the meaning of life circling through his friend's thoughts. As he waited for the French frigate to clear the blocked ice below Baltimore, visions of his future, not always pleasant but still intriguing, circled Thomas's thoughts. He let out a petite laugh as though the idea both entertained and puzzled him, supposing himself a good judge of such matters in general.

# ABOUT THE AUTHOR

**HISTORY HARDENED
ITS WISDOM: SHADY AND DIM
A CALLOUS DAYBREAK**

Growing up in Putnam County, named after General Israel Putnam, I walked its roads and explored the hills and valleys American rebels tread. I often thought, what would I have done when the head of the state, King George III of England, ignored the rights of the American colonies and the rule of law? Would I have marched to the tune of the revolution and been in a regiment commanded by General Putnam or sided with the loyalists?

I have been fascinated by American history since elementary school; days of old run in my veins. I have spent ten years researching and reading about the founding fathers and settled on six men, three boys not yet twenty, and three Virginians who risked having their necks stretched to make the American dream a reality.

In "The World Turned Upside Down," volume 2 of 4 of "Creating A Republic," I wanted to debunk the history of the American Revolution taught from preschool to college. Using creative nonfiction as a vehicle, I intended to unwind the myths of America's founding and take it to a new place. I discovered that History Does Not Repeat Itself; it Rhymes.

Understanding the nature of politics is paramount. The present often breaks into fragments of antique myths. Lying and backstabbing in the quest for power is as old as when our ancestors first walked on the earth.

It is paramount to know nothing is new. Historians stare into the mirror of history but are confused about its creation; thus, the big lie begins. One of the biggest falsehoods was the Revolutionary War when George Washington became commander of the American army.

Neal Friedman (a.k.a. Seth Irving Handaside)

www.historiumpress.com